The Warrior Revealed

The World of Evendaar

Book Four

The Warrior Revealed

A. R. Winterstaar

First Edition, June 2018
ISBN-13: 978-0-9914794-6-7

Evendaar Publishing
www.evendaar.com

More books in the
World of Evendaar Series:

Book One:
The Child Revealed

Book Two:
The Queen Revealed

Book Three:
The Demon Revealed

**Discover more by visiting
www.evendaar.com**

Dedication

P.L.M.

You are the first person who ever asked me to tell a story.
This one is for you.

CONTENTS

CHAPTER ONE
"Shadows Reaching to the Light"

There was a knock, and the door opened. Noise from the busy bar downstairs spilled into the room, bringing the sound of shouting and coarse laughter, interrupting the handsome young man and his older, rotund companion sitting in an uncomfortable silence.

A scruffy head appeared around the door and narrow eyes scanned the room until they found the young man at his desk. Tall and skinny, the man with the narrow eyes ducked into the room, pulling a fellow thug behind him. "Boss, we're back," he grunted. "S'alright if we bring 'em in for you?"

"Ah! Sandy, Francis, my collectors—perfect timing," said the young man. He nodded to his guest on the other side of the desk. "Pere Raven, as requested, I present the best Marchant filth that the slums of the Lower Districts of Concordis have to offer. They should be very useful for your mines."

Pere Raven chuckled, smoothing his simple brown robes down over his generous stomach. "*Our* mines, dear Boss," he said. "We provide the Gift for all the fine old wizards of Evendaar: St. Lucidis, Marchant, and otherwise."

The young man glared at the bald priest. "You asked for my help after losing almost all your workers, and now I have delivered," he said, clearly vexed by Pere Raven's reminder.

"I'm sure you've done an excellent job, but before I get too excited, let's just see what we have here, shall we?" said Pere Raven. He rose from his seat to cross the creaky floorboards of the attic office. The young man followed behind the priest. The two collectors had dragged a motley group of six children into the room and manhandled them into a line. Some of the children were tiny, no more than nine or ten, though the others ranged all the way up to young adults.

The priest walked up and then down the line of children, carefully examining each dirty face.

"What a wonderful collection of workers," said Pere Raven kindly as he looked into the eyes of the frightened children before him. "My dear Boss, I'm delighted to see that you might even have found me a Special." He pinched the chin of a teen girl and forced her head back to show the young man. Her eyes were emerald green and framed by long black lashes.

"Just look at the wide ring of silver," said the priest. He chuckled happily. "Oh, the mines will keep you busy, my dear little kitten!"

The girl squirmed and tried to pull her chin out of his hand. "I ain't going with no priest," she protested. "Itssa priests take the kids away to the Black Mountains to get eaten by the monsters."

The priest smiled down at the girl. "You stupid, special child," he said gently. "I can promise that *you* won't get eaten by any monsters. Instead, you will be worked to death, imbuing gray crystals with your magic. It's all the rest of these nasty little children who will get eaten by monsters."

The children started to whimper and cry, but the priest seemed to enjoy their reaction. "That's right!" Pere Raven smiled broadly, his hazel eyes sparkling with silver. "All the wonderful green magic that lights up your blood will finally have a purpose, and your worthless lives will be given meaning. Though I know you won't be happy in your new home, at least it has to be better than living like fleas on the back of a cat here in Concordis. In the mines you can be proud that you're doing something for society."

Taking all the priest's chatter as tacit approval, the young man called over the two collectors who were shuffling by the doorway. "Get this lot secured in the basement. We'll move them when we have enough for a full wagonload, hopefully by the week's end, if you men are doing your job well."

Dismissed, the collectors began hustling the crying children out the door again and left the two men to their business.

The Boss poured two tiny glasses of Firewhiskey, handed Pere Raven a glass, and held up his own. "A toast," he said, "to keeping the streets of Concordis clean of Green Bloods and their filthy magic."

If Pere Raven took offense at the dig at his Marchant heritage, he didn't show it. Instead, he sipped his drink and kept his gaze on the young man. "It seems that the summer influenza hit Concordis very hard this year," the priest remarked. "Another epidemic like that, and soon all the commoners in Unisia will be dead. I suppose we should be grateful that the Marchant bastards aren't affected."

The young man sat back in his chair and narrowed his blue eyes at the priest. "Yes, it was the will of the goddess, Pere Raven, that the summer influenza should strike down so many of the common folk of Unisia this year," he said. "Yet it was a blessing that I welcomed. One day soon, only the worthy shall walk this world, and it shall be those with strong gold magic in their veins and loyalty to the St. Lucidis family in their hearts."

He leaned across the table, and his expression turned to pity as he regarded the priest. "You say you worship the goddess Serena, Pere Raven, but she has forgotten you. You might be a holy man, but in Unisia, you are nothing but a lackey, serving those monsters up in their Eeyrie, keeping them alive with the magic of their own people. But to what end? We both know that the Eldars cannot be allowed to leave their mountaintop and rule over Unisia as they once did without destroying society as we know it." He sat back in his chair, satisfied with his own logic. "No, the burden falls to us, the pure St. Lucidis knights, to do what must be done. I believe the dream of our goddess Serena was for us, her original tribe, to keep the magic strong and protect Unisia from the corrupted Favored." He pointed a finger at Pere Raven. "And the Marchant family were corrupted the instant they began working with Dark Entities to secure their longevity. Do not forget, Pere Raven, it was your masters who were given the secret to the Gift of Life by the Spider People and devised the hideous way of using gray crystal to harvest magic from their *own people!*"

Pere Raven had evidently heard this speech before, and he sat before the wide-eyed fervor of the young man, nodding calmly as if they were in agreement.

"My dear Boss, I would like you to know how grateful I am for all your efforts to keep our mine on Mount Ecrusius working. You do the goddess's own work for the nation," said Pere Raven. "And yet I feel that it's time that I should do something for you." The priest paused and smiled at the young man's stony expression. "I can only presume that it must irritate you no end to have to live with a queen of mixed blood, and her little children, all running around the Golden Palace like they own the place."

The young man ground his teeth. "It is torture," he agreed. "I curse the day that woman was put on our sacred throne."

Pere Raven grimaced sympathetically. "I heard that Queen Adelena has brought the Marchant prince to live with her, but not only that; I also heard that she is collecting up every stray Marchant bastard she can find and keeping them close to her. There is a young man from Belvoir, a certain Benjamin, who never came home after he delivered the Marchant prince's horse to the Golden Palace. One can only imagine what she is using that handsome young man for."

The young man raised his eyebrows, and his noble nose smelled a plot. "I have no time for your games, Pere Raven. Tell me what you want."

"I have always admired your candor, Boss," said Pere Raven. Pressing his hands into a prayer gesture at his chest, he assumed a humble expression. "If I may, I would like your permission to enter the grounds of the Golden Palace and take something that doesn't belong there: the children of your false queen. I have men who are good with such things, and naturally, our only difficulty will be getting around any St. Lucidis magic protections that might be cast upon the boundaries. I know how you feel about having people like myself and my men tread upon the sacred ground of the Golden Palace, but I cannot tell you how grateful I would be to have those royal children. I have great hopes that they will all be the Specials we so desperately need to keep the mines open that much longer."

The young man pinched his bottom lip, reflecting on this. "The baby is near dead, you know," he said. "The Fire Orchid tonic didn't work, and just this morning, Adelena left on a fool's errand to find a dragon's tear to save her. I was so delighted to have that woman out of the palace again that I didn't consider all the possibilities it could give me."

A deep laugh bubbled up and out of Pere Raven. "Dragons, indeed! One has to admire the determination of that woman to get herself killed for no reason." The priest leaned forward over the desk, sensing victory. "Keep the baby, then," he said. "And I will take the other two for the mines."

"The Marchant prince watches over the children," warned the Boss. "I will need to keep him out of the way for you to do your work, and that won't be easy."

"Marchant princes are easy to distract," said the priest with a wave of his hand. "Just give him an excuse to kill or shag something, and he will leave those little birds all alone in the nest."

Disgusted by the priest's vulgar language, the young man rose from the table and collected his papers, ready to return to his work at the Golden Palace. He picked up the black silk scarf lying on the back of his chair and shoved it into a pocket.

"I will expect a letter from you the moment you're prepared for the kidnapping," said the young man. "Only then will I ensure the proper measures are taken for you to bring your men onto the palace grounds."

Knowing he was dismissed, Pere Raven rose from his chair, repeated his thanks, and held out a hand to the young man, only smiling again when the gesture was ignored.

"I'm sure you can see yourself out, Pere Raven," said the young man crisply.

The priest bowed and left the office.

After a moment's pause to ensure he was alone, the young man slung his official robes across his shoulders and opened the door of the cupboard in the corner of his office, shoving aside the cloth that hid the portal entrance. He then squeezed the thin metal band at his wrist, transforming into his other self. Now prepared, he took a deep breath and stepped into the cupboard, making sure the door slammed shut behind him.

CHAPTER TWO

"The Strange Shapes Love Takes"

Rainere stood at the foot of the bed and watched as the Gift of Life was fed through a tube into Charlie's arm, the potent magic glinting like liquid metal. The teenager twitched fitfully but didn't make a sound. Rainere thought the cure was probably coming too late and Charlie would be dead before nightfall. He could only hope so.

This is a waste of my time, trying to save these children from what is likely a merciful death, thought Rainere. *Charlie knows far too much about the mines, and I cannot let him tell Adelena about the Gift before I get a chance to explain it to her myself.*

Mrs. Dolores Ollenby was sitting by the little girl who had been brought back with Charlie. She tucked a lavender blanket she had knitted herself around the girl and smoothed the hair off her head. "Has this child finished with the health tonic, Your Highness?" she asked Rainere.

Rainere softened his expression for the older woman. Mrs. Ollenby was the only person in the Golden Palace Rainere considered an ally. "Yes, it has done what it can for that one, Mrs. Ollenby." He wondered if she knew what the tonic really was. "It's Charlie who was the worst hit by the dark magic. I do not think he will recover as the child has."

"Charlie is strong," answered Mrs. Ollenby. She joined Rainere at the foot of Charlie's bed. "I'm sure he lived a tough old life before he came to work for the queen." She squeezed Rainere's arm and gave him a smile. "And, after all, he has the best doctor in Unisia caring for him. If you can't save him, then no one can."

Rainere flinched at the compliment. "Quite."

"Your Highness, if you'll forgive my candor," said Mrs. Ollenby, "I know it must be very disconcerting for you to be living as a guest here, away from the Gray Palace and your own life. I also realize that you have been given a heavy responsibility by Queen Adelena for the care of her three children, but I want you to know that you're not alone and that you can depend on me for whatever you need in the coming days. The Golden Palace is not called the Golden Snake Pit for no reason, but I can promise that I have filled the royal apartment with staff proven loyal to our queen, and there you will always be safe."

Rainere understood that Mrs. Ollenby's effort to reassure him was sincere, but his lip curled slightly at her earnest words. "Did you know that the Golden Palace was called the Snake Pit by my ancestors because it was the House of Government when the Marchant kings ruled Unisia?" said Rainere. A tumult of emotions passed through his forest-green eyes. "Yet the fact is that today, I actually sit in the den of the St. Lucidis lions, Mrs. Ollenby, and they are far more dangerous creatures than any snake could be."

"Queen Adelena gave you guardianship of her children because she trusts you, Your Highness, and knows you are completely capable of the task," insisted Mrs. Ollenby with a stubborn optimism. "This is no small thing."

"Yes, but is it my penance or a reward for everything I did to her?" asked Rainere quietly, and his expression showed he did not want to hear Mrs. Ollenby's answer. "I should be with her now as yet again she throws herself into danger's way, but instead I'm here playing nanny."

"You know that Queen Adelena could never have gone to find the cure for Stella unless she knew that her children were safe, Your Highness," said Mrs. Ollenby. "You aren't just playing nanny—you are guarding the most precious treasure in the kingdom." She leaned in close to Rainere and continued softly, "And helping to influence the young people who will lead this kingdom themselves one day. Again, this is no small thing."

Curious at the lady's words, Rainere turned to Mrs. Ollenby with another question on his lips, but she was already bustling to the door.

"I'll go see to Natalie and Aaron," said Mrs. Ollenby. "You take your time here, Your Highness. I can get the children ready for their riding lesson."

"I will join you," Rainere said, but Mrs. Ollenby stopped him with a hand on his arm.

"Not yet," she said with a smile. "You have a visitor."

Instantly, there was a knock at the door, and High Wizard Ohren popped his head in the room. "Hello there! I was hoping you wouldn't mind if I have a word in private with His Highness, Mrs. Ollenby?"

Mrs. Ollenby bobbed a curtsy. "I was just leaving, High Wizard."

High Wizard Ohren entered the room carrying his air of superiority with him like a balloon on a string. Rainere ground his teeth as Ohren went sniffing about the intravenous setup next to Charlie and checked the rate of flow into the boy's arm.

"You certainly know your way around an IV," Ohren remarked. "But I suppose you had all that practice when you were a blue tonic addict."

Rainere drilled Ohren with a glare and, without rising to the bait, waited for the high wizard to get to the point.

"I had heard that we'd gained some extra guests after your little trip to the Black Mountains this morning," said Ohren, keeping his tone light, though he was clearly annoyed by the reappearance of Charlie and the little girl. "But, unfortunately, it wasn't from you, Your Highness. I would like you to understand how important it is that you keep me abreast of your actions while you're living here in my palace."

Green sparks lit the air by Rainere's head. *Adelena wouldn't want me to punch Ohren in the face on my first day without her here,* he reminded himself and pressed his mouth into a hard line, resisting the violent urge.

"I thought we might have a discussion about what happened when you took the queen and her guard through the portal," continued Ohren. "For some bizarre reason, Her Majesty didn't want me to accompany her, though I wanted to be there. So tell me, how did it go?"

Rainere licked his dry lips and steeled himself to deliver the news. "We had made a successful transition from the Golden Palace to the base of the Black Mountains," he said. "But when I had finished building the portal to the tundra, we heard the screams of what I thought was a Marchant Eldar. Before we could leave the area, Queen Adelena spotted Charlie and this little girl in danger. Using a surprisingly complicated spell, Her Majesty saved the children and insisted that I bring them back to the Golden Palace for care as they were both near death, cursed by some sort of weird dark magic."

Ohren frowned and pulled at his beard, yanking handfuls of it as if it annoyed him. "You say the Black Mountains, but which one exactly?"

"Mount Ecrusius," answered Rainere.

"The gray crystal mines," groaned Ohren, closing his eyes for a moment as if pained. "Goddess be damned! These children were being preyed on by an Eldar in those hunting grounds?"

"And so you understand the conflict we create in keeping them alive?" said Rainere.

Ohren yanked at his beard some more. "Yet if they do survive, who would believe them?" he parried. "No one knows the origins of the Gift of Life except those who need it, and there have been horror stories about the Marchant Eldars since time itself began."

"But it would be easier still to let them die," suggested Rainere. *And if the high wizard does it, then Adelena will blame him, and I'll have kept my promise to her,* he thought.

Ohren looked at Rainere with a raised eyebrow. "Are you any good at killing children, Your Highness?"

Slowly, Rainere shook his head.

"No? Well, me neither, though it would have saved Unisia a world of trouble if I had been such a monster," said Ohren, bringing the specter of the Prophecy of the End of the World into the room with his words. "But you know, Charlie appears to be ridiculously loyal to the queen; when he wakes up, you should give him a job, something to keep him close to you until her return."

"The boy is only a street thief from the slums of the Lower Districts of Concordis," replied Rainere, surprised that the high wizard would suggest such a thing. "What use could he be to me?"

Ohren shrugged. "You're a clever man, I'm sure you'll think of something," he said. "Now, more importantly, tell me how far through the Black Mountains did you get the queen and her men? Did they make it to the tundra?"

Rainere stepped away from Ohren and made his way to the window so he didn't expose the guilt that was tormenting him.

"The Eldar sounded so near, and Queen Adelena had already charged me with saving these two children," he said. "I only had time to put them on my horse and instruct Adelena to leave immediately. The queen and her guards were lined up to go into the portal when I left to return to the Golden Palace."

"Are you telling me that you left the queen and her men to travel the portal alone, and you have no idea how far you got them through the Black Mountains or what danger might have awaited them on the other side?" asked Ohren, his anger incredulous. "The goddess damn you, Prince Rainere, how could you be so careless with her life? How could you be so stupid?"

There was nothing the high wizard could say that would make Rainere feel any worse about letting Adelena walk into that portal without him. He had been so angry that she had manipulated him into taking Charlie back to the Golden Palace, and the Eldar had sounded so close, that Rainere had left her behind without a backward glance.

"I have far more inventive insults to use against myself, High Wizard," said Rainere, and his smoky voice shook just a little. "It's no defense, but the situation was so chaotic, and Adelena so insistent, that I followed her orders when I shouldn't have."

The old wizard's expression softened at Prince Rainere's obvious remorse, and he closed his mouth on more recriminations. Reaching into a pocket, Ohren produced a little hand mirror from his robes.

"I have something that might make you feel a little less negligent," he said bluntly, holding it out to Rainere. "I took this from Orestes's stash in his office. I gave one to the queen before she left so I could talk to her while she was away. I haven't used it yet because I wasn't sure Her Majesty would want to talk to me, but we both know she will answer you."

Rainere took the little mirror and ran his fingers over the black enamel cover, a crescent moon carved on one side. Cloaking his excitement behind anger to reassert his dignity, the prince glared at the high wizard. "When were you going to tell me about this?" he sniped. "Or was I expected to suffer in silence while Adelena was away?"

"I'm trying to help you here, Your Highness," said High Wizard Ohren, offended. "It's for your sake that I hope your portal didn't fail the queen and end up killing her."

"And I hope for *your* sake that I didn't fail either," snapped Rainere, his temper flaring. "Because if Adelena is dead, then I will take the three heirs as my own, and you will have lost your entire royal family."

Ohren seemed almost amused by Rainere's proclamation. "I would expect nothing less than such suicidal stupidity from a Marchant prince," he said. "But that doesn't mean I wouldn't have suggested it myself. Without Queen Adelena to protect them, I'm afraid the children wouldn't last long in the Golden Palace when Lord Orgustus crowns himself the People's King."

Rainere's lip curled at the idea. "People's King, indeed."

"Don't think that man isn't dangerous just because he is also a pompous fool," Ohren said. "Orgustus is desperate to claim back his power as regent, and with the vile propaganda flooding the streets of Concordis, our queen is a very unpopular monarch. Tilburn and I will be working day and night to save Queen Adelena's reputation, though it'll be nearly impossible with her so far away. In fact, I think it would be a good idea to present the children to the public to garner some positive interest in the royal family."

"I will not parade the children for the local rabble to gawk and crow at," said Rainere. "Her Majesty would not want me to expose them in that way."

"Her Majesty never realized how much the people hate her," said Ohren with a heavy sigh. "We need to save her crown, or she won't have one to come back to. *If* she comes back at all."

Rainere nodded stiffly, seeing some sense in Ohren's words. "I will consider what you say," he said.

"That's all I ask, Your Highness," Ohren said, and his expression turned cold again. "Now, if you'll excuse me, I have other matters to attend to today. Though, of course, I will see you this evening. I have a habit of taking dinner with the children, and I don't imagine you would be spiteful enough to break any of the routines that they love, with so much change already in their lives, would you?" And with that parting dig, Ohren gave Rainere a shallow bow and left the room.

Rainere stood at Charlie's bedside and looked down at the boy. He could see the blue veins beneath his skin ferrying the Gift around his body and smell the metallic tang of dark magic in the air of the hospital room.

What in the name of the goddess am I doing here? he wondered, swamped by insecurity. *I have no idea how to care for children. I never even cared for myself! Now I have to be a father and a politician and keep Adelena's crown safe without her here.*

Rainere imagined how excruciating it would be to parade himself and the children in front of the citizens of the court and Concordis, and for one bleak moment, he missed Grotto. The old manservant would never have agreed to his master becoming Adelena's nursemaid, but at least he would have helped Rainere understand the Golden Palace court and all its machinations. If there was anything Grotto knew, it was how to manipulate a political situation to Rainere's advantage. Without him Rainere felt woefully ignorant.

I cannot fail Adelena. Rainere tried to find strength in the idea of justifying Adelena's faith in him, but it was too soon followed by the truth of the past. *Because if I disappoint her again, I know this time she really will kill me.* He wondered if Adelena would ask the dragon for a flame as well as a tear and shuddered at the thought.

Having done what he could for the two patients, Rainere realized he should be with Natalie and Aaron instead of dreaming about their mother. Locking the door of the hospital room behind him, Rainere reluctantly headed back to the royal apartments and his new responsibilities.

Chapter Three
"Friends Return as Strangers"

Adele stared up at Queen's Guard Leith anxiously. "Can you see anything?" she asked.

Dawn lit the sky, but the bottom of the valley was steeped in gloom as Leith jumped down from the tree. "I could see the tundra lands, Your Majesty," said the young QG, dusting off his pants. "They are no more than a half-day march down this valley."

"Wonderful!" Adele tried to shake off the anxiety that weighed on her shoulders. "That means Prince Rainere's portal has deposited us right where he said it would, and we are definitely through the Black Mountains."

"Not quite *through*, Your Majesty," corrected General Ohrig. Standing up in his stirrups, he surveyed their surroundings. "This narrow valley would be perfect for an ambush if anyone wanted to attack us. We should scale the side of the valley just to be off the path a bit."

Adele agreed. *Something's not right here,* her instincts told her, and the Chime Voices in her mind tinkled *caution* in their song. Maybe it was the diseased and dying trees around them or the sour tang in the air, but the land itself wasn't healthy.

Adele loosened the reins, and because she wasn't an experienced rider, she let her horse pick the best path through the gray scrub and boulders scattered over the steep wall of the valley.

The six men of Adele's Queen's Guard tried to ride in formation around her, but the narrow track made the going difficult. Adele felt a buzzing at the back of her neck and brushed at it. The Chime Voices in her head began tinkling a little louder, so she twisted in her saddle, searching the scrub around her, but there was nothing there.

"Whoever is humming," said Ohrig irritably, "don't."

The men looked at each other. No one had been humming.

Adele listened intently to the Chime Voices in her head as they began to sing more urgently. She didn't recognize their song, but her heart beat a little faster. Though she was loath to stop their progress out of this horrible valley, the Chime Voices were nervous, and Adele had learned that meant she should be nervous too.

"Ohrig, I think something is coming," said Adele. She was still turning in her saddle to speak with the general when she saw a light flash down the valley behind him. "Shit—something like that!"

The light flashed again and then again, traveling rapidly up the valley floor and bumping around as it made its way toward them.

"Men, cover the queen!" shouted Ohrig. "We have incoming!"

The Queen's Guard fought the terrain to get close to Adele, but it was too tricky, so she waved them off and led her horse behind the nearest boulder. It was poor cover, but she couldn't take her eyes off the light that was getting closer and moving fast. It looked like a great golden fireball, bouncing along in the dirt until it passed Adele and suddenly hit a tree just ahead of her. The ball of light disintegrated in a shower of sparks, and something big dropped to the ground in a heap.

"It's a man!" cried Adele. "And he's injured." The light was gone, but the humming sound was louder now, and she could hear a deep buzzing beneath it, like two instruments playing the same tune at once. It made her skin crawl, and the Chime Voices screeched a warning.

Ohrig jumped down off his horse, drawing his sword as he approached the man lying on the ground.

"You there." Ohrig nudged the man's foot with the tip of his sword. "You alive?"

The man moaned and rolled over. Adele gasped in recognition. "Ripenzo Shale?"

Ripenzo opened his indigo eyes. "Hide," he choked. "Have to...hide!"

The humming and buzzing grew louder still, and Adele turned at Captain Lucky's warning to see a black shadow in midair flying down the valley. "What the hell is that?" she shouted over the noise.

"Damn you—hide!" Ripenzo's voice rasped away, and his head sagged back onto the ground. Clearly exhausted, there was no way he could save himself.

"Bear, get off your horse and help me take this man!" shouted Ohrig. He looked along the steep valley wall and pointed. "Up there. Caves. Let's go."

The Queen's Guard leaped into action, Captain Lucky taking the reins of the horses as QG Bear threw Ripenzo Shale over his broad shoulders. Ohrig led the group up the slope to a collection of shallow caves carved out of the rock.

Adele tried to slow her racing heart as her horse kept losing its footing on the loose rocks underfoot. She only just managed to hold herself in the saddle and cling on until the horse clambered up and over the lip of the cave. Jumping to the ground in relief, Adele handed the reins to Captain Lucky, who took her horse to the back of the cave with the others.

Adele helped Bear lower Ripenzo Shale to the floor and quickly examined him for injuries. She couldn't see any blood, but his shaggy blond hair was dark with sweat, and he looked older than when she had last seen him. His stubbled cheeks were gray with dust, and more gaunt than before. Rip was breathing heavily, but she couldn't work out if he was asleep or just suffering with his eyes closed.

Knowing there wasn't much she could do for him at the moment, Adele joined her Queen's Guard where they stood in a line at the cave entrance, looking out into the valley. The dark buzzing cloud had formed into a swarm of heavy gray figures.

"Are they shadow wasps?" said QG Owens, the first to recognize them. "But the high wizard said they were extinct!"

"I'm sure they'll kill us just the same," grunted General Ohrig. He watched the swarm hover and then dart as one mass along the valley floor.

"But I know they can be killed too," said Captain Lucky, clearly trying to remember back to his magical creature studies. "They have a carapace, or skeleton, covering their bodies, as hard as armor, but there are joints between the plates. Our best bet would be to stab through the joints. Avoid the stingers; they are covered with a neural poison that acts on the brain and nerves, killing in minutes. The eyes—yes, and the eyes!" Lucky shouted over the noise. "Like spiders, they have thousands of eyes. If you can stab them—"

"Chop off the stinger at the base, and stab them through the jaws," groaned Ripenzo as he pushed himself up on his elbows. "It's your only hope."

Adele swallowed, her throat dry. "It looks like twenty wasps in that swarm," she said. "And they're flying right where we were standing. I think they're looking for us."

"Nice," growled Bear, stepping in front of Adele. "Then we get to add shadow wasps to the list of Dark Entities we kill."

The group watched as the swarm of wasps darted along the floor of the valley before separating and flying off in different directions.

"That can't be good," muttered Ohrig. He took a step closer to the edge of the cave entrance to see where the wasps had gone.

Adele could hardly hear the Chime Voices over the hammering of her heart, but she finally managed to focus on their song. At the first sign of danger, her two magics had awoken, the leonine gold and the serpentine green, and fired through her veins, waiting to be used. The Chime Voices sang a spell that filled Adele's mouth with a metallic taste and made her feel sick. It was dark magic they wanted to use, magic heavy with death and destruction. The serpentine green hissed its excitement and filled her hands until she could feel it sparking and fizzing at her fingertips. The Chime Voices pushed the words onto Adele's lips, and she began the chant.

"Adelena," Ripenzo's gasp made Adele turn to look down at him. "Stop what you're doing, now. Protect the men with a web." He struggled to sit up and managed to make it to his knees, his eyes narrowed in pain. "Protect. Not kill."

Ripenzo is wrong, Adele told herself, but it could have been the voice of her magic that spoke. *I need to destroy the threat so my guards will be safe, not hide us like mice in a hole.*

A wasp appeared in the entrance of the cave, surprising the men and making Ohrig shout a warning. The man-sized creature hovered, and they all got a good look at the matte-black body armor and the wickedly sharp stinger dripping with viscous poison. The wings created a huge noise, holding the creature stationary as they beat the air. The wasp's eyes were shiny and huge, swiveling on short stalks as it assessed them and then darted backward and away. The encounter was over in a matter of moments, and then they heard the hideous sound of the swarm regrouping. Twenty shadow wasps dropped into the entrance of the cave, almost blocking out the light.

Adele's human terror made the Chime Voices chant all the faster. The wasps advanced, stingers curled over their heads like scorpions, and pushed the Queen's Guard back into the cave. Given ground, half of the wasps dropped to their six feet and folded back their wings, gnashing razor-sharp jaws at the humans, while the others stayed back, blocking the only exit.

Terrified but prepared, Adele shouted, "Men, behind me!" The magic was vibrating in her voice and had coalesced in her hands, dense and toxic. She raised her hands in front of her chest, and a sphere of black power pulsed within the center of a green haze.

"What are you doing?" Ripenzo's horrified shout distracted Adele for a moment. "You'll kill us all!"

The Queen's Guard had dropped back to form a line in front of her, but with one step, Adele moved through their rank and faced down the looming stinger of a flying wasp. The magic was excited, and the ball was hard to hold. The wasps advanced, and Adele couldn't hesitate. She felt time slow as she held the magic high above her head, ready to kill the wasp.

Suddenly, Adele was flung backward as Ripenzo leaped in front of her, a golden net of magic flying from his hands to cover the humans. Then his mouth opened in a howl as the long black thorn of a wasp's stinger stabbed him through the chest.

The green ball in Adele's hands exploded in the same instant, and everything went black.

CHAPTER FOUR
"To Dream of Gods"

Adele stayed quiet and still. Something was looking for her, something terrifying. She held her breath, and her heart stilled. She could hear the footsteps dragging closer to her. There was a low moan and a grating noise, like the sound of a blade sliding over stone. The beast was already there, limping toward her through the darkness.

"No. I killed you," Adele told the grinning corpse.

"We are coming for you." The Sandarian mage pointed his worm-eaten finger at Adele, and she recoiled in horror. "The great god Dahk'hani will walk this world again."

Adele's vision swirled, and when it settled, she was standing with the mage on an island of rock surrounded by a lake of lava. Hot and cold winds blew about her as Adele looked for a way to escape. There was a movement in the lava, and before her a great hand reached up, dripping molten rock, and the form of a giant man rose out of the glowing lake of fire.

"Do not fear the great god," tinkled the Chime Voices. "He waits for Mother as we do."

The Sandarian mage leaped to plant himself on the leg of the giant still rising from the lava, his head now beyond her sight in the core of the volcano.

"Dahk'hani's time has come," screeched the mage. "You have woken him, angel!"

"No!" Adele shouted, but her voice was only a whisper behind the Chime Voices.

The Sandarian mage laughed. "You will be his!" And the massive hand of the god reached down to shower Adele in drops of fire, burning her alive.

Adele woke screaming, and pain ricocheted around her head, beating her brain to a pulp. She rolled to her side on the stone floor and hugged herself tightly, trying to keep all her pieces together, as she shuddered at the memory of her dream.

"Your Majesty?" Ohrig's voice was filled with dust and grit. "Tell me you're all right!"

"Sweet Christ," croaked Adele and forced herself to sit up, her vision swaying with the nauseating waves in her stomach. "I'm going to throw up."

"That means you're alive." Ohrig was relieved.

Adele looked up from the ground and took in the scene of devastation before her. Twenty shadow wasp carcasses were scattered across the ground, oozing and burnt. The walls of the cave were scorched black with huge chunks blasted out of the rock.

She couldn't believe the carnage her spell bomb had caused. She tried to stand. "The men, Ohrig?"

"All alive, thank the goddess," said Ohrig. "Leith here got a bad knock to the head." Ohrig was already checking Leith's eyes and taking his pulse. "And Lucky has been doctoring a few scrapes and bruises, but the stranger got the worse of it, Your Majesty."

Adele saw Ripenzo lying in the wreckage, the wasp stinger still protruding from his chest. Instantly, the gold magic behind her head came alive, and she found the strength to stagger over to him.

"Someone help me get this stinger out," ordered Adele, and Lucky was there to lift Ripenzo so she could pull the long black barb from his back. When he was laid back down, Adele could actually see the cave floor through the gaping hole in his body. She didn't let it concern her because her Chime Voices told her he wasn't dead. Yet.

Adele laid her hands on Ripenzo's damaged chest and closed her eyes. The gold magic raced out, active and energized. It had played no part in the dark spell, so it was strong and ready for her. Adele cast her gold magic directly into Ripenzo's chest and didn't wait for the Chime Voices to tell her what to do. It was the same spell they had sung when Adele healed Rainere after they had broken through the apex to Prince Rainold's prison dimension.

As the rest of the world faded out, Adele dove into Ripenzo's body, and the first thing she noticed was the sheer scope of Ripenzo's magic. It was like a vast ocean, as deep and gold as High Wizard Ohren's had been. Adele let her magic twine around

Ripenzo's organs, mixing it with the tide of his own magic. In her mind's eye, she could see the red tendrils of the wasp's poison like worms attacking the strong walls of his heart and polluting the color of his magic, tinting it all red.

Adele went to work. The gold magic could heal the damage, but she would need the green magic to suck out the wasp's poison. Though her green magic was depleted, it could sense Rip's power and delved deeply, hungry for what it could get. The green magic absorbed all the red poison, and this let the gold magic work on healing Ripenzo. While it was easy for Adele to set her serpentine tendrils to hunt the red worms out, they became harder to control when they tried to launch themselves into the deep well of Ripenzo's magic. Adele struggled mightily to pull back, not wanting to take any magic not freely given.

The Chime Voices complained bitterly at her decision, but Adele slowly pulled her green magic, and then the gold, from Ripenzo, making sure she didn't shock him.

In the real world, Adele opened her eyes and gazed down at Ripenzo. The wound had left a nasty scar, but he was whole again. Adele brushed the sandy-blond hair off Rip's head and felt his neck for a pulse. Tears of exhaustion and relief dripped down her face at the steady thud of blood under her fingertips. "He's safe," she said.

Lucky knelt on the other side of Ripenzo and confirmed it for himself. The young captain looked up at Adele with awe. "Your Majesty, you just brought this man back to life!"

Adele was too tired to explain that Rip hadn't really been dead, just damaged, as his magic had kept his body going despite the injury, so she only smiled.

I wonder if I could take just a bit of magic back while Rip is still asleep, she thought. *I just need a little to keep going, and he has so much.* Adele ran her fingers over the raised surface of the scar on Ripenzo's chest. She jumped when Rip's hand closed over hers.

Adele looked into his indigo eyes and smiled. "Hello again," she said.

"I'll kill you for this," said Rip, then he passed out cold.

CHAPTER FIVE
"Strangers Become Friends"

They couldn't have left that nasty cave even if they'd wanted to. The men were too bruised and battered, and Rip was in no condition to go anywhere. Night had fallen fast in the valley and taken the temperature with it.

The Queen's Guard had removed most of the wasp corpses, dumping them in a clump of trees at the bottom of the valley, but the smell of their poison still tainted the air with a metallic tang.

QG Pepper had built a fire at the back of the cave, where a natural crack in the ceiling provided a chimney, and set to cooking dinner while the rest of the QGs set up camp for the night. Adele had taken an opiate that their field doctor, Captain Lucky, had recommended, but it was no help for the bone-weary exhaustion and the awful hollow feeling under her heart where her serpentine magic should have coiled.

There wasn't much conversation around the fire, and Adele could tell the men had been seriously shocked by her magical bomb and her ability to heal Ripenzo Shale. They kept casting her sideways glances, as if to watch in case she did anything else dangerous. Ohrig hadn't said a word to Adele other than to ask about her pain, and she didn't know how to begin to apologize for the magic that had almost killed the men along with the shadow wasps.

It must have been the smell of food that woke Ripenzo Shale from his sleep. With a deep groan, he sat up and dusted himself off, fastidiously tying the ends of his shredded shirt together before shuffling between Owens and Bear at the fireside. He didn't seem to mind the stares of the QGs and Adele as he took the plate of food that QG Pepper handed him.

"You decided to stay," said Rip, through a mouthful of bean stew. "It would have been smarter to keep going and get the hell out of this valley."

"We wouldn't leave an injured man behind," said Ohrig evenly. "Especially one who had just saved all our lives."

Ripenzo shrugged. "You don't owe me anything." His eyes flickered to Adele. "Only she does."

"Her Majesty saved your life," interjected Captain Lucky. "You should be thanking her."

Ripenzo turned to Adele, and she reluctantly met his indigo gaze. *He knows what I wanted to take from him too,* she thought.

"So, stranger, why don't we start with your name?" suggested Ohrig.

Ripenzo smirked at Adele's surprise. "They don't recognize me like you do," he said. "To them I always looked like this." Rip grasped his wrist and activated the magic in a thin metal bracelet. Adele saw a green spark, and then sitting before her was a tall man with coffee-colored skin, long brown hair, and deep brown eyes, clearly Sandarian. Rip let go of the bracelet, and he returned to his pale skin and blue eyes. "Tell me, Queen Adelena, did you ever see my disguise?"

Adele shook her head. "I never could understand why everyone believed you were Sandarian. I always thought you looked more St. Lucidis than I did," she said. "But how did you manage to fool High Wizard Ohren and the whole court of Unisia?"

"The spell uses a unique type of green magic." Ripenzo shrugged. "You shouldn't have been able to see through it without a charm to protect your sight from illusions. Or it could be that you're simply very strong." He rubbed the new scar on his chest.

"So you're Ripenzo Shale, the Sandarian ambassador?" asked Ohrig, still catching up.

"My parents call me something else, but I like Ripenzo Shale." He shrugged. "You can call me Rip, if you like."

"What have you been doing since you ran from us on the King's Highway?" Ohrig's tone was curious, but his hand was resting on the hilt of his sword.

Ripenzo cocked his head to the side in his familiar gesture, but Adele knew that she was the only one who could tell that Rip was probing Ohrig's mind with a magical projection. *He can't do that to my general,* thought Adele protectively. She called on her own magic and let it flow into her hands.

Ripenzo held up a hand in Adele's direction, not taking his eyes off Ohrig. "Easy, tiger, I'm just looking at the man."

"Then why don't you look a little less hard," snapped Adele.

Rip turned to Adele, and she could see the wide bands of gold spinning around his pupils. "Why are you always so eager to believe the worst of me?" he asked, acid crisping the edges of his words. "I've been nothing but pleasant to you since we met."

"Because you're a liar," said Adele, too tired to be subtle. "And I could tell you were untrustworthy from the moment I met you."

Rip gave Adele a long, hard look. "You didn't have to destroy my life over a couple of little lies, though, did you? I was just trying to help you, as any fool could see that you were totally lost, dancing to the tune of that St. Lucidis wizard, not knowing what or who you were."

Adele knew that, for whatever reason, Rip was trying to bait her and she should control her temper. "You didn't have to run away from me," she said. "I would have protected you at the Golden Palace."

"Are you kidding me? You can't even protect yourself!" Rip chuckled with genuine humor. "I knew what it would mean to be a prisoner in the Golden Palace, even if you didn't."

Adele couldn't deny that High Wizard Ohren might very well have had Ripenzo killed, or worse, if she'd brought him back to the Golden Palace. Not that she'd had much of a choice at the time.

"Anyway, I've got bigger problems than you right now, Queen Adelena," continued Rip as he held his plate out for another helping of stew. "I have to travel back through these bloody mountains again to find someone I lost this morning. I'd just escaped the—I'd just escaped when those shadow wasps caught my tail and forced me to run to this goddess-forsaken valley." Rip shoveled stew into his mouth, and his eyes scanned the silent group around him. "Now this is the part of the conversation where you tell me why *you* are here, lurking on the wrong edge of the Black Mountains."

"Who did you lose?" Adele's mind instantly flew to Charlie and how he had dropped out of the sky just this morning where Rainere had built their portals. The coincidence was too strange. "Was it a young man and a little child?"

Rip slowly lowered his spoon, and Adele saw a flicker of fear in his expression. "Why would you ask?"

"Because Charlie works for me," said Adele. "I thought I'd lost him, but this morning I caught him falling out of the sky with a Marchant Eldar screaming after him."

"Where is Charlie now?" asked Rip.

"I sent him back to the Golden Palace with Prince Rainere," said Adele, watching Rip cautiously. "He was near dead, bleeding from the eyes, and Rainere said he needed something called the Gift of Life to heal him. I sent the little child back with him as well."

Rip lowered his plate to his lap. "You're going to give Charlie the Gift of Life?" He closed his eyes as if in pain. "Please never tell him that you did that. It would kill him to know he'd had any of the evil potion."

Adele didn't know anything about this Gift of Life, but something in Rip's manner made her inclined to believe him when he said it was evil. "Well, I can't help that now," she said quietly. "If it saves his life, it'll have been worth it."

"Not to Charlie," said Rip.

His accusing tone and Adele's own guilt made her feel defensive. "And why was Charlie falling out of the sky in the first place, Rip?" she asked. "I sent him to the Gray Palace with strict instructions to return to me even if he failed to complete his mission. Did you find him at the palace or in the Dark Forest? Is that where you were hiding?"

"Yes, I had been hiding in the Dark Forest—from *you*, I might add," said Ripenzo, his eyes flashing with irritation. "I was trying to get back home when I was captured by the same cretins who kidnapped Charlie at the Gray Palace. I couldn't even work in their cat-hole place, but they were so greedy for magical humans they kept me anyway."

"What cat-hole place?" asked Adele.

Rip pressed his lips together, and his eyes narrowed in anger. "That's Charlie's story to tell," he said. "But I can tell you that you've put Charlie in great danger taking him to the Golden Palace—those immortal wizards will tear him to pieces when they see how strong he is. That is, if he isn't dead already."

"No." Adele refused to believe it. "I left Charlie in Prince Rainere's care, and the prince will protect him like he does my own children."

"You left your children with Prince Rainere *Marchant*!" Rip's eyes widened at this, and he slapped a hand to his forehead. "You are still as catshit crazy as I remember! Of all the goddess-damn stupid things you could do—" Rip took a deep breath, clearly trying to control his temper. "Well, at least I now know where to find Charlie. I hope you'll have no problem with me going to visit him? I can go in my official capacity as the rogue Sandarian ambassador as long as you give me a royal warrant."

"Of course," replied Adele, eager to give Rip this easy request, until Ohrig coughed loudly.

"Your Majesty, there is still the matter of the theft."

Adele's stomach dropped. "Ah, yes."

Rip looked from Adele to Ohrig. "What theft? I never took anything from you, Queen Adelena."

"I know you didn't, Rip," said Adele. She knew the time had come to tell him the whole truth. "But things got complicated after you left us..."

Ripenzo crossed his legs and put his plate down in the dirt. His eyes were alight with suspicion.

Adele pulled Ripenzo's letter from her pocket, now a little tattered, and handed it to him. "After you left us on the road, we received word that we had to go to the Belvoir Estate instead of back to the Golden Palace, but an unseasonable snowstorm blew in and forced us to turn in to the Dark Forest. We knew that the storm would be dangerous because of your warning, so we asked Prince Rainere for shelter at the Gray Palace instead of continuing on."

Rip turned the folded paper over in his hands. "You kept my letter with you this whole time?" he said. "I'm touched."

"The only problem is that I seem to run into a lot of storms," said Adele with a grimace. "You weren't very specific, you know."

Rip gave her one of his rakish grins, and despite the blood and dirt on his face, he was handsome. "You know that I didn't mean a meteorological storm, right?"

Adele shrugged. "Your warning soon became the least of my worries. After we entered the Gray Palace, my daughter Natalie gave Prince Rainere the Fire Orchid stamens—without my knowledge, of course. Then, when the storm finally broke, we went on to the Belvoir Estate without them."

"What!" Rip was aghast, but Adele's heavy look made him shake his head. "Fine, I'll save my questions for the end."

"For his own reasons, Prince Rainere followed me to the Belvoir Estate, and then for my own reasons, a few days later, I returned with my family to the Gray Palace," said Adele.

"I'm guessing 'for your own reasons' is code for 'I was sleeping with the prince'," interrupted Ripenzo. He seemed satisfied with Adele's glare. "But please, go on; I can't wait for the part about the theft."

"Back at the Gray Palace, there was worse to come," said Adele, her voice rough as she remembered the horror of that time. "Rainere was under contract to the Spider Empress Ka-kik to kidnap and marry me. Instead, he gave Natalie to the empress in my place to complete their deal, thinking that the empress would give Natalie back to him, but she kept my little girl and wanted to eat her to steal Natalie's power, which would allow the empress to walk in the sun. When I found out about what Rainere had done, I led the Queen's Guard into the Nest, and we rescued Natalie and killed the Spider People with Rainere's dragon flame."

"But not all the Spider People," interrupted Captain Lucky. "We left some of the good tree-dwelling ones alive."

Rip raised an eyebrow at the qualification. "How kind of you," he said.

"After returning with my family to the Golden Palace, we discovered that my baby, Stella, was ill with the summer influenza. Rainere realized that he had the Fire Orchid stamens in his possession, and he returned them to me, but not before I had sent Charlie to the Gray Palace to steal them back. High Wizard Ohren made the tonic for Stella, but she was too damaged to recover properly." Adele paused to wipe at the tear that had escaped down her cheek.

"Rainere put Stella in a coma to keep her alive. It was decided that the only cure for her was a Dragon Tear. High Wizard Ohren was sure that Rainere's father, Prince Rainold, would know where the last dragon in Unisia lived, and so Rainere and I ventured into Prince Rainold's prison dimension to ask him where the dragon was, and he gave us the map to the Ice Mountains. We left the Golden Palace this morning, traveling through a portal that Prince Rainere made for us, and then we met you. The end."

Rip shook his head and whistled. "All of that happened in the last two weeks after I left you?" He grinned. "I guess I should count myself lucky that I got away from you when I did. The mines weren't a picnic, but at least I had some laughs with Charlie."

Adele dried her eyes. None of this was funny to her. "I've been queen of Unisia for just over six weeks, and I've had so many attempts on my life I'm losing count," she said. "First the mage in Sandar, then Empress Ka-kik, then an assassin in the slums of Concordis. You might understand why I'm a little on edge finding you again, as the only witness to my murder of the mage. All the decisions I've made as queen have been under the most difficult circumstances…"

"So what's all this about a theft?" interrupted Rip. His intelligent gaze turned on Ohrig. "When you got back to the Golden Palace after Belvoir, what did you tell the high wizard had happened to his precious Fire Orchid stamens? You didn't know yet that Natalie had given them away, right?"

"Well, that's when I was put in another very difficult position," Adele answered. "I told the high wizard the truth about what had happened in Sandar, with me killing that mage and you helping me, but I couldn't possibly tell the Court of the Golden Palace because they would have had me arrested and charged with using dark magic for murder. So I told Lord Orgustus, the ex-regent, well, that you had stolen the stamens from me, and that was the reason you hadn't come back with us, despite being a gift of Empress Sanda'hani."

"So I took the blame for you not being able to control your children." Rip's eyes narrowed. "And now my Sandarian ambassador disguise can't go to either Sandar or the Golden Palace anymore."

"Couldn't you just go to the Golden Palace without a disguise?" Adele suggested. "You'd look right at home with your blond hair and blue eyes."

Ripenzo sighed and wrapped his arms around his knees. "But I liked the ambassador. He's really handsome, and taller than me, and very popular with women. Also, Unisians don't understand anything about Sandarian culture or magic, so I could behave in any way I liked. If I try to enter the palace as a regular Unisian, I'll have rules put on me that I don't want to follow."

"For what it's worth, Ripenzo, I am sorry," Adele said. "I didn't plan to blame you for stealing the stamens—I just kind of blurted it out."

"Like you just 'blurted out' that fatal spell, which would have killed you all if I hadn't been here to protect you from it?" said Ripenzo sharply. "I haven't heard your thanks for sacrificing my life for that yet."

"That's because we would never have been attacked by wasps if you hadn't led them to us," countered Adele. "But tell me, what are you going to do now that I've told you the truth?"

Rip rubbed his chest again where the wasp's stinger had impaled him. "Have you really left your three children under the protection of a Marchant prince at the Golden Palace?" he asked, cocking his head. Adele had no trouble shielding her mind from his gentle psychic prod.

"The wizards at the Golden Palace think I'm a demon," Adele said, watching Rip closely for his reaction. "But they don't know how my magic functions or why it's me in the Prophecy of the End of the World. The only thing that's clear is that I'm not their lost St. Lucidis queen but the daughter of the St. Lucidis king and a demon called Rainestra Marchant. As it turns out, the true heir to the throne was supposed to be the son of Queen Olivia and King Octavius St. Lucidis, who was given to the Marchant Eldars by High Wizard Ohren." Adele bit her lip. "Unfortunately, with me on this journey, Prince Rainere is the only person I trust to protect my children from the St. Lucidis wizards and Lord Orgustus."

"And this is a journey that you are taking only because another Marchant prince told you he knew where a dragon lived," said Rip. "Seems like you are putting an awful lot of trust in some very dangerous men, Queen Adelena."

Adele grimaced. "My choices in the matter are very limited, Ripenzo. Remember, I'm still a stranger on your world."

Rip gave Adele a long look that she couldn't read. The fire crackled and the men of the Queen's Guard watched and listened. The silence stretched.

"You know, I really don't want to get involved in your problems again, Queen Adelena," Rip said finally. "You get yourself tangled up in a nasty prophecy, then betray the only person who can really help you get out of it," he pointed at himself, "fall into bed with a mad Marchant prince, let one of your kids be poisoned by an influenza, and let another child give away the antidote, anger all the St. Lucidis wizards by messing up their prophecy, then break another Marchant prince out of prison to help you deal with the problems you just created, only to leave your children in the hands of the previously mentioned mad prince while you trip off across Evendaar looking for a dragon."

"God, when you use that tone, everything sounds stupid." Adele rubbed her eyes, too tired to argue anymore. "Just so you know, I didn't break Prince Rainold out of his prison. I only broke the apex locking him inside the dimension."

"There you go!" laughed Rip and slapped his knee. "There's the girl I saw sitting next to a dead mage in Sandar, denying all blame for killing him." He wagged his finger at Adele, still smiling. "Just so *you* know, once Prince Rainold realizes that you broke his apex, then it's only a matter of time until he escapes."

Rip waved the letter at Adele. "The storm in my note was a metaphor for the world of shit that was about to come down on your head through the Prophecy of the End of the World, but I guess I should've been more specific. I should have said, 'Don't trust any Marchant princes, don't ever leave your kids alone, and don't listen to a word that a St. Lucidis wizard has to say.'"

Adele honestly couldn't tell if Ripenzo was laughing at her again, because his head was tilted, and he was clearly waiting for her reaction.

"Screw you, Ripenzo." Adele glared at the trickster sitting on the other side of the fire. She couldn't afford to indulge in self-recriminations when so much depended on her strength right now. "You can keep your bloody warnings, and *they* can all keep their bloody prophecy. I'm going to find a dragon and get a tear to save my daughter's life, and the rest of Evendaar can go to hell."

"You do that, Queen Adelena." Ripenzo rolled his eyes again. "Watch how well that attitude works for you." With that last jab at her dignity, Rip pulled his jacket around his shoulders and gave his stew plate back to Pepper. Clearly, the conversation was over, and Adele could only sit fuming as Ripenzo lay down on his coat. Within moments he was fast asleep.

CHAPTER SIX
"Barely Believable Love"

Lady Olivia gasped once more before she judged her ecstasy faked sufficiently. It did the trick, and Lord Orgustus finally rolled off her.

Orgustus lay on his back, his cheeks still pink with his own climax, but already he was regarding the ceiling with a look of distant concentration. Olivia was losing his attention as quickly as she had gained it.

Olivia pushed herself up on her elbow and pressed herself to Orgustus's side. She ran her finger down the side of his face, adoring the curve of his cheeks and the strength of his square chin. She gazed at his beautiful blue eyes, so bright and clear, with the thinnest golden circle around the black pupil. His ancient magical heritage couldn't be more obvious. He was old blood and all the old money that went with it. Olivia sighed contentedly and leaned in to kiss his cheek.

Orgustus flinched from her touch. "Enough, Olivia," he commanded. "I told you I only had a little time for you, and now that time is done."

Olivia pouted but didn't give up so easily. "Why are you so grumpy tonight, Orgustus?" She loved saying his name—it was so daringly familiar without "my lord" in front of it, like it would be after they were married. Olivia pushed herself up to sit so he could get a better view of her chest; she knew just what to say to get his attention back to her.

"The queen doesn't need me until tomorrow morning." She smiled up at him from beneath her lashes. "I bet I could get you to forget your work for a little while longer."

Orgustus snarled, marring his good looks. "You know there is a little job called running the kingdom, and someone has to do it even though our queen seems too busy for the work. Where is she right now, do you know?"

Olivia ran her hand across his chest and played with the small patch of blond hair there. "I told you, she's been in meetings all day with Prince Rainere and the high wizard. I think her kids are with her too. Those little brats go everywhere with her." Olivia let her wandering hand move lower. "But not Stella, of course; she is still hidden away in quarantine somewhere. Only Mrs. Ollenby has the awful job of having to see to her."

"I wonder why the baby hasn't died yet?" mused Lord Orgustus. "The babies in the city are dying left and right, and yet the queen's child clings to life. Meanwhile, the queen is still tolerating the presence of the Marchant prince in the Golden Palace; perhaps she's keeping him here for more than one reason. Perhaps he's helping her keep the child alive with his dark magic."

"Well, you know what I think?" said Olivia. "I think the queen and the prince are in a relationship. The way he looks at her, it's so obvious."

"But how do you know she returns his affections?" asked Orgustus sharply.

Olivia shrugged. "Because she dresses better when she knows he'll be there, she wears perfume, and she really cares what her makeup looks like, for once." Olivia gave Orgustus a sidelong look before she delivered her final piece of information. "And I saw them kissing at the Belvoir Estate. It was right after the ball for the prizewinners, and it was dark, but I saw them together, huddled in a tight corner. They kissed for ages, and he really knew what to do with his hands, if you know what I mean." Olivia giggled but quieted at Orgustus's dark look—he liked his girls to be ladies.

"Did anyone else see them?" Orgustus asked.

Olivia shook her blond tresses, curled just for Orgustus this evening. "Nope, just me. I stayed until they stopped and the queen went back to her room."

"So she favors Green Blood," said Orgustus to himself. "Surely her Queen's Guard would know if there was a relationship there, even if they are sworn to silence." He looked at Olivia with his eyebrow raised and a knowing smile on his lips. "I'm sure the good Captain Lucky would know everything about his precious queen."

Olivia wrinkled her nose at Orgustus's implication. "The captain is so boring!" she whined. "All he ever wants to do is take walks in the garden and talk of his prospects in the Golden Palace, now that he has some actual hope for advancement with a queen to guard instead of just old statues. He's too loyal to his queen to be any help to us, Orgustus. Let me try with one of the other ones. Maybe QG Leith could be more help? Or even that stable hand Benjamin from Belvoir."

But Orgustus was too clever for that, even though she kept her voice neutral.

His hand covered hers on his chest, gripping it hard. "Are you trying to make me jealous, my lady? Even I've heard the rumors about you and that Belvoir stable hand," said Orgustus, giving her the look she hated most. "Now please use your brain, if you have one, and tell me what the hell would a lowly QG like Leith know that his captain would not? Leith would be a waste of your time." He eyed her breasts. "And your improving talents."

Olivia bit her lip. That last comment stung. She had never had a lover who complained about her skills in bed before Orgustus. Yet he was the former regent, and at twenty-five, six years her senior. He would have bedded dozens of women before her. She would just have to work harder than all the others to keep him. She would need to be smart and sexy—but above all useful.

Olivia looked down, attempting to appear chastened. "I just meant that Leith is more susceptible to a little flirting," she said. "The Queen's Guard seem to be very tight. I mean, the general is definitely in charge, but more often than not, it's all the QGs in the meetings with the queen, and they all seem to know what her plans are. Orgustus, if you had seen them coming back from the Gray Palace after the horse carnival, you would know what I mean. I think the queen trusts her guards more than she trusts anyone else. I mean, I know she likes me, but it's so hard to know what she's really thinking. And those eyes! Sometimes I think she can read my mind."

"Sometimes you think she can read your mind!" Orgustus's eyes widened, and Olivia didn't realize he was making fun of her until he got out of bed and backed away from her. "Goodness, Olivia, that is just so spooky! I wonder if this mind-reading queen is going to wear pink to the court dinner tonight?"

Olivia wanted to roll her eyes. Orgustus really liked to belabor a point when he had one, but as it wasn't wise to annoy him, she pushed her shoulders back a little more.

"Orgustus, I only meant that the queen is very reserved. It's going to take a while to befriend her properly to get the sort of information you need." Olivia pouted.

Orgustus wrapped himself in a blue silk robe with an intricate golden lion embroidered on the back. It had been a gift from another lover, and he knew she knew it.

"What I need, Olivia," Orgustus said, coming back to the point of their early evening tryst, "is to have somebody on the inside of Queen Adelena's cortege, and I thought you were that someone. When you came to me, you said that you held the queen's confidence. Where is that confidence now, while the kingdom is dropping dead from the influenza and our queen is sneaking about the palace with a damned Marchant prince?"

"I thought the influenza had stopped spreading now that the vaccines are ready," said Olivia quietly. She didn't want to make Orgustus any angrier than he was, but she did care about all the dying babies.

"They are, *now!*" he shouted. "But no thanks to her. I'm the one who oversaw their distribution to the city and into the villages. I'm the one who consoled the grieving families and attended all the funerals. I'm the one who provided funding to our overrun hospices out of my own pocket, using my own family funds! What has the queen done to help with the influenza? Nothing! She hasn't even left the palace since she got back from Belvoir Estate, and she cares for no one except her own child, who a fool could tell you is going to die soon."

Orgustus's cheeks were flaming, and he stomped around the room, incensed by the trouble the queen was causing him.

Despite having heard all these complaints before, Olivia rose up on her knees and waited for Orgustus to run himself out and catch sight of what she was offering him. Often his anger led to passion, and Olivia wanted to please him with her body now that she had made him so frustrated with her lack of information. As his complaints against the world petered out, his eyes inevitably ran over her supple form and down to the blond triangle of curls between her legs.

Orgustus approached the bed and stood in front of Olivia, his robe open to show his broad chest and growing excitement. Pleased, Olivia leaned forward for a kiss, but then he stepped back just out of reach, his blue eyes turning to ice. Orgustus knew all her tricks already.

"It's time for you to get your beautiful arse out of my bed, my Lady Olivia. I've got work to do." Orgustus gave her behind a sharp slap and left for the bathroom without another word.

Olivia bit her bottom lip as desire and disappointment clashed in her chest. "Yes, my lord." She slid out of bed and collected the clothing strewn about the room. Slipping her dress up over her shoulders, Olivia tied the laces and left Orgustus's bedchamber.

Rushing along the candlelit corridors of the Golden Palace, she made it to her room before the dry sob escaped her.

"Is that you, Livvie?" a sweet voice called from the bathroom attached to the dormitory.

Olivia gulped down another sob and cleared her throat. "It's me," she answered, in a voice passing for normal.

"We're in here braiding Petal's hair. Come in and tell us everything!" The demand was followed by the sound of giggling from her four dormmates. Olivia winced. Walking past the small mirror on the wall next to her bed, she gave herself a cursory look. Her lips were swollen from rough kisses, and her eyes were still red from unshed tears. She pinched her cheeks to put some color in her wan complexion and plastered on a smile. No one would notice if it didn't reach her eyes.

Entering the bathroom, she saw her dormmates chatting and sharing a small slab of caramel fudge. Petal was the only one to give her a guilty look as she wiped her fingers on her nightdress. Olivia pinched off a sigh; if her chubby friend wanted to stay that way, it was no skin off her nose. Petal was sitting on a small wooden stool as two of the other girls, Annelle and Daphne, braided her hair into intricate swirls on her head. Another girl pulled herself out of the bath.

"Well?" said Edith, the tallest and loudest, as she wrapped herself in a towel. "How is lover boy this evening?" The others giggled and looked on eagerly for the details.

Lady Olivia rolled her eyes and sighed hugely. "Well, you know, men!"

"No!" squealed Annelle. "We don't know any men—that's why we're asking you, Miss Lady Love."

"Well, he would like to be my lover." Olivia winked at her audience. "But I make it very clear every time that I will only kiss him. If he wants anything else from this lady, then he will have to ask for my hand in marriage."

All the girls gasped in awe of their friend's dignity and confidence.

Olivia shrugged nonchalantly out of her dress and slipped into the still-warm bath, letting the soapy water wash the masculine scent of Orgustus off her skin. *Not that any of these innocent little girls would know what sex smelled like,* Olivia thought bitterly.

"You are so right, Livvie," agreed Annelle, eyeing Olivia's well-formed, womanly body. "But how do you get him to ask your parents' permission and give you a ring?"

Olivia opened her eyes in pretend surprise. "How do I get him to stop trying is more the question, Annelle! I spent an hour trying to talk him out of writing to my parents this very night. I mean, he is such a handsome man, a wonderful kisser"—this caused more excited giggling among her dormmates—"and the captain of the Queen's Guard at that, but I'm not sure I want to settle down right now. I'm only nineteen years old and the queen's closest friend. Who knows what gentlemen will present themselves before me in the next year or so? Of course, I want to be married by twenty-one at the latest, but there is plenty of time before I need to decide on who."

The four girls sighed with envy at Olivia's romantic life.

"If only I had your luck with men, Livvie," said Petal sadly. "I can't even get that Belvoir stable hand, Benjamin, to look at me, and he is said to have been with all the queen's nannies. And he isn't even a real catch, like your Captain Lucky."

Lady Olivia smiled and stretched a long leg out of the bath just to look at how fine it was, with her perfectly white skin and the long muscles that were much less defined now that she didn't have to work on the farm anymore.

"Not everyone can have a captain," she agreed condescendingly, but she was thinking of Lord Orgustus. "But you know any boyfriend is hard work, whether he's a royal or a servant. You must always keep them wanting more of you and let them make all the promises. As adorable as I think Captain Lucky is, I would never put myself at his mercy without a heavy gold ring on this finger." She raised her left hand to illustrate the point.

Annelle giggled as she tied off another of Petal's braids. "I bet the wedding night will be some fun, though!"

Olivia looked down as an honest flush crept up her cheeks, and she remembered what she had just let Orgustus do to her not even an hour ago. It had almost hurt, and he hadn't even tried to make her feel good, like the boys back home always had, so every one of her cries had been forced.

"Ooh, look at that blush!" smirked Edith. "I bet a girl would wake up pregnant the day after a roll with Captain Lucky-pants!"

Her cackle stirred Olivia out of her reverie. *Edith is getting too big for her boots lately and needs to be taken down a peg.* "Don't be so crude, Edith," she snapped. "A lady doesn't think things like that."

Edith sniffed at the rebuke, but Petal, Annelle, and shy Daphne looked on in admiration.

"Well, I think it would be wonderful to have such a fine man in love with me," sighed Petal as she reached for the block of fudge again.

"Yes," agreed Lady Olivia, suddenly too exhausted for words as she lay back in the water and watched the soap bubbles swirl and jostle each other. "Yes, I imagine it is."

CHAPTER SEVEN
"The Journey through the Tundra"

The next day dawned clear enough, and traveling out of the valley was easy. Far to the north, the Ice Mountains stood tall and imposing on the horizon, gray stone sentinels with snowy white peaks and belts of green at their base, like a scarf around a throat. Yet when Adele gazed upon the vast tundra before her, she was filled with dread. The rocky volcanic soil, while sparsely dotted with ragged gray shrubs and razor-sharp grasses, was also covered with nasty crags and holes that the horses would have to pick their way around, and that meant slow going, which would mean more time on the road—time Adele didn't want to waste.

The sky was a uniform steel gray, and the sun shone like a dull white ball, shedding little light and no warmth at all.

"You all right, Your Majesty?" Ohrig pulled his horse up next to hers and caught Adele trying to massage her forehead. "We can rest, if you like."

"No, I'm fine," croaked Adele. She gave Ohrig a wan smile. "I guess I'm not used to sleeping anymore. It's given me a wicked headache."

"Well, I'm glad you're not worrying about Ripenzo Shale," said Ohrig, a stubborn note in his voice. "I can't say that I feel easy with him loose in the world again."

Rip had snuck out sometime in the night when everyone was asleep, but not before he had helped himself to Lucky's beloved horse, Redfire, and some of their precious food supplies.

"Let's just get on as far as we can today," Adele replied. "Rip wasted enough of our time, and we are half a day behind schedule now."

The going was as hard as Adele had anticipated and then was made even worse by a frigid wind that picked up midafternoon, the cold biting through their heavy cloaks and blowing grit into their eyes. Adele found it exhausting trying to keep her seat in the saddle while fighting the wind, and when Ohrig finally called a halt only a short while later, she didn't complain.

QGs Leith and Bear scouted a place to camp and found a small spring tucked under an overhanging crust of rock. The water smelled of rotten eggs, but everyone was thirsty enough to ignore the odor. They pitched their tents on the uneven ground, shoving the pegs into rock crevices instead of soil, and could only hope the wind wouldn't blow any harder during the night.

Adele and Pepper were given firewood duty. Yet they soon discovered that there wasn't any wood lying around, so they decided to pull a dead shrub out of the ground. It came out with several hard tugs, and Pepper almost yanked the tree onto himself. He dropped it quickly, brushing himself down and cursing quietly.

"If there was a spider on you, I would say," Adele promised Pepper, thinking that was what he might be worried about. She was surprised to see the young QG color bright red and drag the tree back to camp by himself, leaving her to wonder how long he would punish himself for what had happened in the Nest of the Spider People.

Poor guy, thought Adele. *He just hasn't been the same since that night. He used to be so sweet and talkative, but now he hardly says a word.*

Back at camp, Adele found the general staking the horses by himself. She decided to broach the issue with him. "Ohrig, I think I hurt Pepper's feelings just now," Adele said with a frown. "I thought he was worried about spiders on the firewood, but I'm sure the way I said it, it sounded like I was teasing him."

"He'll be all right, Your Majesty," said Ohrig. "The kid's still a bit sensitive. He knows he failed you and the Queen's Guard back in the cavern of the Spider People. It'll take him a while to feel like he's made it up to you."

"But he doesn't have to make up for anything," Adele protested. "Anyone would have been terrified out of their wits by giant spiders and thinking we were going to be eaten alive."

"The fact remains that Pepper hasn't forgiven himself." Ohrig shrugged. "He had a duty, and he didn't do it."

"Are we talking about when the kid shit himself in the Nest?" asked QG Bear, joining the conversation with no invitation. "Kid froze. Didn't do his job. He's too young for the guard, no question."

"It's not his age," Ohrig disagreed. "Look at Leith; he's young too, but he kept his wits. No, Pepper just had a bad turn. There's no shame in fear; it's how you deal with it that matters."

"All due respect, General," continued Bear, a frown creasing his blunt forehead. "I think fear *is* something to be ashamed of. The kid should have put duty first and protected his queen and the guard." Bear shrugged off Adele's glare. "I'm just saying what we're all thinking, Your Majesty."

"If the kid's fears are mythical creatures, then he is right out of luck," said QG Owens with a chuckle, bringing his horse over to the others. "Her Majesty manages to find them no matter what rock she drags us behind."

"Watch your manners, QG," snapped Ohrig. "And Pepper'll be fine. He just needs a moment to prove to himself that he is still a man of the Queen's Guard."

The QGs were silent at this, but Adele could read their various opinions in their expressions.

"Maybe I should have a talk with Pepper," Adele suggested. "I could let him know that I still believe in him and understand why he fainted in the Nest."

"No, Your Majesty," said Ohrig firmly. "QG Pepper might be young, but he's still a man. You come in mothering him like that, you might as well cut off his— well, you know what I mean."

"Yes, but—"

"But nothing, Your Majesty," snapped Ohrig. "I said leave it alone."

Affronted, Adele narrowed her eyes at Ohrig, but he'd already turned his back to her. She caught Bear and Owens sharing a glance and Bear trying to hide his smile.

Adele felt her anger flare at Ohrig's rudeness, but inside her, the green magic struggled to meet it, not feeding the emotion and racing through her blood as it would normally. Disturbed by the weak response, Adele's temper died. *Am I losing my powers?* she wondered.

Trying to fight a growing panic, Adele turned on her heel, marching away from the camp, and sought privacy to properly examine what was left of her magics. She found a quiet place almost out of the wind and sat down on a rock and prepared herself. Yet though Adele called to them, she could only feel a slow response from the two magics.

"Sweet Christ, what's wrong with me?" she whispered aloud, but even the Chime Voices were no help, only chittering in consternation and begging for Rainere's touch.

Thinking of Rainere helped Adele decide that, even depleted, she should practice with her magic to avoid another mistake like the brutal bomb spell she had concocted. She remembered that the magic net Rip had used to protect them had looked similar to the rope which, only yesterday, she had instinctively managed to conjure to catch Charlie as he fell from the sky. *That sort of spell is useful and seems safe enough,* she told herself.

Frowning in concentration, Adele pulled on the gold magic at the back of her neck and coaxed it into her hands. *Simple.* Then she tried to project it out into the space in front of her hands. She concentrated hard on the image of a fishing net, but try as she might, the magic would only coalesce into balls of waving fronds, not stretch out into a net shape. Adele cursed and wiped the sweat from her forehead before trying again, tweaking and changing the magic enough to pull it into a long rope. She then tried to stretch it out horizontally, but it fought her will and whipped out of her hands to hover in midair before dissipating in the evening breeze.

Goddamnit, I gave too much of my power to Rip, and now he's gone, and I can't do anything! Adele spat a filthy curse she rarely used.

There was a cough behind her, and Adele's head turned sharply. Ohrig was standing not two paces behind her with his arms crossed and a stern look on his face.

"You shouldn't be so far away from camp by yourself," Ohrig said. "I know you didn't even hear me walk up behind you. What if I'd been an enemy wanting to put a knife in your back?"

"I knew it was you," Adele lied. "Because even your footsteps sound rude."

Ohrig surprised Adele by chuckling. "Yeah, maybe," he agreed. "The men knew I'd annoyed you, so no one else wanted to come over and have to guard you. My fault, my penance."

Using magic had stolen the last bit of Adele's energy, and she lacked even the strength to keep being annoyed at her general. She pointed at a rock where Ohrig could sit down opposite her.

"You know, Ohrig, we're going to be on the road together for weeks," said Adele. "You and I can always be honest with each other, but you need to stop putting me down in front of the men. It undermines my authority, and, more importantly, it's really irritating."

"A woman who doesn't want to be told when she's wrong? What a surprise." Ohrig rolled his eyes and flinched when Adele threw a pebble at his head and missed. "And you throw like a girl too."

Adele didn't want to laugh, even though Ohrig had a way of delivering his sarcasm that was sort of charming. "I could have hit you with something harder if I'd wanted to," she sniffed.

"I know you could have," said Ohrig, and his smile died. "That's probably why I should let you keep practicing your spells, so you don't hit us next time."

The truth stung, and suddenly Adele was irritated again. "What is your problem, Ohrig? You've been giving everyone hell and nagging me all bloody day."

Ohrig looked like he was going to snap something back, but one look at Adele's expression, and he let out a heavy sigh instead. "I haven't smoked any tabac today," he said, embarrassed to even say the words. "I'm not addicted to it, you know, but giving it up can be hard for the first few days."

"If it would improve your mood, then please, be my guest and smoke," said Adele.

"It's not professional to smoke on duty," Ohrig replied with a frown, like he blamed Adele for that.

Adele gestured to the wide empty expanse around them. "There is no one here to judge you, Ohrig."

"Do you have any idea how far the smell of tabac can travel?" Ohrig asked crisply. "It'd give our position away before we were even seen, and we could be tracked by it."

Adele could see there was no cheering Ohrig in this mood, so she left it alone. Holding out her hands, she tried again to fill one palm with golden magic and the other with green magic. Neither came fast, and only the gold magic could hold the sphere shape.

Ohrig raised a questioning eyebrow at the poor showing. Adele sighed and let him in on her worry. "It took so much of my green magic to make that awful bomb spell, and then almost all my gold to heal Rip, that now I feel like I'm running on empty." She pursed her lips and frowned as the magic fizzed out on her hands. "I'm finding out that my magic is nothing like a wizard's. Rainere's magic is huge and beautiful, like an ocean of power tucked away inside of him, just sloshing around, waiting to be drunk."

"And that's what you do?" Ohrig squinted at Adele in the gathering gloom. "You drink his magic, and then you're strong again?"

"I don't know why I can't make my own magic," said Adele, her voice low with an awkward shame. "I hate thinking of myself as some kind of succubus, draining Rainere of his power, even though he seems to like it when I do," she added defensively.

"Hey!" Ohrig held up his hands. "There's no one here to judge you, Your Majesty."

Adele smiled a little.

"Look, I don't know what a succubus is, but maybe needing fresh supplies of magic has to do with you being a demon," suggested Ohrig, frowning again. "Do we know what's going to happen if you run out of magic altogether?"

Adele swallowed. She'd been trying not to think about that all day. "I've started needing to sleep again," she admitted. "And I feel hollow with a hunger that won't go away but just gnaws and gnaws at me. Beyond that, I just don't know."

"Then we need to get you some magic, and fast," said Ohrig. He slapped his hand on his knee. "I knew I should have kept a tighter hold of that catshit Ripenzo Shale. You were right about him, Your Majesty; that joker was not to be trusted. If only I'd known what you were doing when you saved his life, I probably would have stopped you."

"Sure, Ohrig." Adele gave her general a sardonic smile. "Weren't you the one who kept telling me to give the guy a break?"

"Yes, well, I was wrong," Ohrig said, looking pained at the admission. "I just wish he was here to give your magic back."

Adele was touched by Ohrig's concern but embarrassed to be discussing something so personal when it was clear he didn't realize that, for Adele, taking the magic usually involved sex. "I'll conserve what I have left," Adele said with a surety she tried to feel. "And until I find a new source of magic, I'll have to rely on my wits and charm to get us to the dragon."

"Then the goddess help us all," Ohrig joked gruffly. He stood and put out a hand to help Adele to her feet. "Let's get some dinner into you, and then you can sleep. We've got to keep your strength up."

Adele smiled at Ohrig's back as they made their way to the fireside. He was adamant that she shouldn't coddle Pepper, but he was looking after her as kindly as any father might. The feeling of being cared for put Adele in a good mood throughout dinner, despite the wind, which blew grit into the stew. But later, alone in her tent, Adele's mind turned to her children.

Natalie and Aaron should be in bed by now, she thought. *Did Rainere read them a story and give them enough hugs and kisses? I hope he checked all the closets for monsters and lets the dogs sleep under the children's beds, like I do. I wonder if they miss me yet.*

Adele felt tears sting her eyes as she imagined the cozy scene, then thought of Stella all alone in her secret little chamber. *Just keep waiting, baby. Mummy's bringing home your cure, and soon we'll be all together again.*

Chapter Eight
"The Messages in Dreams"

The bar is busy, and loud clashing music fills her ears. Adele pushes the dishcloth into the waistband of her jeans and shakes the cocktail shaker as fast as she can, then drains the martini into the waiting glass. Orders are being shouted at her, and Adele's hands fly, taking money and ripping caps off bottles, taking money and shaking more drinks together. Someone asks for a frozen margarita. She wants to groan. It's such a cheesy drink to make. Adele grabs the blender filled with ice and alcohol, but it slips, and pink cocktail pours all over her white Converse sneakers.

"Shit, I hope they weren't new!"

Adele turns. He is standing there with that crooked grin, blond curls hanging in his eyes, and a tight V-neck T-shirt that shows off his pecs.

"What's your drink, friend?" Adele uses her usual line, though this guy is so hot it makes her hands shake.

"I'm Justin," he says and leans across the bar like he is going to kiss her already.

Mouth dry, Adele smiles. "What's your drink?" she insists, trying to be cool.

"Surprise me," he says, giving her a wink that could mean he loves her. Adele feels a rush of adrenaline. She surprises herself by leaning across the bar and looking right into his baby-blue eyes, and there's a primal instinct kicking in her guts, telling her to take him home and lock him in her basement—to keep him forever.

This happened on Earth, when I was still ordinary, just a barmaid and a failing student, *Adele thinks in her dream that isn't quite a dream. The hunger burns in her belly, and Adele recognizes Justin as the first St. Lucidis man she ever met. His energy had attracted her dormant magic, and she became emotionally hooked on him, thinking it was love. Now she knew better—Justin had just been food for her magic.*

"Come here and I'll drink you up," Adele says as she pulls Justin to her.

Justin laughs. Then it's Rainere laughing. Then it's Justin. Then it's Rainere again, and Adele dives into him before he can disappear.

The Chime Voices are scratching at her insides, pulling and pushing at her, trying to feed. Yet in a moment, it's all over. Rainere is gone. Adele has eaten every bit of him, devoured his body and his soul. The metallic tang of Rainere's magic lies on her tongue, and she can still smell him on her skin, but he's gone, and the grief is too much to even feel. The mage of Sandar appears by Adele's side. Grinning and rotten, he stands in the middle of her life where he doesn't belong. Adele sees something glowing in the darkness between his ribs and reaches in. It burns in her hand, feeling so good.

"I've got you, angel." The mage grabs her arms, and Adele realizes her mistake. It isn't the mage; it's the hand of Dahk'hani, and he isn't going to let her go. Terror and ecstasy wash over Adele as the god crushes her inside his mouth and swallows her into the deep and loving darkness. "Now you are mine."

Adele woke with the orgasm still thudding through her like a second heartbeat. The Chime Voices chanted in her mind, their song full of yearning and unrequited lust for magic. *Now we are his,* they trilled. Sitting up, Adele tried to feel if her magic was still alive, but even the leonine magic at the back of her head was slow to respond, and the coiled green magic only flickered at her touch. She blamed the dream.

Now I have Dahk'hani eating me in my dreams! Adele shuddered when she remembered the alien presence that held her arms and whose magic burned her to the core before it swallowed her whole. *Sweet Christ, I hope Rainere never feels like that when I feed on his power,* thought Adele, and then she shook it off to think about the new problem now before her. *It cannot be a coincidence that Dahk'hani has arrived in my head the moment I leave Unisia, but what the hell am I supposed to do about it? Maybe the dragon will have answers for me. Maybe Dahk'hani's only here because I'm so weak right now, which means I must find a new source of magic soon.*

Needing to escape her dark thoughts, Adele crawled out of the relative warmth of her one-man tent and into the bitter cold of a tundra morning. Climbing to her feet, she stretched her muscles with a series of expressive groans. The fire was burning brightly, the kettle already set to boil, and Ohrig was hunched with his back to it, watching the bare lands about them as the dawn arrived.

Adele settled herself at Ohrig's side, facing the fire, and began to prepare the tea. "Morning, Ohrig."

"Your Majesty," muttered Ohrig.

"All quiet?"

"All quiet, all night," Ohrig replied.

Adele handed Ohrig his tea, using two teaspoons of their precious sugar supply. Ohrig grunted in appreciation of his favorite brew and gave Adele a rare early morning smile. The fire crackled comfortingly as they sat drinking their tea.

"You all right?" Ohrig cast her a sideways look.

Adele heard the laughter of the dead mage echo in her head. "I had a bad dream," she said.

"Don't tell me about it," said Ohrig.

Adele breathed in the steam from her teacup. "Trust me, you don't want to know."

Ohrig sighed, and Adele knew that her burden was his burden too. "Go on, then," he said. "What's so bad it would frighten a demon queen?"

"The mage I killed in Sandar was in it," said Adele, shuddering. "I was trying to invade Rainere, to get to his magic. Then the mage appeared, and I reached inside him to get his magic too, and…" She looked up at Ohrig. "He was the messenger for the god Dahk'hani. This is the second time I've dreamed of that god; the first time was in the cave after the fight with the shadow wasps."

Ohrig sipped his tea.

"I feel like I'm going crazy," groaned Adele. "This volcano god wants to eat me, and a mage I killed is working for him by haunting my dreams."

"Maybe it's just a bad dream, Your Majesty," suggested Ohrig. "You're exhausted and anxious, that's all."

"Yeah, you're probably right." Adele shifted her behind on the hard ground as the chill crept through her. Rainere devoured. The grinning mage. *Now you are mine.* "I just hate sleeping, that's all."

Ohrig grunted. "I love the stuff," he said. "The only thing I'm dreaming of is my soft bed and feather pillow back at the barracks."

Adele looked up at her general. Ohrig was older than her, maybe fifty or so, though he'd never said. "I'll get us home again, Ohrig, I promise you."

Ohrig poured more hot water into his teacup and did the same for Adele. "I know you will, Your Majesty." He chinked his cup against hers. "Or we'll die trying, eh?"

Adele remembered the speech she'd made before leading the men down into the Nest of the Spider Empress. She was just sorry that Ohrig did too.

"No one is dying," she said. Rainere devoured. The mage glowing with magic. "I'll get us home."

CHAPTER NINE
"The Tender Mark of Love"

Rainere awoke with a gasp. There was a sharp, tearing sensation in the Mark on his side, so intense that he tore his shirt off and searched for blood—and was almost surprised that it was only sweat that drenched his body.

Rainere staggered from the bed and fell to the floor. He bit the back of his hand to prevent the groan that wanted to escape and crawled to the bathroom, locking the door between himself and the still-sleeping children. He knelt at the toilet as the heaves took hold, but they only choked him, and he found no relief. Bewildered by the intense pain wracking his body, Rainere lay down on the cool tiles of the floor and held his rock-hard erection in a loose grip.

"Adelena, Adelena, Adelena." Whispering her name over and over like a prayer, Rainere had no idea if Adelena could hear him as her own call jumbled his thoughts and made his magic roil and race within his veins. The Mark fed him images of Adelena in the throes of ecstasy, and the power of her desire pulsed through him as she experienced pleasure at the hands of another. The Mark twisted sharply again, and then, as quickly as it had come, the pain was gone.

Rainere sat up, panting, and felt the tears well in his eyes. Pulling himself off the floor, he turned the tap at the basin and dashed cold water over his face and chest. Looking in the mirror, he could see the mess that Adelena's call had made of his eyes. The silver circles were spinning fast around his pupils, and Rainere was ashamed of the naked longing that looked back at him. *Adelena is fucking someone else right now.* Rainere couldn't deny what he'd felt her doing, though she was on the other side of Evendaar. *It's only been two days, and already she is in the arms of another. If it's that Captain Lucky, I am going to kill him very, very slowly.*

The Mark twisted again, as if in response to his thoughts, and Rainere heard a whisper call to him. Not the magic hurricane of Adelena's orgasm, but her actual sweet voice, calling his name.

The mirror!

Rainere raced back into the chamber and threw himself on his bed, rummaging under the pillow to find the little hand mirror he had secreted there in the night. Fumbling at the clasp, Rainere flipped the mirror open.

"Adelena!" Despite her betrayal still fresh in his mind, his heart skipped a beat to see her face. Intense hazel eyes stared back at him, her cheeks rosy with windburn. Rainere drank in the sight of his queen and couldn't speak another word. She looked tired and unhappy. *I should have gone with her.* He cursed himself. *She wouldn't have strayed if I'd been with her.*

"Rainere?" Adelena's voice was hollow, as if she didn't think he could hear her. Rainere's heart broke into a million pieces, afraid that she might believe he could disappoint her like that.

Home. Adele pulled out the little hand mirror from the bag at her waist. She ran her fingertips over the crescent moon carved into the lid and wondered who would answer her call. Ohren had the partner for this little mirror so she could communicate with him, but he'd told her that he would probably give the device to Rainere to keep it safe. Still, Adele wasn't sure who'd be there when she flipped the lid open and looked at herself in the round mirror. There were deep shadows under her eyes, and her hair was a mess, but Adele was desperate for home, and so she softly called Rainere's name.

After a long moment, Rainere's face swam into view. He was pale, and all was dark behind him.

"I'm sorry, did I wake you?" Adele cringed at her own silly question.

The mirror tilted wildly, and Adele could see Rainere's smooth bare chest in the yellow light of the lantern that he had just lit. "What is it? What's wrong?" Rainere's urgent tone cut through Adele like a knife, and she almost fell to pieces. She wanted so badly to tell him about Ripenzo Shale showing up, and the shadow wasps, and how she had almost killed everyone with her dangerous spell.

"Nothing's wrong," Adele lied, coughing to clear the catch in her throat. "I just wanted to know how it was going with the children. Are they okay?"

Rainere arched a single brow, and his mouth turned down at the sides. "It's only been two days, Adelena. I haven't lost them yet."

"No, I didn't think you had," Adele protested and wondered why Rainere was being so sharp. "I just miss them so much already."

"Ah, I see." Rainere moved the mirror so Adele could see the two sleeping children, both in a state of sweet disarray, limbs akimbo as they snored peacefully.

"Are you all sleeping in the same bed?" Adele asked, jealousy spiking her tone.

"No, I'm on a cot next to them," said Rainere. "Aaron woke screaming some hours ago and insisted I not leave his side. Natalie slept through the turmoil, but if today is anything like yesterday, she'll be up in an hour or so. Would you like me to wake the children so you can speak with them?" Rainere paused and pulled the mirror back to himself so she could see in his expression the answer he wanted to hear.

Yes, wake them up! Adele wanted to shout. *You've only had the kids for two days; how dare you be so tired already? Try years with them!* But of course, she didn't. Instead, she forced a smile. "No, it's all right. I just wanted to see them, that's all."

"I'm fine too," added Rainere, a little pointedly. "No problems in the court so far. The prisoner has shown no sign of recovery, but he hasn't died yet either. The little girl fares better, but she is still unconscious."

"The prisoner? Is that what we're calling Charlie now?" asked Adele. She became worried, remembering Rip's warning about the danger Charlie would face in the Golden Palace. She could only hope it wasn't true. "I trust you've put Charlie somewhere safe and he's being looked after properly, Rainere. I want him alive when I get back."

"It's on my list of chores," replied Rainere, but his eyes flashed at Adele, and he looked annoyed. "Only Ohren and Orestes know of my return with Charlie and the other child from the Black Mountains, and of course, Mrs. Ollenby was told, but no one else should know he's here. Is that sufficient for his safety, Your Majesty?"

Adele wanted to roll her eyes and tell Rainere to cut it out, but she also wanted him to be in a better mood when her children woke up. "Rainere, you don't have to—"

Adele felt Ohrig tap her shoulder, "Your Majesty, we've got company, and he's coming in fast." Adele's heart dropped into her stomach.

"Rainere, I've got to go. Tell the children I love them." Adele snapped the mirror shut without waiting for a reply and shoved it into her waistband. She stood next to Ohrig and looked out to where he pointed.

"He's standing over there, and with the mountains behind, I almost didn't see him," Ohrig said through clenched teeth. "But he moved just a moment ago, and it looks like he's running toward us."

Adele peered through the gray predawn light. The stranger was too far away to see clearly, but he looked big.

"Wake the men, Your Majesty," ordered Ohrig. "I don't want to take my eyes off him."

Adele did as she was told and was relieved to see the QGs' sleepy expressions instantly become alert when she woke them up with her warning. By the time Adele got back to Ohrig's side, three of the men had assembled, swords in hand, and the others weren't far behind.

The stranger had continued his pace, and now they could all see him properly. He was close to seven feet tall and built solidly. Wrapped in mottled gray skins, he wore a fur-lined hood and a gray scarf over his face that only left space for his eyes. There was a long bow across his back with a quiver of arrows, and a small hatchet and long knife were belted to his waist. His feet were wrapped in furs bound by wide leather bands. The stranger slowed his pace when he came within twenty yards of their group.

"Hi there, stop where you are!" Ohrig walked out to meet the stranger, his sword in hand, and the Queen's Guard arranged themselves three to one side and two to the other, forming a wall and hiding Adele from view.

The giant stranger stopped and shouted something they didn't understand. He raised his hands above his head and slowly removed the bow and quiver and then the rest of his weapons, dropping them to the ground and taking two long paces to the left. He held his hands out in an obvious gesture of peace.

"Sheathe swords, but keep them with you," Ohrig muttered to the men as the stranger moved in closer.

Adele peeked between Ohrig's and Lucky's shoulders and watched as the stranger unwound the long scarf from around his face. She was surprised to see pink cheeks and a huge smile stretched across a handsome face. He knocked back his hood to show a spiky mess of white-blond hair that matched white eyebrows and a scruffy beard.

"We speak the King's Tongue," offered Ohrig. "Do you understand?"

"Hello, visitors!" The stranger's voice was deep, with a strange lilting accent. "I as well speak the King's Tongue. I have come to these lands of Boorenhurdstl to hunt *boorenweiss*, the big white bears." He gestured to the empty tundra and then pointed to his chest. "But I have peace in my heart for men."

Adele didn't realize she had been holding her breath until she let it out in a rush of relief. The stranger was friendly and meant them no harm.

"My name is Jordan Jordansson, son of the chieftess of the Tribe of the Three Sisters Valley." The stranger walked toward Ohrig and threw out a gloved hand, pulled his hand back, ripped off the glove, and offered his hand again. His smile showed straight white teeth, and up close he was younger than Adele had first thought—she guessed no more than early twenties. "I offer a respectful greeting in the Kingdom way to you, the oldest man." Ohrig clasped his hand, and Jordansson shook it vigorously.

"I am General Ohrig St. Lucidis of the Queen's Guard," replied Ohrig. "Thank you for your welcome, Jordan Jordansson."

"Yes, and now we are friends, I will greet you in the respectful way of the Tribe of the Three Sisters Valley," announced Jordansson. He threw his arms around Ohrig, giving him a bear hug that lifted the general's feet off the ground. Ohrig was surprised but tolerated the greeting. Dropping Ohrig back to the ground, Jordansson turned to the QGs on either side of the general and appraised them, looking for the next oldest male, whom he guessed to be Owens. He repeated his welcome to each of the QGs except for Lucky. To Captain Lucky, Jordansson bowed very low and said, "A very respectful welcome to you, my lady."

"I am not a lady! I am Captain Lucky St. Lucidis of the Queen's Guard," snarled Lucky. His square chin jutted in anger, and he clearly surprised Jordansson with his obvious masculinity.

"I am very sorry for my mistake," Jordansson's eyes were clouded with confusion. "You are very beautiful—I thought you were a woman."

Adele heard the sound of Lucky's sword scraping in its sheath and felt it best to step forward before any further miscommunications broke down the meeting. She elbowed her way through the line of men. "Jordan Jordansson, I am Adelena St. Lucidis, queen of Unisia. Thank you for your warm welcome to these lands."

Jordan looked Adele up and down, and his confusion grew until he looked into her eyes. "Oh! You are a grown woman, just very small." He grinned, pleased with his success in recognizing this. "Hello, Queen Adelena of the Unisia People." He held out his hand to shake, and Adele had to grip his enormous one with both of hers. There was a bright spark that flew into the air at the contact, and Jordansson seemed as surprised as Adele. The spark was painless, but energy had flowed between them. She looked up into Jordansson's bright blue gaze.

"That is good," Jordansson decided. "The great god blesses our meeting."

"Yes, I'm sure he does," agreed Adele. She stepped back out of Jordansson's reach in case he wanted to hug her next, but he made no move to touch her again, just examined her, openly curious.

"Jordansson?" Ohrig waved to get the tribesman's attention. "We have come to your lands for a reason."

Jordansson took a moment to understand. "These are not my lands," he replied, grinning as if the idea was funny. "They are the lands of the white bears. I am from the mountains."

Ohrig checked with Adele, and she gave him a small nod of permission. "That is fortunate, as we need to cross these lands and get to the mountains. Would you be able to help us?"

Jordansson shook his head. "It is too hard to talk of this when our stomachs are empty. First we eat as friends." He smiled again, and a beam of sunlight hit his face at such an angle that he looked like he was glowing. Adele could almost see the magic shimmering off the tribesman, and it set her Chime Voices tinkling with excitement. "I will share my food, and you will share your fire, in the way of my people."

Ohrig turned to Adele. "A quick breakfast, then pack up the camp, Your Majesty?"

Adele nodded. "Quick as we can, General."

The QGs fell to their chores, and Pepper prepared the porridge for the camp. Adele invited Jordan to share their breakfast, and he took his bowl of cooked oats politely but didn't look very impressed with it. In turn he offered them small bread rolls, dense and sticky with dried fruit and nuts, and some dried meat that he sandwiched in between the rolls.

"You don't have much water, I think," remarked Jordansson conversationally. "Tomorrow will be a storm, so more snow, then more water."

"You called this land Booren-something," Adele said. "What does that mean in the King's Tongue?"

Jordansson stared off at the horizon for a moment. "My translation is not very perfect, but it would mean 'Big White Bears Hunt and Kill Here Lands' or 'Hunting Lands of the Big White Bears'—something like this."

Adele felt a shudder down her spine. She gestured to the vast lands about them. "The white bears hunt here on the tundra?"

"It is the Season of the Sun, so they are awake and very hungry," said Jordansson. "We will get many chances to fight one because you travel with these animals, the ponies, and they are good food for a white bear."

The other QGs had finished packing up the camp in short order and crowded around the fire to get their serving of porridge and listen to Jordansson talk.

"How big is a white bear?" asked QG Bear. "Bigger than you?"

Jordansson threw back his head and laughed a deep-chested laugh that even made the taciturn Bear smile. "Yes, very much bigger than me." Jordansson chuckled. "Maybe it's like three of your ponies all together and then a big head with much teeth inside the mouth. Very huge is a white bear."

QGs Bear and Owens exchanged an excited look. "How do you kill it?" asked Bear.

"With knives and arrows and much courage." Jordansson grinned, warming to the guards' obvious enthusiasm. "We are very sure to see one, so I will show you how to kill it. We can take the pelt back to the Valley of the Three Sisters and get very much respect from my people."

Adele was finding it hard to swallow her porridge. "Are the bears creatures of magic?" she asked. "Do they have magic they use to fight?"

"Yes, they have bear magic," said Jordansson, and when he smiled at Adele she saw a ring of white suddenly flash and turn around his pupils. "There are very many portals across the Boorenhurdstl Lands that the gods left here. The bears go inside, walking the portals, and they come out again. They also can hide in the portal, and then you can't see them until they are too close. That is how they hunt out here on the open lands and not be seen."

"Sweet Christ," Adele swore.

"How are we supposed to hunt one, then?" asked Owens.

"Or avoid them?" corrected Captain Lucky.

"We pray to the great god Dahk'hani to watch over us to keep safe," said Jordansson with a shrug. "And we pray that no white bear will see us before we see him."

Adele had known that this journey would be dangerous, but now, faced with following a stranger over ice bear hunting lands, she couldn't deny that she suddenly didn't feel quite so up to the task. Her flagging energy didn't help matters. *It's ironic; after they scared me so much, I feel naked without my magics to keep me safe,* thought Adele. The Chime Voices tinkled and chimed, suggesting this giant man could be the answer to her problems, but Adele ignored them and gritted her teeth. *I've got some ways to go before I start attacking strange men to steal their power,* she told herself sternly—and almost believed it.

"How long will it take to get to the mountains?" Adele asked Jordansson. "We must begin our journey quickly, you see."

Jordansson shrugged, using his shoulders and hands. "How fast can a man walk in a day?" He gestured to the tundra around them and then pointed to their horses. "If you ride these animals, it will take two days and one night to cross the Boorenhurdstl Lands and then another three to climb the Fjordkerstahn Mountain before we get to the Three Sisters Valley." He looked to the sky. "Big storms mean less walking. Finding bears means more fighting, less walking." He shrugged expressively again, as if he couldn't know all the complications in between the question and its answer.

Adele turned to Ohrig and saw he was just as concerned as she was. "If we don't know how long it will take, then I suppose we had better get moving, General."

"Let's saddle up, men," shouted Ohrig to the assembled guard. "We've got to get the hell off this tundra."

Without much expectation of competence, Rainere had requested that Tilburn find him a laboratory and stock it with a long list of equipment and supplies for his work. However, he was pleased to discover how adroit the majordomo had been in fulfilling his requirements. The laboratory was not as large as his own back at the Gray Palace, but it was cozier, with wooden beams crossing the ceiling and a pleasant terrace garden that sat just outside the large double doors. The room wasn't on the same level as the other laboratories where High Wizard Ohren worked; instead, it was tucked away in a quieter part of the Golden Palace, far from the busy hallways and gawping courtiers that Rainere so detested.

After his disturbing start with Adelena this morning, Rainere had needed the distraction of organizing magic lessons for Natalie and Aaron. The Mark on his side still tweaked and pinched him occasionally, but the visions of Adelena subsided when he was busy.

It was immediately clear that Aaron was too small to attend to instruction for long, but Natalie was a curious pupil, and her endless questions helped reveal to Rainere where her interest in magic lay. He supposed it was her childhood on Earth that had given Natalie an affinity for machines and any spell with a technological component.

"Like this, Prince Rainere?" said Natalie as she placed her hand in the glass canister and concentrated the green glitter into a ball in her hand, making the globe at the top of the canister flicker. Delighted, she giggled and splayed her fingers so the magic dissipated and the light went out.

"No, you must focus harder, Natalie," said Rainere. "Think of the quality of the light, not of the magic in your hand. The magic is just the path you follow to get where you want to go. Now do it again, and keep the light glowing properly."

Natalie gave Rainere a glare of such fury that Rainere laughed aloud, making the dogs under the table bark. *She is so like her mother,* he thought.

Unable to resist Rainere's laughter, Natalie instantly lost her bad humor. "But I don't want to do this again," she said, hiding her smile with a pout. "It's too hard for me."

"I know it's hard, Princess Natalie," agreed Rainere. "But I learned this spell when I was your age, and I also had to practice every day, because if I ever gave up, then Grotto would beat me with a belt until I got it right."

"Is that what you'll do to me?" Natalie's eyes widened.

Rainere frowned down at Natalie, considering the question. *Could I beat a little girl for displeasing me?* he wondered, imagining Natalie's fear as his hand raised to strike her—the fear he had tried so hard to avoid when he'd put her under a sleeping curse.

"No," answered Rainere firmly. "Grotto was wrong to beat me so often, and all he taught me was to hate him. Though I did learn a valuable lesson, and that is only hard work will make you stronger than those who would try to crush you—or beat you with a belt."

Natalie bit her lip and furrowed her brow. "I will try again," she said, her green eyes clearly searching for his approval.

"*Cormendum,*" prompted Rainere with a smile.

"*Cor-men-dum,*" repeated Natalie. She was delighted when the globe started sparking and glowing. "*Cormendum! Cormendum!*" The globe lit with a solid green light, and when she looked up at Rainere, smiling, he could see the silver ring spinning around her pupils as clear as day. "I did it!" she crowed.

"Yes, you did it." Rainere smiled and brushed Natalie's hair from her face. "Now remember, you must only use your magic with me. Other people in the Golden Palace might be jealous or angry with you for being so strong at your age. We must keep this a secret just between us."

Rainere hated the disappointment in Natalie's eyes. "Is that what Grotto made you do too?" she asked.

Rainere hesitated, unsure how to answer. Natalie was only a little girl, after all. "Grotto knew that no one in the world understands Marchant magic like we do." He pointed at the globe. "That is the beautiful green magic you were just using now. I know it's special, and you know it's special, but most people are frightened of it."

Natalie shrugged, bored now that she had been told she couldn't show off her new trick. "Where is Grotto, Prince Rainere?"

"Down the stones," said a small voice from under the table. Rainere crouched and spied Aaron curled up with the three young dogs, Tra La La, Hero Boy, and Bunny. His eyes looked huge in his pale face. Normally a happy little boy, Aaron hadn't smiled since his mother left.

"What stones, Aaron?" scoffed Natalie. "I think Grotto went home to the Gray Palace."

Aaron shrugged, and the gesture showed he didn't much care what his sister thought. "Tra La La can hear him scream when the moon's out."

Rainere felt his spine stiffen at Aaron's words, but there was a knock at the door, and the prince climbed to his feet again.

"Well, hello there, everyone!" High Wizard Ohren came bounding into the room, covering up his anger with false cheer. "I've had quite a time looking for you all morning. I thought maybe you were trying to hide from me." He approached their table, examining the children and the contents of the room with his laser-bright gaze.

Rainere crossed his arms. "What a paranoid high wizard you are," he said in a tone that mocked Ohren's cheerfulness. "The children were just at their lessons. No cause for alarm, you can be sure."

"Well, I have good news." Ohren glared at Rainere. "I have just heard that Charlie is awake and causing quite the ruckus. He is asking for the queen and threatening the lives of his guards. I think we should go and have a word with him, don't you, Your Highness?"

"Come, children, Charlie is awake," said Rainere, lifting Aaron to his hip and taking Natalie's hand. "We shall go and tell him what has happened since we last saw him."

"Do you really think it's wise to bring the children?" muttered Ohren as Rainere passed him at the door. "He sounds out of control."

"There is no reason why not. I can protect them from one skinny boy," replied Rainere. "Besides, they like Charlie, and Charlie likes them."

"He's Cheeky Charlie," agreed Natalie. "And he is our friend, Ohren."

The little group made their way down the quiet hallways, but it wasn't long before they could hear shouting and crashing coming from the private hospital wing.

"Tell me where I am!" Charlie was yelling as he threw projectiles from his room at the two household guards standing in the hallway. "I want to see the queen."

"Charlie!" roared Ohren. He marched ahead of the group. "Stop this at once!"

"Is that you, High Wizard?" Charlie called out. "Show yourself."

Ohren approached the doorway of the hospital room, waving back the household guards. "Charlie, it's me, look," he said. "I've brought Natalie and Aaron with me, so don't throw anything else, all right?"

Charlie stood in the center of the hospital room, chest heaving and sweat pouring off his pale forehead. A small figure cowered behind him and growled at the people in the doorway. When Charlie saw the royal children in Rainere's arms, his jaw dropped.

"So I really am in the Golden Palace." He blinked the sweat from his eyes. "I want to talk to Queen Adelena. I have a message for her."

Rainere was almost amused. "So much has happened since I last saw you, Charlie," he said as he entered the room and released the children to run and hug the nervous teenager. "I'm so *glad* that we have you back again."

"Yes, quite." Ohren gave Rainere a warning look. "We have some questions for you, Charlie, but I'm sure you have many more for us. How about you sit down before you fall down, son? You're looking a little weary."

Charlie looked wildly from one wizard to the next, anger and fear warring in his eyes. "I have a message for Queen Adelena," he said stubbornly. "I need to speak to her."

"Mummy has gone away, Charlie," Natalie told him as she wrapped her arms around his waist. "She has gone to get medicine for Stella."

Charlie staggered on his feet and pushed Natalie away as he sat back down on his bed. "Then Stella isn't dead," he whispered. "Oh, thank the goddess!" Charlie looked up at Rainere. "So you gave the Fire Orchid stamens back to the queen in time," he said.

"Not fast enough, as it turned out," interrupted Ohren. "The illness accelerated rapidly in the child, and though she was saved, she is still in a precarious condition. The queen is searching Evendaar for the cure to Stella's present state."

"What's 'precarious'?" asked Natalie, but the high wizard hushed her.

"Do you know where the queen is now?" asked Charlie, his eyes narrowing suspiciously at Ohren. It pleased Rainere to see how little the boy trusted the high wizard—it showed he had a brain, at least.

Ohren raised his bushy eyebrows in the direction of Natalie and Aaron. "Lots of questions can be answered later, Charlie," he said. "Right now, we are just pleased to see you well and out of bed. Now, why don't you introduce us to your friend?" The high wizard smiled warmly at the little girl hiding behind Charlie.

Charlie put a protective arm around the girl. "This is Leafy," he said. "I think she's about six or seven."

"Like me!" Natalie was delighted. "We can be friends, Leafy." But Leafy just growled and hid behind Charlie.

"She is a little scared of strangers," said Charlie, looking defensively at Ohren. "And wizards. I found her in the m—"

"In the meantime," Ohren loudly interrupted Charlie, "why don't you two have something to eat and get some rest? I'll come back tomorrow, and we can have a nice quiet chat together then, all right?"

But Charlie wasn't to be so easily avoided. Rainere saw the boy's cat-quick mind turning over his slim options and then picking the most courageous one. "Oh no, it's all right. Leafy and I feel good now," said Charlie, calling Ohren's bluff. "We'll come with you back to the royal apartment. We can wait for the queen there."

"I don't think that's wise while you're feeling so fragile, Charlie," said Ohren sternly, but Charlie only took Natalie's hand in his own and pulled Aaron to his side.

"I would love to visit with the royal children and, of course, see Mrs. Ollenby again." Charlie gave a tight smile, baring his teeth. "So lead the way, High Wizard!"

High Wizard Ohren wasn't happy, but Rainere could see how reluctant he was to force his will when there were so many witnesses in the room. More interested than annoyed now, Rainere was looking forward to seeing how much distress Charlie could cause this manipulative wizard. Things in the Golden Palace were looking decidedly more interesting.

Chapter Twelve
"Trouble Is as Trouble Does"

Lady Olivia cursed Queen Adelena. *If it weren't for her strange disappearance, I'd be working today instead of getting thrown out of the royal apartment by Mrs. Ollenby.*

All Olivia's efforts to find the queen or any of the Queen's Guard had come to naught this morning, and Mrs. Ollenby had confirmed that the queen was indeed abroad, on a political mission somewhere far off, though the old lady couldn't quite remember where.

"Come on, Livvie," shouted her dormmate Edith as she joined the other three scurrying ahead of Lady Olivia. "We'll miss the start if you don't hurry up."

Lady Olivia swallowed a groan. *This is so embarrassing!* She tried not to think about how, just a few short months ago, she had always put on her best dress and hurried out to the stables when she knew Lord Orgustus and his coterie were heading out for a picnic. Sometimes the lords and ladies would take their pick from the young crowd, and a lucky few courtiers would get to spend the day with the social elite of the Golden Palace. Olivia had been picked a few times, but it was only when she had spoken up for the queen at the public showdown in the breakfast room that Lord Orgustus had shown real interest in her and Olivia's relationship with him had progressed to warming his bed and spying for him when she could.

But now I'm going to show up with a bunch of giggling twits, and Lord Orgustus is going to ignore me as punishment for not having any proper information for him, she thought as she dragged her feet along the path to the royal stables.

It was a beautiful day, and the sun was already high in the sky when Olivia found the well-dressed crowd milling around the stable yards, enjoying cold wine and sandwiches from the buffet set up under colorful awnings. Groups of young men who had no hope of joining the picnic party because of their low social standing were instead talking loudly and inaccurately about the quality of the horses being led out on parade. Their only goal seemed to be to impress the equally lowborn girls giggling at their sides. Lady Olivia wanted to roll her eyes. She knew her horseflesh as well as the next Templeton woman from the Blue Hills, by way of Belvoir Estate, and it always irritated her to have to pretend otherwise in front of these city-bred courtiers. Yet, unfortunately, it was very unfashionable for a woman to know anything about horses or horse racing, and Olivia was nothing if not fashionable.

Lady Olivia heard Lord Orgustus's loud, booming laugh over by the corrals and froze for a moment. The same sound used to set her blood racing and her feet running in his direction, but today she was looking to avoid humiliation. She was looking to escape when she spied her dormmates Petal and Daphne hovering in one of the stable doorways and gesturing her over. Olivia quickly joined them.

Petal grabbed Olivia's arm and pulled her into a half hug. "I'm going to try to talk to the stable hand Benjamin again," she giggled, her breath hot on Olivia's ear. "Come and help me get his attention, Livvie."

Lady Olivia felt her nose wrinkle at the smell of manure and warm straw in the stables, but today it seemed comforting instead of claustrophobic. "All right, but just for a minute," she replied. "It's too hot out here for me. I want to go back to the dressmakers' studio and work today."

"Oh, come on!" Petal pulled her hand, yanking the reluctant Olivia through the stables to the last stall. "You can't work every day, and the queen isn't even in the palace—everyone knows that."

The royal stables were much bigger than the ones at home, and Olivia appreciated how clean and tidy they were, though she was very thankful that she didn't have to do that kind of hard work anymore. Most of the stalls were empty as the horses were either out in the yard on display or being saddled for the picnic party.

Suddenly, there was a loud, aggressive whinny from the end of the corridor, which made both Daphne and Petal scream and leap into each other's arms.

Lady Olivia ignored her dormmates' childish display. "Someone sounds upset," she crooned as she approached the stall. "Who has annoyed you so much, my boy?"

The bottom of the stall door was closed, but the top half had been opened, and a huge stallion was pawing at the ground and shaking his mane, stretching his neck over the door. He screamed again.

"Get back, m'lady," warned a voice, and Lady Olivia noticed that someone was in the stall with the horse. "He's in a bad mood today."

Lady Olivia frowned at the stable hand, recognizing Benjamin from Belvoir immediately. "I know this horse," she said, raising her chin. "He is the Marchant prince's horse, Titor. I saw him win the final race of the Carnival at Belvoir Estate."

"Good for you," said Benjamin. He slipped alongside the angry horse, making his way to the stall door. "But he'll take a chunk out of you today, so you'd better back up."

Lady Olivia did as she was told and almost stepped on Daphne and Petal cowering behind her. "Livvie, you great clumsy thing!" Petal laughed loudly and stepped in front of Olivia. "Hi, Benjamin," she simpered at the stable hand but was drowned out by Titor. Embarrassed, she tried again, "Hello, Benjamin!" Petal's shout was too loud in the silence after Titor's whinny and earned her a disparaging look from the stable hand.

"If you could keep your voice down?" he snapped. "The big guy is annoyed enough already."

"I'm Petal," said Petal and held out her hand, but Benjamin had already turned back to his charge.

"Why is he so cross?" Olivia asked Benjamin. Anything to do with the Marchant prince was fascinating to her, and his stallion was almost as impressive as the man himself.

"They took his girlfriends out to parade, and one's pregnant," answered Benjamin. He pulled a handful of carrot pieces from his pockets, but Titor turned his nose away from the treat. "I'm sorry, boy. You'll get your girls back soon, I promise."

Titor butted his head into Benjamin's shoulder and nibbled the leather of his vest. Benjamin laughed and snuggled back. "I know, it's terrible not having your ladies next to you, isn't it?"

"You're good with him," noted Lady Olivia. She reached out a hand for Titor to smell. "I've heard only those with green blood can touch a Marchant stallion." As if to prove her words, Titor stepped away and rolled the whites of his eyes. Benjamin caught Lady Olivia's hand and pulled it down, but didn't let it go.

"Us Marchants have to stick together," Benjamin smiled. "But unlike my friend Titor here, I am very tolerant of other bloodlines." He squeezed Olivia's hand.

"Well, I'm not sure that I am," sniffed Olivia disdainfully, though she made no move to take her hand back. "I've heard that Marchants are nothing but trouble."

"Yeah, but the good kind of trouble." Benjamin's pale green eyes smoldered as they roamed over Olivia's body and came back to rest on her face. He stepped in close and dropped his lips to her ear. "I haven't forgotten Belvoir, my Lady Olivia. Anytime you want to revisit, you just let me know."

"I'm sure I don't know what you mean, Benjamin," said Olivia loud enough for her gaping dormmates to hear, then lowered her voice and looked up through her long eyelashes. "But of course, I'll have to make sure our beautiful queen isn't around to distract you from me again."

Benjamin didn't even have the good grace to look embarrassed. "Can't blame a man for trying," he laughed. "Any rung on the ladder is a step up, isn't it?"

Annoyed that Benjamin had presumed that he was of the same social standing as herself when he clearly was not, Lady Olivia was about to reply when a figure appeared at the near end of the stables.

"Lady Olivia!" Lord Orgustus's voice boomed through the corridor and spooked Titor again. "I've been looking for you everywhere. You are supposed to be coming on the picnic today."

Lady Olivia could tell from Orgustus's expression that he was not happy with her. "I'm sorry, my lord." Olivia wrenched her hand out of Benjamin's and wiped it on her skirt. "I didn't realize that you *wanted* me on the picnic today."

"Unless you are too busy, of course." Lord Orgustus curled his lip at Benjamin's shallow bow. "I'm sure talking to the *Marchant* groomsman is just fascinating."

"What? That's silly!" Lady Olivia forced a tinkly laugh. "I'm coming right now, my lord. I'm so sorry that I made you wait for me."

As Olivia hustled away, she heard Benjamin's quiet chuckle. "Any rung on the ladder, eh, my lady?"

Flushing, Olivia took Orgustus's hand and almost tripped when the lord yanked her along behind him. *My climb up the ladder is going to be so hard today,* she thought ruefully. She plastered a happy smile across her face, knowing no one would bother to see if it was real.

Riding across the tundra in the sunshine was no easier than it had been yesterday. It was just hotter. Jordansson proved to be entertaining company and didn't seem to find walking on foot any more taxing than Adele found riding her horse. He kept up a steady patter and was obviously very curious about the Tiny People of Unisia, as he called them. He had never crossed the Black Mountains before and seemed fascinated by Unisia and its culture. The men were happy to answer all Jordansson's questions and ask their own about the tribe he came from, and soon they were all joking and laughing like longtime friends. Except for Captain Lucky, who kept his distance from the cheerful tribesman and was obviously still holding a grudge over the "beautiful woman" comment.

However much he talked, Adele noticed that Jordansson kept a sharp eye out for ice bears and their portals and more than once stopped dead in his tracks, thinking he'd seen something.

Reassured that enough eyes were on the lookout for danger, Adele pulled the map globe out of her saddlebag and examined the path they were taking. The tundra appeared as a smooth gray expanse inside the globe, but the reality was much different. It grated against Adele's nerves that they had so far to travel over the difficult ground. She rolled the globe in her hands, and the mountain range passed under her fingertips, all the way to the glowing yellow dot where the dragon was supposed to be.

"What's that?" Jordansson had dropped back to Adele. Even with her on horseback he stood comfortably shoulder to shoulder with her, looking at the globe in her hands.

"It's a map," said Adele and rolled the sphere to show him the countryside trapped within the glass. Entranced, Jordansson took it for a closer look.

"It's our world," he said, his blue eyes taking in all the tiny details. "Look, there is my valley, the Valley of the Three Sisters." Adele noticed that the valley did indeed sit between three mountain peaks, a miniature plateau of green in the gray rock.

"And that's where we're going," replied Adele, pointing to the mountain west of the Valley of the Three Sisters. "We are heading toward that little light on the top of the mountain there."

"But that is sacred ground," said Jordansson. He looked up at Adele, his eyes wide. "This mountain is protected by the great god, and it is said that no man shall walk that path."

"I'm not a man," answered Adele with a shrug. "And I need to go there. I am looking for the dragon, Sighmere. Do you know of him?"

Jordansson looked at Adele as though she might be touched in the head. "I know the stories," he admitted. "The terrible, terrible stories that are told to children to keep them in their villages and not going too far from home."

"But you've never been there?" Ohrig joined the conversation.

Jordansson laughed as if it was a joke. "No, General Ohrig, I have never been there. No one has." He thought a moment. "No one except the Dragon Hunters, of course."

"But do you know how to get to the dragon's mountain?" persisted Adele. "Could you take us there, through the valleys? You wouldn't need to come any farther than you wanted, but if you could show us the way, we would be very grateful."

Jordansson shook his head. "You would be grateful, and then you would be dead," he said, and handed Adele the map which she slipped back into her saddlebag. "No one walks the path of the dragon and is seen again."

Adele and Ohrig exchanged a glance. "Sounds promising," said Adele. "If people are getting eaten, then at least that means the dragon is still alive."

"Why do you keep thinking the dragon is some massive creature who eats people?" complained Ohrig. "It's giving me the creeps. What if he's no bigger than a dog and likes vegetables?"

Adele grinned because giving Ohrig the creeps wasn't easy. "I'm only going by the legends from Earth." She turned to their guide. "Jordansson?"

"Down." Jordansson had dropped into a squat and sat completely still, looking hard at a point in the distance.

Adele froze in her saddle and saw the men around her do the same. But the horses were disturbed, and Adele couldn't get her mount to stand without pawing the ground and shaking its mane.

Ahead of them a green gash of magic opened, stretching from the ground straight up, at least five yards high.

"*Boorenweiss*," said Jordansson, and intoned a prayer to Dahk'hani in his sing-song language.

The white bear poked its head out of the green line of magic, and the portal doorway opened wide to free its massive shoulders and torso. Staring at their group with round black eyes, the ice bear emitted a growl so low and heavy that the ground beneath their feet vibrated. The wind changed direction, and the horses caught the scent of ice bear. With a shrill whinny, Adele's horse reared, and she fell off just before it bolted. She rolled to her knees beside Jordansson and didn't even mind the pain.

Adele had seen a polar bear at a zoo once, and because of the name, she had presumed that the ice bears, or white bears, of Evendaar would be similar. Instead, the ice bear looked like a giant, heavily muscled prehistoric kangaroo. Its fur was thick and densely white, only shaded brown around its open jaws. Coming out of the portal, it moved using its front legs to balance itself, then hopped its back legs forward. Then the ice bear sat upright on its back legs and sniffed, scenting the humans and horses in the air.

Jordansson had prepared the Queen's Guard for what they would need to do if they ever saw a bear, but getting the men to move proved difficult. They were frozen with fear, watching the huge beast slowly lollop toward them. A confident Jordansson had advised a simple distract-and-dive maneuver, where Pepper and Lucky would distract the creature by getting close to it and shouting, then the others would make their way around in a circle, surrounding the ice bear. He had insisted that he would be the one to jump onto the bear's back and strike the killing blow. Adele was given the job of staying out of the way. As an inexperienced hunter, she had been happy to comply, but seeing the ice bear changed all of that. She watched its eyes turn from black to iridescent green.

Magic! The Chime Voices began their song of excitement and lust, shrieking like hounds before a hunt. Adele felt the adrenaline pumping in time with her heartbeat and stood tall. She was confused as to how she was meant to accomplish what the Chime Voices wanted, but the hunger burned so deeply in her that all fear was forgotten.

The ice bear let out a dull roar, triggering the Queen's Guard to move again. Swinging its head around, watching the men as they split up to surround it, the ice bear dropped back on its haunches. Jordansson took advantage of the creature's confusion to make his way behind it, his hatchet in one hand and his knife in the other. His face was a mask of grim determination, and such was his distraction that the orders he barked at the Queen's Guard were all in his own language, so no one understood a word of it.

Surrounded, the ice bear growled when it saw QG Owens come between it and the portal. It lunged at the QG, letting out a bellow that sent the rest of the horses scattering with panicked screams. Confused by the noise and running prey, the ice bear leaped in the direction of one of the horses, very near Adele. The horse got away, but Adele did not. She stood exposed and vulnerable before the giant creature as she reached out and beckoned it toward her.

The Queen's Guard yelled, trying to distract the bear from their queen, but it had hooked its gaze on Adele and moved toward her with its strange walk-hop steps. Adele could see the green pupils glowing in its black eyes and knew the power this creature had was wild and strong. The Chime Voices sang a chant that reached Adele's lips, pulling the ice bear in. A snippet of a dream came back to Adele, and she saw a flash of recognition in the bear's eyes. *You are mine, angel,* the voice of the mage whispered behind the singing of the Chime Voices. *Take the power I give you.*

Almost on top of her, the ice bear stared down at Adele, its mouth wide, yellow teeth glinting in its massive jaws. The claws at the end of its hanging front paws were long and black, and Adele could see the dust on its black pads. The Chime Voices were all she could hear as the creature offered itself to her, raising its paws and baring its chest. Adele buried her hands in the thick fur, and her green magic launched itself through the skin, past meat and muscle, deep into the chest cavity of the ice bear. Ropes of magic wrapped themselves around the knot of power under the bear's heart and attached themselves, draining every drop of magic that it could sense. Adele was in deep, sightless and deaf until a white-hot screaming pain disconnected her from the magic.

Diving backward, Adele narrowly avoided the bear falling on her, and she looked up to see Jordansson on the back of the ice bear, his knife buried deep in its neck. Bright red blood gushed out, staining the white fur. Breathless, Adele wanted to howl in frustration. Some of the magic that she had been trying to channel had been released back into the bear at the moment of its death. She tasted metal on her tongue and knew that she hadn't taken enough magic to fill her.

General Ohrig was at her side, his arm around her shoulders, helping her climb to her feet. The Queen's Guard gathered around, and Adele tried to catch her breath.

Jordansson finished hacking at the ice bear's throat and stood up, his arm covered in blood. Eyes bright, he wore a triumphant smile. "It's dead!" he yelled. "I killed it."

The general turned Adele in his hands so she was facing him. "What in the name of the goddess did you think you were doing?" he shouted. "You could have been killed. That bear was a wild godforsaken creature, and you just stood there!"

Angered by his disrespect, Adele felt her eyes light up as the magic fired through her blood. Ohrig suddenly pulled his hands off as if the touch of her skin burned him. "I was draining its magic,"

Adele said tightly. "At least I was, before Jordansson killed it and broke the connection."

Ohrig ran his hand over his mouth to stifle his shocked expletives. "For the love of all that's holy, my queen…"

"Yes!" whooped Jordansson, misunderstanding Adele's words. "We killed the bear, and now he is dead." He grabbed her in a hug and spun her around. "You are alive, and the bear is dead."

"Jordansson, I really needed that ice bear alive for just a bit longer," Adele protested, struggling to get her feet back down on the ground.

"Your Majesty, the portal!" Captain Lucky had gone to investigate the gash of green magic still hovering in the air, and he frantically gestured her over.

Adele rushed to join Lucky. She peered inside, and what she saw made her heart leap, but almost immediately the opening of the portal began shrinking at the edges. "Jordansson," said Adele. "I think that the ice bear was keeping this thing open. Bring it here, quickly."

Jordansson dragged the ice bear toward the edge of the portal, and sure enough, the walls became solid again. "Look, there," said Jordansson and pointed. "We can see the edge of the forest. In this portal we can travel across the whole tundra."

Adele wasted no time. "Men, form a line and hold hands," she said. "We are going through right now. Someone bring that bear carcass with us in case we need it."

Bear and Pepper each picked up a leg of the ice bear, and Jordansson and Owens took a shoulder each. Happy that the creature was secure, Adele reached out for someone's hand. Ohrig slipped his in hers and squeezed tightly to get her attention.

"Your Majesty, are you sure this is wise?" His pale blue eyes had almost disappeared under his frown. "There is a real risk that this thing could collapse with us in it."

"And there is a real risk we'll be attacked by more ice bears on our way across the tundra," Adele snapped back. "Think of the days of travel we are saving, General!"

"Think of the risk!" Ohrig was pale with fear and anger. "Should we die now only to save a few days? Your Majesty, I recommend that we take a beat, gather the horses, and make a proper plan."

"Ohrig, you are wasting our time," argued Adele. "This is our way to the forest, and we are taking it before it closes. End of discussion." She took the first step into the portal, pulling Ohrig behind her, and didn't look back.

CHAPTER FOURTEEN
"Botany and Deception"

In the afternoon Rainere took the children out to the royal kitchen garden for a botany lesson, but mostly they were catching lizards and frogs. Aaron and Natalie hunted through the tall plants, clear glass cylinders in their hands as they looked for prey. Leafy was sitting under a tree next to Charlie, watching the proceedings with a blank curiosity, wrapped in the lavender blanket from the hospital room despite the warmth of the day. Charlie was watching Rainere.

Rainere tripped over a long-legged puppy that was sprawled in a patch of shade. He swallowed his curse and pulled off his jacket, sweat sticking his shirt to his back. He plucked a flower from the nearest plant. "Aaron," he called, "What's this called?"

"Purple," answered Aaron. He showed Rainere the beetle crawling on the back of his hand.

"Impressive bug," said Rainere. "Now, while the color is purple, the flower has a name. Remember, it starts with L," he prompted.

"Lovage," shouted Natalie. She deposited a posy of herbs in front of Leafy, who slowly picked it up and took it into the folds of her blanket.

"Try lav—"

"Lavender!" said Aaron, very pleased with himself. "I need to pee."

"Off you go, then," said Rainere, gesturing to a tree by the edge of the garden.

Aaron toddled off, and Rainere returned to picking more flowers.

"What the hell do you think you're doing?" asked Charlie quietly when Rainere came within earshot.

Rainere took a step under the shade of Charlie's tree. "Holding a botany lesson," he answered.

"No," Charlie nodded at the Golden Palace. "I mean here, in *her* home. What are you doing here? She said she would never forgive you for stealing Natalie, yet she left you as a nanny? I don't get it."

"You don't have to," said Rainere. "You weren't there when Stella was saved."

Charlie mulled this over. "Did she tell you that she sent me to steal the stamens back from you?"

Rainere wiped the sweat from his forehead with a silk handkerchief, folding it before putting it back in his pocket. "Her Majesty told me everything. Including how you tricked your way into her service by pretending that I'd sent you as a messenger. She still doesn't know why you did that, but I would like to find out myself."

"Are you going to kill me?" Charlie asked, curious.

Rainere felt a flicker of irritation at Charlie's offhand tone. "If I had wanted to kill you," he said, "you would be dead already."

"Not if you'd told her that you wouldn't," said Charlie. He chewed on the stem of a weed. "Not if she made you promise to keep me alive."

Rainere turned to look at Charlie, but he only saw confusion in his expression. *At least the boy is smart enough to know that he isn't out of danger just because he's alive.*

"Who do you really work for, Charlie?" asked Rainere. They were interrupted for a moment by Aaron returning and hugging Rainere's legs before grabbing Leafy's hand and leading her over to his sister.

Charlie pulled his knees up to his chin, his eyes hollow as he looked into the distance beyond the Marchant prince. "He'll be coming to kill me soon, anyway," he said. "So saving me was a waste of time."

Rainere wanted to roll his eyes at the young man's sense of melodrama. "I will thank you not to underestimate my abilities, Charlie," he said. "You're safe if I say you are."

Charlie shrugged and returned his gaze to Leafy. "Just make sure Leafy finds a good home, will you? She deserves it after what she's been through."

"Charlie, do not try my patience—" Rainere broke off as a sharp, hot sensation sliced through his ribs. Gasping, the prince fell to his knees on the ground. He clenched a hand over the Mark on his side.

"Hey, are you all right?" Charlie's voice sounded far away as Rainere traveled in his mind to Adele's side. She was close to something dark and wild, like an animal, and she was pulling magic through her hands. He could hear a wondrous music playing, female voices singing a vibrant chorus, as she was swept up in a tide of lust and magic.

"Hey! Hey, Your Highness, you want me to get help?" Charlie was shaking his shoulder. Rainere raised his head from the dirt and brushed his forehead clean. Less than a few seconds had passed, yet it had felt like he had been *inside* Adelena again, where time was endless. Rainere took a deep breath and tried to control his emotions, but excitement buzzed through him and made his hands shake as he pulled the little hand mirror from his pocket. *I have to talk to her and see if she felt the connection too,* he thought.

Rainere was about to flip the hand mirror open when Charlie's hand closed over his. Rainere was surprised by the audacity of the boy, but Charlie only looked horrified.

"Where did you get that?" demanded Charlie, trying to grip the mirror still in Rainere's hand. "Who gave you this?"

"Why?" asked Rainere, snatching his hand away.

"Because that's my mirror!" said Charlie. "It was stolen off me when I was attacked at the Gray Palace. I thought maybe Grottonski had taken it."

Rainere narrowed his eyes at Charlie, still waiting for the trick. "The high wizard gave me this mirror so that I can speak with Her Majesty while she's away. Are you sure it's yours? There might be many like it in the high wizard's coffers."

Charlie pointed at the crescent moon engraved in the enamel. "I watched him carve that," he said. "It's a C for Charlie, so he didn't get us boys mixed up." Charlie reached for the amulet that normally swung at his neck, and his hand closed around thin air. "He gave me a protection from the Eldars too, but it got stolen in the mines—that's why the Eldars came for me."

Rainere was shocked by this outpouring of information. "Charlie," he said gently. "Shut your mouth and don't say another word. We need a place where we can talk properly, not out here where we're being watched."

"It's the Boss," said Charlie anyway, and his eyes scanned the garden as if the man himself might materialize. "The Boss is gonna find me and kill me, and there isn't a goddess-damned thing any of you can do about it. I should've known he would have contacts in the palace. I should've guessed he would be a wizard too."

Rainere raised his finger to his lips and murmured a charm. He caught Charlie just before he fell to the ground, lifting him up into his arms.

"Children, Charlie has fainted in the heat," Rainere called out. "We must go inside where it's cooler for him. Come along."

The children rushed to join Rainere, including Leafy, who snarled at Rainere as if she knew what he had done. *What a strange little child,* he thought as he raised a warning eyebrow in her direction, effectively silencing her. *I will have to test her strength. Like Charlie, she might be much more than she appears to be.*

Stepping out of the portal into bright sunshine, Adele allowed herself a raucous cheer. "We did it!"

She grinned at the pale faces of her Queen's Guard. "See, that wasn't so hard, was it? And now we've saved two days of walking." Adele punched Ohrig on the shoulder in celebration.

Her general was still bent over, holding his knees, and gave her a heavy look in response. "Yes, and you've only taken five years off my life," he panted.

They were standing right on the edge of a lush green forest; the trees were dark gray, their trunks covered in beautiful robes of emerald moss. The ground between the trees was dotted with patches of snow and looked like it would be easy to hike.

Behind them Jordansson exited the portal, dragging the carcass of the ice bear with him. "Don't worry, everybody. It is a nice walk now," said Jordansson as he dumped the ice bear on the ground. "We will rest here, and I will just take the skin off the *boorenweiss*."

Though Adele chafed at any halt in their progress, Captain Lucky took the chance to check Adele's pulse and eyes to make sure she really was all right after her encounter with the wild creature. With QGs Bear and Owens giving helpful commentary, Jordansson and Pepper made short work of skinning the ice bear. Jordansson cut down two saplings and strung them together with rope from his pack to make a sort of sled on which to tie the pelt.

When they'd finished, Jordansson set off into the trees, leading the way and pulling the makeshift sled behind him. The land that had looked so flat from outside the forest soon proved to have quite a steep gradient, and Adele didn't have much breath for talking, so she could only listen to Ohrig's litany of complaints.

"You realize the horses were carrying most of our supplies and food?" the general pointed out. "Not to mention the tents and camping equipment."

Adele nodded, breathless. "That does make things tricky."

"And without horses to ride, we have committed to walking the whole way to the dragon's mountain and then walking home again."

Adele groaned inwardly. "I'm sure we can find some more horses at Jordansson's village," she said. "Didn't he say they had ponies in the valley?"

"So we definitely *are* going to Jordansson's village, are we?" asked Ohrig. "Because the last I checked, we had asked him to take us to the dragon's mountain, and he said he wouldn't."

"Uh-huh," coughed Adele.

"So *why* are we following him, exactly?" the general asked.

Adele grabbed a tree branch and swung herself up a particularly steep rise. "Because no one else knows how to get there," she said firmly. "And Jordansson will take us as far as he can through the mountains. Hopefully, we can get ourselves to the dragon following the map."

"So you did manage to keep your hands on the map, then?" asked Ohrig. "Because I thought you put it back in the saddle bag, which was attached to the horse, which is now two days' walk away."

Adele stopped dead. She looked to the sky and shouted a filthy curse so loudly a flock of birds in the surrounding trees took flight. She looked at her general and saw his grim smile wasn't meant to make fun of her.

"So now you understand the situation you've put us in," Ohrig said. "Right? Well, my work here is done." He pushed through the trees past his queen. "Let me know as soon as you have a plan to get us out of it."

Fuming, Adele had plenty of time to curse herself as they walked but was regularly distracted from her self-recriminations by having to focus on her feet. Hiking uphill wearing a heavy cloak was not ideal, and though banks of soft snow and ice had begun to appear on the ground, the sun filtered down through the trees and created an unwelcome humidity. Although Adele had the shortest legs in the group, she soon began to catch up to her Queen's Guard as they struggled through the forest, stripping off their coats and jackets as they went. It was probably late afternoon when Ohrig called a halt, and they gathered together in a rough clearing, perching on fallen logs to catch their breath.

"So this mountain only goes up, looks like," said QG Pepper, stating the obvious with a groan. He stretched his tired legs. "It's so steep that sometimes I feel like I'm moving backward."

"Where's Jordansson gone?" coughed Bear. He had already taken off his heavy jacket, and his shirt was soaked through with sweat. "How is he so far ahead of us?"

"I can't believe I'm standing in snow while sweating my balls off," complained Owens, ignoring the stern look from his captain. "My feet are frozen, but my armpits are cooking."

Adele barely had the breath to agree. Her lungs were burning, and her legs ached. She had never thought of herself as athletic, but she had hoped she was fitter than this. They all looked up as Jordansson came bounding into the clearing. He wasn't wearing his pack or a shirt.

"Ah, we all tired now, I can see," he grinned and made a show of flexing his muscular shoulders and chest. "The small Unisians are not as strong as mountain peoples." He laughed at his own teasing. "Come, I have found a good camp and made a fire already." He charged off back the way he had come, and everyone reluctantly stood up and followed him through the forest.

"I think it's deeply inappropriate for Jordansson to be half naked before our queen," sniped Lucky to Ohrig, but only got an eye roll in return. "I will tell him to put some clothing on and stop showing off." Lucky dashed up the hill with more energy than Adele thought it possible for him to have.

"No way he got all that muscle from only hill walking," grumbled Leith, sounding a little jealous of Jordansson's physique. "He must train a lot."

"Yeah, it'll be weights," sniffed Bear. "He must do heavy weights and lots of hand-to-hand combat practice. Probably running too. You'd get a flat stomach like that from running uphill."

Adele listened to the men discuss Jordansson's probable training regimen and couldn't keep her mind off his body either. Yes, he was well built, but more disturbing were the tattoos that decorated his upper arms and chest. An alarming thought occurred to her, and she stumbled her way over to where Ohrig was trudging uphill.

"Did you see Jordansson's body, Ohrig?" Adele asked her general.

Ohrig raised his eyebrow at her. "Of course, Your Majesty, but I would say he's a bit top-heavy and should concentrate more on his legs to balance out his form. More repetitions and less weight, if you ask me."

"No, Ohrig, not his muscles—his *tattoos*," said Adele impatiently. "Prince Rainere once told me that his immortality curse was done in dragon's blood. Have you ever heard of tattoos being done any other way?"

Ohrig looked thoughtful. "I know that some pirates draw designs on their skin with ink, but these are temporary. Maybe we should watch and see if Jordansson's disappear too."

"Maybe," Adele considered this, but her Chime Voices convinced her otherwise. "Or maybe we should wonder if a young man like Jordansson is covered in spell tattoos, then what are the others in his tribe going to be like? Maybe they also have those with an immortality curse?"

"It would be wise to find out before we find ourselves walking into a tribe of immortal warriors," agreed Ohrig.

Adele nodded. High Wizard Ohren hadn't been able to tell her anything about the people of the mountains or their customs, so they really were following Jordansson completely blind. Distracted, Adele accidentally crashed into the back of QG Leith, who stood frozen with his nose in the air.

"Do you smell that?" he asked.

"Food!" Bear grinned. "And about time too."

The QGs raced off up the hill, following their noses, and left Adele behind, sunk in her own thoughts. She didn't notice that Ohrig was still with her until he suddenly asked, "Do you like this Jordansson character, Your Majesty?"

Adele tripped on a tree root. "What?"

"I don't know if he is your type, but he seems an all right sort," said Ohrig. "Smart, good-looking, and young enough for you."

Adele stopped walking and stared in disbelief at her general. "Ohrig, are you crazy? I've only known the man for a day." She narrowed her eyes at Ohrig's curious expression. "Why do you think that I *would* like him?"

Ohrig shrugged. "I just think you could do worse than someone like him, that's all. He seems a magical sort." He looked uncomfortable but said what he was thinking. "The sort that might be healthy for you to be with."

Before Adele could answer Ohrig, they came upon a natural plateau where Jordansson had set up camp near a cave. The tribesman had already started a large fire, and several small creatures were roasting above it.

"I thought you had got lost." He laughed and welcomed them to their home for the night.

The camp was a man-made clearing in front of a wide cave, already furnished with a fire pit and cut logs for seating. The sound of water took the QGs off to discover a wide but shallow stream not too far into the forest. Adele traveled up the stream to find some privacy to wash off the sweat and grime of the last few days. Though the water was icy cold, she was grateful to finally be clean again. She stopped short of washing her clothes, as now she only had the one outfit and the sun was already setting.

Dinner was a relaxed affair with the roasted meat and a root vegetable stew. Jordansson had promised that nothing hunted the woods and that, for tonight at least, they were safe.

While they ate dinner, Adele was disappointed to see snowflakes drifting into the flames and dusting the ground around her. She shuffled as close to the fire as she could without actually sitting on it. "I'm going to freeze to death," she muttered and blew on her hands. "I have *never* been this cold before."

"The fire will keep the cave warm, and you have a coat to sleep on," said Jordansson with an offhand wave. "But you can take a big man to bed tonight if you want to be hot, Queen."

As if to prove his own point, Jordansson flexed his bare torso for her. The QGs were all stripped down to their shirts and trousers, perfectly comfortable in the smoky cave.

"I usually sleep next to my children," said Adele with a sigh.

"Well, you can take Pepper to bed then—he is the young man here," Jordansson joked, rolling his eyes at Lucky's protest. "Captain Lucky, your queen is a strong, beautiful woman. Tell me why you all don't fight to be in her bed?"

"Because we are Her Majesty's *servants*," snapped Lucky.

At the same time Ohrig growled, "Lucky, stop letting him bait you."

Pepper blurted out, "Prince Rainere said he'd cut our balls off if we even touch a hair on her head, anyway."

There was a long moment of silence, and it became clear to Adele that the remark was not a joke. "Prince Rainere said *what*?" She turned her whole body to face Pepper.

QG Pepper's cheeks flamed, and Ohrig was forced to rescue him. "To tell you the truth, Your Majesty, Prince Rainere pulled the Queen's Guard aside before we left on our journey. He told us that if any man found himself in a compromising position with you, then he would be cursed on his return to Unisia. I think it's safe to assume the prince has a very loose interpretation of 'compromising,' so for the sake of everyone, we will not lay a hand on you unless your life is at stake."

"Will I have a curse on me for touching the queen too?" Jordansson raised his snow-white brows.

"Yes, but you aren't coming back with us to the Golden Palace, so Prince Rainere won't have a chance to get you," said Ohrig, not taking his eyes off Adele as he watched her anger build.

"Is he very strong, this prince?" asked Jordansson.

"Prince Rainere is one of the most powerful immortal wizards in Unisia," Lucky assured Jordansson.

"Could he curse me from there?" Jordansson looked genuinely alarmed now.

Lucky nodded. "I would think so."

"No! Rainere isn't going to curse anyone," said Adele, infuriated. "And how *dare* he give you orders without my knowledge. How *dare* he try to sabotage my quest." Adele glared around the campfire at her men. "You are all to ignore every word that Rainere has ever said to you. I am your queen, and you follow my orders, not his!"

The men looked unconvinced, but Bear gave Adele a respectful nod. "In that case, Your Majesty, if you need a man to warm your bed tonight, then I'll volunteer."

Adele froze. "Wait. What?"

Bear chuckled, and the atmosphere lightened as he added, "I'm just kidding, Your Majesty," and accepted the cuff on his head from Ohrig with good grace.

Adele felt supremely awkward as the men all chuckled at the idea of Bear in bed with her, but also because she saw Jordansson's eyes light up.

"Would you like me to keep you warm, Queen?" Jordansson ignored Lucky's spluttered protest. "I think you will freeze like a child in the snow tonight."

"Nope, I'll be fine," said Adele. She made a point of getting up from the fire. "As you've said, I can keep myself warm enough, thank you."

"No, I was wrong—you can't." Jordansson shook his head and stood up too. "You are already too cold, and it will get much worse tonight."

"Maybe it is a good idea," said Ohrig, shocking all the QGs into silence. "You stay alive till the morning, and none of us risk a cursing from the prince. I know it's unorthodox, Your Majesty, but we do need to adapt and take fuel where we can sometimes."

Adele felt her cheeks flame and was almost as embarrassed as Captain Lucky was angry. She knew exactly what Ohrig was suggesting she do to Jordansson. "General, I thank you for your concern," replied Adele. "Gentlemen, good night."

Adele collected up her coat and dignity and walked the few yards to the back of the cave, glad of the dark that hid her flaming cheeks.

Chapter Sixteen
"Requited Yet Complicated"

Adele looked about, but no place was better than another, so she dusted off a spot on the floor next to a wall, wrapped herself in her coat, and sat down. She shivered violently, her teeth chattering so hard she almost didn't hear the quiet conversation of the men.

"Jordansson, go and keep our queen warm," Ohrig ordered the tribesman. "But watch where you put your hands, or she will cut your balls off herself."

Jordansson laughed. "I will do as you ask, and she can decide what to do with my balls."

"The queen never agreed to any such thing, General," Lucky protested.

"She didn't say no, either," said Ohrig.

"You will only hear her say *yes* tonight," joked Jordansson, clearly baiting the captain for laughs.

There was the sound of a scuffle and more quiet laughter from the QGs, and then Ohrig's quiet reprimand: "Leave it alone, Lucky."

Adele watched in the dim light of the campfire as Jordansson walked deeper into the cave and found her curled up in a tight ball. "Queen, did you hear us talking?" he whispered and dropped his fur coat down next to her. "It's all right that I am here with you?"

"Sure, why not?" Adele said, feigning indifference, but her teeth chattered too hard, and the effect was lost. She watched as Jordansson laid out his heavy fur coat and used some rods from his pack to make a tent from his shirt.

"You've done this before," she said, admiring his shelter.

"I'm a hunter, so I am out of the village for a lot of the Season of the Sun," said Jordansson. "I know how to live in caves and be happy." He grinned, and Adele could see his teeth glint in the low light. "I do not think that you know this life, Queen."

"I have camped before," said Adele. "But not like this, with no equipment or anything. This is very tough."

"It's a good thing that I found you when I did," said Jordansson. "My land is very hard for the tiny people of Unisia, but I will look after you."

At a gesture from Jordansson, Adele crawled onto the furry mat and positioned her head under the shirt. She made space for the big tribesman, stifling her sigh of pleasure when he pulled her to his naked chest, covering her with a cloud of male-scented warmth.

Lying in Jordansson's arms, Adele felt overwhelmed by the conflict between her heart and her head. She hated being angry with Rainere again. The fury came too quickly and flew too close to hatred. Rainere had betrayed her before by taking control of her life, and now he had threatened her men because of his jealousy. *Rainere doesn't own me. I can do what I want now that we're apart, and so can he.* An image of Stella floated across her mind, and Adele felt the tears well, washing away her anger. *No, I'm lying to myself. Of course, I'll put up with all of Rainere's jealousy and bizarre behavior because he is the only man who can keep Stella alive. Nothing else matters except having Stella well again.*

Adele sniffed and then felt Jordansson's thumb brush against her cheek, catching a tear that had slipped down her jaw. "What makes you cry, Queen?"

"My children." Adele didn't want to talk about them, but Jordansson's voice was so warm and sweet, and the compulsion was too strong. "My baby, Stella, is very sick. She will die if I don't find a dragon's tear to heal her. Stella is why I'm here, freezing my arse off in the wilds of the Ice Mountains looking for a dragon and relying on a complete stranger to help me."

"After that story, now I will cry a little too," Jordansson said, but Adele heard the smile in his voice. She gave him a playful shove, making him gasp.

"Your hands are ice," Jordansson complained. He gathered up both of Adele's hands and held them against the bare skin of his chest, giving dramatic shudders that shook them both. The Chime Voices began a lilting song, and the magic under Adele's heart began to rise, coils slowly sliding over coils. She felt the magic in Jordansson's body, and though it wasn't dark, it certainly wasn't light either. *He would be something else entirely,* thought Adele, and the green magic inside her reared up, insatiable, as if its hunger had only been made stronger by the wild bear energy.

Adele took one of her hands out of Jordansson's grip. "This is dragon's blood, isn't it?" she said, tapping a tattoo on his pectoral muscle. The magic in the lines fizzed against her fingertips. The Chime Voices told Adele that if she traced the tattoo with her finger, she would know the spell that the lines made.

Jordansson shivered under her touch, but not from cold this time. "How do you know this?" he asked.

"Do you really have to take me all the way to your village, Jordansson?" Adele asked, ignoring his question. "Wouldn't it be easier to go straight to the dragon's mountain?"

Adele felt Jordansson hold his breath and could almost hear him thinking. Despite his constant good humor, his pale blue eyes shone with a canny intelligence. "Queen, I have told you that the home of the dragon is a much-protected secret in my tribe," said Jordansson quietly. "We will have to ask the chieftess for the honor of making that journey. It will not be easy to make her do this. You will need me to talk for you."

"I understand," Adele whispered back. "I will appreciate any help you can give us, Jordansson."

"But I really want to come with you and see a dragon too." Jordansson's voice was tinged with yearning. "It will be very dangerous and exciting, I think."

"Then you should come with us," whispered Adele. She ran her hand over Jordansson's cheek, the white-blond whiskers pricking her skin. The Chime Voices begged Adele not to resist—they wanted this man for their own.

When Jordansson's kiss dropped on her lips, it felt like an answered prayer. His tongue flickered between her teeth, tasting of woodsmoke and something green and fresh, like mint. *Just a little,*

Adele told herself as she kissed Jordansson back. *I only want a taste.* But Jordansson had other ideas, and his hand slipped inside Adele's coat, seeking out the curves of her body and cupping her breast in his hand. His kiss deepened, and when he squeezed her nipple, his touch electrified both of her magics, sending them racing through her veins. Adele slipped her hands around Jordansson's face and grasped at the short blond hair at the back of his neck. The green magic unfurled its tendrils, ready and waiting to seek that mysterious magic in Jordansson's body. Curiously, black lines of dragon blood danced through her mind's eye, shifting and morphing into different symbols, and Adele could feel that Jordansson had protections on him that might deflect her invasion.

This isn't going to work, Adele told herself sternly. *Get your hands off the man, now!* She retracted her magic before it could do any damage and turned away from Jordansson's kiss. Jordansson traced his lips down her neck, until Adele pushed at his broad shoulders.

"We have to stop," whispered Adele. "No good will come of this."

Jordansson stared at Adele in the dark, and she wondered what it was he could see. "You wish that I was him, your Prince Rainere."

Adele hesitated. "No, but I won't do this with you. It's too dangerous."

"I will not hurt you, Queen," Jordan sounded offended. "I am not an animal."

"I meant that it would be dangerous for you," said Adele quietly, knowing her words would intrigue the hunter and hating herself for wanting him to pursue her. *Then it wouldn't really be my fault for giving in to him, would it?*

Adele felt Jordansson shift closer, scooping her up to spoon against his chest. She could feel how excited her words had made him.

"Why do you think you would hurt me?" Jordansson asked, his breath warm on her ear as he ran his hand over her ribcage and stroked the soft skin of her stomach.

Adele fought the sensation as lust pounded through her blood. "Because you don't know who I am and what I could do to you,"

Adele whispered, shame making her brusque. "Anyway, you're a stranger to me. I know nothing about you, Jordan Jordansson, except that you are a hunter and a mountain man covered in tattoos."

"I can tell you things about me," said Jordansson, and Adele felt his finger trace her ear. She bit her lip and didn't trust herself to answer. "I will tell you what this mountain man can do for you."

Adele caught Jordansson's hand as it traveled back to her breast. She was feeling uncomfortably hot now. "Just talk." She turned to face him. "You do not have my permission to touch me."

Jordansson smiled and leaned down again, his lips barely brushing Adele's ear. "I feel like there is something between us," he whispered. "Something very big and important. In honor of this, I would like to worship you as the great god has bade his people to worship their women."

Adele almost felt the sparks light her eyes. "Worship me?" she murmured, and the Chime Voices tinkled happily. "I don't think—"

"Yes." Jordansson nuzzled into her neck. "I would kiss you as I did before, down your body, until I could take your"—he touched her nipple lightly—"in my mouth. I would suck and lick this side, and then that side, until you could not catch your breath. Then I would kiss down here"—he ran a fingertip down the center of her stomach—"until I reached this." Jordansson's voice became hoarse, and Adele felt his erection pressing against the side of her thigh. She tucked her hands under her head to stop herself from reaching for it. "I can taste you and lick and suck until you shout my name," Jordansson continued, his fingertips slipping under the waistband of her trousers and lightly brushing the fuzz between her legs. His breath washed over her skin, and Adele ached at the center of her core, the hunger for sex and magic burning in her chest.

Just a little. I promise I won't hurt him too much, thought Adele, trying to placate the reluctant human part of herself.

Adele gasped as Jordansson moved his leg between hers, using his thigh to lever open her knees. His hand hovered over the hot flesh between her thighs. Adele let her hands slip down his broad chest to his stomach and back up to his wide shoulders. The magic all over his skin made her tremble. *I'll be gentle,* she told herself. *He won't even feel a thing.* Adele caught Jordansson's face between her hands and pulled it down to hers. She kissed him, and despite his clear talent for it, Adele couldn't help noting every difference between this tribesman's kiss and Rainere's. *Don't think about him,* Adele admonished herself as she felt the sweat drip down her temple. *You want this man's magic. At least give him a little pleasure before you take what you need.* Jordansson, sensing Adele's new enthusiasm, positioned himself between her legs, his arms folded by her head as he held his weight off her.

"I am big for you, little queen," Jordansson said as he grasped one of her hands and slid it down his rock-hard member. "Don't worry, I will be very gentle."

Jordansson's promise echoed her own as Adele unlaced his trousers and then her own. Jordansson pressed the tip of his erection against her, as if he was going to enter, but then he shifted and slipped his finger inside, reaching deep before sliding out and using her own wetness to rub against the swollen clitoris with his thumb. Adele arched up into his chest and stifled her moan.

"You are so beautiful, Queen Adelena, I will worship you all night," Jordansson breathed. "I promise only to be very gentle."

"I won't be," Adele whispered as she gave in to the desire that swamped her resolve and unleashed a tendril of magic inside of Jordansson. Released into a powerful being, the tendril of green dove deep, only to ricochet off a hard wall of protection. Adele's line of magic recoiled back into her with a clanging shock. Jordansson didn't seem to notice Adele's surprise as he kissed her sweetly, murmuring to her in his own language. Adele tried again, this time using both hands, as she pressed them to Jordansson's chest and pushed a stronger vine of green and gold magic into him. The sensation was like touching ice, and again her magic retracted involuntarily, repelled by Jordansson's odd magic.

Jordansson pulled himself out of their kiss, and his fingers stopped moving in their glorious rhythm. "What are you doing?" he asked sharply. He pulled Adele's hand from his chest. "You did something to my heart. I felt it."

"I didn't mean to hurt you," protested Adele. "Honestly, I'm sorry, I was just—I didn't mean to…" She took a deep breath and felt the intimacy of the moment wane as Jordansson moved further away from her. "I'm sorry, Jordansson. It's my mistake."

Jordansson dropped to his side next to Adele. It was clear he didn't understand what had happened, but his body had reacted to her violation, and he hadn't liked it. "Maybe you will tell me the truth in the morning," he said. "But now I think we should sleep."

"I'm sorry, Jordansson," Adele whispered, and she hoped that she hadn't made their mountain guide angry. She could only imagine what Ohrig would say if Jordansson left them high and dry in the forest because she had been too rough with him in bed.

Jordansson scooped Adele in close to his chest, despite how hot she already was. "I will keep you warm, but I will not worship you now," he murmured.

Adele didn't know if she should be relieved or offended that he started snoring within moments of their abandoned tryst.

She pillowed her head on Jordansson's bicep and felt frustration rattle through her bones. Her conscience might still be whole, but her magic needed more. *God, why did I have to try too hard?* Adele cursed herself as she squirmed, wet and too warm. *I could have at least got some physical pleasure, even if I didn't get the magic from him.* But it was sexual frustration talking, and the grumbling Chime Voices almost tempted Adele to wake Jordansson up and demand he finish what he started. It didn't help to remember that the last time she had been in a man's arms, her magic had rejected Rainere's touch just as Jordansson's magic had rejected her tonight.

It's so stupid to whine, but, Sweet Christ, am I ever going to get laid again? wondered Adele as she prepared herself to wait out a long, frustrating night in the arms of the gorgeous sleeping giant.

CHAPTER SEVENTEEN
"A God in a Grove"

It was around midnight when Adele heard the sound, like that of a gong, ringing through the air. The Chime Voices sang a clear note of joy, and Adele sunk into a deep dream state.

She could feel a presence surround her as she stepped toward the entrance of the cave and into the circle of firelight. Her QGs looked so vulnerable wrapped in their cloaks, huddled together on the ground for warmth, and Adele felt her courage galvanize as she prepared to defend them. She pulled her tired gold and green magics together and tried to cover her body with them like a suit of armor but only managed to cover her back. **That will have to do,** *she thought. She studied the air around her but couldn't detect any disturbances. After a long moment of waiting and watching, Adele was starting to feel a little impatient.*

Come out and show yourself, *she called, and as soon as the words left her lips, the Chime Voices chanted a song that covered Adele in a haze of blue magic.*

"Child of Serena, your step upon my land has woken me."

Adele was flying in a blue sky. The wind buffeted her, but she didn't feel its chill. This was a dream, and there was no need to panic now that her feet didn't touch the ground. Adele could tell that it was not Rainere who had called her, like he had so many times before on Earth. It was another male energy, and it was powerful.

The god appeared in front of Adele, his face as beautiful as the sun. His feet formed a volcano in the earth below. His eyes glowed white hot, and his hands caught her up in their palms, like a child catches a butterfly. "Dahk'hani!" the Chime Voices sang in praise, and this time Adele felt no fear.

"I greet you well, angel. It has been an age since my sister-goddess has sent her messengers to me." The god's voice was like an orgasm that never reached

a crescendo. Adele ached to hear it, wishing it would finish while hoping it would come again and again. She fought to keep her mind and not succumb to the ecstasy.

Adele opened her mouth, but only the Chime Voices sang out, a pealing song pulling from deep inside her lungs and releasing itself into the air like a flock of birds.

The god opened his palms, and Adele dropped to sit upon the base of his thumb. "I seek the dragon, Sighmere." Her ordinary voice whispered below the Chime Voices as if it were only an echo or an afterthought. "I would find a cure for my daughter, and I would see the prophecy ended."

"Will Serena return for me if I grant you these things, angel?" The god lowered his great glowing eyes and examined Adele in a gaze that surrounded her with blue magic and spurred the song of the Chime Voices to greater heights. Somehow, in their words, the god found his answer. "Give me a child so that I may walk again upon the world, and I will give you all that you seek."

Adele gasped in a deep, rushing breath. She was outside of the cave, lying upon the frozen ground. The dream hung about her vision like a fog, and the Chime Voices sang loudly and clearly right at the front of her mind as Adele blinked and climbed to her feet. The men of her Queen's Guard and Jordansson were rubbing the sleep from their eyes and stumbling out of the cave as if they had all been woken at once. Captain Lucky was the first to rush to Adele's side as the tears ran down her face and she fell into his arms.

"What in the name of the goddess happened here?" Lucky held Adele tightly to his chest, and she felt his heart racing in fear as he looked around the forest glade and took in the sight of thousands upon thousands of butterflies carpeting every tree and log like a living painting. Their iridescent blue wings shone in the morning sun as they shivered and fluttered about the glade.

Adele felt drained as she clung to Lucky, but her dignity forced her to her feet, and she took a step out of his protective embrace. She sought out Jordansson's gaze and could see by his pale cheeks that he was as shocked as all the other men.

"Your god was here last night," said Adele, pleased to hear that her voice was no longer the breathless whisper behind the Chime

Voices. "He wants me to give him a child, and then he will grant us safe passage to the dragon. Tell me what that means."

Dropping to his knees at her feet, Jordansson hugged Adele hard. "I will never refuse you my body again," he promised. "You are a messenger of the great god, and I will worship you always, Queen Adelena." He buried his face in her chest.

"Get off the queen," Lucky snarled at Jordansson and drew his sword. The captain shook off Ohrig's warning touch. "No, General! How do we even know that Jordansson didn't bring this trouble to us? This could all be his fault."

Jordansson's blue eyes went even wider at Lucky's accusation. "We need the chieftess," he croaked. He gestured with a hand at the fluttering butterflies. "This is too great for me. I have never seen the hand of Dahk'hani so close before. I don't know what to do."

Adele pulled herself out of Jordansson's embrace. "Well, that makes two of us," she said. "And that's why we are going to keep doing what we came here to do: find that dragon. Dahk'hani can wait."

"But, Queen?" Jordansson was shocked at Adele's blasphemy.

"Dahk'hani can wait!" Adele shouted, suddenly furious. "Pack up the camp now; time is wasting."

Chapter Eighteen
"Hiking over Obstacles"

It was a somber group that left the butterfly-laden glade behind them and continued their uphill trek through the forest toward Jordansson's mountain valley. They made good time with the fine weather, but soon their feet were wet with melting snow, and the seemingly endless ascent made everyone irritable.

Stuck at the back of the group with the general, Adele endured his relentless questions about what had occurred in the night, but she could only answer in snippets of visions and the emotions she had felt. Adele didn't want to tell Ohrig how much at home she had felt in the god's hand, like she could have stayed there forever. Nor did she tell Ohrig about the orgasm that had rocked her core and stolen the strength from her legs. Ohrig was wary of all things magic, and Adele could tell that he was working hard to give her rational explanations for everything that she had seen in her vision, which might have been just a dream.

"For all we know, those butterflies have always lived in that glade," he said as they entered the lunchtime campsite that the men had already built, waiting for Adele and Ohrig to catch up to them.

Jordansson was making a soup with vegetables and a large bird he'd caught earlier, and heard the end of Adele and Ohrig's conversation. "Butterflies are very rare," said Jordansson firmly. "Those creatures were a gift from Dahk'hani for the queen. It was clearly a message from the great god."

Ohrig scowled but was silent as he took the bowl of boiled meat and greens that Jordansson handed him.

Steering clear of her general, Adele chose a seat under a large tree with a mossy trunk and branches that bowed low to the ground. She squinted up into the fluttering heart-shaped leaves that sounded like so many tiny voices whispering around her.

"It's a Tjordanker tree," said Jordansson as he handed Adele a bowl of food and sat close beside her. "It means Tree of Many Hearts. Do you not have them in Unisia?"

"I've never seen one of them before," Adele admitted. "The leaves sound like they're talking."

Jordansson stroked the trunk of the tree. "It's believed that the souls of unborn babies live in the trees. Women who want a baby often sleep under such trees, hoping to be chosen."

Adele pulled herself off the tree. "Does it work?" she asked, immediately remembering Dahk'hani's request that she give him a child.

"Yes, it works," said Jordansson with a smile. "But also because the woman brings the man she wants to father the child with her." He paused and raised his snow-white brows. "And he worships her."

"Well, that normally does the trick," remarked QG Owens. "Women like a bit of worship."

"By the sound of it, every stone on the ground and stick in the trees has got a story on it," said Bear. "Take this tree here. It's got heart-shaped leaves, so in Unisia, we'd call this a heart leaf tree. Done. No story about babies and worshipping anyone needed."

Jordansson laughed uproariously at this insight into Unisian culture. "But that makes no sense," he grinned. "Every name should tell the spirit of the object; otherwise, how can you understand why it is in the world?"

"Waste of time," said Bear stubbornly.

"That really is how Unisians think," said Adele. She couldn't smother a giggle at Jordansson's incredulous expression.

"The forest we are in was the place of the last battle between the great god Dahk'hani and the dragon, so we call this land 'Dahk'hanisturmvog.' What do you call my country?" asked Jordansson.

"In Unisia we call this area, where the tundra finishes and the mountain range begins, the Ice Mountains," replied Bear.

"Because of all the ice on the mountains, yes?" Jordansson couldn't keep a straight face.

"You should ask what they call the black stone mountain range separating Unisia from the tundra," suggested Adele with a giggle. Jordansson shook his head, laughing. "The Black Mountains," Adele's giggles turned into full-blown laughter. "Because from a distance they look—"

"Look, I don't know why you think it's so funny," huffed Bear. "They're just names."

"Are the places in Unisia all named for colors?" asked Jordansson. "That says nothing about the soul of the place."

"Doesn't need to be about its soul," grumped Bear. "It's practical, isn't it?"

"Yes, but you have to admit, it's not very imaginative," chuckled Adele.

"And Unisia?" continued Jordansson. "What does that mean?"

"Unisia is from the old tongue, and it means 'center of the world sanctified by the goddess Serena,'" answered Ohrig, though not with any pique. He seemed to be enjoying the good-humored teasing.

Jordansson and Adele exchanged a look. "Actually, that is quite poetic," said Adele.

"Yes, that is a good name for your land," agreed Jordansson. "Very beautiful." Jordansson's eyes lit up as he smiled at Adele. "Just like its queen."

Adele felt her magic spark at Jordansson's look, but she couldn't afford the distraction right now. "I could use some more, whatever this was," she said, waving her cleaned bone at him.

"I will get it, Your Majesty." Jordansson leaped to his feet but was stopped by Lucky, who had already filled another bowl for the queen and handed it to her.

"I could tell you the story of my name," volunteered Jordansson, taking his seat next to the queen. No one said anything in opposition, so he continued. "My mother had given the tribe eleven strong sons. She had reached an age when she thought that she could not bear another child, so she let a young man worship her, though he did not have the status to father a child. When she felt my spirit move within her womb, she knew that I would be born—" He hesitated and looked to the sky, trying to think of the word. "Wrong, I think. So my mother dedicated my spirit to the great god Dahk'hani, hoping that he would show her mercy for her mistake. But Dahk'hani didn't take my spirit from my mother, even though she drank many strong herbs and did the ceremony to send me back to the darkness. My spirit grew on, and one day, I was born, but too soon for a normal baby, so I was very tiny and weak, and my mother gave me to the village women to raise, expecting me to die every day. I was called Jordan Jordansson because that is the name of the spirit of our village—we are the people of Jordan." He tapped his heart. "I am the son of the village. It was their strength that grew me. The women all gave me their milk, and the men kept me warm, watching over me every night."

His story finished, Jordansson smiled at the gaping expressions of the other men and Adele.

"Your mother tried to kill you before you were born, and she *told* you about it?" QG Leith said, his blue eyes shiny.

Jordansson picked up on the sympathy in Leith's question, and he flushed a little. "I am proud to be the son of all my village," he said. "Dahk'hani wanted me here in this world, and even the power of my mother, the chieftess, couldn't defeat his will. This is what she told me to make me feel special. The great god has a purpose for me, and I will work hard to find out what it is." He looked at Adele, and his eyes were filled with adoration. "Or who it is."

It was Adele's turn to flush. "What about you, Lucky?" she said, quickly changing the subject. "How did you get your name?"

"Yes, what about you, young warrior?" Jordansson turned his attention to Captain Lucky and threw an arm around his shoulders. "Your name means 'good fortune' in the King's Tongue, doesn't it? Is that why your mother named you Lucky?"

Lucky shook off Jordansson's arm, embarrassed as all the men of the Queen's Guard snorted and chuckled at the question. "We should be getting on," he said. "If Her Majesty is finished, then let's pack up the camp." The men followed his lead and broke camp.

Not used to Lucky denying her requests, Adele swallowed the last bite of lunch and climbed to her sore feet, ready to keep trudging up the mountainside. "Hang on a minute," she called, after their group had got going and were already pushing ahead of her. "I still want to know why you're called Lucky, Captain."

Unable to directly refuse her, Lucky reluctantly dropped back to answer his queen's question.

"My full name is Lancelot St. Lucidis, but all Lancelots in my family are called Lucky for short," said Captain Lucky. "It's considered an honor in my family, as our ancestor, Lord Lancelot, was the first and only royal St. Lucidis wizard to have been blessed by the goddess Serena when she walked this world. It is said that Lord Lancelot was so overcome by Serena's beauty that he pledged his life to her teachings, denying all his human appetites, giving away all his worldly possessions, and devoting himself to a life of service and magic." Lucky raised his chin, needing to speak loudly over the guffaws of the QGs. "Though Lord Lancelot might be a joke to history, his direct descendants will always strive to emulate the man who fought the Marchant kings of the time in devotion to our goddess, Serena."

"You do kind of look like him, Captain," said QG Pepper, fighting to get the smile off his face. "I mean, from the pictures that I've seen of Lord Lancelot in schoolbooks and the portraits on the church walls."

"He's the image of Lord Lancelot," agreed Owens, giving Lucky a sidelong grin and copying Lucky's high-handed tone. "And it is said that our captain here follows in all the old man's footsteps, keeping himself pure for the goddess Serena, or Lady Olivia—whoever comes first, I guess."

Leith shook his head. "I still don't get how that makes you pure," said the young QG. "Not touching women just seems weird to me."

"Lucky, have you *never* worshipped a woman?" Jordansson was shocked. "But how will you ever make a child?"

Lucky's cheeks flamed red as he glared at the tribesman. "I don't have to explain my beliefs to you, or anyone else," he said crisply.

Wanting to save Lucky any more embarrassment, Adele quickly turned to QG Pepper. "How did you get your name, Pepper? Tell me it's because of your hair color."

"Ha, ha. I'm sure you can do better than that, Your Majesty," said Pepper, running a hand over his thick auburn locks. "Most old St. Lucidis names begin with an O, but in the Upper Hills, those of the royal line mixed with other families, and we chose our own names. Pepper St. Lucidis was one of the first settlers of the Upper Hills, and he established a great farming tradition for our family." This was the most Adele had heard Pepper say since the night in the Spider's Nest, and she encouraged him to keep going. "Pepper St. Lucidis caused a scandal when he married a royal Marchant—Raincloud Marchant, Your Majesty. Apparently, she could control the weather, and she had a good knowledge of technology, so their farm always thrived when either weather or just magic might've failed them. It's quite a famous story."

"Pepper and Raincloud Marchant," mused Adele. "Does that mean you also have Marchant blood in your veins?"

Pepper shrugged, a little self-conscious as the other men fell silent to listen to him. "I'm not sure that we do anymore," he said. "The magic has disappeared from the most recent generation, like my cousins and me, but before that, the Peppers were known to be very strong."

"Strong, but not very pretty." Bear gave Pepper a good-natured shove into a tree.

"Bear, where did your name come from?" Adele turned her attention to the older QG.

"Bear is short for Obearon," said Bear with a nonchalant shrug. "My mother had pretty grand expectations for us boys, but we aren't anything but a pauper St. Lucidis line, not a drop of royal blood anywhere. Still, the St. Lucidis name has saved my life more times than I can tell you, Your Majesty, and I'm grateful that it was enough to get me thrown into the Queen's Guard. "

"This is true," agreed Owens, chewing on a twig as he walked along. "A good name hides a lot of sins in the army."

"You were never a working lad like me," Bear sneered at his friend. "You were born up in the fancy Guild Quarter with gold dust trailing out of your arse. You only got thrown in this unit because you were unlucky enough to be slumming it with me in the diggers."

Owens shrugged, taking no offense at the suggestion. "It is true that Owens is a good old family name, and one I'm sure my dear father regrets giving to me every day. May the goddess bless his angry soul."

"Gentlemen, language." Captain Lucky frowned at their casual tone in front of the queen, but Adele was only too happy to finally be learning something new about her men.

"And you, Leith?" Adele asked.

Leith looked up, surprised the attention was on him. "Me? I was just named after my father. He's an accountant at the Court of the Golden Palace, Oleitham St. Lucidis. I'm the only St. Lucidis in my family, though; all my sisters are from different fathers, so I guess Mum thought it made me special or something to take the old man's name."

"Lord Oleitham was famous for being the right hand of Lord Lancelot," added Lucky, clearly trying to spread a little of the glory of his old-fashioned name to Leith.

Owens and Bear started chuckling again. "Lord Lucky would've needed a good right hand too," chortled Bear, "what with not touching any ladies."

"That's all ancient history," grumbled Leith, giving Bear a dark look. "My name is about as pure as my hair color." He scrunched up his short brown hair, making the waves stick out. "There's nothing proper St. Lucidis about me."

"If you are all from such different backgrounds, then how were you chosen for the Queen's Guard?" Adele asked.

The men fell silent, and Adele looked to General Ohrig for the answer.

"The Queen's Guard was a dumping ground for all sorts of troubled soldiers the Ordinary Army couldn't keep." Ohrig's tone was even, but Adele heard the passion behind the words that signaled the general was speaking of something close to his heart. "Getting swung into the QG was normally the last step before being thrown in prison. Even to be promoted within the Queen's Guard was seen as an insult to both a man and his service. When I was given the office of general, there wasn't anyone else in the Queen's Guard. The position was a punishment for certain things I'd said and done in the Court of the Golden Palace. Making me general of an empty unit was meant to humiliate me, but I'm not one to let any jumped-up wizard control my fate, so I decided to make the best of a bad situation and used my new rank to go through the army prison yards, called the diggers, and pull out men who I thought deserved the same second chance that I'd been given. That's how I found these two troublemakers." He pointed at Owens and Bear. "Pepper found me quite by accident, but I took him gladly."

"I thought I was signing up at the Ordinary Army office, but someone had played a prank and sent me to the general's office. I was a QG before I knew what was what." Pepper didn't look particularly upset about being tricked into the Queen's Guard and gave General Ohrig a respectful nod.

"Damn right I took you," said Ohrig. "Big strong country boy like you, we needed you in our ranks." The general jerked a thumb at Leith. "Leith's mother dropped him on my doorstep like a newborn lamb, and I only took his skinny behind as a favor to her. Then Lucky joined us by special request of the High Wizard Ohren himself. I think it was the only decent turn the wizard has ever done me."

Adele looked at the faces of the six men who made up the Queen's Guard that she had blindly relied upon for her safety since the day she had arrived in Unisia.

"So being put in the Queen's Guard was a punishment," Adele stated and couldn't ignore the irony of these men being forced into guarding the most reluctant queen in the history of Unisia. "So we are all in servitude together, I guess. I didn't want to be here, and neither did any of you."

Ohrig shook his head, and Adele saw pride shine bright in his pale blue eyes. "We might have been dumped into the Queen's Guard, Your Majesty, but we had our dignity, and we had a rank, even if no one respected it. These men of yours have trained harder and done more tactical exercises than any of those gentle boys in the Ordinary Army. From the day I found each one, five years ago, I have honed them to be one of the best and hardest units that I've ever had the honor to train. On that strange day two months ago, when High Wizard Ohren called us to receive our new queen, I knew that the goddess's hand was guiding our destiny, and I was proud to be ready to present you with the men who are worthy of being the Queen's Guard for Her Majesty, Adelena Olivia St. Lucidis, the true queen of Unisia." He grinned. "Long live the queen!"

The rest of the Queen's Guard echoed his call, and their voices brought tears to Adele's eyes.

Jordansson clapped his hands, applauding respectfully. "I like this story," he said. "There is much love and honor in it." He wrapped his arm around Adele's shoulders. "You are a very lucky queen to have such good men with you."

Adele agreed. She wiped at her tears and took the handkerchief that Ohrig offered her on his way past. "Thank you, General," she said, and she didn't mean just for the scrap of cloth.

"You're welcome, Your Majesty," Ohrig answered, understanding everything.

CHAPTER NINETEEN
"An Omen or a Wish"

It was late afternoon when they reached the end of their trail. The forest stopped abruptly and opened out onto the edge of a wide chasm. The chasm was no more than forty to fifty yards across and crossed by three bridges of ice of varying widths. On the other side of the chasm was an open pass that climbed up into the mountains. Jordansson gestured for everyone to be cautious as they approached the edge and looked down into the chasm. Hundreds of yards down, a fast-flowing river filled the bottom of the ravine, the water red and muddy in the afternoon light.

"This place is called Kachorkian," Jordansson informed them. "It means—" He searched for the words, a deep frown creasing his forehead.

"I'm sure we can live without the explanation, Jordansson," said Bear.

"'The Wound of Dahk'hani Where His Blood Flows out into the World'," continued Jordansson. "It is said that when Dahk'hani discovered that Serena had left the world of Evendaar, he stabbed himself and let his blood run out for eternity, never dying but never being strong again either."

"That's depressing," commented Owens and spat over the side into the rushing waters below. "How do we get across, then?"

"We will walk for half a day this way," said Jordansson. He pointed to their right, following the edge of the chasm. "Then we cross a stone bridge and walk back along the other side for half a day, and then there is the mountain pass we need to climb."

"That mountain pass?" asked Adele, pointing across the chasm directly in front of them. "That very path that we can see right there, cut through the wall of the mountain, not fifty yards away?"

Jordansson nodded. "Yes."

"But we could just cross one of these ice bridges right here," protested Adele. "We'd be done in less than a few minutes and would save ourselves a day of travel."

"No," said Jordansson. "The ice isn't thick and safe like in the Season of Snow, so it is too dangerous to cross. Besides, the long way is very beautiful, and we will have good hunting."

Adele's attention was caught by a blue-winged butterfly that had flown over her shoulder and hovered delicately over the ice bridge before fluttering onward. She smiled to herself and accidentally caught Ohrig's eye.

"If you're going to try to tell me that's an omen from Dahk'hani," growled Ohrig. "You can stop right there."

"No. I was going to make us cross anyway," replied Adele lightly. "But if it *was* an omen, it would definitely be a message to say we are on the right path."

"Maybe," said Jordansson doubtfully. "But I am sure that the long way is safer, and we will not die that way."

Adele thought of Stella lying in her coma back in the Golden Palace. Every day they wasted was a day without Stella healthy and happy. *I have crossed interdimensional portals and lived,* Adele reassured herself. *An ice bridge is nothing to fear.*

"I'll use magic to bind us together," said Adele to her men. "That way I can pull you along behind me one by one."

"No, you will not," Jordansson said firmly and shook his head.

Adele turned to Ohrig. "General, you tie everyone together with the bit of tent rope Jordansson can give us. Then I'll use the rope to channel my magic, just like we normally do when walking through a portal by holding hands."

Ohrig gave Adele a heavy look.

"Yes, of course, it's a risk," she answered his unspoken protest. "But it'll save us a day, and it's time we need to keep."

"Hello! Listen to me!" Jordansson waved his hands to get everyone's attention. "I said, it is not safe to cross here. The sun will melt the ice as we walk. I know you are only small men, but our weight will break this bridge. We *cannot* do this."

Adele turned to Jordansson. "Can I have that rope from your pack, please?"

"General Ohrig!" Jordansson was incredulous to see that this was actually happening. "Do not listen to the queen now. She is crazy to say this should be done."

"You want to try crossing this particular bridge?" Ohrig asked Adele, pointing at the middle bridge.

"It's the biggest," Adele replied, "so likely the safest."

Everyone stared hard at the bridge as if it would give them its secrets. It was only a yard wide and maybe a foot thick.

Jordan threw his hands in the air, as close to angry as they'd seen him. "General, tell your queen she is stupid to do this thing!" he shouted, his voice thundering down the chasm.

The general spun on his heel and pushed himself right up under Jordansson's chin, their chests pressed together. "Now, look here, Jordansson, to us the word *queen* means 'she who will be followed to the ends of the earth without question.' Now, that woman," he pointed at Adele, "is our queen. Do you understand me, boy?"

Jordansson looked into Ohrig's narrow blue glare and nodded. "Yes, I understand."

Ohrig huffed, satisfied he'd made his point, and rejoined Adele at the side of the ice bridge. He looked down into the swirling waters below them. "You really want to cross this death trap and risk all our lives to save a day's march, Your Majesty?"

Adele pulled up the green magic from under her heart and then the magic at the back of her neck. The gold magic growled and twined with the green, giving her strength. Adele felt a rush of power at her fingertips. "The bridge will hold, and I will get you all across, Ohrig."

"Then that's good enough for me," said Ohrig.

"Okay, crazy people." Jordansson held his hands up in defeat. "If we are to cross, then let's do it quick before Dahk'hani forgets about us."

Adele stood at the edge of the ice bridge and examined it for obvious faults as she tied the rope that Jordansson gave her around her waist. There was a distracting buzz at her belt, and Adele took a moment to realize that it was the hand mirror, when she heard a voice squeak her name.

Adele snapped open the cover. "Rainere, I'm kind of in the middle of something," she said. "Can I call you back?"

Rainere's face coalesced in the little mirror, talking as if he hadn't heard her. "Adelena, I felt a disconnection with you last night. The Mark started bleeding…"

Adele felt the tension of the men behind her rise. "Can we talk about this later?" said Adele.

"Adelena, tell me that you are all right," insisted Rainere, his eyes narrowed. "What are you doing?"

"I said I'll call you later," said Adele. "Okay, love you, bye." She didn't even cringe at her inappropriate sign-off but instead took the deepest breath that she could, and hefted her pack higher on her back.

"I'm right behind you, Your Majesty," said General Ohrig.

"Then let's go." Adele kept her eyes on her feet as she took the first step toward the ice bridge.

Chapter Twenty
"Surrounded by Snakes"

Rainere snapped the mirror closed and squeezed it tightly. *Something is wrong with cara mia.* He knew it in his bones. Just like he knew something had happened to Adelena to make his Mark bleed last night. Though he had only seen her for a few moments, he couldn't help but notice the magic in Adelena's eyes sparking oddly, and that her face was pale with fear. *I should be there with her. She needs me, my poor—*

"What did the queen say?" Charlie sat on the edge of the window seat watching Rainere. "Why couldn't you talk to her for longer? She needs to know that the Boss might be here in the Golden Palace."

"Shut up," hissed Rainere. He glanced over his shoulder to scan the sitting room of the royal apartment to see who might have heard. The stewards waited in the doorways across the room, and the last nanny had already excused herself to play outside with the children on the terrace. Only Mrs. Ollenby was left, knitting on the couch as she perused her accounting ledgers.

Charlie had confessed his double life to Rainere, telling him everything that he knew about the Boss: the sort of work he requested, the way he murdered those who failed him, and the way he sent Charlie messages through the mirror. Yet Charlie knew nothing that might help them work out why in particular the Boss wanted the new monarch of Unisia dead. Rainere still wasn't sure if this Boss was the one responsible for the attack on Adelena in the slums of the Lower Districts of Concordis that night, but it was clear that the Boss had connections in the Golden Palace.

Rainere continued studying Mrs. Ollenby. The woman was everywhere at once and knew more about the Golden Palace than anyone besides Rainere himself. He was quite sure that if they were going to find someone hiding in the Golden Palace, Mrs. Ollenby would be the person to help them. Besides, for reasons he couldn't even explain to himself, he trusted the woman.

Rainere approached the lady with Charlie dogging his heels. "Mrs. Ollenby, I hope I'm not disturbing you, but I have something very important to discuss."

Dolores Ollenby looked up with a twinkle in her lavender-blue eyes, and Rainere realized she knew he'd been watching her. "Of course, Your Highness," she said, smiling warmly. "Perhaps we can enjoy a spot of afternoon tea together?"

Without waiting for Rainere's response, Mrs. Ollenby called the steward Hollis over to give him the instructions, and all three of the stewards left at the same time. Charlie collapsed on the couch next to Rainere and threw his feet up on the coffee table.

"I hope you don't mind if I join you both, Mrs. O?" said Charlie. "I have a vested interest in these discussions."

Mrs. Ollenby looked from the ancient Marchant immortal to the young Marchant boy in front of her. "I think you need to tell me what's going on in my palace," she said.

*   *   *

Lady Olivia couldn't hear anything as she watched Prince Rainere and that boy Charlie talking to Mrs. Ollenby through a crack in the queen's bedroom door.

What the hell has the prince got to talk to Mrs. Ollenby about, anyway? thought Olivia. *That woman is nothing but a glorified housekeeper.* Olivia really needed to find out where the queen had gone and why the Marchant prince was still here, staying in the royal apartments with the children. She desperately needed some fresh information for Lord Orgustus, or he would dump her for good, and she wasn't ready to give up on him just yet.

Lady Olivia kept watching, waiting for someone to give her a clue as to what they were discussing. She thought that Prince Rainere was looking more intense than usual this afternoon. He sat tall, his shoulders wide for his slim frame, and leaned forward when he listened to Mrs. Ollenby talk. Thoroughly engaged in the conversation, dots of pink colored his cheeks, and his elegant hands either danced before him or were clasped tightly in his lap. Olivia bit her lip when he undid the top button on his shirt and rolled up his sleeves, revealing muscled forearms. She wondered what it would feel like to have those deep, dark eyes concentrating so hard on *her.*

How can someone so wicked be so handsome? she thought, thrilled by her own daring. *I know I've wanted him ever since that day at the Gray Palace, and if Adelena wasn't a queen, I'm sure I would have had him already.*

The stewards returned to the room in a train, carrying tea trays and a large bottle of golden Firewhiskey with all the glasses and china needed for afternoon tea. Mrs. Ollenby began serving just as Lady Olivia had to duck away and close the door before Hollis saw her peeping.

Not wanting to leave the queen's beautiful bedchamber for her own boring dormitory, Lady Olivia wandered into the dressing room and decided to try on some of Adelena's gowns to cheer herself up. She dreaded having to face Lord Orgustus and tell him that, yet again, she had no new information for him. Olivia picked out a velvet burgundy dress from the queen's wardrobe and held it up in front of the mirror.

I could be a queen, she thought, admiring herself as the gems sparkled on the bodice. *I look the part, and I know how to charm and flatter, unlike Adelena. If I ran the Golden Palace, no one would talk about me behind my back or make fun of me at the balls. Lord Orgustus himself would fall at my feet, and I could have the pick of any man I wanted, even a prince.* Olivia remembered all the time and special acts that she had wasted on Orgustus and felt a wave of self-loathing.

Stop it, she reprimanded herself. *You are not finished yet. Really, who gives a hoot about a stupid lord when you should raise your standards and look at a prince? Even a hated Marchant prince is better than a popular St. Lucidis lord.* She felt her head spin at the very wickedness of her thoughts. *If only I could have Prince Rainere alone for just a moment…*

The door to the dressing room crashed open, and Lady Olivia stifled a shriek. There in the doorway stood Prince Rainere, brandishing a key in his hand like a weapon. He had taken two steps into the dressing room before he realized that she was there.

"What are you doing here?" he growled and shoved the key in his pocket.

Lady Olivia felt her heart leap out of her chest when those dark green eyes found her pressed back against the rack of dresses. She dropped a low curtsy.

"Your Highness," she squeaked. "I don't expect you would remember me—my name is Lady Olivia. I came to the Gray Palace with the queen during the Carnival at Belvoir."

"I know who you are," replied Rainere, his voice smoky at the edges. "I asked what you're doing here."

Despite his straightforward question, Lady Olivia forced a giggle and batted her eyelashes up at the prince. "I'm flattered that I remain on your mind, Your Highness," she said. "Today I am here arranging Her Majesty's dresses and looking for those that need repairs. What can I help *you* with in the queen's dressing room?"

Prince Rainere looked perfectly intimidating as he pulled himself up to his full height and stared down his nose at her. He hadn't run his eyes over her body or given any indication of being affected by her charm, and while this disconcerted Lady Olivia, she had many ways of dealing with difficult men. *Maybe he prefers his women bumbling and pathetic like our little queen,* she thought. *Adelena works that wide-eyed 'please help me' attitude to perfection.*

"I am here to fetch an article of the queen's for Princess Natalie," said Rainere finally. "She has requested something of her mother's clothing to sleep with."

Lady Olivia clasped her hands to her chest to try to draw the prince's eye there. "It is so very sweet how you dote upon the royal children, Your Highness," she gushed. "It's no wonder the queen trusts you with their care."

Olivia opened a drawer of neatly folded shawls and pulled out a length of floral silk. It didn't matter to her that the queen had never worn it. "How much longer do you think it will be until the queen returns, Your Highness? I know we all miss her so much."

"The queen will be home as soon as she is able," said Rainere coldly and reached for the shawl, but Lady Olivia fumbled, and it fell to the ground.

"Oh, I'm so clumsy, forgive me," said Olivia, giggling, and dropped to her knees at Rainere's feet. As she refolded the shawl, Olivia looked up at the prince, her face as close to his groin as she dared. "Your Highness, if there is anything else I can do for you, please let me know."

Prince Rainere looked down at Lady Olivia, and with a sense of deep satisfaction, she saw that flicker in his eye that she had been waiting for. She rose to her feet and gave Prince Rainere the shawl, touching his hand for an instant. "Anything at all," she purred.

The prince gave Lady Olivia a shallow bow. "My lady." He left the dressing room, turning at the last moment to give her a backward glance.

The door closed, and Lady Olivia allowed herself a triumphant smirk. *The prince is just a man, after all,* she thought, but her sharp mind couldn't help but analyze the way the situation had played out. *Just what did he want from the queen's dressing room, really? He certainly didn't come in for a piece of her clothing for the brat.* Lady Olivia remembered the key Prince Rainere had in his hand. *Is that for the door?* She turned to the little door in the corner of the dressing room. She knew there was a small attic room behind it and had once asked the queen to use it for a bedroom. She pulled a pin from her hair and unfolded it in her nimble fingers. "Now let me see what is so important," she muttered as she dropped to her knees and attacked the lock.

*   *   *

"How was Stella?" asked Mrs. Ollenby when Prince Rainere returned to the couch and sat down.

Rainere looked down at the shawl in his hands. "There was a maid in there," he said. "Lady Olivia. I couldn't get past her to Stella's door."

Mrs. Ollenby frowned. "There is no reason that girl should be in the queen's dressing room at this time of day," she mused.

"The maid should be fired," said Rainere, still perturbed by his encounter.

Mrs. Ollenby shook her blond curls. "Lady Olivia Templeton is from the same people that I am from in the Blue Hills, by way of Belvoir, Your Highness," she said, her eyes sharp though a smile dimpled her cheeks. "I know exactly what her life was like there, and I understand what she's had to do to earn a place here in the Golden Palace. The girl is a hard worker, and her talents as a seamstress are only outweighed by her personal ambitions. Personally, I believe that she deserves a chance to make something of herself in this difficult world, and I also find it very interesting to see who she manages to use to exalt herself in the palace."

"More snakes for the pit," said Rainere, curling his lip in disgust as Mrs. Ollenby handed him a cup of tea.

"Snakes who only eat other snakes shouldn't concern us, Your Highness," she said with a gentle reprimand. "Right now, we need to find out who is hunting our queen and how to stop them before she returns."

"Then we kill them," said Rainere, phrasing it as a statement and not a question.

"Of course, then we kill them," agreed Charlie, but he looked at Mrs. Ollenby for confirmation.

"Then we do what we must," said the older lady, offering a plate of cakes.

CHAPTER TWENTY-ONE
"A Prince and a Pauper Reconcile"

After his conversation with Mrs. Ollenby, Rainere joined the children out on the terrace. The three nannies, Seraphina, Siobahn, and Caitlin were playing a chasing game with Natalie and Aaron and their overgrown puppies. Natalie was already screeching that Aaron was cheating, as the three dogs followed his every step and did as he told them to, dodging away from Natalie's hands. Rainere noticed Leafy standing apart from the game, still wrapped in her lavender blanket. She was staring at Natalie as if she had never seen anything like her before. Rainere made his way over to sit near the girl, waving his hand to get her attention.

"Leafy, come here." He gestured to a chair next to his.

"Watchoo want?" asked Leafy sullenly, but she came closer to the prince, regarding him with her dark eyes. She didn't sit.

"I want to know if you would you like to stay here at the Golden Palace," Rainere said. "You can have friends and food and a comfortable bed to sleep in. You won't have to work anymore."

Leafy's gaze followed Natalie as the princess scampered about the flowerpots, laughing as Tra La La jumped and barked around her. Leafy turned back to Rainere, and he saw pale green tears in her eyes.

"I gotta go back to the mines," she mumbled. "Me bruvva Carl is there. I gotta get 'im out."

Rainere regarded the little Marchant child curiously. "What if I told you that I could get your brother out of the mines?" He leaned forward as Leafy's eyes lit up with hope. "Would that make you happy, Leafy?"

Leafy nodded, and the pale green tears traced their way down her cheeks. "Please, sir," she whispered. "The Keymaster will kill 'im."

Rainere reached for Leafy's hand. He turned it over so it rested inside his. He examined the scars and lines on her trembling palm. "You have a lot of magic, don't you, Leafy? And sometimes it hurts you."

"It bites me if I don't use it," Leafy admitted. "And it hurts if I sleep too long."

The magic activates when she sleeps? Rainere was impressed despite himself. *The girl is stronger than I guessed.* "I can show you how to control that, Leafy. Would you like me to teach you how to use your magic so it never hurts you again?"

Leafy scrubbed the tears off her cheeks with the corner of her blanket. "Carl first," she said bravely.

"Of course." Rainere closed his hand over Leafy's and let her feel the vibrations of his power. Her eyes opened wide, and she tried to pull her hand free, but he didn't let her go. "I will do lots of nice things for you, Leafy, but there is just one thing I would like you to do for me." Rainere turned Leafy's chin with a gentle finger to face the playing children. "Princess Natalie is very special to me. Very, very special. I would like you to help me protect her from all the bad people who want to hurt her. You see, Aaron has got his animals to protect him, but Natalie has no one else."

Leafy's eyes were huge above her pale cheeks. "I can use my magic to protect her," she promised. "My biter will stop the bad people." A dense ball of acid-green magic appeared in Leafy's other hand, sizzling with heat. Rainere could see immediately that the biter would cause a lot of damage to the unwary.

Rainere let go of Leafy's hand and sat back in his chair. "Thank you, Leafy. That would make me very happy," he said.

Charlie came out to the terrace, singing out cheeky greetings to the three nannies, who only rolled their eyes at him. He sat himself at the table across from Rainere. "Hey, Leafy," he said. "Go and play with the kids now. I have to talk to Prince Rainere."

"About Carl," agreed Leafy and then left to go and stand next to Natalie, who was engaged in a game of Stuck in the Mud with Aaron.

"What'd she tell you about Carl?" asked Charlie. He couldn't hide his haunted expression from Rainere.

"That he's in the mines and she wants him out," said Rainere. "You need to tell me everything now, Charlie. How you were captured, who by, and what happened to you there."

Charlie scowled at being ordered so perfunctorily to reveal his deepest pain. "Why, so you can go and close the gaps in security?" he sneered. "Don't pretend you want to do one blessed thing to shut that place down, wizard."

Rainere felt his eyes flash, revealing his temper. "Do not presume to know me, boy."

"I know you need the mines more than anyone else," said Charlie, playing with fire. "The Gift of Life is the only thing keeping you properly alive. Without it you'd just be a skeleton, walking the world as a freaking monster."

"I have always known the price that is paid to make the Gift of Life, and I have never misused it," said Rainere defensively. "But I am not the most dangerous creature who needs the potion, and without the mines, the real monsters would wreak havoc across all of Unisia."

"Are you talking about the Marchant Eldars?" asked Charlie but fell silent at a hand gesture from Rainere.

A server had arrived with a tray of tea and biscuits, and both Charlie and Rainere waited until the man poured them two cups. "That will be all," snapped Rainere as the server fussed with a spoon and began ladling sugar into his tea. The man bowed, dropping the spoon, and finally left.

"Yes, I speak of the Marchant Eldars," said Rainere. "They are kept in their Eeyrie by deliveries of the Gift of Life. If that were to stop, then they would look for food elsewhere, and no one with any magic in their blood would be safe."

"But they already leave the Eeyrie," protested Charlie. "At the mines they take all the kids who are too sick to work and put them out on the ledges as food for the Eldars." Charlie shuddered. "I saw one, you know. Long face and horrible, clawed hands. Its eyes were all black and then all silver, and it couldn't really talk, only hiss. It scared the piss out of me."

"You were lucky to survive such an encounter," said Rainere. "The Eldars are powerful predators and will stop at nothing to devour all the living magic that they find."

"Well, it was Rip who threw me off the cliff to escape the monster," said Charlie. "I thought he was trying to kill me, but he saved Leafy and me. He's probably dead now," he added bleakly.

"Rip?" Rainere raised an eyebrow.

"Ripenzo Shale, may the goddess bless his soul," said Charlie. "He was my only friend in the mines, and the only reason I got out of there alive."

"Why do I know that name?" mused Rainere. "It can't be very common. Where was he from?'

Charlie sniffed. "He never said."

"I suppose it doesn't make any difference anyway, if he's dead," said Rainere. He returned to the matter at hand. "Now, Charlie, tell me everything that happened to you from the moment you entered the Gray Palace to steal the Fire Orchid stamens."

Charlie took a slurp of his tea. "Yes, Your Highness," he said, and then he began.

Chapter Twenty-Two
"A Bear Turns Mouse"

Adele stood at the side of the chasm and stared down into the swirling, raging waters below. She heard whispers on the breeze, and the Chime Voices told her that magic was in the air. *Maybe Dahk'hani is near?*

"I will not be a pawn to another bloody god in this world," said Adele aloud, suddenly determined that her path to the dragon would not be thwarted by unnecessary deals with gods. "I will do this myself."

"Looks easy enough, Your Majesty, just keep walking and try not to fall off," Ohrig gave Adele's shoulder a squeeze. He touched her so rarely that when he did, it always made her feel better.

Adele screwed up her courage and took the first step onto the ice. The bridge felt solid underfoot, though she could still feel faint vibrations echoing up her legs caused by each step. *It's the wind that's the worst,* she thought, chewing her bottom lip to shreds as she shuffled forward. The wind pulled wisps of hair free from her braid and whipped them into her eyes. Her clothes flapped against her body and distracted her so much she almost looked down over the void she was crossing. Adele forced herself to speed up, and it seemed to take forever and then no time at all before she stepped off the other side onto the mountain ledge.

The men hadn't wanted to use the rope in the end, but instead volunteered to make their own way across the bridge individually. They arranged to let Jordansson cross in second place, and though Adele raised an objection, they all seemed pretty set on the idea. Captain Lucky insisted he would follow Jordansson, and then the rest of the men one after the other behind him.

Jordansson resettled his pack and raised his arms over his head, letting out a wild shout that set the Queen's Guard chuckling. "This is going to be very amazing!" he yelled, clearly terrified and ridiculously excited at the same time.

Jordansson edged out onto the ice, his boots shuffling along the bridge as he dragged his precious ice bear pelt behind him on its sled. He reached the middle and raised a hand in a backward wave, hesitating, and Adele let out the breath she had been holding in a big rush. Sweat prickled her brow, and she realized how much she didn't want Jordansson to die.

He almost ran the last half of the bridge. Leaping off, he grabbed Adele and swung her around joyfully. "We are alive, you crazy queen! We are alive!" he shouted, then set her down on her feet and wiped the sweat off his forehead. "I really thought I was going to die this day." He whooped again and made Adele laugh with his infectious joy.

"And we saved a day of travel." Adele grinned, thrilled that her gamble had paid off.

"Yes, we did!" said Jordansson. He wrapped his arms around her as they both turned to watch the other side of the bridge. "Now let's get your guards across."

Captain Lucky made the crossing quickly, followed by Owens, then Leith, Pepper, and General Ohrig. The old general stepped onto solid land with a mouth full of expletives that made Jordansson laugh uproariously, and even Lucky chuckled at the creative imagery.

"Just one to go," said Owens as he looked across the bridge at Bear, who hadn't even taken the first step. The sun was just cresting the trees now and lit the mountain wall above them. In a short time, it would shine down on the bridge, and that wouldn't be good.

"QG Bear, come across now!" Ohrig shouted as calmly as he could. "We are running out of time, so pace it, soldier."

Bear crossed his arms and stood a step back from the bridge. Adele could see by his white face and the way he was muttering to himself that Bear was terrified. Everyone began shouting encouragement from the other side, but Bear took his time. Clearly steeling himself, he took a tiny step onto the bridge, hands extended in front of himself, and slid each foot along the ice like he was walking in the dark.

"That's it, Bear! Don't look down, just look at me, mate," Owens urged his friend.

Then Bear stopped moving. All the men of the Queen's Guard began shouting again, but the QG was frozen with fear and wouldn't move or answer anyone. Adele looked up and watched the progress of the sunlight, slowly slipping down the mountain face behind them.

"Bear, you have to do this," shouted Ohrig, silencing the other men with a wave. "You step one foot in front of the other right now, QG!"

"I can't," stammered Bear. "My feet are stuck on the ice. It's too high and the wind—"

"Bear, listen to me. I'm going to come out and get you, all right?" said Ohrig. He dropped his heavy jacket as if its weight would make him that much lighter.

"No, General!" Adele grabbed Ohrig's arm. "I'm the lightest; I'll go and get him."

Ohrig shook her off. "You think I'm going to let the goddess-blessed queen of Unisia cross this fucking bridge a second time, you're wrong," he growled.

"But that's why I can do it," said Adele, slipping past the general and stepping out onto the bridge before she could think about what she was doing. "Serena needs me alive, and so does Dahk'hani—they won't let me die."

The general saw it was too late to change her mind. "Please shut up and watch your feet, Your Majesty," Ohrig begged.

Adele felt dizzy as the adrenaline lurched through her system and made her hands shake, but she knew that Bear felt worse than she did, and so she concentrated on calming her racing pulse and talking. "Bear, I'm coming to you. Just stay where you are."

Despite her bravado, Adele inwardly cursed at how close Bear was to the wrong side of the bridge, and it took her a long minute to shuffle over to him, shouting his name.

"Your Majesty?" Bear finally opened his eyes and locked his gaze on Adele. "What're you doing here?"

"Coming to save you, Obearon," said Adele, holding out her hand.

"Only my mother calls me that," said Bear, staring at her hand as if he had never seen one before.

"Well, you are acting like a child," Adele scolded. "Come on, I'll take you to the other side."

"I can't move my feet," whispered Bear. His small blue eyes were filled with fear. The wind gusted about them, making Bear whimper and instinctively take a step back.

"But that's it, Obearon," said Adele. "You're moving your feet right now. Just take a step this way, toward me, all right?"

Slowly, slowly, Bear slid one foot in front of the other and then placed the other next to it. Adele inched forward to meet him. "I want to hold your hand, Obearon. Give me your hand."

"No," Bear whispered, freezing again. "I don't want your magic touching me."

Adele was surprised. She hadn't known that Bear was frightened of her powers, but she saw her opportunity. "Well, if you don't want me to touch you, then you are going to have to move it, right now."

"Your Majesty, the sun is close!" Adele heard the shout behind her and almost instantaneously felt a shudder beneath her feet that vibrated up through her whole body. Bear's eyes flew open and met Adele's frightened glare.

"I said now, Obearon!" shouted Adele. Still keeping her eyes on Bear, she shuffled backward as fast as she could.

Seeing his lifeline moving away, Bear began following Adele. They had gone almost two thirds of the way when Adele heard the creaking groan of ice breaking apart. The Chime Voices clanged loudly, and Adele knew there was no time to think. Reaching within herself, Adele grabbed a coil of gold magic and threw it around Bear's shoulders, anchoring him as she sent a blast of green magic to her legs. The bridge began to tremble and shudder, a second crack rent the air, and Adele took a running leap and jumped. The gold magic rope reached the end of its length and

Bear's weight yanked hard, but Adele pulled harder, and Bear flew along the bridge after her. She landed with both feet a good two yards onto the mountain ledge and only had a moment to straighten before Bear came barreling into the back of her and sent the two of them crashing to the ground.

The side of Adele's face was pressed against the razor-sharp gravel, and she saw stars before her eyes. When QG Bear was finally lifted off her back, Adele was too weak to do more than gasp as the air started leaking back into her lungs.

"Your Majesty!" Ohrig knelt by Adele's side, and she could see all the boots of the other QGs gathered behind him. "Can you hear me? I'm going to turn you over, so don't try to move."

Adele felt Ohrig and Lucky roll her over as carefully as they could and lay her on her back. Lucky ran his hands over Adele's head and down her neck and shoulders, his cold fingers probing for breaks or swelling. "She seems whole, General," he said. "But that was a nasty fall—she will have a concussion for sure."

Ohrig brushed the shards of gravel from Adele's cheek and requested the medical kit, which someone handed him. Jordansson peered down at Adele, and he looked like he was glowing with the sun lighting him from behind as he kept it out of her eyes. "I saw your magic, Queen. You were very clever, and you saved your man," he said, but Adele could only close her eyes against the pain of Ohrig dabbing a stinging ointment on her cheeks.

"Let's see if we can sit her up," suggested Lucky.

Adele felt herself lifted and folded into a sitting position. Surprisingly, it made breathing easier, and she came closer to her senses. She couldn't turn her head properly, but her gaze found Bear where he sat, hunched over his knees, white-faced and shaking. Owens was handing him a flask of Firewhiskey and rubbing his shoulders.

Every bone in Adele's body ached, and her face stung horribly, but she felt something protective rise up in her at the misery in Bear's expression. She had just made him do something that had terrified him, and now he felt like a failure. Adele didn't want to lose another QG to his sense of shame. "Bear, are you all right?" she croaked.

Bear wouldn't look at his queen. "Fine, Your Majesty."

"Bear!" Adele's sudden shout made every man look at her. She stretched her sore face into a smile. "I asked, are you all right?"

Bear managed a sideways grin at Adele. "Never been better, Your Majesty," he answered.

"You could stand to lose some weight, though," Adele quipped. "Maybe lay off the cake for a while."

"I'll try, Your Majesty," said Bear. He forced his gaze to meet hers. "I, uh, should—"

"Very good," Adele cut Bear off and gave him a nod that hurt her neck. "And Ohrig, I accept your apology."

"What apology?" said Ohrig, looking at Adele with an expression that told her she might have lost more than her looks in the fall.

"It was a wonderful idea to cross the ice bridge," said Adele. "No danger to us at all."

Ohrig huffed a laugh. "I will never disagree with you again, Your Majesty," he replied dryly.

"We should get a move on, then," said Adele. "Don't want to lose much more of the day." She struggled to her feet, trying not to look feeble as Ohrig and Lucky muttered about concussion and its effects. Adele straightened her back and took some experimental steps forward.

"Jordansson, if you could lead us to your village, I'd like to have a talk with the chieftess before I get another nighttime visit from Dahk'hani."

Jordansson gave Adele a gentle, one-armed hug. "You are crazy," he said respectfully.

"I know," Adele agreed, refusing to let herself cry.

Chapter Twenty-Three
"A Room at the Inn"

The path through the mountains was wide, though sheer cliff faces on either side hemmed them in and blocked the sun. Jordansson explained that this road was the only way from the forest, or the Dahk'hanisturmvog, into his valley, and that it would be watched from above by sentries. The road ran at a steady incline, not too steep, but Adele's head pounded with every step, and she fought off waves of nausea. She thought about the way her green magic had helped launch her feet in a jump that should not have been possible and wondered what else she could do with it that would give her the appearance of being superhuman. Considering this, Adele didn't mind using just a little of her green magic to keep her legs moving and her back straight, grateful that she could keep a slow and steady pace under her own steam.

They took a break to light some torches when the sun had almost disappeared. "Queen, you know that I can carry you?" suggested Jordansson, slowing his pace to match Adele's short steps. "We are not far from my village. Maybe another hour walking like this."

Adele couldn't smother the groan that escaped her. *Another hour!* She winced. "Somehow, I don't think it would look very dignified to appear before your people as someone who can't even walk on her own two feet."

Jordansson waved away her concern. "But it would look very good for me that I carry a queen in my arms through the village, like a champion. I would show my older brothers that the little brother is a big man now."

Adele blinked at the brief shadow of rage that clouded Jordansson's eyes. "But it would still make *me* look weak," insisted

Adele. "I don't know what your issues are, Jordansson, but this is a political mission, and I don't want the chieftess to think that I am less of a woman than she is."

Jordansson shrugged, back to his usual cheerfulness. "She *could* think you were stupid to keep walking after you were squashed by your guard."

Adele could sense Captain Lucky's disapproval without having to look at him. "I will carry you myself, Your Majesty," he said. "It would be more appropriate."

"No, I'll do it. I'm bigger and stronger, Lucky," said Jordansson, and as if the issue had been decided, he swept Adele up into his arms, causing her to yelp in surprise and Lucky to protest vigorously.

"Captain, leave it," instructed Ohrig. "We'll make better time now that the queen isn't walking, so everyone can pick up the pace."

Embarrassed, Adele hadn't realized how much she was slowing the group down. She could only try to look dignified as she was carried like a child in Jordansson's arms. He kept up a steady conversation, talking about his village and the people in it. Adele let the motion of his stride and his slow heartbeat thud in her ear until she closed her eyes, relaxed.

The Queen's Guard were complaining about shortness of breath and feeling tired, and that made Adele feel slightly better as they slogged the last couple of miles. Jordansson pointed out that the altitude was making the air thinner than in the forest and not to worry about it. It seemed to amuse him that the men were gasping and sweating while he remained quite comfortable.

Adele was only dozing when she felt Jordansson's lips against her forehead. "Your mirror is talking, Queen," he murmured.

"It'll be Rainere," said Adele. She gingerly touched her swollen cheek and puffy eyes. "I can't let him see me like this. He will worry too much, and I need him concentrating on the children."

Adele shoved the mirror deeper into her waistband and sent Rainere a mental apology, hoping that he wouldn't panic that she didn't respond this time.

A great wall blocking the path marked the end of their journey. In the middle of the wall, an enormous gate had been cut out and intricately carved. From first glance, it was clear to Adele that the gate was heavily warded with the same dark blue magic that swam deep inside Jordansson and signified Dahk'hani's presence.

"That's some tricky magic," muttered Adele, catching Ohrig's raised eyebrow. "On the door. I can see it's guarded with some tightly woven spells."

"I'll trust you on that," said Ohrig. "I guess we let Jordansson announce us now."

Jordansson wasn't waiting for permission. He dropped Adele gently to her feet and walked to the far side of the doorway, where he found a long white staff that might have been a bone. He blew into it, and a high, carrying note rang out. A window high up in the wall opened, and a torch attached to a head poked out, looking down at the group. The newcomer shouted something, and Jordansson responded with a long story that apparently the other tribesman wasn't interested in listening to, as the window was shut again.

"Ah, good!" Jordansson covered his embarrassment well. "He has gone to tell the chieftess that we are here and will ask the warriors to guide us to her."

The Unisians nodded but looked at each other, unsure if this was completely true. The group waited, stretching out their backs and legs and taking a drink from their dwindling water supplies. Adele tried not to sway on her feet, but there was nowhere to sit, so she endured. They waited five minutes, then at least another ten before there was movement. It was getting very dark and cold when a smaller door carved within the gate itself opened, and a dozen guards came out carrying torches and formed a long line. The men were huge, maybe close to eight feet tall, and uniformly blond. The tribesmen wore their hair in neat buns and were dressed in the same gray furs and leather that Jordansson wore. They had no weapons that Adele could see, but when the tallest of the guards approached her, she gave him a wary look anyway.

Jordansson stepped up to do introductions. "This man is like your general of the village guard. His name is Azagard Sword, and he is my third older brother."

The man called Azagard Sword gazed down at Adele like a bird regarding a worm. The planes of his broad face were hard, as if he had been carved from stone. Frosty blue eyes looked Adele up and down with none of Jordansson's warmth. In fact, Sword barely gave his own brother a glance before instructing his guards to form a phalanx around the Queen's Guard and gesturing for Adele to step forward.

Adele was grateful that she kept her feet in front of this giant man. She barely reached his chest but tried her best to look dignified despite her bruised face and filthy travel clothes. "Azagard Sword, my name is—"

She got no further. Sword raised his hand for her silence and snapped something at Jordansson that made him gush an answer, pointing at Adele and obviously needing to give proof that she was who she said she was. Jordansson gestured to the ice bear fur he carried on its little stretcher, and apparently this was enough to earn the big man's grudging trust. Sword shouted something, and the phalanx moved forward.

"Don't be frightened," said Jordansson, with an apologetic shrug and glance up at his older brother. "They are just being cautious because you are strangers."

"Jordansson, you said that your people would be pleased to see us," muttered Adele.

"My people will be, but the guards are never happy to see anyone at the gate," said Jordansson. "It will all be well after the chieftess has seen you."

Adele and her men were herded through the door in the great stone gate, and Adele felt a distinct sizzle across her skin as she passed. She hadn't known what to expect when she saw Jordansson's home, but nothing could have prepared her for the vista that unfolded before them.

Here within the open plateau of the Valley of the Three Sisters, the sun had only just set, and Adele could see three shallow valleys that met the plateau, fanning out like the arms of a half sun. Clusters of tiny lights showed where hundreds of homesteads ranged across the shadowed lands and in a wide spread as high as the gray peaks of the mountains. Adele could hear the faint sounds of the ringing bells of livestock in the hills and the calls of their shepherds as they were gathered in for the night. Stars sprinkled the sky, large and luminous above them.

"Jordansson, I had no idea your village would be so big," remarked Adele.

"Thank you, and welcome," said Jordansson. He smiled proudly. "The Tribe of the Three Sisters Valley is very big and strong in these mountains. Our tribe controls a very large area and far more land than the Tribe of the Hunting Fox and the Clans of the Temple of Dahk'hani."

Though night was falling fast, Adele looked around, fascinated, as the group made their way down a rough path to meet a much better maintained road that took them through a patchwork of neat paddocks and rows of vegetable gardens. Any doubts that Adele may have had about the guards being the biggest tribesmen were lost when she saw other villagers come out of their houses to watch the strangers pass. The women seemed to be as tall as the men, and everyone dressed similarly, in pants and sleeveless jackets. Jordansson was right—compared to his compatriots, he did indeed look small, though sadly that made the Unisians even tinier by comparison.

"*Ho-hij!*" Jordansson called out cheerfully to the villagers standing in doorways, but there were only a few hands raised in return, aside from the children, who gave the group the warmest welcome. They jumped around Jordansson, pestering him with questions and staring at the strangers with open curiosity. The guards made no move to shoo the children away, and a little girl, probably no more than five or six from her appearance, even took Adele's hand and held it as they walked.

Jordansson couldn't have been prouder as he dragged the ice bear pelt and led the foreigners into the village like a returning hero. The guards bade the group stop at a large open square, and

Jordansson continued shouting greetings to everyone. A young boy with shiny blond hair and a dirty shirt ran over and threw himself against his legs.

"*Ho-hij!* This is my nephew, Staxis," said Jordansson with a laugh. He swung the boy up onto his hip. "Say *hij* to the Unisians, Staxis."

The boy dropped his head to Jordansson's shoulder. "*Hij*," he said.

"*Hij*, Staxis." Adele gave the boy a smile, which he returned with shining eyes. Behind him Adele noticed a group of ten red-robed people forming a line across a low stage in the large village square. She looked to Jordansson, questioning with a twitch of her eyebrow.

"This is the council of leaders of our tribe," explained Jordansson, dropping Staxis to his feet. "They will want to speak with you. I will translate, so do not worry."

"Are you the only one in your village who can speak the King's Tongue?" asked Lucky, alarmed.

"Yes," said Jordansson. "Some others have a few words, but none can speak it like I can. Now we should all stand in a line and bow to the council of leaders."

Jordansson took a moment to smooth his spiky hair down with the flat of his palm. Though he was still smiling, he had a decidedly anxious air about him as he approached the watching council members and started his introduction of the Unisians.

Suddenly, the Chime Voices in Adele's head began an excited tinkling, and she could feel unfamiliar magic swirling through the air. Then, from between the robed figures, a woman stepped to the front of the stage. The chieftess may have been very old, or she could have been a woman of middle years who had attained her gravity with heavy experience. Tall like her people at eight feet, her shoulders were broad, but she was very thin, almost skeletal. Her long white hair was braided and rested over one shoulder in a thick rope. She wore a white robe that pooled at her feet and exposed the edges of pendulous breasts where the neckline met in a deep V. Finely drawn tattoos decorated her high cheekbones, as well as her neck and chest, in various floral and geometric designs. The chieftess's eyes were a blue so pale it was almost white, and she looked directly down her high-bridged nose at the Unisians before her. She was as terrifying as any wizard, and the tattoos of powerful spells that covered her body seemed, out of the corner of Adele's eye, to dance. *Dragon's blood,* the Chime Voices tinkled with excited notes.

Adele couldn't understand a word of what Jordansson was saying, but his body language left her in little doubt that he was feeling uncomfortable. Hunching his shoulders, Jordansson answered the questions thrown at him by the council, and Adele could only watch as he became more and more defensive with his replies.

"Do you get the sense that our friend Jordansson might not be so respected in his own tribe, Your Majesty?'" Ohrig muttered in Adele's ear, echoing her own fears. "Maybe you should say something on our behalf?"

Adele tried instead to return the fierce gaze of the chieftess and communicate with all the dignity that she could muster that she was herself a force to be reckoned with, despite the fact that her left eye was swelling shut and her face was bleeding.

Finally, the chieftess raised a hand, and Jordansson fell silent. She began to speak. Her voice was gravelly and creaked like an old door; nevertheless, she commanded the attention of the entire square and put an end to the muttering among the councilors. She pointed at the Unisians and announced something that made the gathered tribespeople cheer in agreement. Jordansson stepped back in line to tell Adele and the Queen's Guard what had happened.

"This is good news," said Jordansson, though his smile didn't quite reach his eyes. "You are being given a house to rest and time to eat, then the chieftess has invited you to sit in council with her at a blood-burning ceremony."

"Why is it always blood?" Adele muttered, feeling utterly exhausted.

"Come, we must let you rest." Jordansson gathered Adele protectively under his arm and gestured for the Queen's Guard to follow him. "I will take you to your lodge."

"You said something about eating?" Bear said.

"Yes, come with me, quickly." Jordansson led them to a low, domed building at the edge of the square where they were to stay.

"Looks like our friends are staying with us," noted Ohrig when he saw the guards who had accompanied them from the gate arrange themselves at every window and flank the door. "I don't imagine we are encouraged to explore the place?"

A frown creased Jordansson's forehead as he too watched the guards remain at attention, blocking all the exits. "These are mountain people, and they do not know your ways, or most truthfully, they know too much of Kingdom wizards to trust them at the start." He forced a smile. "But after the ceremony, all will be well, and you can ask the chieftess to tell you the way to the dragon." Adele gave Jordansson a doubtful look. "I promise," said Jordansson, nodding more than necessary. "All will be well after the ceremony." But he looked almost as worried as she felt.

Chapter Twenty-Four
"A North Wind Blows a Summer Breeze"

Ohren studied Gorrik standing at the open window and wondered what the old man was thinking about, staring into the night sky and wearing an expression of such intense concentration.

The two men had made themselves at home in Orestes's office and were eating all his cake and biscuits while they waited for him to join them. They had been waiting for a while now, and Ohren was getting irritated. If he hadn't had so much to talk to his twin about, he could have been enjoying dinner with the royal children and continuing to keep his eye on Prince Rainere. Though Ohren had been watching the Marchant prince closely with the children for days now, he still didn't quite trust that Rainere wouldn't manage to hurt one of his vulnerable little charges or whisk them off to the Gray Palace without telling anyone.

"Are you all right, Gorrik?" asked Ohren, breaking the long silence. "You're very quiet tonight."

"I'm just listening, boy," said Gorrik, turning from the window with a sigh. "There is a strange energy in the air tonight whispering violence and hate in Concordis, and it's unsettling my old bones. It's that dratted North Wind, you know."

Ohren decided to take Gorrik's word for it. He had enough to worry about in the Golden Palace without concerning himself with "strange energy."

"I don't know about any North Wind," said Ohren. "But I know that Lord Orgustus is more than whispering his hatred for the monarchy through the corridors of the palace. With the queen away for goddess knows how long, we should keep that lion cub close, Gorrik. I don't like how much support among the young courtiers he is gathering for his cause."

"The lion cub is only a St. Lucidis politician," said Gorrik with a tired groan. He dropped into an armchair opposite Ohren. "This energy dashing around tonight has a more sophisticated edge, and by that, I mean properly magical and purposeful, Ohren. I don't know who is stirring up this trouble with the citizens in Concordis, but it's no common bit of rabble-rousing."

Ohren cocked his head. "Gorrik, do you think Prince Rainere is the one behind all the antimonarchy propaganda flooding the streets? I'm sure if he wanted it, he would have the power to raise the slums of the Lower Districts to his side."

Gorrik guffawed with genuine amusement. "Use your brain, my lad, if it hasn't melted in your head." He cackled again. "The Marchant prince is too busy trying to win back the heart of his darling girl to bother about her crown. Why else would he have given her the title rights to his Gray Palace and released her from the betrothal? It was Grottonski who wanted the crown for the prince. Rainere just wants Adelena to warm his bed again. The boy is clearly besotted with our little queen."

"Yet he was prepared to sell her out to a Spider empress, Gorrik," corrected Ohren. "I don't think we should forget that this prince is still a victim of his Marchant upbringing, and old hatreds die hard in his family. Maybe this is all part of some long-term plot of his."

"You think while our Marchant prince is wiping baby faces clean and chasing after little ones on ponies, it's all some scheme to lull us into a false sense of security and then he will strike—*how*, exactly?" asked Gorrik.

Ohren frowned. "Certainly, he is good with the children," agreed the high wizard reluctantly. "But I will breathe much easier when Adelena gets home and that prince is further away from the seat of power."

"Any word when our girl is getting home?" asked Gorrik.

"Yes, I would love to know that too," interrupted High Magistrar Orestes as he entered his chambers from an inner door.

"Orestes, you've been here the whole time!" said Ohren. "But I checked your private rooms—you weren't there before, were you?"

"When is the queen getting back, Ohren?" asked Orestes, ignoring his twin's pique. "Do we know if she is still on her journey, or even still alive?"

Ohren pulled at his beard, annoyed that he had to reveal himself as a soft-hearted fool. "I felt sorry for the prince," he began, "so I gave him the mirror and—"

"And he is the only one who can speak to Queen Adelena!" Orestes took the seat behind his desk and glared at his twin, furious. "Now we have no line of communication with our hapless monarch, and Rainere has even more power. I know you are biased to Marchant men, Ohren, but please stop putting us all in jeopardy by trusting yet another psychotic prince!"

"No, it wasn't like that," argued Ohren. "I knew Adelena wouldn't speak to me unless she had to, but she will speak with the prince because he has her children. I thought it would be much easier to get Rainere to trust me while he is living here in the palace than it would be to get Adelena on our side again when she's a world away."

Gorrik produced a phlegmy chuckle. "And how is the 'trust' campaign going, Ohren? Are you and Rainere good mates yet?"

"Not yet, but we will be," Ohren spoke loudly over Orestes's angry sigh. "I'll start with Dolores Ollenby. Rainere seems to have a soft spot for her, and she might have some ideas for me."

"She is a sweetheart, and it's no wonder he likes her. Of course, all of her delicious, old gold magic would help the bond," agreed Gorrik. "But boys, what are we going to do about this violence in the city?"

"What violence?" asked Orestes, his blue eyes bright with alarm. "You never go down to the city, Gorrik; how do you know what's going on there?"

"The North Wind tells him, apparently," joked Ohren.

"You'd do well to respect your elders once in a while, boy," replied the old history teacher, offended. "I'm telling you that there is something bad in the air, and you'd be wise to heed my warning."

"Very well, Gorrik," said Ohren apologetically. "I've got a contact in the Lower Districts I can get hold of. I'll ask him for some information tonight, if that will make you feel better."

Gorrik only sniffed, still annoyed at Ohren's teasing, so the high wizard turned to his brother, wanting to share the joke, but Orestes was looking worried.

"Who is this contact of yours, Ohren?" asked Orestes. "I hope you aren't doing anything that could get you into trouble."

Ohren shrugged. "His name is Sandy, and he is always involved in something unsavory. If there is something afoot on the streets of the slums, he'll know about it. I haven't spoken to the man in months, but I know how to find him."

"Right, well, you'll have to excuse me, gentlemen!" Orestes jumped to his feet. "I still have work to do tonight and can't stay chatting with you both, as much as I'd like to."

"We aren't chatting, Orestes—we are taking a *meeting*," said Ohren, annoyed to see his brother packing up papers and readying himself to leave. "I still want to talk to you about how we should contain Lord Orgustus and all his gossip in the palace, as well as the issue of Grottonski, while he is still in our dungeons. It's going to get very awkward if Prince Rainere discovers him down there."

"I don't have time for this now, Ohren," snapped the high magistrar. "Let's take another meeting tomorrow. I'll send you a note with what time I'm free. Now I will say goodbye to you both. You can see yourselves out."

Ohren and Gorrik looked at each other in the silence following the door slamming shut behind Orestes.

"Fine! I'll just do what I want, then," said Ohren, defensively. "Without our high magistrar's sage advice."

Gorrik raised his snow-white eyebrows at the sulky high wizard. "Don't you always, m'boy?"

CHAPTER TWENTY-FIVE
"Preparations for a New Death"

Jordansson left Adele and the Queen's Guard inside the main area of the lodge that was their home for now, and everyone chose a room of their own.

Adele was cautious after their cool welcome to the village, but she found two giggling young women in her room filling a large wooden tub with hot water and fresh herbs, clearly meant for her to bathe in. As she waited for the women to finish their work, she attacked the plate of cold meat slices and pickled vegetables that had been laid out. A flagon of cold water was scented with something like mint, and Adele drank it all before the bathtub was filled.

Thankfully, the young women didn't offer to help her undress but left quickly after refilling her water jug with another from outside the door. Adele dropped into the hot water with a loud and effusive sigh of joy, then yelped as she registered the pain of her stinging injuries.

"Your Majesty, are you all right?" Captain Lucky's head appeared in the doorway, his gaze scouting the room until he found Adele sitting in the bath, crossing her arms over her chest.

Adele was too relieved to be in hot water to be annoyed with her overzealous captain. "Lucky," she said firmly, "go find something else to do."

"Of course, Your Majesty, my apologies!" With a blush Captain Lucky ducked out of the room and left Adele, finally, in peace.

The bath gave Adele time to examine every scrape and bruise caused by the accident with Bear, and she found there were almost too many to count. She gingerly washed herself, alarmed at the amount of dirt in her hair, and got all her wounds clean. A young woman darted in and grabbed Adele's dirty clothes, only giggling when Adele tried to protest, and dumped an armful of new ones on the bed before ducking out again.

Reluctantly, Adele pulled herself out of the bath with a pained groan and immediately heard a voice call from next door. "I'm fine, Lucky!" she shouted back.

The dress she'd been given was clearly meant for a much taller woman, as the neckline swung lower than she liked, and she had to use her belt to gather all the billowing fabric in. For a moment Adele thought longingly of her team of dressers and makeup artists back at the Golden Palace, not to mention Lady Olivia's gorgeous gowns that always made her feel as if she were wearing a dream. Yet there was no help for it now, so Adele made the best of it and searched for any grooming tools she could find on the dressing table in her room. Cringing at her image in the mirror, she pulled at her tangled mess of hair with a sharp comb and managed to brush it out before binding it in a tidy plait.

Adele couldn't help but grin at the mess of red and blue bruises on the left side of her face, not to mention the pockmarks from the gravel on her cheek. *I look like a war-torn warrior.* She felt a little spark of pride at the idea. *Though it's a pity that no warrior can run in a dress this long and heavy.*

Jordansson entered her room just as Adele was pulling her boots on and helped himself to a long look at her naked legs. He was also freshly washed and had shaved off his patchy white-blond beard. The dark blue vest he wore was trimmed with fur and showed off his well-muscled arms. His dark suede trousers were just tight enough to flatter what she knew was between his legs. Jordansson noticed her taking him in, and a broad smile spread across his face that made Adele want to smile in response. She didn't.

"Queen Adelena, are you ready?" Jordansson came to stand behind Adele in the mirror. He placed his hands on her arms, and they warmed her through the fabric of her dress. "How do you feel?"

Adele grimaced. "About as good as I look, Jordansson," she said, shrugging off his touch. "Is there anything you can tell me about this ceremony of the blood? Anything that will help me prepare?"

Jordansson looked uncomfortable. "The blood ceremony is a powerful and rare magic," he said. "I have been taught that it is only used to test the power of new chiefs and chieftesses for our tribe. I have no idea why the chieftess would want to show our tribe your power if it could be greater than hers."

"Unless she has no intention of keeping me alive," said Adele, sounding bitter in her own ears. "It's very easy to kill someone in a blood ceremony."

Jordansson's eyes widened. "No, Queen, I would never have brought you here if I thought you are in danger from my people."

"But if I was in danger?" asked Adele. She looked up at Jordansson, stepping a little closer to let him see the magic circles spinning in her eyes. "Whose side are you on, Jordansson? The foreign queen who needs you to guide her to the dragon to save her family and break a prophecy that controls Evendaar? Or your mother, the chieftess, and a people who consider you to be the feeble last son of a powerful woman?"

The magic sparked in Jordansson's own eyes at Adele's summary, and she didn't know if it was wise to push the man this hard, or if she even felt right about asking someone to betray their family. Yet her own family needed her to do what she had to do, and Adele knew, no matter the price, she would pay it.

"When you go, you will take me with you," said Jordansson. His expression was grave.

"Of course," said Adele. "You are our guide."

"No." Jordansson kept his gaze on Adele, watching her intently. "When you go back to your home in Unisia, will you take me with you then? I want to get out of these mountains and see the world. I want to come with you, Queen, and stand by your side as your equal."

Adele sucked in a breath. "Done."

"Do you promise me?" Jordansson held out his hand to shake.

Adele folded both of her hands around Jordansson's. "I promise to take you with me back to Unisia if you help me survive this blood ceremony and get me to the dragon, Jordansson." A spark of magic lit the air above their hands.

Jordansson's expression became soberer still, and a veil lifted in his eyes as he decided to share a truth with her. "The chieftess told me that there is a map to the dragon's home, but that she will never give it to you," he said. "The chieftess believes that it is blasphemy to allow any foreigners to disturb the dragon in his mountain and that you will cause chaos in the world, chaos that cannot be fixed."

Adele swallowed, her throat dry. "Get me that map, Jordansson."

"I will, Queen," he whispered. He brushed Adele's lips in a surprise kiss. "We need each other now."

"Your Majesty!" Ohrig entered Adele's room after a brief knock, surprising her in Jordansson's arms. Captain Lucky followed the general into the room. He looked hard at Jordansson, a snarl curling his lips.

"One of the guards out front said that we must go to that ceremony now," said Ohrig. "At least, that's what it sounded like he said."

Adele cursed, and dread made her stomach muscles clench tightly. She felt the weight of her promise to Jordansson resting on her shoulders, and the information that he had shared made her feel even worse about going into this blood ceremony with the chieftess. Try as she might, she also couldn't shake a horrible feeling that the god Dahk'hani would have a hand in all of this, and she could only pray that Serena might have one too.

CHAPTER TWENTY-SIX
"No Place for the Timid"

Adele and the Queen's Guard made their way through the village along a torchlit path, crossing the square to a much larger building that she guessed was like a town hall. The hall was one enormous room decorated with yellow lanterns and bright blue bunting that hung from the ceiling and was tied to the wooden posts that held up the curved roof. At least two hundred curious villagers filled the space, and all were dressed for a festival in colorful clothes. The women even wore flowers in their blond hair. Adele couldn't help but feel tiny among the giant men and women of the Tribe of the Three Sisters Valley as her group wove through the crowd, guided by their guards.

Jordansson waved as people called out to him from the crowd, but his smile was strained, and the comments thrown back sounded more mocking than friendly to Adele's ears.

A red-robed female councilor met them in the center of the room and, with minimal fanfare, led their group to a narrow doorway at the back of the room, where the rest of the councilors were waiting for them to arrive. Adele peered through the doorway and was surprised to see that the floor of the next room was lined with grass and the ceiling was open to the night sky. A large conical tent had been placed in the middle of the open-air chamber, its white skin walls almost glowing as it was lit from within.

General Ohrig stepped to Adele's side and peered in with her. "Only one doorway, but open access from the roof," he noted with a deep frown. "I don't like it."

The female councilor put her hand on Ohrig's arm and shook her head, obviously protesting his inspection of the room.

"Oh, no, the queen isn't going in there alone," said Ohrig firmly. "The last time I let her out of my sight for one of these ceremonies, she was almost killed. This time I'm going to be there."

Jordansson took Ohrig at his word and translated his message to the councilor, who in turn discussed it with her fellow councilors, causing much head shaking and animated conversation.

Adele waited while they came to a decision, though she didn't hold out much hope for a positive result. She was very surprised when Jordansson translated the councilors' decree.

"They said that you may take in one man with you, but that he should have magic in his body so not to insult the great god," Jordansson said. "Have any of your men got magic in them? If not, I will come in with you, Queen."

Lucky stepped forward and glared at Jordansson. "I am Her Majesty's Queen's Guard, and I will have the honor of protecting the queen in this ceremony. She can trust me to look after her in there, unlike you."

Jordansson looked annoyed. "The queen can also trust me, Lucky."

Lucky raised his chin. "So if there was a choice between your mother, the chieftess, and Queen Adelena, you would protect our queen?"

Jordansson opened his mouth, but nothing came out, so he shut it again and shrugged. "You should be in there with her, but it will still be better if we both are," he said finally.

The decision made, Adele and Lucky tried to enter the room, but they were stopped by the councilor putting her hand out across the threshold and giving them instructions.

"You must undress before you enter the sacred space," said Jordansson and started pulling off his vest straightaway. "You need to be naked before our god. To be as we were born, you see."

Lucky and Adele exchanged an alarmed glance that made Jordansson grin as he pushed down his trousers. The councilor impatiently mimed undressing to Adele so it was clear that this wasn't some prank of Jordansson's.

"Let's just get it over with, Lucky," said Adele, eyeing the tent in the room beyond. The light within showed that the chieftess was already preparing the ceremony. Adele undid the belt on her dress and pulled the heavy fabric over her head, standing in her chemise, underwear, and boots. Her Queen's Guard had already turned their backs so as not to see her naked, but Adele caught Bear's eye as he snuck a peek at her and winced.

"Goddess, she's all bruised up," he muttered, and that made all the other men sneak looks at her. "I'm so sorry I did that, Your Majesty."

"I don't know why you guys are all pretending to protect my honor," snapped Adele, simultaneously irritated and paranoid as she yanked off her boots. "Everyone else in the room is staring at me."

While this might have been true of the curious villagers, the councilors were clearly examining Adele for concealed weapons or tattoos. She slipped her chemise over her head and dropped her underwear to the ground. Lucky was already half-undressed and stoically joined her in dropping his shorts too, though it was clear how much it pained him. As he stood there cupping himself and staring at the ground, his embarrassment only highlighted to Adele how silly it was to care about modesty when they could be entering a very dangerous situation.

"You aren't going to be much help as a guard if you can't look at me, Lucky." Adele managed a lopsided smile. "This is the only time I will say it, but do not take your eyes off my arse in there."

"Yes, Your Majesty," said Lucky, forcing himself to look in Adele's eyes. "Of course."

"Yes, Lucky! You are strong for a little man." Jordansson slapped Lucky hard on his naked back. "Lots of muscles and—" he looked down to where Lucky was having trouble hiding his manhood. "—the little women must be very happy with you too." He chuckled, and Lucky muttered something that wasn't thank you.

The councilor clapped her hands to announce that they were now ready to enter the sacred room. There was a path they had to follow, delineated by small candles in the grass, and Jordansson was the first to enter, followed by a shivering Adele and then Captain Lucky. Though a huge crowd gathered in the meeting hall, as soon as they had crossed the threshold the noise dropped away and sounded muffled. *This room had better not be in another dimension,* thought Adele, already regretting her decision to trust the chieftess.

The grass felt spongy and soft underfoot. Adele followed the naked Jordansson and tried not to notice that he had a small tattoo on his left butt cheek that looked like a bow and arrow, but the arrow was shaped like a male appendage. Adele didn't need a book of spells to know it was a fertility spell. She wondered if it was odd for a man of this tribe to be so obsessed with having children or if they were all like that.

Jordansson opened the flap at the side of the tent to expose a triangular doorway, and bending double, Adele slipped inside. Lucky followed behind, almost stepping on her heels.

The tent was filled with steam that was almost too dense to see through. Adele shuffled around, looking for a place to sit, and stumbled on a pile of cushions on her way to the other side of the tent. As her eyes adjusted to the gloom, she saw that she had picked a seat uncomfortably close to the naked chieftess, who was staring at her with large pale eyes. Feeling it would be too awkward to move away again, Adele studied her surroundings.

A large pot of water was bubbling over a smokeless fire. *Sacred fire.* Adele recognized it right away. The steam was billowing out of it in antiseptic-smelling clouds. Jordansson settled himself on the other side of his mother, and Lucky moved as close to Adele as he could, sitting cross-legged and covering his lap with his hands.

The chieftess spoke quietly to Jordansson, though she didn't spare him a glance, and he obeyed her instructions. Using heavy cloths, he moved the hot pot off the fire and replaced it with a triangular frame with a circular bowl at each point and a larger bowl in the middle. Adele had a horrible case of déjà vu, and the same fear claimed her as in the Holy Caves of Sandar as her stomach dropped away and her skin began to crawl.

The chieftess filled each bowl on the tripod with a mixture of fresh herbs and salt crystals. Immediately, the smell of Sunday roasts filled the air, and Adele flinched when the chieftess picked up a black stone knife and held her hand out for Adele's arm. Adele looked through the mist into her great pale eyes.

She only needs to make one move against me, and I will kill her, Adele promised herself as she felt her two magics hiss and growl, though they couldn't manage much more than a weak protest, and she silently cursed herself for using them too hard after saving Bear and walking up the mountainside today. The Chime Voices sang their own strident support, but Adele knew she wouldn't be able to follow their instructions if her magic was so depleted.

Adele breathed deep and felt the antiseptic steam burn all the way into her lungs, then echoed the hiss of her magics when the chieftess tightened her grip on her wrist and pulled it out over the larger pot in the middle of the tripod. The slash was wide and shallow, and the blood welled quickly, dripping and sizzling in the bottom of the bowl.

Adele wrenched her wrist back when she felt that enough blood had been given. Yet instead of looking angry, the chieftess merely handed Adele a handful of clean cloth strips and some wadding to dress her wound. Lucky did the job for her quickly and silently.

All four participants watched the smoke form above Adele's burning blood, but none more closely than Adele herself. A column of gold sparkles appeared in the smoke, and then another of green. The two columns twisted together and rose to the peak of the tent. Adele watched them roil and spread, as if trying to find a way to escape, then she saw something she had never seen before. The chieftess waved her hands and pulled the two magics back down to the tripod. The Chime Voices in Adele's head chittered, angry at the blasphemy that she was witnessing, though Adele didn't understand why.

The two magics hovered, seemingly contained back in the pot, when the chieftess pulled out a long pipe from behind her back. After blessing the pipe and bathing it in steam, she used a taper from the fire to light the bowl, which was filled with a dark, sticky resin. The chieftess took a long inhalation, and Jordansson leaned forward to explain what was happening.

"This is called the Smoke of Visions, and it is a custom of my tribe. Through the smoke the chieftess calls to the god Dahk'hani. If your soul is not loosed from your body when he arrives, then it will hurt you, so please smoke deeply. Close your eyes, and you will see only truth around you," explained Jordansson, but Adele thought he might only be repeating things he'd had explained to him before and not from experience. "No one who has taken in the Smoke of Visions can lie. This could be your only chance to ask the chieftess for the knowledge of the dragon and where he lives."

Adele held the pipe when it was offered to her and took a shallow pull. The smoke tasted like a mix of grass clippings and cinnamon, and it rushed into her mouth and down her throat before she had a chance to blow it out again. Adele coughed hard and handed the pipe to Jordansson. Jordansson took a pull and then gave it to Lucky, insisting that the captain smoke too.

Adele braced herself for the arrival of Dahk'hani, but first she wanted her blood back. Adele reached out to reclaim her magic from the pot on the fire when she heard a loud shout of protest from the chieftess and everything went black.

Chapter Twenty-Seven
"To Speak with Gods"

Adele was standing on an ice floe that rocked and trembled beneath her feet, moved by the endless ocean that surrounded her.

Though she knew this had to be a vision, Adele felt the icy cold seep into her bones, aching and sharp. Behind her there was a roar, and when she turned, she saw a lion perched on a much smaller ice floe, maybe ten yards from her. The lion glowed with a warm golden light, his mane full and glittering with magic. Adele caught the gaze of the creature and could see the intelligence and determination in his eyes. He roared at Adele again and pawed the air, almost tilting the ice floe and himself into the black water.

"Shhh," Adele hushed her leonine power. "I will come to you, just wait."

Then Adele heard a hiss and turned around to see a giant serpent, her body coiled and head reared, ready to strike. The serpent's head waved side to side, and her forked tongue flickered as it tasted the air. Adele could see her serpentine magic was preparing to launch itself across the black water to be with her. Just beyond the serpent, a white cloud hovered above a different sheet of ice. This cloud tinkled and shrieked in hysterics. Adele instinctively held a hand to her head. The Chime Voices! The very idea that she had been separated from her powers made Adele furious and burned away the cold that held her still.

"I will save you all," she shouted and looked for a way to reach her magics. She knelt to paddle, and that was when she saw the chieftess traveling toward her, flying across the ice floes. The woman was naked, but her magic danced upon her skin, all the tattoos lit up and burning with a blue light.

Adele felt the ice beneath her rock, and she fought to control it as the roars and hisses behind her rose to a deafening noise.

"Calm yourself, angel." The chieftess's voice was just as cold and croaky as in the world, but she now spoke a language that Adele understood. "I would speak with you without fear of reprisal—that is why I have asked Dahk'hani to separate you from your power."

Adele yanked on her magics and felt the ice floes moving slowly across the tide to her side like magnets. "And now you have me here," said Adele, staring into the winter-blue eyes of the chieftess. "What do you want to say?"

"I wanted to see the woman who would talk with dragons." The chieftess came to the edge of the ice. "And I would ask her why she would endanger the world and defy a god?"

"My child is dying, Chieftess," said Adele. She felt colder just saying the words. "I will have her healed and returned to me at any cost."

"Will you destroy the world for love of a single child, angel?" The chieftess opened her arms wide. "Would you destroy what the great god has given our people?"

Adele flexed her strength, and now the ice floes came shooting toward her. The lion and the serpent leaped to her side as the cloud of Chime Voices descended above her. Adele felt secure and strong as she stroked the beasts of her magic, feeling their power, her power, through her hands. "It was the prophecy of your gods that brought me here," said Adele. "They are welcome to send me home again."

The chieftess dropped her arms, and her face crumpled in despair. "If you do not take responsibility for what you are, then I cannot help you." She looked behind, and there was a figure limping toward them. The chieftess disappeared with a flash of light, and in her place stood the emaciated and whey-faced mage of Sandar.

Adele recoiled, horrified to again see the first man she had killed standing before her in this weird otherworld. "What do you want?" she shouted.

The mage's leering grin sickened Adele. She could see the wounds where she had blasted her power through him, draining him of his life. "I am servant to my god Dahk'hani," creaked the mage. "And I will follow you throughout the worlds to see his will done." The mage pointed down to his ankle, where Adele could see a shiny red splotch on the gray skin. "You gave me your blood in death, angel," he grinned. "We are one."

Adele had a vague memory of carrying the dead mage to the back of the holy caves in Sandar with Ripenzo. She remembered the bandage on her wrist coming loose and her skin touching the body.

"You have been much honored, angel. Dahk'hani wants you to have his child, and he has chosen his people of Jordan to father that child." The mage looked up and down Adele's naked body covetously. "Your blood and the son of Jordan will make a vessel strong enough to bear the spirit of Dahk'hani in the world of Evendaar. Reborn, Serena's favored Dahk'hani will take your throne and bathe the world in his fire, cleansing the pestilence of lesser men from those of her magic. This is his sister-goddess Serena's prophecy, and he will see it done for love of her."

Anger and fear clashed inside Adele, stealing her wits and making the Chime Voices sing in panic. "That is not the prophecy, and I will not follow..." But her voice was a whimper, pitiful in her own ears. "Leave me alone."

The mage threw his head back and laughed a hideous gloating laugh. "That is the one thing I cannot do," he cackled. "You have bound us for eternity, angel."

CHAPTER TWENTY-EIGHT
"After the Blood Has Burned"

"Queen Adelena, wake up!"

Adele sat up and found her face pressed to Jordansson's bare chest. Disoriented, she pushed herself away and gazed around the tent. The chieftess had left already, and Lucky was lying on a pile of cushions, his mouth open and snoring. The steam had dissipated, and Adele felt chilled in her nakedness.

"Jordansson, how long was I out?" she asked, her dry tongue almost sticking to the roof of her mouth.

"It's almost midnight, so a few hours," he said, helping her to her feet. "You go and see your men—they will worry for you. I will carry your captain out of here."

Wobbling on unsteady feet, Adele retraced her steps to the big room where her men waited. Ohrig was watching the chamber, so he was the first to notice she was back and held out a robe for her to wrap herself in. Jordansson carried a naked Lucky in his arms, and Adele was pleased for the captain's sake that he was still out cold to save him from the embarrassment.

"I see Lucky did a bang-up job of guarding you in there, Your Majesty," growled Ohrig with a heavy frown. "A lot of good his bit of magic did him."

"The chieftess made us smoke some strong herbs, General," replied Adele, batting at the glowing butterflies flapping around her head. "I'm not sure anyone is meant to escape their effects, and honestly, I'm still feeling a bit odd even now."

"Strong herbs?" grunted Bear. "Should've sent Owens in, then. He can handle all that stuff."

Owens grinned and offered to take Lucky out of Jordansson's arms. "I have had a certain amount of experience with herbal opiates, it's true." He looked down at Lucky. "This poor lamb never stood a chance."

Adele gave her Queen's Guard a sharp once-over, taking in their pale, suddenly very young faces and the dark shadows beneath their luminous eyes. "You children all look exhausted," she said, wagging a finger. "We should return to our quarters and get some rest. Despite making me bleed for her, that chieftess didn't get me any closer to finding the dragon. It'll be up to little Jordansson to get what we need now."

"You want to tell me what happened in there, Your Majesty?" asked Ohrig, frowning.

Adele blinked hard as she watched Ohrig scratch at the long rabbit ears now poking out of his head. "Nothing I haven't seen before," she replied grimly. "It's always the same shit, just a different day."

Ohrig raised an eyebrow at Adele's language. "Sounds ominous," he said. "Are you sure you're all right, Your Majesty? You look a little…wobbly, wobbly, barm-bah."

"Stop talking nonsense, Ohrig," sighed Adele as she ducked her head to avoid another cloud of blue-winged insects. "I'm going to bed. I need to get away from all these butterflies." Adele turned and began weaving through the crowd, ignoring the giant men and women as she mounted the cloud path that floated in front of her, her legs already aching on the soft steps.

"Her Majesty is as high as a kite," noted Owens. "You lads better make sure she gets back to our lodge, now."

Pepper, Leith, and Bear quickly took off after Adele, but when Jordansson tried to follow, Ohrig put his arm out and barred the way. "Tell me what happened in there, Jordansson."

Jordansson checked that they could not be overheard. "It was a spirit quest," he said quietly. "I did not see what the queen saw, and I do not know who she spoke to. When I woke up from my vision, I heard her say, 'Leave me alone.' She was crying, so I did what I should not have and woke her up."

"You did well, kid," said Ohrig. He gave Jordansson an appraising glance. "You like her, don't you?"

Jordansson held Ohrig's gaze, "We have been fated by the great god to be together," he said.

Ohrig gave Jordansson a sardonic grin. "You know there's a queue, right?"

"Yet I know that one day she will be mine," replied Jordansson with a shrug.

"Good enough," said Ohrig, patting Jordansson on the arm. "Now, why don't you put your pants on, son, and come back to the house. We're going to get some rest, and I could do with a translator around if those other guards return."

Chapter Twenty-Nine
"Queen on a Cloud"

The world had started spinning horribly by the time Adele returned to her room. She sat on the bed, the silence ringing in her ears, and she almost missed the tiny sound of someone squeaking her name. Reaching under her pillow, Adele found the little hand mirror where she had hidden it earlier. She opened the mirror and looked at the image of Rainere's pale face. His eyes were flashing with sparks of magic, and his forehead was creased in a deep frown.

"Rainere!" Adele coughed to clear her steam-burned throat. "It's so good to see you."

"Adelena, where are you?" Rainere narrowed his eyes. "What happened to you? Are you crying?"

"I'm not crying," said Adele and wiped the tears from her cheeks. "I'm in the mountains, staying with a tribe called the Clan of the Three Sisters Valley. I don't think they like me very much."

"Who hurt you, *cara mia*?" Rainere sounded angry. "Did someone try to kill you again?"

The image in the mirror swung wildly as Rainere moved, and Adele saw a wide expanse of white skin tight over the bones and muscle of his chest.

"Sweetheart, are you naked?" asked Adele, distracted by a sudden surge of desire. "Can you please show me your body? I miss your beautiful body and your magic. God, how I miss your magic. I'm so hungry and so tired without you here, Rainere."

Rainere's mouth softened, and he moved the mirror to show his naked torso before returning to his face, his gaze gentle now. "Please, *cara mia*, tell me what has happened. Maybe I can help you," Rainere spoke slowly and clearly. "I can feel you through the Mark, you know. I ache when you ache."

"I don't see why everyone's life has to be connected to mine," mused Adele, waving away the little butterflies that had returned to dance around the mirror. "I'm just doing my thing, trying to save Stella. Stop putting your shit on me."

"Adelena, I want to know what happened to you," pleaded Rainere. "Tell me what I can do to help you, my love."

"You can't help me, my beautiful Rainere," Adele said. She felt streams of water fall from her eyes. "All roads lead back to the fucking prophecy. More blood ceremonies that hurt me." She waved her cut wrist at Rainere. "An angry chieftess, an angry mage, and more crazy gods." She suddenly thought of something important to tell him. "We can't let the light come, Rainere, because this god will cleanse the world with his fire. We need the dark days, and the shadows as well. You should tell the old Wizard Whatsisname about that."

"I will, *cara mia*, I will tell Ohren about the fire." Rainere's face wobbled as much as his voice. "What else should I tell him, my love?"

"Oh, the children!" Adele could hardly talk through the tears spilling down her cheeks. "My poor baby, Stella. I fought for her at the beginning when Justin wanted her dead, and I'm fighting for her now after Evendaar tried to kill her," Adele explained to Rainere's flashing green eyes. "Dahk'hani wants me to have his baby so he can take my throne. He'll burn you all, and I won't be able to save you because I forgot to ask about the dragon. Where's that goddamn dragon, Rainere? Help me find the dragon."

"I want to help you, *cara mia*." Rainere's voice fell like raindrops on her ears. "Please, keep talking to me."

"I wish you were here, Rainere," sighed Adele as she climbed into the middle of her huge bed and buried herself between the two pillows. "Tell me you love me, and I'll put you next to me."

"I love you, *cara mia*, so very much," Rainere said. "Keep me close…" His voice wove a spell in Adele's thoughts, and she let him wrap her up in his words of love.

The darkness clawed at her, and Adele dreamed deep and frantic dreams. *Rainere was there, and her children too. Stella was well again, but the dragon was looking for them. Or was she looking for the dragon?* Several times Adele awoke drenched in sweat, and once she even imagined seeing Jordansson sitting at the side of her bed, but then she closed her eyes again and slept.

Rainere sat on the side of the bathtub and clutched the hand mirror, staring into its depths, waiting for another word from Adelena.

"May the goddess grace you, *cara mia*," he whispered. He could only see an expanse of cotton where she had left the mirror somewhere in her bed. Rainere couldn't hear her breathing or see any sign of life, but he kept his mirror open just in case.

Knowing he wouldn't be able to sleep again that night, Rainere crept out of the bathroom and pulled a robe over his shoulders. The three children lay asleep in his big bed, Leafy curled in a tight ball between the sprawled bodies of Natalie and Aaron. Awake, Charlie stood at the window, looking out on the shadowed gardens of the Golden Palace.

Rainere didn't speak, but he wasn't surprised when Charlie followed him out of the bedchamber and into the dimly lit sitting room, empty of servants at this hour. The terrace doors had been left open to catch the nighttime breeze, and Rainere noticed that a bottle of Firewhiskey with matching glasses had been set on a table between a pair of overstuffed couches. Rainere sat down on one of the couches and poured himself a glass of the golden liquid. Charlie sat on the opposite sofa, and after a moment's pause, Rainere poured the boy a glass of whiskey too. The prince handed Charlie his drink and slouched back in his seat, his gaze on the mirror still in his hand.

"So." Charlie coughed and traced the pattern on his crystal glass. "Did you get to talk to the queen?"

"I did," said Rainere, his voice hoarse with emotion. "But she was injured and was in no condition to tell me what had happened."

Rainere leaned forward over his knees and ran a hand over his stubbled scalp, clearly agitated. "She said something about a ceremony of the blood, and she had a bandage on her wrist where she'd been cut. She also said that they had made it to the mountains and are with the Clan of the Three Sisters Valley."

Rainere looked into the mirror again, but the image of cotton sheets hadn't changed. He threw the mirror onto the coffee table, where it spun on its back. "I presume she is trying to find a guide to the dragon's mountain from there," he added, chewing his bottom lip.

Charlie took a sip of his whiskey. "I guess that's good news," he said. "Did she happen to say how the Queen's Guard were faring?"

Rainere shrugged. "She was crying," he said quietly. "She has already been through so much without me. I should be with her right now." He pressed a hand across his eyes, not wanting to share any more of his private pain with Charlie.

Charlie clearly felt awkward expressing his sympathy to a man he hated, so instead of speaking, he slurped at his whiskey, more quickly than he meant to. He spluttered as the fiery liquid leaped into his throat.

Rainere uncovered his eyes and looked over at Charlie, raising an eyebrow. "This is the high wizard's brew," he said. "Try sipping it."

Charlie coughed again. "Noted," he croaked.

"*Ho-hij,*" a little voice called out. Rainere and Charlie both reached for the hand mirror, but Rainere got there first. Charlie jumped over the coffee table to sit next to the prince.

"Adelena?" Rainere held the mirror tightly.

A pair of sky-blue eyes set in a broad masculine face greeted Rainere and Charlie. "My name is Jordan Jordansson. I am a friend of the Queen Adelena. Who are you?"

"What are you doing with her mirror?" snarled Rainere, ignoring the question. "Where is Queen Adelena?"

"The queen is safe in my bed," said Jordansson, smiling, and turned the mirror to show Adelena's naked back where she slept beside him. "I will not wake her, as she has had a very hard day and endured much."

Rainere stiffened when he saw Jordansson's hand stroke the hair off Adelena's shoulder and rest on her bare skin. "Get your hands off the queen," he growled. "How dare you touch her while she sleeps."

"Ah, now I know you," chuckled Jordansson, returning the mirror to his own face. "You must be Prince Rainere Marchant. She told me all about you." He chuckled again and shook his head. "She is very angry with you after what you said to her guards. They are all angry with you."

"Who is this joker?" whispered Charlie. "Tell him you'll kill him." But Rainere waved for silence.

"Jordansson, is it?" Rainere said, and his voice was cold enough to chill stone. "Are you the man who will lead Her Majesty to the dragon?"

Jordansson gave Rainere a wink. "Yes, this and other things," he said.

Rainere dropped his face closer to the mirror and studied Jordansson for a long moment. He smiled a smile that made Charlie flinch from him. "You're a liar, Jordansson," Rainere said. "She hasn't laid a hand on you, because if she had, I would know. You, boy, are as pure as the driven snow."

Jordansson dropped his nonchalant act for just a moment before he plastered on another smile. "She *will* be mine," he said. "She needs me, and I will be here for her." Jordansson let Rainere see him kissing Adelena's neck. "Here, you see, she is in my bed, while you are all the way over there in your Unisia. Good night, prince." The screen went black.

"Did he just hang up on you?" Shocked, Charlie returned to his seat, knowing it was only sensible to give the prince as much space as he could after that conversation. "What a cat's prick!"

Rainere sat silently gripping his glass of whiskey and staring hard at the blank mirror.

"What sort of name is Jordan Jordansson, anyway?" sniffed Charlie. "Bit weird, if you ask me."

"It's the name of a dead man," said Rainere, and his eyes sparked with a green flash. Then he slugged his whiskey and shook off his anger, regaining his cold calm. "Now, to business, Charlie. Clearly, it's essential for us to discover who this Boss is as quickly as we can and neutralize his threat to Queen Adelena before her return to the Golden Palace. To do this, we will need to make bigger inroads into discovering where the Boss lives and works and who he works with."

If Charlie was disturbed by the radical change of subject, he didn't show it. He just looked at Rainere, his hazel eyes curious. "I guess you'll want to use me as bait?" he said.

Rainere was pleased that Charlie didn't seem to be as stupid as he often looked. "Yes, of course," he replied. "You are the only one who knows him. We will devise a way to set you up, and he will reveal himself to us."

"Do you really think that the Boss lives in the palace?" asked Charlie. "Or do you think that Orestes could be working for him too? He did have my mirror, but it doesn't mean that the Boss didn't just give it to him."

"It was actually Ohren who gave me the mirror," said Rainere, pouring himself another Firewhiskey. "He only *said* that Orestes gave it to him. I don't want to discount that our most manipulative high wizard is trying to kill Adelena if she has run out her usefulness for him."

Charlie considered this. "Surely there would be easier ways for a powerful wizard like him to get rid of Her Majesty while she was in the palace? Sending her away and trying to get assassins to kill her doesn't seem to be working out for him too well."

"Maybe he is using someone else to organize the attacks so that his hands stay clean," mused Rainere. He got up to start pacing behind the couch. "Lord Orgustus seems stupid enough to be manipulated into trying to kill the queen to get his regency back again. I've also heard that he's behind all the antimonarchy propaganda that has recently flooded the streets of Concordis and its outlying towns. He works in the palace and is seen frequently in the city, a perfect cover for any criminal activities that he might set in motion."

"If it is Lord Orgustus, then he'll already know I'm in the Golden Palace," said Charlie. "But that shouldn't stop me having a sniff around to find out if he's working with Ohren and Orestes."

"And if it is Ohren or Orestes, then they might very well suspect that we will try to find out who the Boss is too," said Rainere, turning and pacing the other way. "They will probably throw up roadblocks at every turn. It will be useful to accept that your life is forfeit, Charlie."

Charlie gave a nonchalant shrug. "That's nothing new," he said, and the ghost of a smile crossed his lips. "Might as well do something useful with the time I've got left. Couldn't think of anything better than helping our Queen Adelena."

Rainere narrowed his eyes at Charlie's proud confession. "Yes, well, the longer you stay alive, the more you can do for her. Right up to the minute that your lying heart decides to betray me."

"Look, with all due respect, Prince Rainere, if I wanted to betray you, I would have done it long before now," Charlie said, showing his irritation. "And just so you know, I have been working for the Boss and hating him for years longer than you even knew he existed. Now he's threatening the life of the only person in this world who means anything to me. I'm going to do everything I can to find out who he really is and make sure Queen Adelena knows it too. So," he climbed to his feet, "when do we start?"

"Now," said Rainere. "Stick close to Mrs. Ollenby, and try to find out the next time Lord Orgustus goes into the city. Then you will follow him to where he works, watch what he does, and learn who he works with."

"What'll I do with Leafy while I'm doing all this?" asked Charlie, frowning. "I don't want to drag her into Concordis; she'll slow me down too much."

"Leafy can stay here with the children," said Rainere. "I will keep doing what I have been and will try to find out more about Ohren and Orestes. Those twins are unnaturally similar, to my mind."

Charlie swallowed hard. "So I'm meant to trust that you won't let me be captured by the Boss or give Leafy to the Church for the mines?" he said. Rainere could tell from the terrified look in his eyes the boy wasn't used to trusting anyone. He understood too well—he had the same terror.

"And I will trust that you won't turn me over to your Boss and sell information on the queen and her quest to find a dragon," answered Rainere.

"Agreed." Charlie extended his hand, and Rainere looked at it for a long moment before he reached out and shook it.

"Agreed," said the prince.

Rainere had let Charlie take the big bed with the children while he grabbed a few hours of sleep on the cot by the window. The children woke early, and Rainere felt an ease with them this morning that hadn't been there previously. Despite his stressful night, he found that he was ready for their noise and enthusiasm when Aaron and Natalie snuggled in next to him for a morning cuddle before getting up for breakfast.

I'm getting used to these needy and affectionate children, Rainere thought, as he avoided a tiny elbow flying at his nose. *I had no idea life with them would be so enjoyable.*

A nervous nanny poked her head around the door and found the Marchant prince tickling the royal children into hysterics. Charlie had pulled a pillow over his head to muffle the noise, but Leafy was sitting up on the big bed, smiling shyly at the antics of her new friends with the dangerous wizard.

"Siobahn, isn't it?" said Rainere when he noticed the shocked brunette standing in the doorway. "You can take the children to get dressed now."

"No!" Natalie and Aaron both howled. "We're puppies; we don't need clothes!" But Mrs. Ollenby had made her way into the room behind Siobahn, and she wasn't to be trifled with.

"Whew! What a smell with all these children and puppies in such a small room!" The royal housekeeper waved her hand in front of her nose, making the children giggle again. "We are going to have to get these children back into their own nursery again, Your Highness. You cannot expect to have this gaggle of mess-makers cluttering up your bedroom every night."

Rainere got out of bed. Siobahn almost tripped over a puppy when she saw that the prince was only wearing pajama pants and an open silk robe.

"Careful, Siobahn." Mrs. Ollenby tutted at the gaping nanny. "Now let's get the children dressed and the room empty for the maids to air." She helped hustle all the children and dogs out into their own suite.

Rainere took time in the small window of privacy to shower and dress himself. As much as he enjoyed the minutes alone, all too soon, his mind began imagining what could happen to the children while he was out of sight and earshot of them—minutes that an assassin could plan their death or kidnapping. Yet as soon as he was out of his bathroom, he heard shouts and laughter and breathed a deep sigh of relief as his heart rate slowed again.

Breakfast was taken at the dining table in the enormous bay window of the sitting room. It reminded Rainere a little of the Glassroom at the Gray Palace, and he enjoyed the feeling of being in the sun as he ate a rich breakfast of eggs, toast, and a dish of minced sausage meat served with fried potatoes that he was slowly becoming addicted to.

High Wizard Ohren entered the room and sat down before the surprised steward could even announce his name.

"Must be a new boy," said Ohren as he poured himself a cup of tea and winked at Aaron. "But you'd think even a new steward would recognize *me*, though, wouldn't you?"

"I did," agreed Aaron.

Prince Rainere glanced over at the steward hunched by the door and then caught Mrs. Ollenby's eye. "I wasn't informed of any new staff," he said.

"The new steward is a fill-in for Turner while he is off sick, Your Highness," said Mrs. Ollenby. "Though I had thought he had better training than this." She immediately hustled over to the servant to give him a piece of her mind.

As happy as Rainere found himself with his new domestic arrangement, he still couldn't get used to having High Wizard Ohren sitting at the same table with him day and night.

"Did you hear from Her Majesty yet?" Ohren asked, reaching across the table for the marmalade.

Rainere was shocked that the high wizard would ask him about Adelena in such a public arena as the breakfast table. *What is the old man playing at now?* "Yes, I did," he replied stiffly. "She was very well and has managed to get to their destination very quickly."

"Will Mummy be home soon?" asked Natalie, handing Rainere a glass of juice he didn't want.

"Very soon," Rainere promised the little girl. He took a sip of the juice to please her. "She sends her love to you all."

"Well, that is wonderful news," said Ohren, smiling, but his electric-blue eyes never left Rainere's. "I'm not sure what your plans are today, Your Highness, but I would very much like to have a meeting with you and Charlie, if that's possible?"

"No." Rainere shook his head. "The children are my priority, High Wizard. They have their riding lesson, then I have some matters to attend to while they take lunch, and after that, they have magic lessons for the rest of the day."

"But no nap," Aaron reminded the prince. "No naps for me."

"We will discuss the issue again during the midafternoon," said Rainere to the little prince before turning back to Ohren. "As you can see, High Wizard, my day is quite taken up."

"Oh, you'll want to see this, Your Highness," said Ohren. "I have something very special for you. It's about a certain matter you discussed with Mrs. Ollenby."

"Have you got a present for Prince Rainere?" asked Natalie.

"Of sorts," replied Ohren, giving Natalie a wink. "Perhaps Your Highness can give me a few minutes while the children take their riding lesson. I'm sure Mrs. Ollenby is quite capable of supervising them." The housekeeper had returned to the table and nodded in acquiescence.

Rainere felt cornered. His gaze happened to fall on Leafy. She had stopped eating her breakfast and was staring at the high wizard with a snarl on her lips. He could tell that she was clenching her hands under the table, no doubt one of her magical biters on its way to forming.

"Mrs. Ollenby, take Leafy with the children to their lesson," Rainere said. "She is to stay with you at all times and can have a riding lesson too." He turned to Leafy. "Leafy, do you remember what we spoke about yesterday?" Leafy nodded her dark head. "Good." Rainere felt he had made the best of a bad situation. "Then let us go, High Wizard, the day is wasting."

High Wizard Ohren stood and bowed. "I'm right behind you, Your Highness," he said.

CHAPTER THIRTY-TWO
"Snakes Who Eat Other Snakes"

Lady Olivia waited impatiently for Lord Orgustus to notice her. The large sitting room of his apartment was filled with his lackeys, and Orgustus had a giggling Lady Clare of Carparell sitting on the edge of his desk, twittering in his ear as he signed the scrolls handed to him, one by one, by the majordomo, Tilburn.

Olivia was so excited to give Lord Orgustus her news that she could barely concentrate on the gossip circulating in the room. "You should have seen it, Orgie," said Lord Pine, throwing a long leg over the arm of the chair he slouched in. "Fires everywhere and all those peasants chanting their hearts out. The queen is really in for it, if she ever shows up again."

Lord Orgustus looked up at the Carparell lord, his eyes narrowed. "You think the decline of our beloved capital into chaos is amusing, Lord Pine?"

Lord Pine threw a nut into the air and caught it in his mouth. He shrugged. "They really hate the queen down there, you know," he said. "Maybe you won't even have to wait much longer before the people *demand* that you are given the regency back."

Lord Orgustus threw a glance up at Tilburn as the majordomo's cheeks flushed a deep red. "That is treasonous talk, Lord Pine," Lord Orgustus said, though a smile softened his words. "I'll thank you to show some loyalty to our currently appointed queen."

Tilburn slammed another scroll down in front of the acting regent and pointed a manicured finger at the place where he was to sign, his lips pressed in a hard line.

"I think we are finished for the morning, Tilburn," said Orgustus as he signed his name with a flourish. "Why don't you take Mr. Gorrik with you and give me a moment's peace."

Lady Olivia hadn't actually noticed the old man standing at the window, his cat perched in his arms as they looked out over the palace gardens. Gorrik turned at Lord Orgustus's words and tottered over to the great desk.

"The fires are still burning in the city, my lord," he said mildly. "Did you happen to be in Concordis last night? I'm looking to fill in my records, you see. This is the first riot this city has seen in over a hundred years."

Lord Orgustus sat back in his chair and steepled his hands at his chest, clearly uninterested in speaking with an old man and his cat. "I wasn't even in the city last night, Mr. Gorrik," he said. "The first I heard of the unrest was this morning when I woke."

"Can anyone vouch for that, my lord?" asked Gorrik, earning himself a baleful glare from Orgustus.

"I can," giggled Lady Clare. "His lordship was with me all night."

The admission set off a chorus of catcalls from the young men in the room and titters from the ladies. Olivia burned with rage as Lady Clare proudly claimed the honor of Lord Orgustus's bed. Olivia had waited for him to show up for their pre-arranged meeting all night, but now she knew where he'd been.

"Well, I suppose you wouldn't have had anything to do with such a nasty business," said Gorrik, stroking his cat. "When the queen returns, she will expect that her acting regent will have behaved with loyalty and respect."

"You are known to have the ear of the high wizard, Mr. Gorrik—do you have any idea when the queen will be back in the palace?" asked Lord Orgustus. "I can't seem to get a straight answer on it from our majordomo here."

Gorrik smiled, but his cat narrowed its pale green eyes. "I'm sure as soon as the high wizard knows, then he will tell you of the queen's return," he said mildly.

"Which is to say that you do not think the high wizard knows when she'll be back either," Lord Orgustus said, triumphant to have gained this much knowledge. He dismissed Gorrik with a wave of his hand. The old history teacher took the elbow that Tilburn offered him, and they made their way from the suite, followed by Tilburn's two squires carrying the scrolls and papers. The cat perched on Gorrik's shoulder, and Olivia caught its pale green gaze. She thought that if cats could smile, then this one was certainly smiling at her as it was carried away.

"Lady Olivia, why are you here?" Lord Orgustus's question snapped Olivia to attention. She flushed.

"My lord, you wanted me to measure you for your new suit," she said, using the code that Lord Orgustus had given her to use if she had any information on the queen.

"Right, yes, so I did." Lord Orgustus stood at his desk, his expression warning Olivia that this had better be good. He absently kissed a pouting Lady Clare on the forehead and then gestured for Olivia to enter his private chamber.

Olivia enjoyed giving the undernourished and overbred Lady Clare a haughty glance as she followed Lord Orgustus out of the room.

As soon as the door closed, Orgustus pulled Olivia into his arms and kissed her deeply. Normally, his kisses took her breath away, but today she only waited until she could pull herself free of his embrace.

"Lord Orgustus, you'll want to hear this," said Olivia. She smoothed down her skirt as she stepped away from him. "I have found where they're keeping the baby, Princess Stella."

She was rewarded with Lord Orgustus's look of shock. "Seriously?"

"They're keeping her in a tiny garret room that can only be accessed through the queen's own dressing room," said Olivia, the excitement to be revealing such a big secret making her voice shake. "The door is locked, but I could open it with just a pin. I saw the baby on her bed." Olivia swallowed. "I think she might be dead."

Lord Orgustus's blue eyes narrowed as his mind raced. "Then why keep the child isolated?" he asked, chewing his bottom lip. "Surely a state funeral would be better than keeping the decomposing body of the child in the Golden Palace?"

"She wasn't decomposing," said Olivia. "The baby looked very normal, actually; a little pale, but I couldn't see any damage to her."

"Do you think it might be because of magic?" asked Lord Orgustus. "Did you see signs that might make you think they were doing something awful to the child or using her for dark magic?"

Olivia paused. *This is the first time Orgustus has spoken to me as if I might have a brain in my head,* she thought. She realized she didn't enjoy the honor as much as she would have a week ago. "I wouldn't know," she replied. "But I know it's not healthy or right to keep a little child locked up in a secret room."

Lord Orgustus reached around Olivia to grab the door handle. "Can you take me there now?" he said. "Where are the Marchant prince and the other children?"

"Right now, they are finishing up their breakfast," said Olivia. "But the prince will soon take them down to their horse riding lesson, so we can easily get in and out without being seen."

Lord Orgustus took Olivia's hand and squeezed it. "Lead the way, my darling."

Lady Olivia smiled and took her hand away. "Of course, my lord."

Chapter Thirty-Three
"Shifting the Focus"

Lord Orgustus's apartment was only a few corridors away from the royal apartments, so it wasn't long before Lady Olivia could see the high magistrar shouting at a steward by the door to the queen's bedroom.

Olivia was shocked that Lord Orgustus didn't hang back as she wanted to but immediately marched toward High Magistrar Orestes. "Good morning! What seems to be the matter, High Magistrar?" he asked.

"Lord Orgustus, good morning," the high magistrar replied through clenched teeth, clearly furious. "This steward has been lax in his duties and hasn't passed on a message that I required. Now I have to find the high wizard myself, and I've got no idea where he is, as the apartment is empty."

Humbled, the steward in question bowed his head low and shuffled his feet. Lady Olivia didn't recognize him as one of the usual stewards, though Hollis and Franks hovered behind him.

"I know the high wizard had breakfast with the Marchant prince and royal children, High Magistrar," squeaked Lady Olivia, hoping she wouldn't get into any trouble for revealing this. "I saw them not an hour ago."

The high magistrar shifted his frosty gaze to Lady Olivia, and she immediately regretted speaking. Orestes gave her the creeps. His eyes scanned her body and came to rest on her face again. "Do you have any idea where they might be *now*, child?" he asked.

Lady Olivia dropped into a curtsy. "No, High Magistrar, I'm sorry."

"I suppose you know all about this riot in the city last night, High Magistrar?" said Lord Orgustus loudly. "I would love to hear what you intend to do about it."

"Do about it?" The high magistrar raised both gray eyebrows. "The riot is over. Deaths were minimal and in the sole domain of the Lower Districts of Concordis. There is nothing the crown needs to do, Lord Orgustus."

Lady Olivia shot Lord Orgustus a furtive glance when she heard his sharp intake of breath. His cheeks had already colored, and his fists tightened at his side. "There was a *riot* in our peaceful city, High Magistrar," snarled Lord Orgustus, waving his temper like a flag. "Riots do not happen in isolation; someone or something caused it. Our very own citizens died in the ensuing violence, and whether they lived in the slums or not, they shouldn't have lost their lives. Concordis has been rocked by the tragedy of the Summer Influenza, and now our people are expected to tolerate riots in their streets with no reaction from the crown? This, sir, is an outrage!"

The high magistrar looked from Lord Orgustus to Lady Olivia, though she hardly raised her eyes from the floor. "What business do you have at the royal apartment today?" he asked, completely ignoring the lord's diatribe.

"Well, we are here to see to the good health of the royal children," blustered Lord Orgustus, thinking on his feet. "They have been left in the care of an immortal wizard with known tendencies to dark magic. I would like to see for myself that they are still well and happy."

The high magistrar took in this information, but Lady Olivia didn't think he looked like he believed Orgustus. "Yes, the children, of course," he said. "Make sure you check in on little Princess Stella too. I'm not privy to where they are keeping her, but if you find out, I'd be delighted to be kept informed of her health. It's supposed to be very fragile still."

Orestes's gaze lit on Olivia again, and she dropped another curtsy to avoid it.

"I'll be sure to tell you, as soon as I discover her whereabouts, High Magistrar," said Lord Orgustus, giving Orestes a shallow bow. "The safety of the royal children should be our first priority with the queen away from the Golden Palace and only a Marchant wizard as their guardian."

"Quite." The high magistrar looked almost amused before he turned sharply to face the three stewards standing against the wall. "You two, Hollis and Franks, take this new boy to wherever Mrs. Ollenby is and make sure she knows I want him fired for his mistake today."

Franks and Hollis bowed deeply from the waist, and immediately pulled the new steward between them, and marched him off down the corridor.

The high magistrar turned back to Lord Orgustus and Lady Olivia. "There," he said, smiling thinly. "Now there really isn't *anyone* at home. Have a good day, my lord, my lady." With that he turned and stalked off up the hallway in the opposite direction from the stewards.

"What luck!" crowed Lord Orgustus. "Come on, let's go in before any more servants come along."

Olivia followed Orgustus into the queen's bedroom, but something didn't feel right. "My lord, do you not think it was a bit odd how the high magistrar sent all the stewards away? It was almost as if he knew what we wanted to do here."

"Don't be paranoid, Olivia," snapped Orgustus, but she could tell he was nervous despite his bluster. "Show me where this baby's room is."

Lady Olivia took the lead and guided Orgustus into the queen's dressing room. She ignored his grumblings about selling the queen's shoes to pay off the crown's debt and showed him the little door at the back of the room. She pulled a pin from her hair and dropped to her knees to handle the lock.

"Where in Evendaar did you learn such a horrible trick?" Orgustus asked, not bothering to hide his disgust. "Sometimes I forget you grew up on a farm instead of in a palace."

Olivia pushed herself to her feet and opened the door. "My apologies, Lord Orgustus," she replied, and they both heard the anger behind her words. "I will try to be more ladylike when I do your spying for you."

Lord Orgustus shouldered past Olivia, giving her a dark look as he climbed the narrow staircase before them. He paused at the top, and Olivia joined him on the last step.

The room was windowless, with bare wooden walls and a parquetry floor. The only furniture was a large bed draped with a white silk canopy and a small night table with a leather armchair next to it.

Olivia led Orgustus to the side of the bed, and they both looked down on the baby. "I thought she was sleeping at first," said Olivia softly. "But then I looked closer, and I couldn't see her breathe."

Lord Orgustus reached out a hand, a golden glow lighting his fingers, and tried to touch Princess Stella. He was only an inch from her face when the matrix lit up and acid-green lines of magic filled the air around the bed, forcing the lord and lady to back away to avoid touching it.

"Dark magic!" gasped Lord Orgustus. He stared at the glittering web in shock. "They have trapped the child in a hideous spell, locking her in some kind of demon dimension and hiding her from the grace of the goddess. May Serena have mercy on her poor soul."

"What should we do?" asked Olivia, wondering why Orgustus was jumping to the conclusion that Stella was in danger because of the magic. The baby looked pretty peaceful to her.

"We need to rescue Princess Stella, and fast!" said Lord Orgustus. "I will try to find someone who can deal with this sort of magic, and we shall move her where that evil prince can't get to her. Maybe the high magistrar can be of some help to us."

"You want to tell the high magistrar we broke into the queen's secret room and kidnapped her child?" asked Olivia, surprised by Orgustus's rashness. She thought for a moment. "What about that old history teacher, Gorrik? He's about a thousand years old, so I bet he knows something about dark magic and how to fix it. We should take the child to him first."

Lord Orgustus looked at Olivia with a new respect. "That is a brilliant idea, Olivia," he said. "You wait here with the child, and I will go and fetch Gorrik. I'm sure he hasn't gotten far since the meeting in my chambers." He gave her hand a squeeze. "You won't be too frightened waiting for me here?"

Olivia found herself trying not to roll her eyes at Orgustus's new affection. "Of course not, my lord," she said. "Just please hurry!"

"I'll be back in a flash," said Orgustus, leaving her alone in a silent room with a baby wrapped up in dark magic.

Chapter Thirty-Four
"Unexpected Allies"

"Mrs. Ollenby told me everything last night," announced Ohren as he closed the door to his laboratory, shocking Rainere and Charlie into silence. "I know now that you both believe that a character called the Boss is responsible for the attempt on the queen's life in the Lower Districts and that you intend to search for him. Naturally, I have heard of this character, but no more than rumors, so I tried to find someone who knew him. Unfortunately, my contact turned up dead."

Ohren watched the two Marchants exchange a glance as he led them to a long table, covered in canvas cloth, stationed under a window.

"I want it to be clear, Prince Rainere, that I am on your side," said Ohren. "Despite what has passed between us, you have to know that I love our queen and believe she really is the salvation of Unisia. If someone is out to kill her, then I will do everything I can to help uncover the assassin."

Rainere stood very straight, sparkling green magic surrounding each of his fists. He drilled the high wizard with a hard stare. "So much talk, yet so very little action," he said.

With a wild sweep of his arm, Ohren pulled the canvas sheet off the table and revealed what was underneath.

"Someone found the body of my contact under a bridge on the edge of the slums, and it's well known that he was working for the Boss and of Marchant descent. Green Bloods, I believe they are called," said Ohren. He gestured at the mangled body on the table. "Probably the man was strangled to death, and the cats have already had a go at him. But I was hoping…"

"What were you hoping, High Wizard?" Rainere didn't recoil from the body, but he did flinch at the sound of Charlie heaving into a waste bin. "That I might have the hideous spell necessary to bring the dead back to life? I would not taint myself with such evil."

"No," said Ohren, yanking on his beard. "I simply thought Charlie might recognize him." He gestured for Charlie to pull himself together and come examine the body.

Reluctantly, the teenager approached the corpse, holding his hand over his mouth. "Yeah, I know him. It's a guy named Sandy," he said. "He's a blue addict and has a habit of stabbing people in their sleep, so I'm glad he's dead."

"Why would he have been killed, do you think?" asked Ohren, getting close to the body and examining the wounds on its face.

Charlie shrugged and made his way toward an open window. "The Boss'll kill you if you screw up a job. He'll kill you if you do too well and he thinks you disrespect him. Or he'll kill you to prove to everyone else that he can. The man is psychotic. Maybe Sandy had started taking some of the tonic he was meant to be selling? All I know is that he's been working for the Boss longer than I have, maybe five years or more, and it wouldn't have to be serious for the Boss to take him out like this."

There was a knock at the door. Ohren shouted, "Go away, I'm working."

The door was flung open, and Orestes stood in the doorway, a thunderous expression on his face. "Brother, we have a problem," said the high magistrar, but he fell silent when he saw that Ohren had company, and his jaw dropped when he saw the corpse on the table. "Ohren, what is the meaning of this?"

If Ohren felt perturbed that his twin had discovered the dark work he was doing, he hid it well. "An anatomy exam," he said brightly. "His Highness was going to show me another method of surgery and stitching. We needed a corpse, naturally. The boy is here to observe."

Orestes's expression showed his disapproval, and he avoided looking at the body by holding out his hand to cover his peripheral vision. "We have more important matters than doctoring this morning," he growled. "I sent you a note to meet me in my offices at the ninth hour, but you never showed, so I had to come looking for you. That useless steward in the royal apartment was still holding the letter when I got there."

"Sorry, Orestes, he's new," said Ohren. "Let me just finish up here with His Highness, and I will join you shortly in your rooms."

"You said that there's a problem," interrupted Rainere, directing his question at Orestes. "What is it?"

"Nothing that concerns you, Your Highness," replied Orestes, but then his electric-blue eyes narrowed at the prince. "Or maybe it does, considering your place in it all. There was trouble in the city last night. An effigy of the queen was burned in the town square near the Guild Quarter. There was a mixed crowd protesting and singing, but the City Guard managed to contain it with a few arrests. There was a group of carousers who went into the slums, and a few deaths were reported, but none of note."

"You mean no one from the Guild Quarter was killed," muttered Charlie, glaring at the high magistrar.

"Good goddess!" Ohren was shocked.

"The effigy was wearing a bridal gown doused in green paint," continued Orestes. "And the chants called the queen a Marchant whore and an evil magician, among other things."

Rainere crossed his arms across his chest. "The whining of peasants," he snapped.

"Peasants who have never had occasion to riot before," said Ohren, looking worried. "Who inflamed this situation last night, Orestes? Who is organizing the peaceful people of Concordis to act like this?"

"Lord Orgustus was allegedly in the city last night," said Orestes. "He is known to frequent the clubs in the Guild Quarter, and it's been said that the antimonarchy propaganda is being funded by deep pockets. It's also well known how he feels about the queen, and you know as well as I do, Ohren, that he is just arrogant enough to make a reach for his regency again."

His message delivered, Orestes turned to leave. "I'll see you in my chambers as soon as you're finished, Ohren," he said. "But tell me, where are the royal children just now? I hope you've left them somewhere safe while you attend to this 'work.'"

"They're having their riding lesson at the stables, and Mrs. Ollenby is watching over them," replied Ohren, but he was distracted now, pulling at his beard and tangling it in the rings on his hand. "See you in a minute, brother."

The door closed, and two pairs of narrowed Marchant eyes locked on Ohren.

"Why did you lie to your brother about why we were examining the body?" asked Rainere. "Do you not trust him?"

"I trust him to be wildly angry," said Ohren with a rueful grimace, covering the body with the canvas again. "As much as I respect and admire all kinds of magic, my brother adheres very much to the traditional St. Lucidis ways. He strongly believes that the queen is being tainted by her connection to you. You must understand the gossip and fear that your presence in the Golden Palace inspires, Prince Rainere. I don't want to worry my brother any further by telling him that we're actually working together to find this Boss character. He wouldn't trust your motives."

Charlie hiked himself up onto a stool. "You're an immortal, aren't you, High Wizard?" he asked boldly.

Ohren was annoyed at being interrupted by Charlie. "Yes, I am," he said. "What of it?"

"How'd you get that way, then? Did the Marchant Eldars curse you too?" Charlie asked.

Ohren's face closed like a door slamming shut. "That is none of your business, boy," he replied.

"So that means your twin has to be immortal too, no?" continued Charlie recklessly. "So if he hates Marchant magic so much, why'd he let the Eldars do that to him?"

"It's *why* he hates Marchant magic so much," said Ohren, and his electric-blue eyes were frigid. "He never asked for immortality—it was given to him by mistake. My mistake."

"That's one hell of a mistake," said Charlie, hopping off his stool and walking toward the wizard. "But what could you possibly have done to make the Marchant Eldars curse you with immortality?

You're St. Lucidis; they'd have no reason at all to make you one of them. What'd you do for them, High Wizard, that they cursed you?"

"Watch yourself, Charlie," warned Ohren. "You are speaking of things you don't understand and never will." But he was backing up as Charlie advanced on him, the skinny boy cornering the tall wizard.

"You're all a bunch of liars, you royal St. Lucidis," sneered Charlie. "You play so innocent and spit on our green magic, but you wanna be immortal, so you use the worst spell in creation to lord yourselves on high, then make the same magic illegal for the rest of us."

"Get away from me," whispered Ohren, though his blue eyes were wide with pain instead of anger. Charlie was wrenching secrets from him one after the other.

"You and your brother run this kingdom like a toy garden." Charlie was close enough to poke Ohren in the chest. "We are just your playthings. Marchant bad, St. Lucidis good, and no one can argue because all the immortals win."

"No," protested Ohren, shaking his head. "It's not like that."

"What did you do for the Eldars, High Wizard?" asked Charlie. "Why'd they make you immortal?"

"They didn't!" shouted Ohren as he violently pushed Charlie away. Charlie flew across the room and crashed into a table. "Rainold did this to me when I—" Ohren fell silent, shocked by his own confession, his eyes melting into pools of blue. "When I asked him to," he finished. "I never knew that it would affect Orestes too. He hated my Rainold and anything to do with dark magic—he blamed it for all the violence in the kingdom. He hates it still, though it's the very thing that is keeping him alive to fight."

Charlie dragged himself to his feet and kept a wary distance from the high wizard. He licked at the cut on his lip. "Who's *your* Rainold?"

"My father." Rainere's voice rasped in the ringing silence.

"Yes, your father," admitted Ohren, hanging his head. "We were young and foolish. We thought that together we could control the power. I asked Rainold to go to the Eeyrie so he could learn the curse and find the dragon's blood we needed. Of course, the Eldars caught him trying to steal from them and cursed him before his time. But he still stole the blood for me, and he still cursed me."

"Then why have you aged?" asked Charlie. He spat a gob of blood onto the floor. "You got old when you should have stayed young."

"Don't be an idiot, boy," snapped Ohren, showing the rings on his hands. Most were heavy gold with chunky gray crystals set in them. "No one wants to be reminded that their high wizard is alive by the grace of dark magic." He gestured at himself. "I have to wear this stupid beard and act the old man to keep the people happy, and so does Orestes."

"Show me what you look like," demanded Charlie. "I want to see who you really are."

Ohren toyed with a ring on his finger and seemed tempted. "What's the point?" he said. "You only need to know what I *should* look like if I hadn't been so greedy in my youth."

"I insist," said Rainere, his gaze intense. He took a step toward the high wizard. "Show us what you really look like."

Ohren sighed, exasperated. "Very well, just for a moment." He pulled the charmed ring off his index finger, and then the next two off his other hand. There was a bright shimmer, and suddenly, standing before them was a tall, handsome young man. Ohren was still broad in the shoulders, but his robes hung differently on a skinny frame. Blond hair flopped into his electric-blue eyes, and his high cheekbones blushed bright red. Ohren ran a hand through the loose curls at the back of his neck.

"You have no idea how good it feels to take that charm off," he said sheepishly, rubbing his red cheeks. "I don't miss blushing, though."

"You're just a boy!" said Rainere, shocked. "You couldn't have been more than twenty when you were cursed."

Ohren shrugged, uncomfortable. "I always looked young for my age," he said, with a lopsided grin at the irony.

Charlie clapped his hand over his mouth, covering his shock.

Ohren slipped his rings on and morphed back into the familiar old man they knew as High Wizard Ohren. "It's like wearing a hair shirt," he complained, yanking at his beard. "The charm on my rings can't be strong enough to trip any dark magic alarms in the Golden Palace, so I have to wear the beard to help disguise myself."

He shrugged, embarrassed in the silence of the two staring Marchants. "Now, if you don't mind, I should go and find Orestes." Ohren smoothed his robes, suddenly filled out with an old man's figure. "The problems of the past can wait, and I should be working out how to control Lord Orgustus before he launches a coup in the Golden Palace. For now, I'll leave you two to find what you can on the Boss, but report back to me when you have something."

Ohren left the laboratory. Charlie and Rainere turned to each other, reflected looks of shock on their faces.

"Well done, Charlie," said Rainere. "I think that's more information than I would have got out of the high wizard in a lifetime of awkward conversations. I'm not sure it helps us with our problem, but it has certainly answered a few of my own questions."

Charlie shook his head, almost choking on his next words. "That's him, Your Highness. That's the Boss."

Rainere swore, and his pale cheeks blanched further. "Charlie, are you sure?"

"Normally, he wears a scarf on his face," said Charlie. "But those eyes—I know those eyes. It's him—High Wizard Ohren is the Boss of the Underworld."

CHAPTER THIRTY-FIVE

"Fragrance of Love's Memory"

Rainere raced along the hallways of the Golden Palace, ducking in and out of the secret corridors to make it to the door of the royal apartment. More rattled than he wanted to admit to himself, he'd decided to check on Stella before going down to the stables to see Natalie and Aaron. He comforted himself that Mrs. Ollenby and the little terror, Leafy, watched over the children and Charlie was on his way there now. Unusually, there was no steward at the door of the queen's bedchamber, so he slipped inside with no trouble.

Rainere's head was spinning with a thousand questions but he couldn't pick apart the complexity of the situation. *If Ohren is the Boss, and he knows that Charlie knows the Boss, then why would he reveal himself so casually to the both of us? Yet Charlie was so sure.* Rainere knew the high wizard was a brilliant liar, but even so, there hadn't been a shred of duplicity or fear when he revealed his true appearance.

Rainere put his hand on the door handle to the queen's dressing room, but it turned before he could move it. Startled, Rainere stepped back as the door opened and he came face to face with Lady Olivia.

"Your Highness!" Lady Olivia dropped into a deep curtsy. "I hadn't expected you in the queen's chamber. Can I help you with something?"

Rainere bit back the curse on his tongue. *Everywhere I turn, there are interfering servants getting in my way,* he thought, furious. "No, you cannot help me," he snapped. He turned to leave, refusing to let his eyes search for the secret door in the dressing room behind Lady Olivia.

"Wait, Your Highness! Please look at me!" Lady Olivia called out, and Rainere stopped at the desperation in her tone. He turned to face her, curious at the young woman's hysterical tone, when Lady Olivia caught Rainere by the elbow and led him to a narrow couch by the glass doors open to the queen's private terrace. The prince was too surprised by Lady Olivia's audacity to refuse to sit when she pulled him down next to her.

"Please forgive my candor, Your Highness," gushed Lady Olivia. She still hadn't let go of Rainere's arm, and he noticed it. "But I have to tell you that I know your secret and the reason why you are always in my queen's chambers."

"I'm sure I don't know what you mean," protested Rainere, but Lady Olivia only looked up at him from beneath her long lashes, a smile curling her lips.

"You miss her, don't you?" said the lady. "And I think that your heart is broken without Queen Adelena here. This is why you are always in her room, to be close to her things, even though you can't be close to her. Am I right?"

Cornered, Rainere could only nod. "You have discovered me, my lady," he admitted. He noticed that Lady Olivia was wearing a burgundy dress that he was sure he had seen on Adelena at some point, and he remembered how easily it had come off in his hands. *Now someone else is undressing Adelena.* The thought came unbidden into his head and brought the memory of Adelena's unbridled lust. *That Jordansson is keeping her very happy while she's away from me.*

Lady Olivia smiled sweetly and squeezed Rainere's upper arm, lingering on his bicep. "May I offer a suggestion, Your Highness?" Without waiting for a reply, Lady Olivia went to Adelena's dressing table and fetched a tiny purple bottle. She pulled out the jeweled stopper, and the fragrance of Adelena's favorite perfume filled the air.

Lady Olivia giggled at Rainere's rapt expression. "Perfume is a strong cognitive trigger," she said, giggling again, as if surprised at herself. "What I mean is sometimes just the smell of a lover's perfume can make you feel like they're right next to you," she simpered.

Rainere tried to take the bottle, but Lady Olivia moved it just out of reach. "Here." She dabbed the scent on her arched neck. "It smells better when it's warm. See?"

Rainere leaned forward and closed his eyes. The memories of those lost nights with Adelena filled his mind, and his body responded immediately. His lips touched the warm skin of Lady Olivia's neck and felt her pulse race. Eyes still shut, he raised his hand to her shoulder, pulling her closer as he buried his nose in the fragrance of his beloved. He felt feminine hands on the back of his neck, stroking his head and then gently pulling his face up to hers.

"Your Highness." Lady Olivia's whisper sent chills across Rainere's skin. "I have admired you for so long. I want to be here." She kissed his cheek, her lips sticky with gloss. "For you." She kissed Rainere on his mouth, and desire flashed through him with an intensity that left him blind.

Pushing Lady Olivia back on the couch, he muttered the spell that loosened the dress from its hooks and bindings. He yanked it down at the front, and creamy soft breasts filled his hands, making him moan with pleasure.

"Oh, Your Highness," gasped Lady Olivia. "Yes, I want this too!"

Rainere needed Lady Olivia to stop talking, so he kissed her again. In her kiss he searched for the taste of what he'd wanted since Adelena had woken him up with the magic screaming through the Mark. *Adelena is fucking that ice man,* he reminded himself again and felt defiance swamp his good sense. *She is taking her pleasure where she wants it, and I will take mine.*

"Your Highness, please," Lady Olivia begged. "Tell me what you want me to do." Her voluptuous breasts filled his grasp, her nipples hard against his palms as she pressed up to meet him, offering him her youth and her body. The desire raged in Rainere's veins, but in Lady Olivia's sky-blue eyes there was only a shred of gold not quite strong enough to spin around her pupils. *This woman is just a simple St. Lucidis girl.* Rainere ached with suppressed lust and knew there was nothing Lady Olivia could do for him.

"Please, I want to make you happy, my prince." Lady Olivia began undoing the buttons of Rainere's shirt, running her hands over the muscles of his chest, presuming she had won him before the game had truly begun.

"You want to make me happy?" Rainere's voice rasped, and Lady Olivia looked up at the danger in his tone. She nodded, and there was a flicker of triumph in her eyes.

Suddenly, as fast as it had come, the desire turned to rage, and Rainere lost his breath trying to control it. Gently, he put one hand around Lady Olivia's throat. The other slid under the small of her back, pulling her up to sit astride him. "You're used to riding all those little St. Lucidis ponies, Lady Olivia," he said. "You've never had a real stallion before, have you?"

Lady Olivia had lost some of her surety, but she wasn't ready to back down. She pulled Rainere's hand from her throat and shook out her blond tresses. "No, Your Highness," she panted. "I've never had a prince like you."

"But I don't play games with little girls," Rainere warned. He let the magic spark in his eyes and fire through his voice.

"I'll give you anything." Lady Olivia pressed herself against Rainere, excited by his challenge.

Her bravery and ambition almost made Rainere smile. Almost. And for one wild moment, he thought the girl might actually be able to replace Adelena. *It would be so easy to have a woman like this at my beck and call.*

"Can *you* hurt *me*?" growled Rainere as he twined his fingers in Lady Olivia's long blond hair. He pressed her hand to his chest and forced her to feel his power as it fizzed and burned across his skin. "Can you?" he begged.

"I want to," whispered Lady Olivia, and her eyes lit with a dark desire. "I want to hurt you, my prince." She closed the distance between their lips.

Then the door to the bedchamber crashed open, and a steward ran into the room, tripping over the rug and cursing.

"Get out," shrieked Lady Olivia, crossing her arms over her naked chest. "Get out, you fool!"

The steward didn't listen, only crossed the floor to where the would-be lovers were sitting. He pulled a tiny bracelet off his wrist.

Indigo eyes shimmered through sparkles of gold magic as his disguise was broken, and a slightly shorter, rugged blond man appeared before them.

"You'll want to get that girl off you, Prince Rainere," the not-a-steward said, and his gaze watched Lady Olivia struggling to stand up and get her dress back on. "The children have been taken, and we need to hurry."

"What!" Rainere exploded out of his seat. "They should be at the stables."

"That's where they were kidnapped," said the man, already making his way to the door. "I saw it all."

Rainere joined the stranger in a few long bounds and grabbed him by the arm just before the door was opened. "Who are you, and why are you helping me?"

The stranger shrugged off Rainere's grasp. "The name is Ripenzo Shale, and I'm helping *you* because those kids are *my* family. I've left Charlie looking for clues at the stables, but the quicker we can find the kids, the more likely they are to survive."

Though Ripenzo's response gave Rainere more questions than answers, he decided to risk whatever trap might be ahead and sprinted as fast as his immortal legs could carry him.

Chapter Thirty-Six
"Odor of Foul Play"

"Tell me what's happened!" Lord Orgustus burst back into the queen's bedchamber, surprising Lady Olivia where she was still slumped on the couch.

"Oh, Orgie, it was terrible!" whimpered Lady Olivia as she retied her bodice ribbons with trembling hands. "The prince attacked me like an animal."

"I don't mean to you!" snapped Lord Orgustus. "I meant to the children! What was the steward shouting about?"

Lady Olivia felt cold under Orgustus's icy stare. "The children have been kidnapped from the stables," she said quickly. "But that new steward wasn't really a man. Well, I mean to say—I think he was a wizard."

"Another wizard!" Orgustus swore. "That's all we need." His calculating gaze swept the room as he considered their options. "I will go and investigate this crime and try to learn what I can," he decided. "You will stay here and await Gorrik. I sent for him and have been told he'll meet you here within the hour." Lord Orgustus spun on his heel, his cape whipping out behind him.

"So now I have to wait here again with the dead princess?" shouted Lady Olivia, fear giving her anger a voice. "But my lord, what if Gorrik thinks I'm the one who did that to her, or that I'm part of it?"

Lord Orgustus only laughed as he turned the door handle. "I don't think you need to fear being overestimated, Lady Olivia." He threw her a glance over his shoulder. "Remember, you can always just show him your tits."

Orgustus slammed the door behind him and left Olivia gaping as his insult hung in the air. "Now I hate you," she said aloud. "And you will be sorry you said that."

Finishing up with her dress ribbons, Olivia poured herself a glass of Firewhiskey from the queen's own bottle and slugged it back. She pondered how best to appear when Gorrik arrived. *If I'm crying, it might look better.* She made her way to the queen's dressing table. *A bit of powder to pale my cheeks and*—she held up a mascara wand—*a quick poke in the eye should do it.*

The Firewhiskey warmed her nicely, and it hardly hurt when Olivia did what she had to with the tiny brush and the acidic paste. She decided to throw herself on the floor at the door to the queen's dressing room, eyes streaming and cheeks wan, as she waited patiently to deliver her greatest performance to date.

Chapter Thirty-Seven
"Nightmares in the Day"

The scene at the royal stables was like something out of Rainere's worst nightmares. The bloody body of a gray pony lay heaped with splintered logs where it had been blasted by the side of the corral. He saw two young squires lying in the middle of the training ground and could only hope they weren't dead. Charlie was nowhere to be seen.

Mrs. Ollenby sat in the dirt. She was bleeding from a gash on her head, and her pink dress was streaked with blood and mud. Rainere rushed to kneel beside her.

"What happened here?" Rainere took Mrs. Ollenby's hand, but she snatched it back, glaring up at him.

"If you really don't already know, Your Highness, we were outnumbered, and the enemy had terrible dark magic in their hands," said Mrs. Ollenby accusingly. She was trembling with rage, the wide band of power spinning and sparking around her pupils. "There was one dressed like a priest, and he had men with him dressed like the Household Guard, but they weren't. They threw a bomb at the children as they rode in the yard, and then they grabbed them. They used evil spells and mechanical weapons."

"It was a concussion bomb," said Ripenzo behind Rainere. "The priest is a man called Pere Raven, and he'd dressed up a bunch of Rangers to look like Household Guards to get them through the palace grounds."

Rainere's head snapped round to Ripenzo. "Rangers from the Dark Forest Squad?" he asked. "But the Marchant family stopped financing them years ago. They shouldn't still be working."

"Obviously, there are people in the Dark Forest with deeper pockets than yours," said Ripenzo, squatting beside Rainere at

Mrs. Ollenby's side. "But it sure is handy that they're known to only work for Marchants. If I wanted to frame you for kidnapping the royal children, I would think using them was a great idea."

Rainere finally caught up. "No," he croaked, horrified. "I would never…" But he had, once before.

Rainere faced Mrs. Ollenby's furious gaze. "Mrs. Ollenby, I would never do anything to harm the children. I made an oath to Adelena—my life is forfeit if I break it."

Dolores Ollenby grabbed Prince Rainere's hand, clutching it tightly in her own. "If you really didn't do this, then stop whining and go and save those children," she snapped. "I'll do what I can here to try to disguise the evidence so it won't immediately point to you, Prince Rainere." He helped the woman to her feet, holding her steady. "And you, Ripenzo, we've met before, though you won't remember it because I only served you tea. But I know that you saved my beautiful Adelena when she was in a lot of trouble in Sandar, and I'll thank you to do the same for her children now."

Ripenzo smiled. "Of course I remember you, Mrs. Ollenby," he said. "You are one of the strongest wizards who's ever handed me a plate of biscuits."

Mrs. Ollenby winced at the compliment. "Well, a fat lot of good it did against those Rangers. My magic just dissipated over their shields," she said. "But I think I got the priest one on the face, which is something for my pride."

"Mrs. Ollenby, where is Charlie now?" asked Rainere.

"I sent him after the children," answered Mrs. Ollenby. "Hopefully, he caught their trail out of the palace grounds." She paused. "You know, they took Leafy too, Your Highness. The poor child was terrified, but she fought them as hard as she could, throwing nasty balls of magic at them. If a Ranger hadn't grabbed Natalie and held a weapon to her head, I'm sure Leafy would have kept on fighting, but she went to help the princess instead, and they got her too."

"Well, at least we know where they're going," snarled Ripenzo, clearly hurt by the news of Leafy's kidnapping.

"How do we know that?" asked Rainere.

"Because they need kids as strong as Leafy and Adelena's children," said Ripenzo.

Rainere muttered a foul curse, but Mrs. Ollenby was still puzzled. "Where are they taking them, Ripenzo?" she asked.

"The crystal mines, Mrs. Ollenby," said Ripenzo. "They are taking all the children they can find with Marchant magic to the crystal mines at Mount Ecrusius, and may the goddess help them if they turn out to be Special."

"The Boss is behind this set up." Rainere was sure. "While I was out of the way talking to Ohren this morning, he must have taken his opportunity. That means Pere Raven is working for Ohren or Orestes—or both of them!" He swore savagely.

Ripenzo looked thoughtful, his denim-blue eyes puzzling this over. "Maybe you are at the center of this," he said. "But we should rescue those kids before Pere Raven takes them away where we can't reach them."

Frustrated by his ignorance, Rainere shook his head. "Charlie says that the Boss has an office somewhere in the Lower Districts of Concordis," he said. "I don't know the city well, but I've been to the slums once before. I'm sure the Boss of the Underworld isn't too hard to find."

"Oh, the prince has been to the slums *once*, has he?" Ripenzo rolled his eyes. "You'll get us killed in minutes, no doubt demanding that he meet us for lunch at a restaurant of his choosing."

Rainere was just about to fire back at the sarcastic Ripenzo when a figure limped out of the stables, capturing his attention. The young man pushed his black curls off his forehead and tried to bow. "I know where the Boss will be," he said. "I can take you to him, Your Highness."

"Who are you?" asked Rip, holding out his hand to shake. "You look like you could be Rainere's son."

The young man looked from one wizard to the next, and his pale green eyes were wide with fear. "My name is Benjamin, sir," he said. "I was in the stables when the attack happened. I ran out when I heard the explosion, but I just froze, you know. I didn't even try to save the royal kids from those guys with the dark magic." He took in a shaky breath. "And if I don't help you now, then I'll never forgive myself."

Rainere glared at the handsome stable hand. "Your failure before means we don't need your assistance now, Benjamin," he said. "Stay with Mrs. Ollenby, and make sure she gets help for that injury."

"Wait just a second there, tiger," said Ripenzo, holding his hand out to Rainere. "The kid knows the city and who the Boss is. Let's take him with us."

"I would kindly suggest you all stop jabbering and go now," snapped Mrs. Ollenby. "Benjamin, saddle three horses. I'm going back to the palace to do damage control, because when the court discovers that the Marchant prince and the children are not at home, all hell will break loose." Shaking off Rainere's supporting arm, she turned to limp away. "I want you all gone in ten minutes."

"You heard the lady, fellas," said Ripenzo, heading into the stables. "Let's go rescue those kids."

Chapter Thirty-Eight
"The Path to the Dragon"

Adele had been dreaming of Rainere. She noticed things about him in her dream that she didn't consciously know. The noise he made when he was kissing her, that whispery moan she could never hear because she was already too far inside him. His hands were warm on her skin and stroked her so gently, yet no matter how she reached, his magic was just too far away…

The sound of quiet conversation dragged Adele out of her sleep. She squinted in the candlelight at the sight of General Ohrig and QG Leith packing bags on the floor and lining up equipment against the wall in her room. Adele felt a gentle hand on her back and turned quickly, still sleepy enough to believe it could be Rainere, but it was a shirtless Jordansson.

"What are you doing in my bed?" croaked Adele. "Get off me, Jordansson."

"I was chosen to wake you up," smiled Jordansson, laying a kiss on Adele's naked shoulder. "You were sparking magic everywhere, and your men were scared to touch you."

Adele groaned and rolled away from the tribesman's embrace. "What are you all doing in my room?" she complained. "It's still nighttime—let me sleep."

Ohrig sat himself at the foot of her bed. "You've been asleep for over a day and a half, Your Majesty," he said. "The only reason I knew you weren't dead is because you kept talking in your sleep."

"It's the Vision Smoke," Jordansson clarified needlessly. "It put you to sleep, and your body needed the sleep to heal."

"Yeah, I got that," grumped Adele, rubbing her forehead. "It also gives you a wicked headache. I seem to be able to remember everything about the visions I had, but I can't remember asking the chieftess about the dragon." She looked over at Jordansson. "Did I?"

Jordansson shrugged. "You would have only spoken to her in a vision, and I couldn't hear that."

"And how is Lucky feeling after all those opiates?" Adele asked Ohrig, pulling the sheet over herself and sitting up.

"He is having trouble staying awake, but I believe he is no worse for wear," said Ohrig. He was watching her closely, and Adele could feel the heavy cloud of questions that he carried about him, just waiting for the go-ahead to ask them.

Instead, Adele gestured at Leith, who was darting glances at her as he finished stuffing equipment into a pile of backpacks. "Are we leaving already?"

Jordansson climbed off the bed and went to the door, looking around for eavesdroppers, then checked the window, peering out into the gloom, before coming back to kneel by her bedside. It was strange for Adele to see him look so serious.

"The chieftess still has not said a word about what happened in the blood ceremony but has gone to her camp on the mountainside," whispered Jordansson. "There has been much arguing in the council. Some say you are cursed by Dahk'hani, and some think the same signs suggest you are blessed by him. While they wait for the chieftess to return, the summer is closing, and the heavy snows will soon come. Your general said that he thought you would want to leave when you woke. You have slept long, and we hope you are strong enough to travel now."

Adele squared her aching shoulders. "Yes, I'm strong enough," she lied. "If the council is still arguing, perhaps it's best if we get the hell out of the way and get back to our journey. Did you manage to do what we talked about?"

Jordansson pulled a scroll that had been folded in half out of his back pocket. "I found the map of the Dragon Hunters," he said, grinning. "It wasn't hidden very well."

"You stole it from your mother?" Adele was impressed that Jordansson had kept his word to her.

"I will take you to the dragon, Queen Adelena," said Jordansson. "And you will keep your promise to me too."

Adele nodded. "Before we get started, how can we be sure that the dragon we're going to find is really Sighmere? There are legends about him, but no one in Unisia knows for sure."

Jordan winced at her question. "Yes, this is the dragon we speak of now, but please do not say his name because it will anger the great god Dahk'hani."

"Why?" asked Adele. Anything that Dahk'hani didn't like made her suspicious.

Jordan shrugged. "It is said that the dragon and Dahk'hani were once involved in a great battle, and each one came close to defeating the other, but they were both wounded and still hate each other."

"That's an interesting bit of information," said Adele to Ohrig. "So while I search for one, the other visits me in my dreams. That can't be a coincidence." Ohrig only frowned more deeply. "When will anything ever be simple?" groaned Adele. "Every time we turn around, this journey just keeps getting more complicated."

"Maybe you *are* cursed," chuckled Jordansson, but Adele didn't think that was very funny.

"Will the chieftess come after us when she finds that the map is gone?" Adele asked Jordansson.

"I left a copy that I made," said Jordansson with a wink. "It will trick her."

"Jordansson said that, according to the map, the journey should only take two days," Ohrig told Adele. "Hopefully, bringing a gift of dragon's blood will smooth things over when we come back this way."

"Sure." Adele felt a hot flash of anger. "And I'll just add blood to the shopping list of what I need to take from a mighty dragon, will I?"

Ohrig found Adele's foot under the covers and gave it a squeeze. The gesture calmed her as much as his rare smile. "We are so close now, Your Majesty," Ohrig said. "You've brought us further than anyone thought possible. Just a few more days trudging through the mountains, and then we'll have the cure for Stella. Easy."

QG Leith laughed, making everyone in the room look at him. "Yep." The young QG grinned at his queen. "Sounds like a piece of cake, Your Majesty."

"Ah-ha," chuckled Jordansson as he pushed himself off his knees and made his way to the door. "I said the trip would be short. I did not say it would be easy, did I?"

Adele groaned and fell back onto her pillows.

"Come on, troops, there's no time like the present," said Ohrig with his usual gruffness. "Get dressed, Your Majesty, and we'll be out of here before dawn. I'll give you ten minutes."

CHAPTER THIRTY-NINE
"The Longest Road to Hell"

The journey to Concordis was slow and painful for Rainere. They had to take the back ways, through small towns and between hedgerows so as not to be noticed, and that took time that he could only fill with imagining the nightmares befalling Natalie and Aaron.

Benjamin was silent as they traveled, but Ripenzo Shale couldn't stop talking. The man seemed determined to fill Rainere in on all that had happened between himself and Adelena in Sandar and their history together. Rainere fought not to show any emotion when Ripenzo revealed that Adelena had killed the Sandarian mage in a blood ceremony and then tricked Empress Sanda'hani into believing that Ripenzo had raped her. *Adelena has as many secrets as I do*. Rainere remembered all the opportunities she'd had to confide in him and had chosen not to.

"What do you think Adelena'll say when she finds out that her children were stolen on your watch?" asked Ripenzo. "Think she'll believe that it wasn't your fault?"

"It was my fault," muttered Rainere, pulling up the hood of his borrowed cloak as they entered the outskirts of the city. "I allowed myself to get distracted trying to find who arranged her assassination, so I wasn't with the children when they were taken. High Wizard Ohren saw to that."

"Someone else in the Golden Palace is trying to kill Adelena?" Ripenzo chuckled, then laughed out loud at Rainere's glare. "Admit it, she is a magnet for trouble, that one."

Rainere turned in his saddle, ready to lash out at this irritating man. "I do not find the threat to Her Majesty's life amusing at all," he said. "The fact that you do strikes me as very suspicious."

"Well, maybe I'm just not as serious as you are, Prince Rainere," said Ripenzo. He winked, his eye flashing in the sunlight. In that moment Rainere could see that Ripenzo didn't just have a circle of magic around his pupils—the entire iris was gold, and the indigo was just a disguise. Rainere blinked in surprise.

Benjamin coughed. "Gents, there's someone on horseback ahead. I think they're coming for us." He frowned and looked around the quiet road, muttering, "Charlie's a slum kid, so I bet he guessed I'd take you this way."

The rider was a young boy on a skinny pony. His black hair was tied back in a messy braid, and his jeans were torn through both knees. The boy slowed when he spotted their group and checked a piece of paper at his waist.

"Hi there!" called Ripenzo. "You lost, kid?"

"I'm looking for friends of Charlie," the boy called back. "You friends?"

"Sure are," smiled Rip and pulled his horse up alongside the boy. "What's your name, kid?"

"Piss off," said the boy. He screwed up his face as if he meant to spit. "Charlie said you'd pay me for this, and then more after."

Ripenzo Shale pulled a silver coin from his pocket. "Right you are, Piss Off."

Rip flicked the coin through the air, and the kid caught it without seeming to even look at it. Then the boy sat upright in his saddle, and his eyes glowed with a soft green light.

"You have to come now," said the boy in a voice that sounded like Charlie speaking through a tunnel. "The Boss has the kids in the cellars under his pub, but they're being moved tonight. I saw our kids go in and not come out, so I think they're down there too. They are still alive. I repeat, for fuck's sake, come here now."

The young boy blinked and shuddered at the end of the message. He was pale beneath the dirt on his cheeks. "That spell'll cost ya," he rasped. "Another silver bit, right?"

Rip tossed the kid another coin, and the three of them watched the boy turn and race away through the fields on his pony.

"We need disguises and to get rid of these horses if we're going into the heart of the slums," said Benjamin. "The Boss'll get word straightaway if there are three well-dressed gents walking around the Lower Districts looking lost. I've got an idea, if you'll trust me."

Rainere's lip curled at the idea but Rip quickly agreed. Their horses picked up the pace, though Benjamin warned they were still at least half an hour away from their destination.

Rip started humming in a broken chant, which Rainere found even more irritating than his chatter.

"You told me that you are related to Adelena's children," Rainere said, interrupting Rip's next song. "How?"

"It's complicated," said Ripenzo, and he turned his eyes to the road to hide his expression. "When I first heard that Adelena was here in Unisia, I didn't want to get involved. I've got things to do in this world too, you know." Rip sighed heavily. "But then I got curious and arranged to meet her and the kids through my situation in Sandar. From the minute I saw her, I could tell that Adelena was completely vulnerable and stupid, and that was when I realized that I couldn't stay out of the way any longer. She can find trouble under every rock in this world, and she has no idea at all of how she is being used by those St. Lucidis wizards. Goddess in heaven! I couldn't believe it when I saw her on the edge of the tundra and she told me that the high wizard had actually sent her to stay at Belvoir Estate and also that her baby had almost died from the influenza. That should never have been allowed to happen!"

"Why didn't you tell me at the beginning that you'd seen Queen Adelena recently?" Rainere rode up next to Shale and tried to grab the reins of Shale's horse, desperate for news. "Is she all right?"

"Easy, tiger," Ripenzo said, and his chuckle returned. "I saw Adelena on the other side of the Black Mountains with her motley crew of guards." He threw Rainere a sideways glance. "She told me that she had sent Charlie back with you to the Golden Palace and how much trouble her kids were in. So, I thought it was time I faced my responsibilities and came back to watch over them."

Rainere stiffened in the saddle. "Did Her Majesty ask you to check up on me?"

"Nope," said Ripenzo. "I knew you would need me, though. None of those bloody St. Lucidis wizards can be trusted for long."

Rainere didn't know what to say to that, so he stopped asking questions and let Ripenzo return to his incessant humming. The time stretched as they rode past the outlying farms and fields of Concordis, finally coming to a turn in the road where they passed under a rusty metal archway. "We're here," announced the stable hand.

Benjamin had led them to a community of buildings perched on the side of the riverbank like a genteel shantytown. Though the houses were built from blackened wood and rusted metal, they each stood at least two stories high and looked solid enough. Some of the windows were even decorated with flower boxes, and each dwelling had a clean front step, though it was surrounded by muddy yard. A long barn had been built next to the homes and by the smell was clearly a working stable.

"This is the Second City Stables, where most of the nearby public houses board their horses," said Benjamin. "We can leave our horses here while we travel into town on foot, which'll be safer than riding through the slums. Beautiful horses like this will attract too much attention for us."

A man came out of the stables, wiping his hands on a rag that he shoved in his back pocket as he approached them. He was tall, with cropped black hair, and was wearing coveralls with patches on the knees and bib.

"What's all this, Ben?" said the man, his mouth tucked in a sour line. He squinted at the royal stable hand and then up at Ripenzo and Rainere. "You in some kinda trouble?"

Benjamin dismounted. He was slightly taller, but he hunched in front of the older man. "Nah, Dad, I'm just helping out some friends," he said. "We need to leave the horses here for a day or so, and it'd be good if no one found out where they came from."

Benjamin's father ran his hand over the neck of Rainere's horse, Titor. "Bit hard to hide this sort of breeding, Ben," he said. "He's a beauty, aren't you, love?" This last he directed at Titor as the horse nuzzled his hands.

"Dad, we also need to borrow some clothes," said Benjamin, gesturing at the house nearest to the barn. "Has Mum done the washing this week?"

"Your mum's always washing," said his dad, then nodded at Rainere. "That fella's a bit taller'n me, but I should have some coveralls that'll fit. The other guy'll be easy. You mind telling me why I'm giving board and clothes away with no talk of recompense?"

Ripenzo stepped forward. "Sir, thank you for your help this afternoon. Please rest assured you'll be paid fully for your services." He held out his hand to shake. "This is a nice place you've got here."

Benjamin's father looked at Ripenzo as if he was touched in the head and ignored the proffered hand. "Take these horses to the back of the stables and put them in stalls twenty through twenty-two. They've just been mucked out, but you'll have to give them the feed yourself."

Benjamin nodded with a grunt of thanks. "This way," he said to Rainere and Ripenzo, pointing to the stables.

"Ben," his father called out. "When are you gonna come back to work? We could do with another hand around here."

Benjamin hunched his shoulders tighter, and his handsome face fell. "I told you, Dad, I work at the Golden Palace now. It's full-time in the stables there."

"Sure you do," said his dad, derisively. "Last week, you told your mum you had a job at Belvoir Estate as a guard. That didn't last long, did it?"

Benjamin flushed with anger and continued walking away from his dad.

"Family, eh?" said Ripenzo sympathetically and gave Benjamin a clap on the shoulder. "They're never happy for you, are they?"

Benjamin only shook his head, embarrassed, and led them into the stables.

Chapter Forty
"The Magician's Wand"

They were ready within the hour, and Benjamin organized a ride to the edge of the slums on the back of an open feed wagon filled with sun-warmed hay.

Feeling supremely awkward, Rainere was dressed in old coveralls that smelled like soap and horse. He filled out the shoulders so much that he couldn't do up the buttons over his chest and so had to wear a vest that had seen better days underneath. Benjamin had said that Rainere's severe haircut was helpful because it made him look like he'd just got out of prison, and the irony of that wasn't lost on Rainere. He'd shaved his head two weeks ago to dissociate himself from his royal Marchant heritage, and now he looked like every other Marchant laborer in the Lower Districts.

However, it wasn't the clothes that bothered him as much as the thin metal band on his wrist. The charm it carried made his skin feel itchy and tight while it disguised his features, making his nose less prominent and his brow a little heavier and dusting his clean-shaven chin with a dark five o'clock shadow.

"I'm just saying," said Ripenzo to Rainere as they made their way onto a main thoroughfare. "Try to blend in a little. You're still walking like a prince when you should be walking like a stable hand at the end of a long shift."

Rainere slid his hands into his pockets and dropped his head to soften his usual ramrod posture, and it annoyed him when Rip laughed anyway.

Rip had shoved an old denim cap over his blond hair and rolled up the sleeves of his coveralls to show a few tattoos that would, hopefully, inspire any street magician to walk the other way. He said they were temporary ink, but Rainere thought he saw the patterns flicker and shift when he was nearby.

The three men kept close together while Benjamin took them through the narrow streets into the slums proper and then into the rough area where Rainere had been before when they'd been searching for a portal to Prince Rainold's prison dimension. The sun was setting, and the odor in the streets was of hot garbage and cat urine mixed with cooking smells from the restaurants that had begun to open for the dinnertime trade.

The streets were busy with ragged children darting around the groups of men and women all dressed in the dull uniforms of their trades, heading either home or out to spend their hard-earned coin. Turning another street corner, Rip, Rainere, and Benjamin found themselves on a wide promenade lined with pubs, clubs, and several tall buildings with red shutters on the windows. A few of the shutters were already open, and barely dressed women and young men were hanging over the windowsills, calling out to passersby who might be in need of an early evening diversion. Rainere couldn't take his eyes off a particular young woman leaning out of a second-story window. No more than a girl, she was wearing a long black wig and a violet dress that was cut to expose much of her breasts.

"Just call me Queen Adelena, baby," she was shouting to a passing group of men. "I'll lie on my back if you can show me your Marchant magic!"

"I've got my Marchant magic right here, love," shouted back one of the men and grabbed between his legs to the raucous laughter of his friends and the prostitute.

Rainere felt his blood boil at the insult to Adelena's honor. *Yet these peasants would have no cause to ridicule her if it hadn't been for me,* he thought, and guilt mixed with his anger. *Our relationship has been so detrimental to her rule.* The knowledge that she would be better off without him in her life suddenly hammered home to Rainere.

"We should talk," said Ripenzo suddenly, and Rainere threw him a ferocious glare, wanting to keep his thoughts to himself. "To each other, I mean," added Ripenzo with an eye roll. "It looks strange to see three guys walking together after work and not having a laugh. Ben, come on, he won't bite—ask our Marchant friend here a question."

The stable hand, normally so cocksure and proud, was now hunched and nervous. Benjamin gave Rainere a quick glance. "What should I call you when we're inside?" he asked. "I don't want to be disrespectful, sir, but using your title would give us away pretty quickly."

Rainere thought a moment. "Gray," he said.

"Gray? That's not a name, it's a color," said Ripenzo, smiling at group of pretty ladies waiting outside a cafe and jovially waving away their invitation to join them.

"It's one of my middle names," said Rainere. "And I'll react quickly if I hear it."

"Right, well, we're almost there," said Benjamin. "The pub the Boss works out of is at the end of this street."

They were approaching a large and noisy public house. The sign hanging over the door proclaimed the establishment The Magician's Wand and had a picture of a magician holding his robes up, his pants down around his ankles.

Rip squinted, "Is the magician in the picture holding his own—?" But Benjamin gestured, and they all ducked down an alleyway.

"The Magician's Wand is where the Boss holds court," whispered Benjamin. "I'm not known here, and neither are you, so we might get clocked for that. It's better to go in, claim a table, and order drinks like we have business there. We've got to hear if the Boss is at home or if he's left town already."

"This is pointless," growled Rainere. "We don't need to buy drinks if we just walk in there, kill everything that moves, and then go downstairs to find the children."

"As cheerful as I am about killing a load of innocent people, which I'm not, Charlie's note said we will find the kids in the cellars below this place," Ripenzo reminded him. "But because we don't know where that is, exactly, we'll need to scout it out. We should be prepared for any magical protections on the place. You'll be in charge of any green magic that comes flying our way, Gray, and I can handle the rest. If anyone of us sees the Boss, then try to keep your head down and tell the others. If Charlie is right and Ohren really is the Boss, then we'll have a hell of a fight on our hands tonight."

"This still is a terrible plan," protested Rainere. "I simply don't see why we need to walk in together. I should scout the building and sneak in through the back door while you two cause a disturbance in the bar."

"Causing a disturbance in this bar will get us killed," said Benjamin, with a nod at the four bouncers standing at the pub's front door. "And there is no back entrance to this place. It's just the front. The back is—well, I don't know where the back is, but there just isn't one."

"Keep your eyes open for Charlie, too," said Rip as they moved out of the alleyway and began walking toward the pub. "If he hasn't been caught out already."

The bouncers on the door barely spared Ripenzo Shale a glance as he slipped through, but one of them put a hand out to stop Rainere midstride. "No spells, no charms," the bouncer warned him, looking the prince up and down. "I see you with one spark of green magic, and I kick your arse from here to the Gray Palace. You got me, Green Blood?"

Rainere made to answer with a threat of his own but felt himself none too gently pushed from behind by Benjamin and straight into the noisy front bar of the public house.

The room was wide and spacious and filled with hundreds of people. There was a bar running down the long side of the room, with a set of double stable doors leading to the kitchen next to it. On the wall behind the bar were shelves fully stocked with bottles of various narcotic beverages, and in the center of the room was a large, square area filled with bench tables and dotted with smaller circular tables. A haze of smoke rested above the din like a cloud, and the place smelled of beer and unwashed bodies.

Rainere had never seen so many commoners all together in one place, and he was ashamed to feel a little overwhelmed by the noise and the sensation of being touched by strangers all around him.

Ripenzo headed for a table at the side of the room furthest from the bar, and the others followed him. A man was already sitting at the table when Rainere and Benjamin arrived.

"This table's taken," said the seated man, sneering at Ripenzo. "Piss off."

"It's taken by us," snarled Ripenzo as he planted his fists on the stained wood and leaned across the table. Rainere almost didn't recognize the cheerful Rip with his face contorted by a look of dumb violence. "Move it."

The man seemed to crumple, all his bravado leaking away when he caught sight of Rainere glowering at him over Rip's head. He grabbed his bottle of beer and quickly left.

As soon as the three of them were seated, a server appeared and took their drinks order. When he left, Ripenzo announced he was going to find Charlie, and left Rainere and Benjamin alone to scope out the crowd. Foaming mugs of beer arrived almost immediately, and Rainere took a long sip.

"It's not…unpleasant." Rainere took another sip.

"You've never had beer before?" Benjamin was surprised enough to ask, swinging his glance away from studying the room.

Rainere shook his head. "Nor have I ever been to a public house such as this," he said. "It's disgusting in here, but there is a certain quality to the atmosphere that feels lively and potentially lawless." He scanned the room again, his eyebrow raised. "I suppose that's what these peasants are seeking after a day of labor."

"Yeah, sure," agreed Benjamin, his own eyebrow raised sharply at the prince. "Us peasants like a bit of lively lawlessness after working all day."

"There's Charlie!" said Rainere. He stood up suddenly, surprising a man who had been carrying two mugs of beer on his way past their table. The man tipped his beer down the front of himself and quickly turned on Rainere.

"Oi!" he shouted, pushing his beer-soaked chest into Rainere's. "You owe me two beers." Rainere stepped back, but the man followed his movement. "I said, you need to buy me two beers, darlin', or you're getting my foot up your arse."

Rainere pushed into his assailant, sliding the man's feet backward a couple of inches along the wet floorboards. "Try it," he hissed, letting the magic spark in his eyes. "Please."

"There you go, mate," Benjamin interrupted and shoved his hand in the man's face, showing him a couple of coins. "That's for the beers and your trouble. I'll sit my friend down again before we have the bouncers over here, you got me?"

The man looked from the money to Rainere's eager gaze and snatched the coins out of Benjamin's hand. He made a few disparaging comments about Rainere's genitalia and then retreated back through the crowd.

Charlie slipped into a seat at the table just as Rainere and Benjamin sat back down. "Is this it?" Charlie said by way of greeting. "You're the fucking army come to save the kids?"

"We are all that's needed," snapped Rainere. "Now report."

Charlie was white as a sheet and sweat stained the underarms of his blue shirt. He'd tied his coat around his waist and mussed up his hair so that it stood up in tufts on his head. "Here's my report: We're fucked," he said, grabbing one of the beers. He took a hearty slug before slamming it back down on the table. "She is going to kill us all in terrible ways when she finds out her kids got taken on our watch." Charlie wiped his mouth and stared off into the horror of his invisible future. "She won't listen to our excuses. She'll just tear bits off us and drag the magic right out of our bones."

"Charlie, calm down, mate." Benjamin looked nervously at Rainere as the prince's temper clearly sparked in his eyes. "You sent a note that the kids are somewhere underground. Where?"

"That's just it," said Charlie. "I followed Pere Raven and the Rangers to this pub. They were carrying the kids in sacks over their shoulders. I saw them go through the kitchen doors, but when I went back there, I just thought they'd gone down to the basement." He took another gulp of beer. "So I decided to send you fellas a message. I ran out, found a curse carrier, and sent him to you. When I tried to get back through the kitchen and down to the basement, it had gone."

"What had gone?" Rainere hissed. "Be clear, boy."

"The basement," said Charlie, his eyes wide with fear. "The basement was gone, and so were the kids."

Chapter Forty-One
"Ever Onward and Upward"

It was still dark as Adelena shouldered her pack and put her hand on Ohrig's arm to steady herself.

"Quiet now," whispered Jordansson. "Make no noise."

The seven of them slipped through the village in near darkness and followed Jordansson to a path that took them along the outside of the village and up a winding road into the second of the three valleys. In the dark Adele kept getting startled by the noise of bells, but it was only the small goats that dotted the valley floor.

The group trekked as hard as they could until dawn and had made it high up onto the side of the valley before they took a much-needed break. Despite her thumping headache and sore body, Adelena couldn't help but be struck by the beauty of the sun rising over the mountains. The green hills blended into gray rock, and everything was bathed in an almost celestial glow.

"Beautiful, yes?" Jordansson had dropped back to walk beside Adele.

"It's amazing," said Adele. "On a morning like this, you can certainly believe that this country really was created by the gods."

"And it was," said Jordansson. "When the gods walked the world of Evendaar, Dahk'hani, the volcano god, made this land of ice and snow as a balm for his fires below the earth. Some of his tribesmen didn't like this cold, so they followed the mountain range and traveled to the lands of water—what you call Sandar. The other tribes learned to live in the snow, hunting the animals that Dahk'hani made for our food and using the magic he gave us to honor him. He gave each tribe a chieftess or chief to govern the people, and he gave us the blessing that allows us to make children."

"Tell me more about the magic Dahk'hani gave you," said Adele. "What color is it?"

"The magic has no color," said Jordansson, giving Adele a look so that she understood how strange her question had been. "It is magic and is strength inside of us, here." He pointed to his heart. "Some are born with more than others, but all of Dahk'hani's people are born with magic. It is used for hunting, food gathering, building, protection, and to charm a mate to your bed."

"Why do you have tattoos?" asked Adele. "Who drew them on you?"

"Each marking is a spell for strength and hunting skills," said Jordansson. "My mother, the chieftess, gave them to me as a protection."

"I didn't see anyone else except the chieftess with tattoos in your village," said Adele.

"That is because they are only for those who need them," Jordansson said. "I am small and weak. I would not have survived the trials of a young man's life without help from the dragon's magic. My mother told me since I was very young that I would always need extra magic to protect me."

Adele's interest sharpened. "Why is that?"

Jordansson shrugged and kicked a pebble along the ground. "She said that Dahk'hani would reveal his purpose for me one day and that I was to be ready. I have been waiting for a message from the great god all my life, and now I think you are that message, Queen Adelena."

Adele was too breathless to respond to Jordansson's announcement as the flat trail along the side of the valley suddenly veered up the steep side of the mountain. There was nothing Adele could say to him, anyway, and neither could she deny it. After all, it was in her own vision that the mage had told her that Dahk'hani wanted her to have a baby by a Jordan or mountain tribesman. *But that's definitely not my plan,* thought Adele. *Even if Jordansson thinks he wants me. The poor guy is just getting mixed up in all this trouble that keeps following me around Evendaar.*

The sun rose behind them and warmed their backs as the air became even thinner than before, and Adele's headache became a dull throb. Stars swam in her vision, threatening her equilibrium. Determined to make it up the mountain before she collapsed, she dug deep, spearing what little remained of her green magic into her legs to keep them going up the steep, rocky slope.

The sun had reached its zenith when they finally crested the mountain peak and stood on top of the world. Adele was in awe of the sheer magnificence of the vista before her. She dropped her heavy pack and breathed in the crystalline beauty of white-capped mountains bathed in sunshine. Behind her lay the iridescent green valleys of the Three Sisters Tribe, and before her lay the pristine, snow-covered mountainside that sloped into the next valley and another beyond that.

"There." Jordansson pointed into the distance. "That is the mountain where the map says the dragon sleeps." The tribesman had stripped down to his trousers and boots again, and the white skin of his torso was shiny with sweat. "This wind is very good, nice and cold," said Jordansson, spreading his arms out wide to catch the breeze blowing around them. "Thank you, Dahk'hani, for your mountains!" he shouted, then shouted something exuberant in his own language that made everyone chuckle, though they didn't understand it.

"So Jordansson?" Ohrig interrupted the party. "How are we going to get through these massive valleys to the dragon's mountain? To my eye there is no way this journey is only going to take two days. That looks like a week-long trek at least."

"We will *slepozana*," said Jordansson, bending his knees and elbows and bopping up and down. "Yes?"

"No." Ohrig shook his head. "We've got no idea what *slepozana* is."

Laughing as if Ohrig were teasing him, Jordansson reached into his pack and pulled out a collection of short, narrow planks of wood. He unpacked them, folding out the planks until they were about as tall as he was. He grinned. "*Slepozana*."

"Skis?" Adele didn't know why she was so surprised, but the concept of skiing just felt so out of place in this world. "You want us to ski down the mountains?"

"Yes, skis," agreed Jordansson with the one-shoulder shrug he normally gave when hearing their translations. "This is a very fast and very fun way to travel. You will like this."

With that declaration he had everyone unpack their skis and poles. Pepper started a fire with the charcoal he'd brought and made tea to have with their lunch of bread and cold cuts while Jordansson explained the basics of skiing.

Her lunch was not sitting well in her stomach as Adele wrapped her boots in the complicated strappings attached to the skis and bounced up and down, like Jordansson showed them, to get a feel for the bindings. Somewhat secure, Adele shuffled to line up next to the Queen's Guard as they all heard the last bits of advice from Jordansson. QG Bear, keen to make up for his humiliation crossing the ice bridge, was the first to volunteer to ski down the hill.

"The light here is very flat where there is no sun," warned Jordansson. "Keep your hands close to your hips, and ski to the sun—this is safest."

"But don't go straight down, right?" said Bear, frowning in concentration. "I have to try to turn in a curve, then curve again."

"Yes," said Jordansson. "Now watch me, and come and join. Follow exactly my tracks in the snow."

Jordansson settled his pack on his back, his coat and shirt tucked in the top under a strap. "Watch me!" he shouted and then, with a loud yell, slid off the edge of the plateau and down into the shadowed valley below. Owens whistled through his teeth, and Leith swore quietly as they all watched Jordansson gracefully swoop through the powdery, soft snow and turn out from the base of the slope into a line curving toward the sunlight. Once he reached the sunny area, he stopped, sending a huge spray of snow sparkling into the air. He waved his pole back up the hill as the signal for Bear to take his turn.

"Your Majesty, you'll excuse my language, please?" said Bear as he took a deep breath and lined up his jump.

"Go for it, Bear," laughed Adele. "Do your worst."

Bear shouted a curse, both terrified and exhilarated as he plunged down the slope, and almost immediately fell on his side, tumbling and rolling until he came to a stop at the base of the shadowed slope.

"That would've hurt," said Ohrig, wincing, but everyone cheered when Bear struggled to his feet, waving his poles, apparently unharmed, only to fall on his face in the snow again.

"I'll go next," suggested Adele. "I'll see if I can get to Bear and help him up."

"I'll come after you, Your Majesty," said Lucky.

Adele took a deep breath of the thin air and readjusted her pack so it was balanced on both shoulders. "Right," she said. "Off we go, then."

Adele launched herself down the hill just a little too fast. Her first instinct was to lean back to slow herself down, but she remembered Jordansson's advice and leaned forward, trying to balance on both feet, and then pressed down on one leg to turn herself slightly uphill. Nervous, she flailed with her poles and almost caught the ground coming around in a curve, but thankfully regained her balance once more. Adele could see Bear in the distance and made a beeline for the pile of snow he was churning trying to dig himself out.

Adele managed to pull up in a clumsy stop and almost got the pointy end of a pole in the face from the QG. "Bear, I'm here," she said. "I'll try to help you up."

"Your Majesty!" Bear looked comically surprised at Adele's appearance. He had snow in his hair and on his eyebrows, and she couldn't help but laugh.

"No, no way, not this time!" The big man shook his head and kept struggling in the soft snow. "I'll not have my queen drag my useless arse out of trouble a second time."

Adele looked up the hill as Lucky came careening down toward the two of them. He came to his own clumsy stop by throwing himself at the ground, but the captain was smart enough to allow

Adele to help him up out of the snow, and then Lucky managed to lever Bear back upright on his skis.

"Let's get down to Jordansson," said Adele. She waved at the tribesman as he waved up at them. Adele took off again, finding the slope much gentler here, and it really was easier to ski in the sunshine than the shade because she could see all the bumps and divots in the surface of the snow.

Pleased that she only fell over once on her way to Jordansson, Adele looked behind herself and was very amused to see her Queen's Guard dotted all over the mountainside, either in a pile of snow or slowly making their way in wobbly curves.

"You did this *slepozana* before," said Jordansson, giving Adele an admiring smile. "I can tell you know how to lean away from the mountain instead of into it."

Adele leaned on her poles, which she'd planted in the ground, and got her breath back. "Well, I did spend a couple of winters in the snow when I was a teenager," she said. "I loved it, but I didn't know if I would remember how to ski, and this equipment is not at all what we had on Earth. These are very strange boots to wear while being tied to wooden skis."

"This is good," said Jordansson and wrapped his arm around Adele's shoulders, planting a quick kiss on her head. "This will be very fun for you and me." He looked back to the flailing Queen's Guard. "This will not be so good for your men. Lucky will be very angry that I am better at this than him. He does not like me very much, and now he will hate me more." He looked at Adele for her opinion on the matter.

"Lucky is very protective of me as his queen," said Adele, not wanting to be disloyal to her man, and leaned out of Jordansson's embrace. "He takes his duty very seriously. I think he sees you as someone who might distract me on our journey, that's all."

"And do I distract you?" asked Jordansson, but there was something about the way he held his mouth that made Adele feel he was looking for a proper answer and not a joke in return.

"I refuse to be distracted," said Adele, carefully choosing her words. "I am here for my daughter Stella. If I didn't need to find a dragon for her cure, then I wouldn't be here. I would leave the dragon alone, and I would leave your people alone."

"The great god Dahk'hani brought me to you for a reason, I think," said Jordansson. He put his hand on Adele's back so she would look him in the eye. "In the ceremony of the blood, I had a vision that a bear with a heart of magic waited for me on the Boorenhurdstl, or tundra. In the dream I took my spear and knife and ran at the bear, but it stood up, and I was very afraid. Then it handed me a"—Jordansson gestured with his hands—"a gold hat with no middle."

"A crown," suggested Adele.

"Yes, this crown," said Jordansson. "He gave me the crown and then gave me his heart of magic. I had never felt such joy as when I held that magic in my hand. I felt my heart flying and music in my whole body. I was happy." Jordansson shuffled over to Adele, and she knew what was coming. "Like when I kissed you that night in the cave, I felt the same way as I had in my vision," he said. "My heart danced, and I heard that music again. I think it is a sign from Dahk'hani that we should be together as man and woman."

Adele bit her bottom lip. "I have learned not to trust the gods of this world, Jordansson," she said. "Let's see what Dahk'hani wants in exchange for this 'gift' of his."

"What gift?" asked Jordansson, confused. "The crown is you, and the magic heart is what we could have together—love."

"No, Jordansson, it's not love, it's magic," said Adele, trying not to sound bitter. "You are the gift, not me." He smiled, not understanding at all, and Adele didn't have the heart to break his.

Chapter Forty-Two
"At the Top of the World"

Jordansson set a fast pace for the beginner skiers, but Adele was pleased to see her younger QGs pick up the basics quickly. Ohrig, Bear, and Owens took more time and slowed down the group considerably. It was late afternoon when they came to the end of their skiing lesson.

Jordansson had consulted his map and pointed up the side of the valley to where he said there would be a collection of caves where they could spend the night under cover.

It was exhausting climbing uphill after hours of skiing on shaking legs, but everyone agreed it was far less nerve-wracking.

They made the high caves just as the sun had crested the mountains on the opposite wall of the valley. The cave that Jordansson had chosen was nice and wide, with a hole in the ceiling just perfect as a chimney for their fire. Remains of old blankets and a pile of dry wood showed that this was an infrequently used hunters' lodge.

The fire was started and camp set up just as darkness fell. Pepper prepared the dinner, and Owens and Bear sat groaning by the fire, comparing bruises and insisting that Captain Lucky doctor their potential sprains and muscle tears. Ohrig medicated his own pain with a slug of Firewhiskey and his usual stoicism. Pepper and Leith had delighted themselves with picking up skiing so well, and Jordansson promised to show them some more advanced tricks the next day.

Exhausted, Adele sat by the fire, drifting in and out of the various conversations, when the Chime Voices started singing very suddenly and very loudly. Then they stopped, then started again in a weird staccato song. A strange energy flooded her fatigued body, and Adele left the cave to go stand on the landing outside, hoping the cold air would clear her senses.

The darkness around her seemed absolute, but as soon as her eyes adjusted, she looked up to see the lights of a thousand stars blanketing the sky. A familiar scent tickled Adele's nose, and off away to her right, she spotted a tiny glowing ember floating in midair.

"My apologies, Your Majesty," grunted Ohrig, who came closer, carrying the little orange ember with him. "I brought a smoke with me in case there was an emergency. Today was it. I've never in my life had to do that *slepozana*, and I won't lie—I thought I was going to die."

Adele chuckled. "Don't worry, Ohrig. You earned that cigarette." She breathed deeply, letting the fragrant smoke fill her nose, but shook her head when Ohrig offered her a puff. "I don't need another vice," she said. "Mine are dangerous enough."

Adele smiled when she heard Ohrig's dry chuckle, though she couldn't quite see his face in the dark. Then Captain Lucky came out to join them, carrying three tin cups of tea and a smoky torch. They moved away from the mouth of the cave and over to a trio of uncomfortable boulders to sit down. Ohrig drew in the last of his precious tabac and stubbed out his smoke in the dirt. Captain Lucky stared up at the sky and then glanced at Ohrig. He coughed, clearly signaling to the general to say something.

Ohrig didn't reply, but Adele felt the weight of his thoughts hang in the darkness. She sighed. "Ohrig, just ask me whatever it is you and Lucky have been talking about today," she said. "It's driving me nuts, you waiting for the right time to say what's on your mind."

"All right, Your Majesty, I'll be honest: we don't think you look good," Ohrig said and winced when Adele jabbed him in the ribs at the insult, but continued on. "I know you've got yourself fooled, and I'll agree you did well on the *slepozana* today, but you are not yourself, by a long shot. Your black eye isn't healing despite the rest you've had, your hands shake, and your cheeks are almost gray. Whatever you smoked in that blood ceremony did you no good, and it's clear you don't want to admit it, but we all know what you should do tonight." He took a deep breath, clearly uncomfortable with what he was about to say next. "You should see if Jordansson can give you what you need."

"You are talking about taking his magic, Ohrig," said Adele flatly. "You're talking about me stealing his strength and making him weaker to make myself stronger."

Ohrig's silhouette showed him leaning forward, elbows planted on his knees. "But he's a young man with a lot of strength," he said, "and you are tiny and exhausted, with a long journey ahead of you."

Adele bit her lip and chewed this over. "Would you do it?" she asked finally. "Would you sacrifice someone else's strength for your own purposes, Ohrig?"

"Yes," he answered quietly, "if I thought he wanted to give it to me out of love and then I would have the strength to save my daughter."

Adele did not like the way this conversation was heading. "I might be a demon, Ohrig, but I know it's wrong to trick someone who has feelings for you."

"That's the truth, Queen Adelena," replied Ohrig. "But if it means the difference between your strength and his, I would take it from him myself to give you. So I'm telling you to do this."

Adele couldn't stand it. Frustration and exhaustion made her hands shake even harder, but her magics only responded weakly to the flurry of emotions. "I am not a monster, Ohrig," she spat. "Don't ask me to act like one."

"That man will do it willingly for you, Your Majesty," insisted Ohrig. "It doesn't make you a monster to let him."

Adele turned to Captain Lucky, glaring at him through the darkness. "And do you agree with the general, Lucky?"

"Your Majesty, I won't mince my words," said Lucky. "The general has made me aware of your situation and your special *needs* concerning magic. I have some knowledge of the study of magical power, and as you know, I have a decent amount of strength in my own St. Lucidis strain of gold magic."

Adele froze and not just from the cold. "Do all the men know about my 'needs'?"

"No, Your Majesty, the general and I have kept it between ourselves," Lucky reassured her quickly. "But we have all noticed your worsening condition and the faded color of the magic in your eyes."

Adele raised her hand to her eyes, though she couldn't touch them.

"However." Lucky coughed, glancing across at Ohrig. "Unlike the general, I do not believe that Jordansson is the right candidate for you. We have no idea of the quality or nature of his magic, which, as we can both see, isn't green or gold. I know you have moral objections to becoming involved with the tribesman, but I too have a practical objection: we just don't know what he'll do to you." He coughed again. "So I would like to offer myself to you as a source of magic to re-fuel you."

"Re-fuel me." Adele felt like crying. "Lucky, no."

"Your Majesty, I think Lucky presents a good alternative if you are determined not to touch Jordansson," said Ohrig, and clapped the captain on the shoulder. "For one thing, you know you can trust him; for another, he is just as young and strong enough to take whatever you would need to do."

Adele realized she had just been neatly outmaneuvered by her general. Ohrig had purposefully made her admit she wouldn't touch Jordansson and now he threw Lucky in her path, giving her little room to refuse him by the same arguments. *I have to stop this madness before I actually give into the temptation.*

"Lucky, do you know how a demon takes the magic out of a man?" said Adele, unable to keep the tremble from her voice. "Do you have any idea *at all* of what I could do to you if I lost control?"

Only half of Lucky's face was lit by the light of the torch, but Adele saw his determination in the set of his finely chiseled jaw. "My queen, you are not the only one who had a vision in the blood burning ceremony," said Lucky. "In my dream I saw you lost in a vast land, lying in the snow. You were so still and so very near death, and I was terribly afraid but then I heard the *actual* voice of the goddess Serena telling me to worship you and give you back your life. Light and music filled my soul, singing with righteous joy, and

I knew that we were blessed by the goddess." He reached out to touch Adele's arm but stopped just short. "Your Majesty, whatever you need to do to me, I am not afraid."

"No, but I am," whispered Adele, shaking even harder as adrenaline raced through her blood and the excited Chime Voices urged her to find out what the handsome, young captain would taste like. She ignored them, clenching her fists against the rush of lust. "Lucky, if it was easy I would be happy to take you... but the magic is wild, and I find it very hard to control. Intimacy is a big part of it. My magics want everything another body can give, physically as well as magically."

"Oh, you mean, sex?" said Lucky. He coughed and glanced at the general again, losing a little of his confidence. "Well, still, I will do what is necessary to keep you well, Your Majesty, no matter the price."

Adele shook her head trying to dislodge the Chime Voices's urgent song. "I know you have a strict moral code and I refuse to take advantage of your duty like that, Lucky," she said. "I just couldn't."

"Your Majesty, let's stop playing around! Captain Lucky is a healthy, young man," huffed Ohrig, frustrated. "He'll be happy to get over his moral qualms if it means he has served his queen."

Adele didn't hear Lucky's reply because right at that moment the Chime Voices screamed, and the sky exploded. She fell to her knees as her head filled with a song so heavy and so powerful that she couldn't hold it up any longer.

"Your Majesty, can you hear me?" Lucky shouted as he wrapped his arms around her shoulders. "We need to get her back into the cave," he said to someone else.

"Then pick her up, man," shouted another voice.

"I can't." Lucky's breath was hot on Adele's ear. "She keeps slipping. I think there's some magic protection on her so I can't get a grip. Get Jordansson now!"

Then the song changed, and Adele could raise her head again.

"Goddess, look at her eyes!"

Jordansson was there next to her. In the light of the exploding stars, he glowed blue, his tattoos writhing and flowing across his skin, sparking darkly. "Queen Adelena." He pulled her up to her feet, and Adele saw his magic meshing with hers where they touched. "This is the Aurora Gottessteppen, the Path of the Goddess." Even Jordansson's voice danced, the words twining with the song of the Chime Voices. "Every year it shines, lighting the sky with the magic of the goddess and flowing across the sky like water. Our people believe that it brings fresh magic to the world. Look up at it, take it in."

Adele clung to Jordansson's hands and looked up. The night sky above her was bathed in clouds of violet and green lights. Rivers of green magic, blended with waterfalls of gold and waves of blue magic. Stars exploded between the clouds of magic, and the inky black sky opened with dozens of different portal doorways.

Adele was lifted from the ground. Her feet weren't dangling but instead standing on solid air, as if she stood on the palm of a god. *Dahk'hani!* She had to escape his clutches, so Adele reached up her hands and whispered the powerful chant of the Chime Voices to the sky. "Home, mother," she begged. "Give me the power to take me home." A vision of a place like an oasis in a desert flashed into her mind. Adele was bewildered. *I don't want to go to a desert—I want my family!*

Adele felt herself propelled higher into the air, and a lightning bolt of gold fire arced through the sky and struck her. Vines of green and silver light snaked down the bolt of energy and joined it. Adele felt herself burst into flames as the wild and savage magic lanced every cell in her body, electrifying her.

Then it was over.

Adele dropped from the sky and landed gently back on the earth. She took a deep breath, and her lungs filled with clean, cold air. She watched as the clouds of magical chaos floated away across the heavens and over the mountains like a giant ship.

"Well, that was something," Adele croaked. She turned to face her Queen's Guard. They were all staring at her, their expressions filled with shock and fear in the way that she was coming to hate.

She led the way back into the cave and dropped by the fire to warm her hands.

"Your Majesty," said Ohrig. He sat next to Adele, not taking his gaze off her. "What the hell just happened?"

Adele rolled her shoulders but felt no pain. She put her hand to her eye, and the swelling of the bruise had gone. "I feel like I've got my strength back," murmured Adele as she felt for her other bruises, now gone too.

"You look unreal," said Ohrig, but it didn't sound like a compliment. "I mean, you're almost glowing and the magic is spinning in your eyes silver and gold, but really fast. I'm not sure it's supposed to do that."

"I feel better than I have since I last invaded a wizard." Adele hesitated to use the word "fed,"—it was too animal. "Even that ice bear didn't make me feel like this."

"It's the magic of the goddess Serena," said Jordansson reverentially. "I have never heard of any chieftess or human being able to drink directly from the source of the goddess herself. I saw the presence of Dahk'hani tonight. He was here, with us, holding the queen up in his hands."

"You saw the god Dahk'hani?" Adele's voice was sharp as she turned her gaze to the tribesman where he paced by the fire, almost hopping with excitement. "I did feel something carry me into the sky up to the magic clouds, and I know I can't fly by myself."

"You were singing too, Your Majesty," said Lucky. "It was in the old tongue, but I caught the words 'home' and 'mother.'"

"That was a song of the Chime Voices," said Adele.

"The what voices?" Jordansson asked.

"Nothing," Adele stretched her arms above her head and felt Ohrig flinch next to her. She rolled her eyes at him. "Ohrig, I'm not going to hurt you. I feel totally normal now, I promise."

"But you even smell good," said Ohrig accusingly. "Not unwashed and sweaty, but with some kind of perfume."

Adele sniffed her arm. "I can't smell it," she said.

"It's like flowers and fresh rain and sunshine and whiskey..." QG Pepper trailed off, embarrassed, as everyone turned to stare at him.

"I still feel cheated that it was Dahk'hani who must've helped me get this magic back," said Adele with a frown. "He's sure to want something in return, and I know I won't like it."

Everyone was silent, thinking their own thoughts and staring at the fire. Ohrig was the first to clear his throat.

"We should get some rest," said the general. "Anyone who cannot get cosmically recharged by the sky should get out their bedrolls and try to sleep."

"There is no way I can sleep now so I'll stay up for the first watch," suggested Adele.

"We should leave someone with you in case your friend Dahk'hani shows up and tries to take you away again," said Ohrig, and Adele finally saw her general's real fear. He had thought she was being taken away when she was lifted into the sky, and he'd been helpless to do a single thing to stop it.

"I will stay up with the queen," offered Jordansson. "I have many questions, and I am too excited to sleep as well." He laughed as he planted himself by the fire, shaking his head. "You must all be so used to your queen being this amazing, but I have never seen such a thing as tonight."

Lucky opened his mouth to protest, but Ohrig gave him a shove. "Bed, Captain," he instructed. "There isn't much we can do to protect her if a god shows up, anyway."

Adele stared down at her hands and watched as her fingertips sparked with little puffs of green and gold glitter. *Would this be enough power to heal Stella?* she wondered. *Or is it that I normally have this much power after I've been with Rainere but never knew how to recognize it?*

Adele suddenly felt a wrenching pang of homesickness. Fumbling at her waist, she found the little hand mirror and pulled it out. "Rainere," she called softly. "Rainere, if you're there, please answer." The mirror only reflected her own sad eyes back at her. "Rainere," she begged. "Rainere, please, answer me." But the mirror stayed silent. Adele shoved it back in the pocket at her waist.

Jordansson shuffled over next to Adele and put his arm around her. He kissed her hair and let his cheek rest on her head. "Don't worry, my queen," he murmured. "You still have me."

But Jordansson wasn't *home*, and his kindness didn't make Adele feel any better.

Chapter Forty-Three
"An Echo So Heavy"

Rainere blinked up at the iron-studded rafters, and only then realized he was lying on his back on the sticky floor of the front bar in the Magician's Wand. He took in a breath and felt like he'd been kicked in the chest.

"Are you all right?" asked Charlie.

At the same time Rip exploded in a furious whisper. "What the hell d'you think you're doing, *Gray*?"

Benjamin helped Rainere off the floor and back into his seat. "I just felt something incredibly intense through the Mark," Rainere rasped, still breathless as his chest heaved. "It's Adelena, she—"

"What mark? What's he talking about? Actually, you know what? I don't give a fuck," muttered Rip, casting his gaze about the pub and watching for signs that anyone had seen Rainere acting oddly. "Whatever happened just negated your disguise charm for a few moments. We can only hope no one recognized you."

The four men froze as a tiny piping voice began calling from the pocket of Rainere's overalls. "It's Adelena," whispered Rainere. "I should answer it."

"Yes, go on," Rip snapped. "Use the magical device the Boss had in his own hand and give us all away, why don't you?"

"She might need me," said Rainere, still shaking from the effects of the fit that had taken him just a moment ago. "I have to answer."

"You could tell her you lost the kids while you're at it," said Rip, his sarcasm starting to bite. "In fact, let me have a chat with her."

Pained, Rainere shoved the mirror down deeper in his pocket. "I'll call her as soon as we rescue the children," he told himself but flinched guiltily when he caught Charlie's eye. "I have to make this right first," he said.

"We need to get into that kitchen," said Rip, getting back to business. "Charlie, why don't you and Benjamin create a distraction by the front door, and when everyone is looking at you, Rainere and I will jump the bar and slip through those doors behind it."

Charlie shook his head. "Won't work. I got into the kitchen by stealing a uniform and mixing in with the glass-pot boys, so I know there are guards on the other side of those doors, watching the kitchens and making sure no one from the dining room comes in."

At Charlie's words Rainere suddenly noticed the young boys dressed in green vests and caps collecting glasses from the tables with deft hands. He looked down at the bracelet on his wrist. *The spell is simple enough: a spark of green trapped within the bounds of iron and a little wish.*

Casually hiding his hands under the table, Rainere let a little more magic flow into the bracelet and imagined the disguise in his mind. He felt a nasty twisting sensation in his organs, and suddenly he couldn't see so much of the world as he shrunk down in his chair.

The first to notice his transformation to a teenage boy was Charlie, who whistled quietly and gave Rainere a grin. "Is this how scrawny you were two hundred years ago?" He cocked his head to the side. "I think I could take you now."

"Watch it, boy," snarled Rainere, irritated when Rip and even Benjamin chuckled. "I'm still me." But his adolescent voice cracked on the "still," and the threat lost its menace.

"Now we can both be glass-pot boys," said Charlie, seeing straight through to Rainere's plan. "We should go now, while the dinner rush is still on and we can slip into the kitchens to investigate the basement situation. Maybe you can see the spell that I couldn't."

"Nope." Rip shook his head. "That's far too risky for you, Charlie. Let Rainere and me do the dangerous work here. Normally, I have a talent for passing unnoticed when I want to, but—shit! Unfortunately, that time isn't now."

Out of the corner of his eye, Rip watched two big men approach from the door. "Watch it, lads. Someone noticed our friend Gray being an idiot, and they look like they want to chat about it."

Charlie gave Rainere a hard slap on the back. "I'll show you down to the side of the kitchen where the boys keep their uniforms." He moved faster than a cat out of his chair and through the crowd.

Rainere scurried after Charlie on awkward legs. "This is *not* a plan, Charlie," he squeaked angrily.

Rip looked up, smiling, as the two big men stopped at the side of their table. Identical in height, one had a crew cut, and the other had scraggly black hair to his shoulders. Both had mean, narrow eyes and were dressed in black leather and denim.

"The Boss would like a word with you about your friend," said the long-haired bouncer, his voice unexpectedly high. "He broke the rules of this establishment."

"That wasn't our friend," said Benjamin, forcing a snarl. "That was some kid trying to sell us blue tonic. We weren't having it, so he caused a scene and scampered. Nothin' to do with us."

"Not our problem," said the bouncer with the crew cut. "Boss wants a word, he gets a word." He gestured behind himself with a thumb.

Rip raised his eyes. Where once there had been blank wall, now there was a wide balcony. A young man, tall and lanky, with blond hair neatly brushed back, had his hands on the wooden balustrade and watched over the whole room.

Rip almost groaned with frustration. *The Boss has been watching the room this whole time!* Then a second figure joined the Boss on the balcony, and Rip was unpleasantly surprised to recognize the rotund form and perfectly bald head of Pere Raven. He cursed his luck that the evil priest should catch him in this stronghold while he didn't even have his bracelet to disguise himself anymore.

"All right, lads, we'll come with you," Rip agreed. He climbed to his feet, then stumbled and tripped forward into the two waiting men. "Oh, excuse me, gents!" Both of the bouncers sucked in a harsh breath and fell to the ground a moment later.

It was a testament to the roughness of the bar that hardly a patron did more than step to the side for the falling bodies.

"You knocked them out," said Benjamin.

"In a sense," said Rip, but something about his expression triggered Benjamin.

"You killed them?" the young man gasped, his eyes wide.

"Only their mothers will mourn them, Ben," said Rip, and his eyes traveled to the balcony again. "Let's duck out of here before—"

A set of crystalline blue eyes found Rip's through the crowd and widened in surprise. "Shit, I shouldn't be able to see him on his balcony," said Rip. "Not having my disguise means I can see through his enchantments, which means he's used gold as well as green magic. Benjamin, run and find the others, tell them—"

Rip didn't get to finish as Benjamin threw a wild punch at a man next to him, and Rip had to duck as another man tripped over the two bodies on the floor. Benjamin was laying another roundhouse into the next man, before Rip realized what he was trying to do. Joining in, he flailed at a man next to him and connected with a painful crack, toppling into a table full of drinkers who were not best pleased with their spilled beer. The bar erupted in a brawl that had every bouncer in the place running toward the ruckus while Rip and Benjamin took their chance to escape.

CHAPTER FORTY-FOUR

"The Glass-Pot Boys"

Rainere and Charlie heard the chaos in the bar as they shuffled trays of glasses around on the counters near the kids lined up at the sinks washing dishes. They were delighted to see the four bouncers in the kitchen dart out into the bar to help maintain order. Most of the staff in the kitchen ran to the doors to see what was happening as well.

Charlie showed Rainere to the back corner of the kitchen where he had last seen the basement door. "It was right here," he said, pushing his green cap up on his forehead. "There were two big double doors in the floor and steps leading down."

Rainere scanned the floor for any cloaking magic, but it was either too clever or Charlie had been mistaken. There was a shout, and suddenly everyone who was watching the bar from the kitchen doors jumped back to their stations. Charlie and Rainere ducked behind the sinks and watched as the Boss came into the kitchens leading Pere Raven and a group of Rangers.

"Calm down, my lord, the fight is just a coincidence. No doubt the rabble is still angry after the riot my rangers caused last night," Pere Raven was saying. He had a long red gash on his cheek but was wearing his usual mild expression. "But there is no way that anyone followed us from the palace. My Rangers left a nasty trail behind us that would thwart anyone who wanted to know where we were going."

The young man pulled his scarf further up his face, making sure it was secured. "Your arrogance will be the failure of this enterprise, priest."

Rainere was surprised by how firm and mature the Boss sounded for such a young man, yet it wasn't High Wizard Ohren's voice. "The false queen has many in her employ who are very strong in dark magic and quite capable of following a fat priest and his black dogs."

"If my arrogance is misplaced, then so is your caution," said Pere Raven, with no evidence of irritation. "The children are safely contained, and I will ship them out in a few hours when the portal aligns."

Despite his assurances, Pere Raven had to wait while the Boss waved his hands in a series of complicated gestures, green and gold magic flaring as he muttered a chant to make the doors to the basement appear.

"That's an interdimensional portal," whispered Rainere to Charlie. "Fortunately for us, I know how to break through one of those. Adelena showed me."

"See, the doors haven't been tampered with!" said Pere Raven. He frowned in a way that suggested he didn't want to get angry, but he might be thinking about it. "Of course, if you are using this disturbance as an excuse not to discuss the new terms of our agreement, then that is a different thing entirely."

The Boss ignored the wily priest and cloaked the basement doors with a violent gesture. The group of dangerous men left the kitchens.

"I'll need Rip's gold magic working with mine to open that basement door," whispered Rainere. "Let's go find him."

"Oi, you two! Get back to work!" shouted a voice, and before they could leave the kitchen, Rainere and Charlie had wooden buckets thrust into their hands by a ruddy-cheeked woman wearing a long apron. "Go out and clean up all that broken glass with the others," she scolded them.

Rainere stumbled when he was shoved from behind by another glass-pot boy. "Please, missus," he whined. "I've hurt me ankle. I need a minute."

The woman didn't have time for this. "Take him out back," she instructed Charlie. "But you'll both be docked for time wasted, so be quick about it."

Charlie put his arm around Rainere while the prince feigned a limp, and they went out a back door that led to a large, busy courtyard. Three black armored wagons were lined up, identical to the one that had taken Charlie to the mines. The only good news was that the wagons weren't ready for departure—the horses were still housed in their stables. At the far end of the courtyard, there was an archway, and the area within the arch crackled with potent green magic.

"That's an old permanent portal," whispered Rainere to Charlie as he leaned against him. "It must be how they can get the children in those wagons and out of the city without being seen, but also why they have to wait for it to line up with their destination."

Charlie looked up and saw that the sky above them sparkled green. "There's a protection net up there, as well as guards patrolling the roof. No way we can get in or out from the top."

Charlie and Rainere made their way around the courtyard to some benches by the stables and sat down. The prince peered in through the stable window behind him when he heard a familiar whinny. "Those are the Marchant breed," he said, affronted. "Those are *my* horses."

"Those are *Rangers'* horses," said Charlie. "So keep your bloody voice down."

Rainere looked around to see if they'd been overheard, but everyone around them was far too busy to worry about two lazy glass-pot boys slacking off.

"We need to get the children out before they're taken through the portal," said Rainere, his young faced creased with worry. "They could end up anywhere near the mines or in the Dark Forest."

"Yet this is still a busy pub," mused Charlie. "There must be some way for supplies to come in, if it's not through the front door or that archway there." He scanned the walls of the courtyard and was lucky enough to see a man pushing a wheelbarrow walk through a brick wall in front of them. "Right, there! It'll be charmed. Let me go find out the code word."

Without asking permission, Charlie picked up a sack of potatoes from the kitchen door and hustled over to the brick wall. "I've got to get this back to the delivery wagon," he said to the man pushing the wheelbarrow. "Chef says they're rotten."

"It's only me on tonight, so I'll thank you for your help, son," said the tired carter. "But I'll tell your chef it's not my fault if the whole load is bad. There's been too much sun this season, and all the potatoes are drying out." The carter told Charlie the code word and made his way to the busy kitchens. Charlie dropped his sack of potatoes and hurried back over to Rainere.

"Hopefully, Rip and Benjamin made it out of that brawl by now," he said, helping Rainere to his feet. "Let's go get them and show them how to get back in here."

Rainere kept up the limp, and Charlie held his arm over his shoulder. At the wall Charlie picked up the sack of potatoes again and murmured the code word, "tits of the queen." He pulled Rainere through the wall before the prince's fury gave them away.

The alleyway was at least twenty yards long and wide enough for two wagons to pass each other, but it was empty at this time of night. Lanterns hung on the walls bathed the alley in a green light that gave the boys a sickly pallor as it lit their way.

Charlie and Rainere made it to the end of the alley, slipping through the second curtain of magic at the exit, and found themselves faced with a group of City Guards, cudgels clasped in their hands and swords swinging from the hip.

"All right, lads?" yelped Charlie, almost dropping the sack of potatoes on his toes.

"Wot you two doin'?" asked one of the City Guards, a scar running through the crew cut of his brown hair. "Skiving?"

"Went off shift," said Charlie. "Me mate hurt his ankle in the brawl in there."

"You know you're meant to use the front door at all times," said another City Guard. This one had a gold handle on his cudgel, and his rounded vowels suggested a more educated background to Charlie, so he'd be their leader. "I'm going to report this. What's your names, boys?"

"Charlie Row, sir," said Charlie. "And this here's me mate, Gray."

"Gray *what*?" asked the guard, poking Rainere in the chest with his cudgel handle. "Quickly now, boy."

Pulling the bracelet off his wrist, Rainere raised his chin and looked the guard dead in the eye as he regained his adult form. "Rainere Rainov Lucien Gray Marchant," he said. "But you can call me *what*."

"What?" said the guard, just before the blood exploded from his mouth. The other guards had no time to realize what had happened to their leader before they too died in an implosion of blood and pain.

Charlie spat out the blood the City Guard had just vomited on him. He wiped at his eyes with his shirt-tails. "You made a fucking joke?" he said, incredulous. "The first joke I've ever heard you make, and then you kill four men."

Rainere slipped the bracelet back on his wrist. "I was tired of being humiliated by this scum," he said, fastidiously dabbing at the blood on his shirt.

Charlie was pale. "You've been a working kid for no more than half an hour, and you're already tired," he said. "Try a lifetime of it!"

Ripenzo and Benjamin appeared around the corner, coming in from the street. "Ah, I thought I'd find you two standing in a pool of blood, surrounded by bodies," said Rip.

Charlie spat out a gob of copper-colored spit. "Really?"

"No, not really." Rip rolled his eyes. "This was incredibly stupid, so I guess Rainere is to blame."

Rainere shrugged. "I'll clean up the mess," he said, and with a wave of his hand picked up the dead bodies and speedily propelled them through the air to a couple of large trash bins, dumping them inside and slamming the lids closed. Then he separated the blood from his and Charlie's clothes and sent the droplets into an old bucket resting against the bins. "Done." He morphed back to his teenage form.

The potato carter reappeared through the wall and gave Benjamin and Ripenzo a suspicious once-over. "Oi! You leave these boys alone," he said. "These lads work in the pub already, you don't want nothin' with 'em." The kind old man gave Charlie a quick scruff on the head. "You two get out of here—I'll not let 'em get you."

Charlie and Rainere both ran out of the mouth of the alleyway and found a shadowed doorway in which to wait for Ripenzo and Benjamin. It wasn't too long before they saw Rip and Ben getting hustled out of the alleyway by the old man, waving his hands at them and threatening to call the City Guard.

The street they found themselves on was mostly deserted except for the odd delivery cart rumbling down the rough brick road. Ripenzo and Benjamin soon joined them in the doorway.

"So people here steal kids right off the street, do they?" Ripenzo asked Charlie.

Charlie shrugged. "Or he thought you were propositioning us," he said. "Two kids with black hair and no amulets, we'd be fair game in this quarter after dark, for magic or sex—or both. The Boss is the only top shelf predator; no other crime boss would dare to cross or touch his merchandise. That's why he's *the* Boss, and the others are just bosses."

Ripenzo turned to Rainere. "These are *your* people!" he said accusingly. "Are you happy to just let them be abused and subjugated like this on the streets of your own city?"

It was Rainere's turn to shrug. "They aren't my people any more than they are yours," he said. "I am royal, and they are peasants. We are two different breeds of human."

"I could punch you right now, and you would probably go down with those weedy arms of yours," murmured Charlie, but he didn't raise his fists, only looked out on the quiet street.

"You really are a special guy, Rainere Marchant!" spat Ripenzo. "You'll kill yourself for a couple of kids who aren't even your family, but those who share your actual blood you'll just leave to die like so many cats in the street."

"Natalie, Aaron and Stella *are* my family," replied Rainere, returning Ripenzo's anger. "Adelena made them my family. It's you who are the interloper here."

"Interloper!" Ripenzo shoved the smaller Rainere back against the wall of the doorway so hard his head bounced. "You have no idea how much *I belong here,* Marchant."

"Shhh," Benjamin hushed the pair of them as a squad of City Guards went past. "New guards. We can sneak back in with the next lot of deliveries if we're quick. Now, fellas, what's the plan?"

Chapter Forty-Five
"Simple Plans of Complicated Men"

The plan was simple. Charlie and Rainere were to go in first through the front door and into the kitchens like they were returning to work. Then Rainere would stun ("Not kill," as Rip kept repeating) all the kitchen workers and lock every door except the one that led out to the courtyard.

Benjamin and Ripenzo would come in through the alleyway and stun anyone they encountered who might stop them. Then Benjamin would harness the horses to one of the wagons as their getaway vehicle while Ripenzo entered the kitchen.

Ripenzo and Rainere would use their combined magics to open the interdimensional doorway to the basement. Charlie, Ripenzo, and Rainere would descend, find the children, and carry them out into the prepared wagon and escape back to the Golden Palace.

"What if there are other kids down there?" asked Rip after the plan had been decided. "We should save all of them, not just Adelena's."

"What if Adelena's children are being raped or tortured as we speak and you are wasting our time!" hissed Rainere. "We need to go now. We have waited and planned long enough."

Rip glared at Rainere, but he nodded his agreement. "I'm still going to grab all the kids I find," he added. "Now let's go. May the goddess have mercy on our souls."

Rainere and Charlie streaked off down the road and circled back to the front entrance of the pub. Everything went according to plan right up until Rainere and Charlie entered the kitchen. The place was packed with cooks and servers waiting on the evening crowd, so Rainere didn't see the danger until he had wrenched off his bracelet and released his spell. The staff all fell to the floor, unconscious, and only then did Rainere see what he had missed.

The group of four Rangers, conspicuous in their black leather uniforms, were unlocking the unshielded basement doors. The Boss was nowhere to be seen, but Rainere took a moment to bar the kitchen doors, making sure only the one to the courtyard stayed open.

The prince approached the Rangers with Charlie cringing behind him. "You are to leave the basement door open," Rainere instructed them. "And let us walk the children out of here."

The Rangers didn't even exchange a glance with each other. By an unspoken agreement, one of them stepped forward. "No," he said simply and opened fire.

Rainere only had a split second to get his shield up to protect himself and Charlie. He could see the Ranger's weapon through his transparent shield, but it was something he had only seen before in his mechanical weapons manuals, never in real life.

Rainere spared Charlie a glance. "You know these men, Charlie—kill or capture?"

"Kill, kill!" shrilled Charlie. "Quick! All of them."

Rainere turned his shield concave, and the projectiles returned to the attacker, pelting him in the chest and body until he fell to the floor, bleeding from a hole just above his eye.

In the silence of the aftermath, Rainere heard the screams and cries of the children in the basement. He didn't waste another moment but moved forward, casting spell after spell at the three standing Rangers while they separated and tried to flank him, shooting flames and metal projectiles from their own weapons. It was loud and chaotic, the action happening too fast to be terrifying.

Rainere lost sight of one of the Rangers in the smoke from his spells, which worried him as he was still waiting for the Boss to come charging into the kitchen at any moment with the strength of a St. Lucidis wizard's magic. He counted the Rangers on the ground as the third one went down, a victim of a decapitating spell. The last Ranger appeared at Rainere's left, a flaming knife in his hand as the man lunged for the prince behind his protective shield. Rainere turned just as the knife sliced past his ear and slammed a ball of magic right into the Ranger's chest. The man coughed blood and collapsed.

Still holding his shield up and not taking his eyes off the open door to the courtyard, Rainere made his way over to the open basement. "Charlie, go down and get the kids," he said. "We have little time."

Charlie leaped into the hole, slipping down the balustrade of the narrow staircase. Rip poked his head in the door of the kitchen and looked around. He saw the dead Rangers and raised an eyebrow. "Four of them," he said, impressed. "Nice work."

"Get the children out of the basement," Rainere said through clenched teeth. "Charlie is already down there."

"Benjamin found a wagon already hitched," said Rip. "I'll pass the kids up, and you throw them in the back."

Rip hurried into the basement, and soon he and Charlie had passed out all fifteen children who had been trapped down there. Charlie led the little princess and prince up last of all.

"Prince Rainere, you came!" sobbed Natalie. She was holding Aaron in her arms, and tears streaked her dirty cheeks.

Rainere felt his own tears prick the back of his eyes as his heart broke. "Of course I did, my darling," he rasped. "I will always come for you."

Dropping his shield, Rainere scooped the children into his arms and carried them out to the waiting carriage. He squashed them in with the other children, promising the nightmare would be over soon, and then looked around for the others.

Rip came out of the kitchen, and Charlie came running behind him.

"Where's Leafy?" asked Charlie, already panicking. "Who's seen her?" He made to dart back into the kitchen, but Rip grabbed his arm, pulling him back.

Suddenly, a Ranger stepped in the kitchen doorway. He was clasping Leafy in front of him and holding one of their mechanical weapons at her temple.

"Hello, Charlie," said the Ranger. His cold voice froze the men in front of him. "We've been looking for you, kid. Caused us a right bit of trouble. You'll have to pay for that."

"Hello, Cedric," replied Charlie, as calmly as he could. "You've lost, mate. I've got a Marchant wizard here who can kill you where you stand. Give us back Leafy, and I'll ask him to let you live."

"That's why I always liked you, Charlie," said Cedric in his monotone. "You've got a sense of humor." Then he raised the weapon and fired a shot at Charlie's heart.

Charlie expected instant death, but instead he was shoved backward by Rainere leaping in front of him. The prince grunted in pain, and Charlie fell through the doorway of the wagon, on top of the screaming children.

Ripenzo took advantage of the chaos to aim a bolt of gold magic at Cedric's head and grab Leafy out of his hands. Throwing the tiny girl in the wagon after Charlie, Rip slammed the door shut and shouted for Benjamin to get the hell out of there.

There was only enough room on the sideboards of the wagon for Rip to stand, so Rainere climbed up next to Benjamin on the rider's seat and held on for dear life as they raced through the alleyway and then out through the badly lit streets of the Lower Districts.

With the rattle of the wagon's wheels on the cobblestones and the screaming of the children in the back, there was no way Rainere could have heard the thin voice piping from the hand mirror in his pocket.

CHAPTER FORTY-SIX

"Danger as a Sport"

Gorrik was giving Lady Olivia the creeps, staring at her as she stood by the window in Lord Orgustus's bedroom. His cat was purring around her ankles, so she picked him up and cuddled him to distract herself.

"Lord Orgustus should be back soon," she repeated, looking away from Gorrik's toothy smile and at her own reflection in the dark window glass. "I hope that he has found out who took the royal children."

"Well, we've got one left, haven't we?" Gorrik nodded at Princess Stella lying on Lord Orgustus's bed. "Not that she'll be much use to us without the cure, but I'm sure we can find some purpose for a sleeping princess."

Goddess, but he is so weird! Olivia hugged the cat under her chin. *When is Orgustus going to get here? It's well after midnight now and I've been waiting for ages.*

"Thank goodness you could disarm the curse that kept Stella stuck in that awful attic room and move her here, Mr. Gorrik," gushed Olivia, covering up her fear by feigning admiration. "What did you call it, a Sleeping Guard? I never knew that you could control such powerful dark magic before now, Mr. Gorrik. It's just a shame that you can't break this last curse so she can wake up and tell us who did this to her. Don't you think, Mr. Gorrik?"

"Please don't feel the need to flirt with me, child," said Gorrik mildly. He took a silver flask of Firewhiskey out of the inside pocket of his robe. "I am very old and couldn't really care less if you bat your lashes at me or not." He took a long slug of whiskey and smacked his lips.

Olivia felt her own lip curl in disgust and glared at the decrepit old man. "I'm not trying to flirt with you, sir," she said. "I only wish to—"

She was cut off by the door to the bedchamber slamming open. An angry Lord Orgustus appeared in the doorway. "What the hell are you doing here?" he shouted. "For the goddess's own sake, Olivia! Why did you bring the child to my personal chambers?"

Lady Olivia opened her eyes wide, appearing confused and hurt. *So all the blame will be on you when the queen finds out we've taken her baby, Orgie,* she thought. "I didn't know where else to take her that would be safe, my lord," stammered Olivia. "Master Gorrik didn't have any other suggestions."

Lord Orgustus turned on the old history teacher and managed to calm himself enough to be respectful. "And what do you think, Master Gorrik?" he asked, walking to the bed to look down on Stella. "Can you undo this wicked spell that holds the child in stasis?"

"Well, maybe," creaked Gorrik, showing his yellowing teeth in a rueful smile. "But I doubt Her Majesty would be grateful for the interference. The child wasn't completely healed by the tonic, and this coma is protecting her from dying a rather painful death. To top it off, the Marchant prince has created a very powerful limit on the spell, and very clever too."

"What is it?" Orgustus rounded on the smaller man, irritated to hear anything good about the prince he hated.

"Well, the spell can only be broken by true love's kiss," said Gorrik. "Or rather, by a surge of a magic particular to Queen Adelena applied to the matrix of the spell, which has been situated on the child's lips. Romantic—and very impractical for anyone other than her mother to use."

Orgustus snarled in triumph. "So for this spell to work, the queen must have ordered the prince to perform this dark magic on her child, or at the very least been aware of what he had done."

"Oh, yes," said Gorrik, nodding as he took another slug of whiskey. "You can be sure that Her Majesty knew all about it."

"Would you testify to that in the Court of the Golden Palace before the High Wizards' Council?" asked Orgustus.

This time Gorrik only shrugged. "That depends on what you are trying to achieve, my lord."

A loud shout was heard in the adjoining chamber, and Orgustus raced to the doorway to come face to face with the high magistrar, Orestes.

"I heard that the royal children have been kidnapped," said the high magistrar without any preamble. "I also heard that you were there too and may have seen who took the children. So, did you?" He stepped forward, aggressively pushing Orgustus back into the room, and only then noticed that Orgustus had company. "Gorrik, what are you doing here?"

"The queen's secret has been discovered," said the old man. He gestured at the baby on the bed. "Queen Adelena has been using dark magic to keep Princess Stella alive. Though I do seem to remember a certain meeting when someone suggested that they would take the fall for her if this was ever discovered by the court." He waggled his shaggy brows at Orestes, his milky eyes unamused.

The high magistrar blinked. "I can't think what you mean, Gorrik," he answered coolly. "The queen would know of the law prohibiting the use of dark magic in the Golden Palace as well as anyone else in her exalted position. There can be no exceptions."

"It's despotism!" shouted Lord Orgustus and struck his fist into his palm. "We can have that woman off the throne for this. Finally!"

"Just to be clear, tell me what you saw down at the site of the kidnapping, my lord," insisted Orestes. "Was there any evidence of dark magic used?"

Lord Orgustus's blue eyes lit with a strange fervor, and Olivia could practically see him rewriting history in his head before answering Orestes's question.

"I heard from a steward that there had been an attack on the children during their riding lesson," said Orgustus. "I raced to the stables and saw the damage to a corral, blasted apart by an unnatural fire. There were two fatally injured squires on the ground, and witnesses among the stable hands told me that the

Marchant prince, some boy called Charlie, and another Marchant stable hand called Benjamin had been seen leaving the area on horses as if running for their lives. No one saw the children disappear, but no doubt they were transported through a portal."

"Then why would Prince Rainere be riding a horse?" Olivia surprised herself as much as any of the three men with her question. "I mean, it doesn't make sense that he would put the children through a portal and then escape some other way, does it?"

"Were you there, my lady?" asked Orestes. Olivia felt herself pinned by his laser-focused stare. "Did you see what happened to the royal children?" His tone suggested that she must have if she would dare to question Lord Orgustus.

"No, I wasn't, High Magistrar." Olivia dropped her gaze to the cat in her arms, and his pale green eyes seemed to understand her fear as he purred at her. Olivia's survival instincts were screaming at her to run, and she wondered when she would be allowed to get the hell out of this room.

"High Magistrar, what is our next step here?" asked Lord Orgustus. "Do we have grounds to issue a warrant of arrest for the Marchant prince and his cronies? What about the queen? Surely, she has to be made to answer for her crimes against the crown and the court? And you cannot tell me that the high wizard hasn't had a hand in this all along—"

"Silence, boy!" The high magistrar's shout was as sudden as it was violent. "Do not *dare* to say a word against my brother, you sniveling lion cub!"

Though he hadn't changed expression, the air around Orestes pulsed with the waves of rage rolling off him. Olivia shrank back against the window seat and hoped he wouldn't look at her like he was looking at Lord Orgustus right now.

"There is chaos in my palace," said Orestes quietly, but his head jerked in a tic that set the gold rings spinning around his pupils. "I *hate* chaos. Do you hear me, children? *I hate chaos.*"

No one in the room said a word. Even the cat stopped purring.

"I will tell you what is going to happen right now, before things get any worse," said Orestes. He turned his glare to the sleeping baby on the bed. "I will issue a warrant for the arrest of Prince Rainere Marchant, and when he returns to the Golden Palace, we will put him in chains and crush him under the full weight of St. Lucidis law. The false queen will be held accountable for her own and the sins of the evil Marchant prince. She will pay for the pain she has caused my brother. She will pay for everything that she has made me do to our people. She will pay for everything she has done to destroy the status quo of my Unisia. And I will see her pay with her life—that I can promise you."

"Killing a Marchant immortal is one thing, but are you really going to try to kill a demon, Orestes?" Gorrik asked, seemingly unperturbed by the wide eyes and spittle-flecked beard of the high magistrar. "We don't even know if the queen is ever coming back again."

Orestes pointed a long finger at the baby. "She's coming back for her." He seemed to settle back into his more civilized persona, hiding the madness away behind a frown. "And if the queen is made to believe that the Marchant prince kidnapped her children as he has done before, then she will kill him for us. Then I will deal with the demon myself." He brushed his hands together as if the matter were settled and turned his cold gaze to Lady Olivia. "Now, does this young woman have any further use to us?"

But Olivia didn't get to hear if anyone was going to defend her, as there was another knock at Lord Orgustus's chamber door, and one of the high magistrar's stewards poked his head into the room.

"High Magistrar, there has been word that Prince Rainere Marchant has returned to the royal apartment and is wounded. The high wizard is with him now and has asked that you join them immediately."

Orestes turned to Lord Orgustus. "Ready, my lord?"

Lord Orgustus looked more nervous than triumphant, and Olivia thought he might actually have realized how dangerous the high magistrar was. "I am ready, sir." Orgustus wiped sweaty hands down the side of his pants. "I will always do my duty for the Crown of St. Lucidis."

"Good boy." The high magistrar nodded, his blue eyes flickering with madness again. "Gorrik, watch the girl while I'm gone."

The two men left the room, slamming the door behind them. In the silence the cat started purring again, and Lady Olivia turned her white face to Gorrik. "Was the high magistrar talking about me or the princess?" she asked.

Gorrik gave Lady Olivia a long look and sighed at what he saw in her eyes. "I'm sorry, kid," he said. "But you are really going to have to pick a side."

Lady Olivia swallowed hard and didn't even pretend to be confused. "Whose side are you on?" she whispered.

Gorrik shrugged. "I've got me, kid, and I've got my Master." He pointed at his cat, who jumped out of Olivia's arms with a mewl and ran over to him. "Honestly, the rest of you can go hang."

Chapter Forty-Seven
"Seeing Through the Darkness"

Adelena put the hand mirror away in her waistband and stared into the fire. *Why isn't Rainere answering me?* she wondered, swamped by anxiety. *I hope I did the right thing leaving my children with him. If any harm comes to them while I search the kingdom for this dragon I will never forgive myself. Or him.*

Jordansson had fallen asleep hours ago, after asking Adele a million questions about her power, where she was from, and her plans as queen of Unisia. It was as if watching her drink the goddess power from the sky had opened up something inside of him too, a hunger to know the world and what moving to Unisia could mean for him. It had been uncomfortable for Adele to reveal exactly how careless she had been with her responsibilities as a queen and how little she could tell him about her powers. Of course, there was a lot she kept back from the infatuated tribesman too. It wouldn't be wise to frighten him so much that he didn't want to lead them to the dragon anymore.

To distract herself from darker thoughts, Adele practiced flexing her fresh, new magic. Reaching in with her mind, she grasped the leonine power by the mane and her serpentine magic by a coil and brought them, fizzing and pulsing, into her hands. It was such a joy to have them respond to her call, and the feeling of strength was wonderful after so many days without it.

Little clouds of gold magic coalesced on her palms, and Adele dropped them on the floor of the cave. She was delighted when a tiny mound of dirt shifted and a green shoot parted the soil and grew up before her very eyes. The green stem sprouted two leaves, and the blossom at the top unfurled five white petals. The flower trembled as if in a breeze, and Adele renewed her concentration to hold it steady and coax it even taller. Then a tendril of green magic wound its way between her fingers, interrupting the flow of gold magic sprinkling down on the flower.

Adele marveled at the beauty of the heavy green glitter as it flowed like a liquid vine. She released it, and it descended slowly onto the flower, twining around the stem and embedding itself in the base of the blossom. The petals changed, becoming denser and waxier. At the heart of the flower, the pale blue stamen became a pointed thorn, and the petals closed in around it like a mouth. The flower swayed in the current of magic, turning its face to the source.

Curious, Adele reached out with a finger and touched the mouth of the flower. She snatched her hand back with a yelp as the blossom snapped at her, the stamen stabbing out like a flicking tongue. Angry, Adele sent another thread of green magic coiling down to the base of the flower and sucked all the magic back from it until there was only a stringy dried husk where the blossom had once stood.

Sensing a presence, Adele's head shot up. She looked straight into the pale blue gaze of General Ohrig. It was clear that he had seen her little experiment.

"I'm a monster," said Adele. She felt her eyes fill with tears. She had to get away from Ohrig's judgment before he could lay it down on her already-burdened shoulders. She grabbed her heavy coat and headed for the mouth of the cave. The night was still pitch-black, but the blanket of stars and a new moon illuminated the sky and made silhouettes of the mountaintops before her. The Path of the Goddess was nowhere to be seen.

Ohrig followed her out and stood next to her in the dark. Adele wrapped her arms around her shoulders, holding herself tight. She heard Ohrig's intake of breath.

"Ohrig, please," said Adele. "I know I'm a monster, and you can't tell me otherwise."

"I wasn't going to deny it, Your Majesty," said Ohrig. "You definitely are some kind of monster."

"It's why I don't want to expose Lucky to this horrible dark magic within me. I would hurt him without meaning to, just like

I did to that flower," whispered Adele. "But then how can it be possible for a fucking god to carry me in his palm and help me drink from the *sky*?" Adele swallowed a sob. "Every time I think I can cope in this world, something else happens to freak me out, and I'm lost again, Ohrig."

Ohrig sighed and wrapped his arm around Adele's shaking shoulders, pulling her in for a hug. He rested his cheek on her hair. "Look, I know you're a demon but I also know that you are a young woman with a heart of gold, who always tries to do right. That makes you two things—just like everyone in this world, no different. Believe it or not, when I lose my temper, I can be a bit of an arsehole. I'm not a demon, but I'm not nice to be around then, either, so I learned to control my temper. It's that simple."

Could it really be just that simple? Adele pressed her face to Ohrig's chest, absorbing his warmth and breathing in the smell of the tobacco and woodsmoke that clung to his shirt. There was just a hint of peppermint covering the man smell of his skin. The hug went on until Adele felt it should probably end. "I thought you didn't coddle your troops," she joked, her voice muffled by his shirt, and felt Ohrig's chest shake in a silent chuckle.

"I hug all my soldiers when they need it, and I knock them around when they need that," he said. He kept his arms around her. "Now, you know I will happily follow you into hell and back again, Queen Adelena, but later today, when we climb the last mountain and meet the dragon, I only want you bringing the demon queen with you. This sweet young mum Adelena can go hide in a corner and cry all day, because we are going to need Queen Adelena, slayer of Sandarian mages, devourer of Spider empresses, and vanquisher of immortal Marchant princes. Queen Adelena the arse-kicking defender of her children is just wily enough to trick a dragon into bleeding for her and then crying in thanks for the honor. You bring her today, and we are going to be all right. Do you understand me?"

"Yes." Adele nodded and felt a smile stretch her lips. "Yes, I understand you, General."

"Good." Ohrig finally let her go and headed back into the cave. "Now, make us some tea, demon."

"Don't push your luck, human," replied Adele, giving Ohrig a nudge in the ribs that made him wince in mock pain. "That was a good speech, though," she added. "A little poetic, even."

"I meant it," said Ohrig firmly. "You are the only one who can get us home again. So do it."

Chapter Forty-Eight
"The Way Grows Harder"

The trek through the mountains was more difficult the next day. The skiing was steeper, and the climbs were higher. Owens almost broke a wrist tumbling down a slope and required strapping and a dose of Firewhiskey to continue.

Jordansson didn't seem to be much concerned with pace and even took a longer path away from the mountain that loomed large on the horizon, which led to much frustrated groaning by the entire group. The air became thinner the higher up the mountains they went, and the men tired more easily than the day before, meaning more rest stops were needed. Lucky was the first one to start vomiting from altitude sickness, and Pepper and Owens soon followed.

"I think this climb is going to kill us before the dragon can," complained QG Pepper, wiping his chin and slugging down some water. "No wonder no one ever visits him. He's so bloody hard to get to."

"We could have *slepozana* down the valley and across the floor, climbing the other side with ice axes," suggested Jordansson, shirtless as always and glowing in the afternoon light. He pointed down the valley from the mountaintop they had just traversed. The side was sheer to the bottom of the valley, and then another sheer mountainside matched it to the top of the dragon's mountain.

"You can climb that?" Lucky asked, disbelief clear in his tone.

Jordansson showed the captain his pickaxes and mimed clawing through the ice. "It's too hard if you have never done it before," he said. "You men are strong, but for this you must know the spirit of the ice before you can trust the mountain."

"So how much further?" Ohrig was gasping despite the rest stop, his cheeks bright red with exertion. "Can we make it there before dark?"

Jordansson was already shrugging before Lucky groaned. "Don't ask him that; he'll just ask how long can a man walk in snow, or how much snow can fall from the sky in a day."

Jordansson grinned at Lucky. "Hah! Finally, the tiny people are learning the ways of the mountains," he said. "But I think if you can keep pace, we can make the caves by nightfall. I do not think we can enter the dragon cave today, unless you want to meet a dragon when you are tired and ready for rest."

Adele bounced on her toes. She still felt strong and energized after last night. Knowing how to direct the green magic into her legs and arms made for easy hiking, and only her shoulders ached under the heavy pack. She was keyed up and eager for the challenge to be met and done.

"Let's see how we feel when we get to the campsite," Adele said. She was met with a chorus of groans and whispered curses. "I know you guys are tired, but we are so close now. Just think, the quicker we get there, the quicker we get to go home!" No one answered her, and Adele forged on ahead with Jordansson, pushing the pace and enjoying his equally enthusiastic company.

The last few hours of the day were magnificent. As the sun dropped in the sky, it bathed the world in gold and colored the snow peaks in myriad shades of apricot and pink. Struck by the incredible beauty of the world around her, Adele lost track of the time and was surprised when Jordansson pulled them up to yet another plateau at the base of a white peak and announced that here was the cave where they would set up camp.

The cave was far bigger than the one they'd used last night, and, more importantly, it was already occupied. Smoke puffed out of the chimney, and piles of bones had been neatly stacked on either side of the clearing in front of a man-made wall with a wooden door.

Adele was concerned to see that Jordansson looked anxious. He licked his lips and scanned the entire area before he let them enter the place in front of the cave, a circular space that had been cleared of snow. He gestured silently that everyone should keep their packs on. Jordansson even put his shirt and jacket back on and made an effort to flatten his spiky, sweat-soaked hair.

"Why are you so nervous, Jordansson?" Adele asked. "Is this person dangerous to us?"

"No! What? No!" Jordansson laughed, but it sounded forced. "I haven't seen them in a long time, that is all." He raised his fist to knock on the door of the cave and hesitated. "But it would be good if you keep some of the green magic in your hands, just for the introductions." He knocked before Adele could protest.

There was a long and tense moment of silence before Jordansson knocked again. "*Ho-hij!*" he shouted.

"*Ho-hij.*" The growl came from behind them. Everyone turned around to see two giant men coming up the same path they had just climbed. Towering over the Unisians, and even Jordansson, at close to eight and a half feet tall, the two men were perfectly identical. They had long platinum hair bound in plaits and tied with white leather strips. Their skin was alabaster pale and contrasted wildly with their cornflower-blue eyes—sharp eyes—that took in the intruders standing in front of their home. Now that she had some experience, Adele could tell that both twins were clothed in ice bear fur and had weapons made of bone and tooth shoved in their belts or slung over their backs. One of the twins carried a brace of furred creatures that looked small in his hands but were actually snow hares as big as dogs when he dropped them on the ground.

"Get on with it, man," growled Ohrig. He gestured for Jordansson to start the introductions before the ice giants decided to have an opinion about the intruders.

Jordansson hurried forward, shouting greetings, and the twins tolerated him hugging them around their chests, even giving him gentle pats on the back. Jordansson talked fast in their own tongue and waved at Adelena and her guard many times, introducing them one by one. The twins didn't speak or respond to any of the things Jordansson said, except to nod once when he asked them a question. Jordansson hurried back over to the Unisians.

"These are my brothers, Stormchaser and Tempestborn," he said with a smile, looking more relieved than before the conversation. "They are the Dragon Hunters and have said that we can stay in their home tonight before seeing the dragon tomorrow."

"The Dragon Hunters are your brothers?" Adele didn't like the surprise. "Why didn't you tell us that?"

"It doesn't matter," Jordansson said. "They hold the sacred duty to hunt for the dragon and watch over him as he sleeps. That we are brothers does not mean they will help me. Also, I am the youngest and weakest of our family—this doesn't bring them any honor."

"You don't suppose they might have some dragon blood or a tear lying around the cave, do you?" asked Ohrig out of the corner of his mouth to Adele, but Jordansson still heard him.

"Do *not* ask this question!" Jordansson hissed, aghast. "The Dragon Hunters do not take from the dragon, they *serve* him. It's a sacred duty," he added, as if Ohrig had suggested that it might not be. He hurried off back to his brothers.

"Jordansson looks like he's losing his nerve, doesn't he?" said QG Bear over Adele's shoulder.

"And yet suddenly so full of information about what the hunters do and what they don't," said Adele with a frown. "I wonder what else he's kept from us."

The twins, Stormchaser and Tempestborn, had settled down at the side of their house to skin and gut the creatures they'd killed, and there was a tense waiting period while the Queen's Guard talked among themselves and Jordansson talked to his brothers in a one-sided yet very animated discussion. It was dark by the time the twins finished trimming the animals and opened their front door, allowing the strangers inside their home.

Chapter Forty-Nine
"In the Home of Giants"

Adele had no reason to be surprised, but she still felt alarmed at being in a home where she had to climb onto a chair and couldn't quite reach to put her elbows on the table. The fire in the oversized chimney had burned down to huge glowing embers, and the four carcasses were arranged on a rotisserie over them. Jordansson brought out the rest of the food and cooking supplies that everyone had carried in their packs and presented it all to the twins as if it were a gift. Only one of the herbs won a visible reaction from the twins, and they held it to their noses for the longest time before sprinkling it all over the roasting meat.

The Queen's Guard had been surreptitiously surveying the single-roomed cave, finding a back exit and a very deep hole just outside where the toilet had been dug. There were two long beds situated on either side of the chimney and a square dining table with a bench on each of the four sides in the middle of the room. A long workbench curved around the wall, covered with all sorts of woodworking tools and sawdust. Snow was melting in buckets on the hearth, and the Queen's Guard helped with hauling more in to serve with dinner.

Adele noticed that the twins didn't talk to each other at all. They showed each other things for approval or disapproval and looked to the other when Jordansson had obviously said something that surprised them. Yet most of the time the two massive men moved around each other like clockwork, seeming to know where the other was and how long he would be there.

By the time dinner was served, the new moon had risen high in the sky. Each guest was served a quarter of a roasted beast and a pile of stewed root vegetables heaped on trays that served for plates.

Adele had no hope of eating through her pile of food despite her ravenous hunger, though the Queen's Guard dug into their meals with no hesitation.

Jordansson was warned with a hand gesture by one of the twins not to say a word while the meal was in progress, and he finally stopped his constant chatter, though Adele could see it was almost painful for him to do so.

After dinner the twins fastidiously tidied away the cooking equipment and did all the dishes, refusing to let anyone help. Jordansson did get to push the dining table and chairs up against a wall and unroll a couple of large fur rugs on the floor in front of the fireplace. He signaled that Adele and the Queen's Guard should set themselves down and wait for the twins to join them.

"What have you been talking to them about?" Adele asked Jordansson, while watching his huge brothers move quietly about the room.

"I've been telling them about home," said Jordansson. "The last time I saw them, I was only as tall as you and very young. They haven't been back to the Valley of the Three Sisters in all that time. A lot has happened in my family: new babies, new partners, and new farms. The chieftess, our mother, has aged and gained new powers, but no one knows how. There is a rumor she is storing strength to take over the next valley, the Valley of the Hunting Fox—" Jordansson remembered himself and who he was talking to. "But that is not Unisia's concern, of course."

"Of course," replied Adele. "What did you tell them about us?"

"I told them everything about you. How you helped me kill an ice bear with your bare hands and rode the lightning of the Goddess Path. I also said that you were guests of our tribe from the lands of Unisia and you seek the dragon in his lair." Jordansson took Adele's hand and gave it a reassuring squeeze. "Now that they have been good hosts, feeding you and giving you a bed for the night, they will ask you questions, and you will not lie to them. Will you?"

Adele ran her eyes over the collection of weapons on the wall of the cave. "*I've* got nothing to hide, Jordansson." She left the suggestion hanging, but Jordansson was too distracted by his brothers to pick up the subtlety of her accusation.

Finally finished, the twins dropped down on the rugs, sitting next to each other. Tempestborn started speaking, his voice gravelly from lack of use, in the sing-song language of their people.

"First, they want the queen to show them some magic so that they know she is the great warrior wizard that I have claimed," Jordansson translated. He shrugged at Adele's nonplussed expression. "They are simple men. They need pictures with their words."

Adele thought for a moment. She downed the water in her metal cup and picked up her knife. Nicking the tip of her finger, she let a couple of drops of blood fall in. Then, using the fire tongs, she held the cup over the fire while the Chime Voices gave her the chant to bless the fire in the name of the goddess Serena and make it sacred. Within a moment her blood burned and rose out of the cup, two thin strands of green and gold sparkles mixing and separating in a perpetual helix.

"By the grace of the goddess Serena, I stand before you, blessed as the blood that runs in my veins." The words were the last line of the chant of the Chime Voices, and Adele knew that it wasn't the King's Tongue but the old tongue that used to be. Yet she could tell by the clarity of their expressions that the twins understood her.

Stormchaser began speaking, his voice slow and deep. Jordansson translated almost at the same time.

"The dragon, Sighmere, has slept below the ground for over a thousand years. He waits for the goddess Serena to come for him and take him back to the Realm of the Gods. Though we are the people of the great god Dahk'hani, we serve the dragon, watching over him and keeping him from leaving his home beneath the world.

"Queen Adelena, if you really are a messenger of the goddess Serena, then that means the time of the goddess is at hand and that Serena will soon return to the world of Evendaar. When she arrives, Dahk'hani will wake, healed and ready to continue his battle with Sighmere, with the goddess, Serena, to stand witness. The Dragon

Hunters will have fulfilled their duty to the great god when Dahk'hani kills the dragon, and peace will reign in the valleys of Dahk'hani's tribes."

The story continued, but Jordansson took a long drink of water. "I hope that Stormchaser has a point to make with all this story telling," he said. "Because I'm starting to think he just likes talking."

Adele's head spun. *If Sighmere is asleep and Dahk'hani is asleep, but Dahk'hani can talk to me, does that mean Sighmere isn't as powerful as Dahk'hani, or is he just not interested in talking to one of Serena's messengers?*

"Jordansson, ask Stormchaser if Sighmere is a god, or if the dragon is considered to be as strong as a god." Adele carefully watched Stormchaser's expression when Jordansson translated the question, but the tribesman's face could have been carved from the ice for all he gave away, and he only answered with one word.

"He says he doesn't know, as he is just a humble tribesman," said Jordansson.

"Really?" said Adele, frowning. "If I've got the story right, Sighmere and Dahk'hani hate each other, but they don't want to fight each other without Serena to watch who gets to be the winner. So they are both napping, waiting for her return. Dahk'hani has set your people the sacred task of keeping an eye on Sighmere, ready to tell in case Sighmere should wake up before him, and Sighmere wants to stay underground because—why?"

"Look, Queen," said Jordansson, giving her the impression that he didn't believe the story either. "These brothers of mine have been up here in the mountains with a sleeping dragon to watch over for the last twenty years. They are a bit crazy and might even be mating each other—I don't know." He couldn't help but grin at his own humor. "We should take everything they say with some space."

"Salt," interrupted QG Pepper. "You take what is said with salt, to make the story taste better even though you don't believe it."

"All right, salt," said Jordansson impatiently. "I don't know why my mother favored the twins. They might be tall and handsome, but they share only one brain. You do not need to listen to all their stories. I will take you to the dragon tomorrow, and we will get the tear and the blood from him. It will be done."

"Jordansson, if there is something you aren't telling us that could endanger this mission, then I'm going to be very angry," Adele warned him. "You have no right to hide any information that could be useful to us."

Jordansson glanced at his brothers out of the corner of his eye. He obviously didn't want to have this conversation with Adele in front of them. "Can we go outside and talk about this?"

"No, it's freezing out there," said Adele firmly. "Tell me here."

Jordansson took a deep breath and swore under his breath. "Look, they think that if you enter Sighmere's home, you will all be eaten by the dragon because he is still angry with Serena for leaving him here in Evendaar. They believe he hates the tiny people of Unisia because you are all her tribes."

"Ah, see," said Adelena. She felt her cheeks pale. "This is important information."

"So Sighmere will be an *angry* dragon," said Ohrig, noting the facts. "An angry dragon who hates little people and our goddess."

"But this is only a story," protested Jordansson. "You need to take the salt now, lots of it. The Dragon Hunters also said they haven't seen Sighmere even once in their time, nor did the Dragon Hunters before them. They think he might be dead even, except the carcasses they leave in his cave are still disappearing."

"Then he isn't dead," corrected Ohrig.

"Or something else is eating them," said Bear. "Hopefully, another Dark Entity we could kill."

Adele would have weighed her options, but there was only one. "Whatever is under that mountain, Jordansson, I will have to go anyway and see for myself," she said. "I didn't come all this way to back out now. Stella needs a tear, and I will get her one."

"Yes!" Jordansson grinned. "We will go and see a dragon tomorrow."

"Yes, *we* will," said Adele. "But *you* will not."

Chapter Fifty
"Fear and Follies"

Adele didn't sleep a wink during the night, but nor had she expected to. Instead, she had wrapped herself up in a jacket belonging to one of the twins like an enormous robe and sat outside for hours watching the glory that was the Path of the Goddess as it rippled across the night sky. Occasionally, one of her QGs would come and check on her, but Adele felt as safe as she ever had sitting at the top of the world and enjoying the magical electricity that made her Chime Voices sing their most beautiful songs.

The men rose early, so just after dawn, and a hearty breakfast of scrambled eggs and leftover stew, they set off on the next stage of their journey. The twins led the way, their giant strides eating up the distance as the rest of the group struggled to follow behind.

"No," said Adele, for the hundredth time that morning.

"But what if the dragon does not speak the King's Tongue?" said Jordansson as he tried to match step with Adele and almost tripped on his own feet. "I can translate for you."

"He was supposed to be Serena's lover, and the King's Tongue is her language, so I'm sure we'll cope," replied Adele. "Now, how much further?"

They were walking along a long, narrow path that spiraled up Dragon Mountain. Jordansson had laughed when the men had first started calling it Dragon Mountain and translated a very long and hard-to-pronounce name in his own tongue, but they had ignored him and still called it Dragon Mountain.

"But what if he eats you?" asked Jordansson, desperately seeking any excuse to make Adele take him in with the Queen's Guard.

"Look, Jordansson," said Adele. "I'll say it one more time: The Unisians are one of the tribes of Serena, and despite the story, I want to think that the dragon will very probably be happy to see us. You are from the people of Dahk'hani, and he probably won't be happy to see you. Plus, even though you are very charming, I'm not sure I really trust that you want to see the dragon for the same reason that we do. We will go in and talk with Sighmere, and if you still want to talk to him so much, you can go in after we leave."

Jordansson blinked. "What is 'charming'?" he asked.

"It means that you are full of charm," Leith answered, helpfully. "That you are brave and polite and especially attractive to women. Like me, I'm always called charming." He took Bear's cuff across the head with a laugh.

A slow smile crept across Jordansson's face. "Queen Adelena, you think I am this charming? Really?"

Adele rolled her eyes. She wasn't in the mood for Jordansson's flirting right now. "And if Sighmere ends up eating us, then you can be the person left alive who can tell our great and noble story."

"Can I put the part in about how we kissed and you think I'm charming?" laughed Jordansson.

"You got a kiss in with the queen?" Ohrig looked impressed. "When was that? I thought I was watching you two pretty closely."

"Ohrig, don't encourage him," said Adele. She stalked off up the hill to avoid the laughter of her men congratulating Jordansson on his luck.

The twins had stopped some way up the hill, and the thin air made Adele think that the top of the mountain was so close she could touch it. When she joined the twins, she saw why they had stopped.

The mountaintop had broken away from the rest of the mountainside, cloven as if by an axe. A long ice bridge connected the mountaintop to the edge where they were standing. The rest of the men came slogging up to join them.

"Shit, really?" Bear had already paled, and Adele felt a stab at the memory of the last time they had all crossed an ice bridge.

She had nothing but sympathy for her QG, but when she turned to him, she caught Ohrig's eye and saw the tiny shake of his head. She rethought her strategy and poked Bear in the chest. "You are going to suck it up, QG Bear. We need you on the other side of this bridge, and right now. You can go after me."

Bear nodded. "I'll go first, if it's all right with you, Your Majesty," he gulped. "Make sure it's safe."

The twins were confused about the exchange between the strangers, and though they asked Jordansson for a translation, he declined to comment, only giving Bear an encouraging hug to send him over the bridge.

Not wanting to take away from his victory over a personal fear, Adele failed to mention that the ice bridge was five times wider than the other they had crossed and at least that thick again. The other QGs walked three across, sauntering casually behind as QG Bear slowly set the pace, sliding one foot along in front of the other until they reached the other side.

"Thanks, Bear," said Pepper with a respectful nod. "It was good to have you out front."

"Yeah, you were a windbreak for us, so the walk was steady," added Owens.

Bear was doubled over, holding his knees and panting with the effort of the crossing. "Glad to be of help this time, lads," he said.

The twins had walked away from their group and set themselves near the entrance to an ice cave. Adele's stomach dropped away, and the Chime Voices started a worried tinkling. She reached inward for her magics and grasped at them firmly, comforted by how strong they still felt.

"That is where the dragon, Sighmere, sleeps," said Jordansson as he came to stand next to her.

Adele took a deep breath, but the air was so thin, it sounded like she was gasping. She looked into the cave before them and couldn't see anything but blue ice traveling down a long tunnel before curving around a corner. It'd be slippery and dangerous going down, and the cave looked like nothing so much as the giant maw of some creature, ice stalactites hanging over the entrance like teeth ready to chew them up.

Adele felt a nudge at her side and saw QG Owens holding a tiny notebook in his hand. "What do you think, Your Majesty?" he said, chewing a pencil in the corner of his mouth. "Normally, I don't write bets down as my memory is so good, but I was thinking I'd better this time so there's proof that I got something right."

Adele frowned. "What're you talking about, Owens?"

"How big this dragon is, Your Majesty," said Owens, tapping the book. "Lucky is saying as big as a cart horse, Pepper thinks it'll be the size of an ice bear, and Bear said as big as a cat, just to be contrary. Leith couldn't bet as he lost all his money on thinking you and Jordansson would've…on another bet, and the general doesn't gamble."

Adele pointed in the entrance of the cave. "You think a cat would need a door that big?" she asked.

"Technically, that was Bear's bet, Your Majesty," said Owens.

"The dragon will be the biggest creature you've ever seen," said Adele, losing her breath again in the thin air. "It'll stand as tall as…and as big as…" But she couldn't think of any way to describe a dragon that they would understand. The word "dinosaur" wouldn't make sense to anyone. "It'll have eyes as big as shields and teeth as long as swords," she added.

"Care to wager on it?" asked Owens.

"No," spluttered Adele. "I'm not going to bloody wager on it."

"I'll give you good odds, Your Majesty," grinned Owens. "Eyes as big as shields and teeth like swords will have ten to one odds, the longest yet."

"All right, go on then." Adele handed over the small bag of coins at her waist. "Hopefully, I'm wrong."

"So shall we go in, Your Majesty?" said General Ohrig, joining Adele at the mouth of the cave. "No time to waste now that we're here, I suppose."

Adele cast Ohrig a sideways glance to make sure he was joking. "I love your enthusiasm, Ohrig," she said, forcing a smile. "Personally, I'm not sure I would want to follow someone like me into a dark cave with a dragon when I've got no idea what to expect and no idea how to make him cry. Probably safer to stay up top with the ice twins and braid each other's hair."

"Probably," Ohrig sniffed and tightened his belt. "But Bear wanted to add another mythical creature to the growing list of dead, and this is just too good a chance to miss."

"Spider people, shadow wasps, ice bear, dragon," Bear counted them off on his fingers.

"The ice bear wasn't mythical," scoffed Lucky. "We knew they still existed before we killed it."

"One that big, though?" asked Bear, his eyes narrowing.

"I believe it was a common enough size for a full-grown bear," answered Lucky.

"That's not how I remember it," said Bear smoothly. "It was mythically huge, like Jordansson's brothers here. Maybe we could chop down one of them too."

Jordansson laughed and pointed to Tempestborn. "Take that one first. I won't miss him."

"We aren't going to kill the dragon," Adele reminded her men. "We just want to torture it emotionally until it can't take it anymore and bursts into tears."

"Spoken just like a woman," said Ohrig, chuckling to himself until he realized that all the men had fallen silent and were staring at Adele as she turned her hazel-eyed gaze on her general.

There was a long moment before a huge grin spread over Adele's face and she threw her head back and laughed. "Well, I'm sick of practicing on you lot," she said, and all the men broke apart laughing, relieving some of the nervous tension building between them.

Stormchaser exchanged a glance with his twin, Tempestborn, and received a shrug in return. He nudged Jordansson for an explication of the Unisians' odd behavior.

"They laugh so they do not fear," explained Jordansson in the King's Tongue and smiled at his friends. "That is the way the tiny people make the big world seem smaller for themselves."

Adele wiped her eyes and pulled out the hand mirror from her waist. "I just want to call home, and then we can go in," she said. She walked away from the group. "You men could start praying to Serena to protect us from her dragon lover to see if it helps."

Adele opened the mirror and took a look at herself. She was pale, and her pupils were only pinpricks in the glare of the sun at the top of the mountain. Her greasy hair had been pulled back into a tight braid, and she could only be grateful that Rainere wouldn't be able to smell her.

She called his name softly and was surprised at how quickly Rainere responded. She could see his head and shoulders and the purple velvet curtains behind him. He was clearly in the royal apartment, and Adele felt a sharp pang of homesickness, wanting to be exactly where Rainere was too.

"Rainere," Adele gasped, cursing the thin air for her breathlessness. Her heart hammered in her chest as she looked upon his finely carved face. "We have found the dragon, I just wanted to tell you before I went in and..." *tried not to die,* Adele thought but didn't risk saying. "Could I see the children, please?"

Adele watched Rainere's gaze flicker to the room beyond her vision. "They are a little indisposed just now, Your Majesty, perhaps—"

"Rainere, please, I need to see them before I go in," begged Adele. "I'm frankly terrified, and I can't do this without talking to them first. It'll give me courage."

A thousand expressions flitted across Rainere's face, but the last settled into sympathy. "Yes, Your Majesty," his voice rasped. "Let me fetch them for you."

The image went black as Rainere covered his mirror, and Adele waited a long minute before she saw the small faces of her children, their heads together, trying to see her in the mirror.

"Natalie! Aaron!" Adele felt the tears catch in her throat. "Oh, my babies, how are you? Are you good? I miss you both so much!"

"Mummy, we had a bad day," whimpered Aaron, and Adele saw the tears fall down his face, leaving tracks in the dirt on his cheeks.

"What?" Adele's heart constricted. "What do you mean 'bad day,' sweetheart? Tell Mummy what happened."

"They put me in the dark, Mummy." Aaron couldn't say any more as he broke down in sobs and arms embraced him, taking him away from Adele's gaze.

"Natalie, tell me what happened," ordered Adele.

Natalie's eyes were wide, and she shook her head. "Come home," was all she could manage before she buried her face in her hands, her little shoulders shaking.

The image swung wildly back to Rainere. "The children are safe now, Your Majesty," he said. "The men responsible have been punished, and I want you to know I have the situation in hand—"

"Rainere," Adele spoke through gritted teeth, choking back the horror that something awful had just happened to her children without her there to protect them. "I don't care what it takes, but you keep those children alive until I get home, and you tell those St. Lucidis wizards that I will burn their entire kingdom DOWN TO THE GROUND, IF ANYONE TOUCHES ANOTHER HAIR ON MY CHILDREN'S HEADS." She dropped her voice and poured every ounce of menace that she could into it. "Do you understand me, Prince Rainere?"

"I understand, Your Majesty," Rainere croaked. "I will let the wizards know."

Adele snapped the mirror shut and stood up. Her magics fired through her blood, rage and fear mingling as she looked for an enemy to fight.

"Your Majesty, are the children all right?" Ohrig called out, as every man got to his feet to join Adele.

"There has been an incident," snapped Adele. She tried to regain control of the magic that fizzed from her hands, dripping to the ground and melting the ice. "I need to get home now."

"We're ready, Your Majesty," said Captain Lucky, and the men assembled behind him.

"Right." Adele shook off the last sprinkles of magic from her fingertips. "Let's go see if this dragon is frightened of demons."

Adele stepped into the entrance of the icy cave and felt no chill with the magic coursing through her blood. Though she still didn't know what to say to the dragon, she felt her own fears recede as the image of Natalie's and Aaron's sad little faces were stamped in her mind. *I will not fail them again,* she promised herself and held on to that fierce thought, forcing her feet forward down the throat of the tunnel.

Chapter Fifty-One
"Strategies of the Desperate"

"Well, that went as well as could be expected," said Ripenzo, watching as Mrs. Ollenby hustled the weeping children out of the room and into the comfort of their nursery. "Adelena was going to hear about it eventually—better from you, Prince Rainere, than anyone else, I guess."

"No, the timing couldn't have been worse!" cursed Rainere. Leaping to his feet, he began pacing the room. "Didn't you hear? Adelena is about to enter the home of the dragon Sighmere, and now she is feeling furious and reckless. You have no idea what she is capable of when she gets angry. She is a danger to everyone, including herself."

A ringing silence followed his words as Rainere, Ohren, Ripenzo Shale, Charlie, and Benjamin all considered what that meant.

"I just thank the goddess that you weren't stupid enough to mention that we've lost Princess Stella too," said Ripenzo. "I know you said your spell signal says she is close by in the palace, but it's no coincidence that she goes missing on the same day as her siblings."

"The Sleeping Guard protecting Stella was activated sometime very early this morning and if anyone tries to take her out of the Golden Palace then they will die, very painfully," snarled Rainere, and mopped at the blood still trickling from the bullet wound on his arm. "As soon as we decide how to proceed, I will find her and punish those responsible."

Ripenzo nodded. "Seems fair."

"It will be a messy and lingering death," promised Rainere, wrapping a fresh bandage around his arm.

"Enough!" groaned Ohren. "I cannot legally hear you planning to commit murder in the Golden Palace, Prince Rainere."

Silence fell over the group again.

"If Adelena gets herself killed, who gets custody of the children?" asked Ripenzo, looking thoughtful. "She has no close relatives left on her St. Lucidis side, and I doubt any demons will come forward for them."

"I would take them," said Rainere. "I am actually their closest relative by marriage on my stepmother's side, as well as the fact that Her Majesty left me as their legal custodian."

"Would the high wizard let them go to you, though?" asked Ripenzo, stepping up to poke Ohren in the back. "Or would you try to keep up the charade of the kids being your pedigree heirs? I only ask as I know you have a history of throwing children away when it suits you."

With an angry shout, Ohren launched himself at Ripenzo Shale, just as the younger man sprang behind a chair, narrowly avoiding being caught by the supernaturally fast wizard.

Ripenzo wagged his finger. "Tut tut, High Wizard, your dark magic is showing."

"Who the hell *are* you?" Ohren spat with fury, magic sparkles forming a gold halo around his head. "And where the hell did you come from? You sneak into the palace pretending to be a servant, and then we are just supposed to believe that you have the same name as the Sandarian ambassador and thief Ripenzo Shale."

"I'm family, mate," grinned Ripenzo, winking at Rainere like he was in on the joke.

"You are a *liar*," spat Ohren. "And I'll have you imprisoned until we find out who you really are."

"Ohren, you will not," interjected Rainere. He moved to stand between the two men. "Ripenzo helped us rescue the children, and Adelena will want to—"

"How do we know that he didn't orchestrate the whole thing himself just to get near her children?" said Ohren. The halo above his head had turned into a little cloud of gold sprinkled with green flecks.

"Stop acting a fool, Ohren!" snapped Rainere, his tone heavy with derision. "Why would Rip kidnap the children and then stay around to help rescue them? The goddess herself would weep at such stupidity!"

"I wasn't kidding," said Ripenzo, pointing to the roiling cloud above Ohren's head. "Your dark magic is showing."

With an irritated swipe of his hand, Ohren dispersed the magic into the air. "Well, if we are going to *trust* that it wasn't the mysterious stranger with the odd name who kidnapped the children," he replied, still glaring at Ripenzo as he sat back down in his chair, "who was it?"

"Well, it has to be the Boss," replied Rainere, looking hard at the high wizard. "And he has to be someone in a position of great power in the Golden Palace right now. Someone privy to all our conversations and plans. Maybe someone even masquerading as a friend, while at the same time plotting Adelena's murder."

The high wizard frowned, but it was clear he was taking the suggestion seriously. "But for the Boss to have orchestrated such a thing as the kidnapping, he would also have to have an intimate knowledge of the Golden Palace and the children's schedule. Obviously, he lives or works in the palace. Does anyone have any idea of what this Boss even looks like behind his fierce reputation?"

"I've seen him," said Charlie. "In fact, he kind of looks like you, High Wizard."

"Me?" Ohren was shocked.

"Not like you are now," corrected Charlie. "But like you really look—without the magic."

Ohren instinctively rolled his hands together, clicking his heavy rings. "But that's not possible," he said. "There must be some mistake. Surely there are at least a dozen young men who look similar to me in the palace."

"Not similar to you—*like* you," insisted Charlie, pale with the bravery it took to confront the man who he thought had tortured him for years.

Ohren saw the pain and fear in Charlie's eyes and stopped protesting. "Charlie, I'm sorry, but I am not the Boss. I wouldn't do anything to hurt Adelena or her children on purpose."

Ohren looked around at the other men, who were all staring at him, the question in their eyes. He raised his chin, prepared to defend his honor with logic. "Besides, with the exception of Prince Rainere, I would have been able to kill you all in a heartbeat to protect myself if I was, wouldn't I?"

"Makes sense." Ripenzo shrugged as he got up to help himself to some grapes from a fruit bowl. "But you have a brother, don't you, High Wizard? A certain high magistrar who is your identical twin?"

"You need to stop making ridiculous accusations, Shale!" said Ohren, but his demand lacked conviction, and his cheeks paled above his gray whiskers. "Orestes would never betray his family. He is high magistrar because he respects the law of Unisia and upholds it to the letter. He wouldn't betray *me*."

A furious pounding on the door interrupted the high wizard's denials, and Ripenzo hurried to answer it. Lady Olivia pushed her way into the apartment, her eyes searching wildly until they found Prince Rainere.

"Prince Rainere, your girlfriend's here," called Ripenzo needlessly as Lady Olivia dashed to Rainere and threw herself on the ground at his feet.

"Your Highness, I have come to warn you!" Olivia's hands shook where she rested them on Rainere's knees. "Two dead squires have been found in the stables, killed by dark magic, and the royal children are believed kidnapped. Lord Orgustus also found Princess Stella hidden in a secret room and trapped in a sleeping curse. He has taken her into custody and is keeping her in his own chambers. Mr. Gorrik said you are the only one who could have performed such dark magic and with that evidence Lord Orgustus is coming here right now to arrest you. You must leave the Golden Palace at once!"

Prince Rainere rose to his feet, and green magic fizzed into his hands as he squared his shoulders turning to the door. "He can try," he snarled. "But he will find his death comes early today."

"No, Rainere, you can't!" shouted Ohren desperately. He jumped in front of Rainere and grabbed the prince's wrists as if to restrain him. Rainere instantly shook Ohren off, but before he could strike at him, Ripenzo was there, pushing his way between the two wizards. Lady Olivia scrambled off her knees and found a safer seat by Benjamin.

"I will not be arrested and thrown in prison like some common criminal!" shouted Rainere. His dark green eyes glowed with anger. "I am a Marchant prince and immortal wizard. No mere St. Lucidis commoner has the right to judge me."

"I love the confidence, mate," said Rip. "But you fight them off, or run, and you just prove your own guilt in their eyes."

Rainere crossed his arms. "I will burn this palace to the ground before I debase myself with imprisonment," he snapped.

"If you burn this place down, then you will take the only home the children know, and that Adelena has got to come back to," said Ohren, but he looked more anxious than angry with the prince. "Prince Rainere, please think! You just rescued the Natalie and Aaron from the Boss, and Stella is still unwell. Even if you could get them all back to the Gray Palace, you would have the full force of the Unisian Court and every army in the country on your doorstep declaring war on the Marchant family."

Rainere raised a single eyebrow and smiled an awful smile. "You think I'm frightened of war, High Wizard?"

Ohren threw up his hands in despair. "Prince Rainere, you cannot use your power to destroy our nation. It would cause absolute chaos, and our world as we know it would end."

"I don't care," Rainere enunciated each word carefully so the high wizard and everyone in the room was completely clear on his position. "I don't belong to your world, and I would be happy to see it end."

"But Adelena wouldn't," interrupted Ripenzo. "She wouldn't want you to kill everybody to save your own pride, would she? She belongs here, and the children belong here. They might only be half St. Lucidis, but they are the good half of it."

Rainere opened his mouth and thought about what Adelena would do if she came all the way home from her voyage with the dragon tear in hand, only to find Rainere and her children prisoners in the Gray Palace with the whole of Unisia having declared war on them. He shut his mouth again.

"So I should let myself be arrested?" snarled Rainere. "Leaving the children free for anyone else to attack while I'm locked up?"

"Hey! If all Lord Orgustus needs is a scapegoat because Marchant magic was used, I can just say it was me," said Charlie, joining the tense group. "I'm an outsider, no one in the palace really knows me, and I could prove that I'm strong enough to use dark magic to kill someone—maybe not two at once, but they were only young fellas. So blame me." Charlie swallowed hard and flicked the hair out of his eyes with a sharp jerk. Rainere could see what it cost the boy to speak without crying.

"You make a good point, Charlie, and it would be more useful to sacrifice you instead of the prince," agreed Ohren, but Ripenzo was already rounding on the boy.

"Oh, for fuck's sake, Charlie!" Rip shouted. "See, this is how you get yourself into these dangerous bloody situations. Stop working so hard at being a martyr for your goddess-damned queen, and use your head for once." Rip turned back to Rainere. "Come on, Rainere, don't let the boy go down for you. Let them arrest you and give us time to think of a way to get you out. We can keep Adelena's little ones safe. It's the only way."

A heavy silence fell over the room. "If you really didn't do it, Your Highness, and Natalie and Aaron are still alive," said Lady Olivia in a small voice. "Then I'm sure the high magistrar will find you innocent."

"You thought Rainere might've killed the children?" Rip cocked his head to the side and looked down at the young woman. "Yet you came to warn him anyway? What a loyal girlfriend you turned out to be! A little coldhearted, sure—but loyal."

Lady Olivia blushed and looked down at her lap, almost managing to hide the triumphant gleam in her eye.

"Lady Olivia is not my girlfriend," snapped Rainere. He stalked to a side table and poured himself a Firewhiskey. "She is just some harlot who threw herself at me."

"And you knew just the way to catch her, if I saw that right," said Ripenzo, winking at Rainere despite the hot glare he received in return.

High Wizard Ohren was irritated at the turn the conversation had taken and coughed meaningfully. "So back to the point, can it be said that we are agreed? Prince Rainere, you will go quietly, and we will work to free you from the prisons as soon as we are able."

Rainere swigged back his Firewhiskey. "And if the high magistrar turns out to be the Boss and refuses to let me out again? How far do we take this thing before I have your *permission* to get myself free?"

Ohren shrugged helplessly, so Ripenzo answered for him. "You have my word, Rainere Rainov Lucien Gray Marchant. I will see you freed before a week is over." There was a puff of gold sparkles on his lips to signify the gravity of the oath he uttered.

Rainere pressed his mouth in a hard line and nodded. "*Seven days.*"

The argument ended there as the door crashed open, and Lord Orgustus, followed by the high magistrar, Orestes, and a dozen Household Guard in their purple and gold uniforms filed in.

Lord Orgustus found the center of the room and surveyed the group staring at him, his canny gaze calculating the threat each person posed to him. His lip curled at the sight of Lady Olivia sitting on the couch beside Benjamin, but he didn't deign to speak to her. Ever the orator, it was clear he was soaking up every moment of the drama. Unfurling a scroll, Orgustus didn't take his eyes off the Marchant prince as he read his prepared speech.

"Prince Rainere Marchant, you are being arrested in the name of the queen, Adelena Olivia Serena St. Lucidis, on charges of kidnapping the royal children, Princess Natalie and Prince Aaron, and two counts of murder by dark magic. You are also accused of being responsible for using dark magic to imprison Princess Stella in death. We have witnesses to each of your crimes and evidence to support them."

"Lord Orgustus, the children are alive and accounted for," said High Wizard Ohren, drawing himself up to his full height in front of the pompous lord. "Princess Natalie and Prince Aaron are in their nursery now. I can show you myself."

"The reappearance of the children still won't explain the two dead squires down at the royal stables, High Wizard." Lord Orgustus's tone was as cold as his eyes. "Nor does it account for Princess Stella. Our queen is missing, and in her absence, I have the power to arrest the custodian of the royal children if I believe they are in danger while in his care. I can claim custody of the royal children in his stead or until he is proved innocent of all charges." He waved a hand at Orestes, who stood at his right shoulder. "Isn't that what you told me, High Magistrar?"

High Magistrar Orestes nodded and gave his twin an apologetic glance. "That is the law of Unisia, my Lord Orgustus."

Raising his chin proudly, Orgustus prepared to recommence reading his scroll.

"As delightful as I find your little parade," interrupted Rainere. "I would like it noted on the official record that I dispute all charges, but that I will agree to being arrested under Unisian law and will go"—he tasted the word like it was something foul—"quietly."

If Lord Orgustus was surprised by this easy victory, he didn't show it. Instead, he raised a finger for silence. "I will also announce that all those of a known Marchant bloodline, or recognizable as being from a Marchant bloodline, will be imprisoned until it can be proven that they were not accomplices in the acts of which the Marchant prince has now been accused."

"What? That's not lawful," protested the high wizard. "Orestes, we can't arrest anyone just for having Marchant blood."

"Actually, yes, we can, with due cause," replied his brother. "The laws that were written after the last Marchant exodus were stringent and binding."

"That means that I'm taking the boy, Charlie, as well," said Lord Orgustus. "He is an alleged ex-consort of Queen Adelena and, as such, would have been privy to the confidence of the children. He was also seen at the site where the children were taken earlier today and now here at the site of their return."

"I never!" spluttered Charlie, but Ripenzo hushed him with a hand on his shoulder.

Lord Orgustus's eyes scanned the room again, jumping over Ripenzo and landing on Benjamin. "I'll take him too," he said, but his triumphant gaze fell on Lady Olivia. "The Marchant stable boy has been working directly for Prince Rainere as his personal groom. It won't be hard to prove any collusion between them. Guards, put the prisoners in chains."

Rainere stiffened when two guards approached him, proffering handcuffs before them. He looked each man in the eye and held out his wrists. "Who is going to risk touching me first?" he asked, his voice heavy with menace. The two guards looked at each other and pulled back.

"For the sake of the goddess, I'll do it myself!" Lord Orgustus stormed over and grabbed the irons as the other guards hurried to handcuff Charlie and Benjamin behind him.

He approached Prince Rainere and slapped the cuffs on his outstretched wrists. "This is for the kingdom, and this is for your false queen," hissed Orgustus so no one else could hear. His crystal-blue eyes looked directly into Rainere's dark green gaze as he sneered, "Imagine all the stupid things she is going to do when she finds out I've put you in prison. I will have her off that throne so fast her little head is going to spin."

"Do not underestimate *your* queen, Lord Orgustus," replied Rainere. "I mean less to her than you might think."

"Really?" Orgustus raised his eyebrows and feigned thoughtfulness. "Well, if you're out of the way, and I have custody of her children, I might as well go ahead and marry her, then. She's a bit old for my tastes, but I'm sure she's lively enough. I'll have her pregnant before the year is out! I can do that, you know—father children."

It took every ounce of Rainere's self-control to see through the bait and not kill the man where he stood. "You are a bit late to the party on that, my lord." Rainere forced a thin smile. "Once you've had a Marchant man between your legs, there's no going back. Just ask Lady Olivia."

The fury on Lord Orgustus's face was all the response that Rainere needed to calm down, and he gave High Wizard Ohren a polite nod before being escorted from the royal apartments. "You have seven days, High Wizard, that's all."

Chapter Fifty-Two
"The Dragon Sighmere"

The ice beneath their feet changed to mud and then to dry dirt as Adele and her men crept down the long tunnel. The only light was from their torches, and the only sounds were of their harsh breathing. Once again, as before any great challenge, Adele knew that only she could hear the music in her mind. It was playing a complicated melody in a rollicking tempo that filled her head and made her magics dance as the Chime Voices sang along.

"Your Majesty, I think there's something up ahead," whispered Captain Lucky when they stopped for a break. "I can feel vibrations in the wall."

Adele nodded and wiped the sweat from her forehead. "It's getting warmer down here," she said. "Any idea how long we've been walking for?"

"Hard to say," said Ohrig. He shoved a canteen of water into her hand. "Maybe twenty minutes, but this curve never stops, so I guess we're spiraling down into the earth, like a giant corkscrew."

Everyone took a drink and continued walking, following the wall. When the dark began to lighten, the group automatically slowed their pace. Adele thought every curve would be their last as her eyes adjusted to the growing light, but they went even further down, having to strip off jackets and scarves as the temperature climbed.

At last they reached an enormous cavern where the air itself glowed with golden light. Shuffling back to cling to the wall, Adele felt horribly exposed, with nothing to hide behind. The music in her head had come to a sudden stop, and that didn't bode well.

Adele took in the vast cavern, taller even than the tunnel. The walls stretched so far away that she could barely make them out around the dozens of finely carved columns that supported the ceiling. What looked like glowing stars hovering among the columns provided the light that reflected off piles of gold coins and jewels scattered on the ground.

"The dragon's hoard," whispered Adele. She hoped none of the other myths about dragons that she'd heard were true.

"Must be the gifts Jordansson told us about," Ohrig whispered back. "Looks like the dragon has had a fair few visitors over the last centuries. Hopefully, that means he's friendly, after all."

Adele scanned the area for any movement or dragon-shaped forms, but she saw nothing. "I think I'm going to have to knock on his door," she whispered. She looked back at the white faces of the Queen's Guard hunched together behind her. "If he tries to eat us, it's every man for himself, all right? You will run—that's an order."

The Queen's Guard exchanged nods with each other, and Adele almost sighed. She knew they were all agreeing to ignore her.

She stepped out of the tunnel and into the cavern. "Hello! I seek the dragon Sighmere!" she shouted. "I am Queen Adelena Olivia Serena St. Lucidis, and I would talk with you."

There was a sound like wind rushing through trees, and out of thin air, a bright golden ball of light shaped itself into a long, sinuous form. The dragon had arrived. Protecting her eyes from the glare, Adele moved deeper into the cavern and heard her men shuffle after her. The light finally dimmed enough for her to see what faced them.

The dragon was massive and covered in sparkling gold and bronze scales. His head was as big as a carriage, and when he grinned, teeth as long as swords appeared over his lower lip. An eye as big as a shield blinked slowly, and the dragon dropped his gaze to Adele and her men. He made a sound like a motor purring, and a tongue as long as his tail unfurled and tasted the air above Adele, making her instinctively duck into a squat.

"Look here, I have an angel come to visit me." The dragon's voice rang out like a bell, but his mouth didn't move from his terrible smile. "Or am I dreaming her?"

Adele trembled as adrenaline coursed through her system and she looked upon the greatest predator she had ever seen. Power vibrated the very air around the dragon. His magic didn't just spark but flowed in solid waves of gold over the claws of each of his four feet. Despite his size, the dragon settled himself like a cat, the clicking of his scales the only sound in the chamber.

Adele forced herself to stand upright. "Sighmere, I come from—"

"I know where you come from, little angel," sang Sighmere, angling his head so he could look at her more closely. "I want to know why you are here."

"I have come—" she began again.

"It's been an age since I saw an angel in my domain," Sighmere sang, and his sigh ruffled Adele's hair like a warm breeze. "They used to come and sing to me, but now I am left all alone. I have nothing more to give them, and they have nothing more to say."

"Sighmere!" Adele raised her voice. "I cannot sing to you, but I will tell you why I have crossed the world of Evendaar to seek you out."

"Strange, little ugly thing you are," Sighmere's voice chimed. "Not at all like the others, but you smell of the stars and dust and sadness and the stink of motorcars."

Adele felt her jaw drop. "What do you know about motorcars?" she blurted out.

The dragon blinked slowly. "We visited so many worlds, my beautiful goddess and I," he sang. "Earth was so dull, though her children wanted to stay and play." He began to hum a lilting tune.

The Chime Voices began to echo the song of the dragon, confusing Adele's thoughts and filling her head with music again. With an effort she pulled upon the green magic beneath her heart and felt the strength of it help settle the confusion.

"I hope you will forgive me, Sighmere, but I have come to ask something of you," Adele shouted over the dragon's humming. "I need a tear to save the life of my daughter. Will you give me one?"

Sighmere stopped humming, and the silence was hideous. The dragon moved his head even closer to Adele so that if she had wanted to, she could have reached out and touched one of his long, glittering eyelashes. His sinuous russet tongue unfurled and ran over his lips.

"A tear, says the ugly angel," huffed Sighmere tunelessly. "A tear will not fix your face or help your mind unknot, nor purify the taint from your blood. A tear will not heal your broken heart, ugly angel."

"Please," begged Adele. "I do not ask for me, but for my daughter. Stella caught the Summer Influenza in Unisia. She is terribly sick and will die without your tear, Sighmere. I only need it to save her life."

Sighmere hummed, and in a shimmer of light, he twisted his neck and gazed at her from his other eye. "My heart is hollow, and as even you can see, my eyes are dry, ugly angel. Though you are one of her children, and I could almost weep to see you so disfigured."

The dragon's insults made Adele curious. "Are the other angels so very beautiful?" she asked.

The dragon raised his head and breathed out a sphere of magic as large as Adele herself, its sides shimmering with rainbow ripples. Inside the bubble one figure after another spun. Women with long hair of every color, lithe and tall, with muscular forms—they glowed with health and were so beautiful that Adele almost cringed into herself. Almost, but didn't. She had a job to do.

"You are right, Sighmere," Adele agreed. "Angels are beautiful. I don't know why the goddess Serena made me so ugly, if that is what my sisters look like."

"Her ways are mysterious," hummed Sighmere. "Though I have known her across the eons, still she will not reveal herself to me."

"Nor do I understand why she let me give birth to a child without any magic in her body, even though I am so strong," replied Adele, shifting the topic back to the only one that mattered to her. "Perhaps Serena makes mistakes sometimes?"

The dragon Sighmere spun like a cyclone, the wind knocking everyone from their feet, before settling back into his form. "You dare to question your mother, the goddess?" he shouted, loud enough to shake the coins in their piles, sending them cascading to the dirt. "You dare to blaspheme before me?"

Adele imagined Stella in her bed and took a deep breath. Angry or not, this dragon would give her what she came for.

She decided not to be frightened. With only a thought, her magic spread, coating her skin in an invisible armor that not only protected her physically but helped keep her mind sound too. The gold magic fired every synapse in her brain, and the green magic filled her blood, sending her heart pumping and giving her the feeling of being invincible, even before a dragon. The human part of Adele whispered that she was being stupid, that someone as tiny and weak as she was shouldn't be challenging a dragon, but the demon queen ignored it. She needed this dragon to cry, and she wouldn't stop until he had. It was clear he was obsessed with his goddess, and that was where she would start.

"I know someone who has spoken to Serena," said Adele. "Just recently."

Sighmere dropped his head and scented the air around Adele's head again, his tongue almost brushing her hair. "You lie, angel," he whispered. "My goddess does not speak with mortals on this plane; she cannot come here anymore."

"He isn't mortal," replied Adele. She wasn't sure the dragon could see her properly down on the ground, so she scrambled up to stand on a nearby chest inlaid with rubies and gems. "Prince Rainere Marchant is an immortal wizard. He was traveling on a spell through the universe to find me, and he became lost. Rainere thought he was going to die, but the goddess caught him and told him that he must return to Evendaar and save me from those who would see me dead. She said we were fated to be lovers."

"Then it is your lover who lies, that Marchant prince," sang the dragon, his melody stubborn and sure of itself. "The goddess does not know what passes on this world—she could not. It's impossible."

"No," Adele raised her arms, reaching to the sky. "It's her prophecy that we follow. It's her prophecy that guides her people in Unisia."

The happiest sound in the world rang out in peals, shaking the stars hovering in the ceiling and vibrating the air so hard that Adele fell off her chest and into Lucky's arms as he dove to catch her.

"What's happening, Your Majesty?" Captain Lucky's eyes were wide with the fear and wonder to which Adele was immune with her magical shield.

She looked up to see Sighmere stamping his front feet into the ground, his tongue lolling from his mouth and his great eyes closed. "He is laughing at me," she replied. "Lucky, look! I see a tear, get the bags!"

Lucky passed the word, and despite their fear, the Queen's Guard did as they were told and grabbed the bags they had brought in with them. Only Leith and Lucky got under the dragon's head in time to catch the giant drop of liquid as it spun shimmering from the eye of Sighmere. Adele jumped in next to her men but was a moment too late, so she was drenched by the falling liquid, along with the two QGs. All three of them lit up with a glow that covered them from head to toe. The Chime Voices shrieked for joy, and Adele felt the dragon's magic soak through her magical shield and absorb into her bloodstream. She tasted the tear on her lips and watched Lucky and Leith do the same.

"It's so sweet," said Leith. "It tastes like fruit and flowers and my mother's perfume all at once."

"How about you all back up to a safe distance?" said Ohrig and frowned at the three of them standing beneath the maw of the dragon, grinning at each other and licking the tear off their chins. "Your Majesty, we've got what we came for—we should get out of here."

The peals of dragon laughter died away, echoing sweetly in the corners of the vast cavern. "You stupid angel." Sighmere grinned, and hundreds of teeth gleamed in the golden light. "What you call prophecy is only a conversation with Serena. Your silly minds cannot comprehend the songs of the stars or the beauty of the future and the dreams of a goddess. She sings you a song, and you cling to it like some sort of truth."

Adele clambered up onto the trunk again, narrowly avoiding Ohrig's grasp as he tried to pull her back to his side.

"Tell me, what is the truth?" Adele felt drunk and high. The words dripped from her lips like notes, and the Chime Voices sang joyfully, weaving the magics in her blood until the three powers formed a shimmering, pulsing fabric. Adele felt the beauty of the magic like silk dragged over her skin, and the sensation was so delicious that she could hardly focus on the enormous dragon before her.

"My truth is an eons-long tale of love and betrayal," sighed Sighmere, blinking his golden eyes. "But you have brought me the gift of laughter, my ugly angel, and I have rewarded you with a tear, though it surprised us both. You will want to leave now. You are your mother's daughter, after all."

Though she heard her men shuffling behind her and Ohrig giving orders to check the seal on the two large bags, each holding almost a gallon of the tear, Adele shook her head. "Tell me your story, Sighmere," she said. She looked up into the dragon's huge golden eye. "I want to understand you better and know the path Serena has set for us."

The dragon Sighmere took in a deep breath, and Adele felt the air rush past her and whistle between his teeth. "There is no path set for us, angel," he said. "I sit and wait for my lover to return, and you will be only dust before Serena remembers that she made you at all."

Adele sat down on the chest and crossed her legs. She waved behind her for her men to settle in and threw a glance at Ohrig, trying to communicate all that she was thinking: *This is important, Ohrig. The dragon can solve the riddle of the Prophecy of the End of the World and explain who I am. After Stella is healed, I can make sure that we are never in danger again if I can tell all those wizards that there are no "dark days" coming to Unisia and that we are just caught up in a game of the gods.*

Ohrig only frowned, his pale blue eyes glaring at Adele. "Let's go," he whispered, not understanding at all. This was magic, and it made his skin crawl to be at the mercy of it.

"Sighmere," said Adele, and it was the Chime Voices who sang his name, calling the dragon to attention. "I am listening."

Chapter Fifty-Three
"And in the Beginning"

"In the beginning there was only darkness. The darkness grew until it became so infinite that it created a Thought, and that Thought became Light. Light cast a glow, pushing back the darkness, and the glow became Hope. Light and Hope made love a million times and then a billion times over, until suddenly Life sprang from the breast of Hope and spread throughout the darkness, defining the Universe, harnessing Father Light to make the stars and planets and forming galaxies and its own strange and tiny universes."

Sighmere breathed out. "This is more than I have sung in over a hundred years," he said, with a happy chuckle. "I am enjoying myself."

"From Life the gods were created, and they worshipped Father Light and Mother Hope, as good children should worship their parents. The gods created more of themselves, and with their very own hope, they began to emulate creation, building their own worlds and universes.

"Father Light was pleased with the gods and showed them many things, but he worried for his children, as fathers do, and he created Time to contain the gods and their creations so they would not hurt themselves. Time was the shadow of creation, defining the difference between forever and a moment. The gods didn't like Time, as everything they made was harnessed by Time and would eventually pass out of eternity. So they worked hard to create new worlds unconfined by the limits of Time, worlds that would last forever. But alas, the harder they worked, the longer Time became.

"The god Dahk'hani felt the pull of Time so hard that he sought to escape it by experimenting with perspective. There was a world that he had built in a galaxy not far from the Realm of the Gods.

He contained himself in a tiny form and settled his feet on the new world. There he walked the earth and lived as long as his mortal form could sustain itself. After just a short time, the body fell apart, and the god was released. Yet in that moment of mortal death, the god had held the breath of freedom from Time. Delighted with his discovery, Dahk'hani shared the knowledge with his sister, Serena. She joined Dahk'hani in the mortal world and took the form of a tiny being that she called 'human.' Serena and Dahk'hani lived in joy, naming the world 'Evendaar' and creating tribes of humans and animals—all for the purpose of watching them die and seeing them pass through the instant of Timelessness that so fascinated the gods.

"Serena never tired of playing at mortality, and though she treasured the creatures she had created and loved watching them die, she needed to return to the Realm of the Gods from time to time to release her power from such a tiny form. It was during one of these visits that I met Serena. Her power was wild and glorious, and our lights blended as beautifully as a song. Our love lit the universe around us, and Serena wanted to show me all that she knew of mortality and Timelessness. In Evendaar I was not as practiced as she at condensing my power into so small a form, so I took this shape, which Serena called 'dragon' to honor me. Serena taught me the magic of creation, and I made my own tribe under the light of the full moon and called them 'elf,' but they were ugly, and their power was as warped as their minds, so I made them servants of the favored tribe of Serena, a gift to her little Marchants. Dahk'hani was angry to see his beloved sister's new lover and the life we made together, and he tried to compete with me, creating more complex creatures than ever I could.

"Serena could never understand jealousy, between gods or mortal animals. She played lover to both of us, then between her tribes of humans. In retaliation Dahk'hani let Dark Entities enter Evendaar, seeking to destroy all that she had built. I discovered Dahk'hani's malice and told Serena. She was distraught to see her creatures die so quickly without any joy of life, and so we sought to close all the portals where the Dark Entities entered the world.

Dahk'hani saw Serena's sadness, and he became sorry. In his attempt to win her back to his side, Dahk'hani created a new race of humans, a handful of tribes bigger and stronger than Serena's tribes, and gave them a strange magic that made them impervious to both the gold and green magics of the natural world. He gifted them to Serena and begged her forgiveness. Serena was delighted to have peace with her brother again and asked me to create a paradise in Evendaar for these new tribes of Dahk'hani. While I went to level the mountains and melt the ice of the northern lands, Dahk'hani followed me with his tribes, and they attacked me.

"Our battle was fierce. He fought me with fire, and I fought him with ice, but our cries drowned out the calls of Serena as more Dark Entities invaded the land of Evendaar and killed her creatures. Alone, Serena fought the Dark Entities and was forced to gift martial skills to her own tribes of humans to allow them to defend themselves. Finally, she left Evendaar, sealing the last door to the Realm of the Gods behind her and leaving Dahk'hani and me together to fight our eternal war for her love."

Sighmere stammered to a stop and rolled his great eyes to the ceiling of the cavern, the lights dancing across his face. "My lover left me because I allowed Dahk'hani to trick me, and so I didn't hear her call for me. After she left I buried myself under the ground, heavy with shame, and decreed that I would not walk her beautiful world without her. Now I wait for her forgiveness." The dragon sighed. "Even if I must wait until the end of Time itself."

Adele felt a sharp jab in her back. "Your Majesty, it's time to go," hissed Ohrig. "If you won't walk, then I am going to bloody well carry you out of here."

Adele gave Ohrig a nod and climbed to her feet on the chest. "Sighmere, thank you for your story." She bowed from the waist. "I too understand heartbreak and betrayal, but you should know that your story has not ended. If you had been to the surface of Evendaar, you would know that the goddess Serena sent you a path home to her. We saw it."

Sighmere's reaction was swift and violent. After the whirlwind died, Adele found herself dangling in the air, held by magic that felt hot around her waist. Sighmere looked down his nose at her, a snarl curling his russet lip. "What do you know of Serena, little malformed angel?"

"Please." Adele could hardly breathe. "Look inside me—I have seen it. There is a path across the sky, with lights that shine blue and green and purple and gold. It will take you home."

Adele could see the flash of the dragon's magic coming at her, but despite her two magics, she couldn't stop the invasion as her mind exploded under his touch.

In agony Adele relived every day of her life at light speed. The only comfort came from flashing images of her children, their births and laughter, and the unadulterated joy they brought her. Then it was Rainere turning from a wisp of a dream into a flesh-and-blood man, loving her and igniting her magic with his. Then the pain was gone, and air rushed into her lungs. Finally, Adele opened her eyes and felt herself falling ever so slowly to the ground. General Ohrig was holding her up and cradling her head in his hands, but she couldn't hear what he was saying, only feel his love and fear as it rippled off his skin.

Adele felt fragile and hollow, as if the euphoria had filled her body only to leave a deeper emptiness behind. Tears leaked from her eyes, and she ached to have the power of the dragon inside her again. Wanting to beg for it, Adele could only open her mouth and gasp, clutching at the front of Ohrig's shirt as he pulled her up into his arms.

"Little angel, you have seen much," whispered the dragon Sighmere. "I will follow you to this path of my goddess. Tell me, does Dahk'hani wait for me up there?"

Adele couldn't comprehend any being with an entire universe of power within his form being afraid of anything. She managed to shake her head. "Only his tribe is up there waiting for us," she croaked, then closed her eyes as darkness filled her vision. "You can ask them…"

Sighmere took a deep breath. "Then let us go and see this sky path and meet these people."

"Sighmere!" It was Ohrig shouting, and Adele felt his fear morphing into anger. "You have hurt our Queen Adelena. Please make her strong again."

Sighmere seemed to notice the Queen's Guard for the very first time. "Yes, little warrior, an angel is a fragile thing, yet if I feed her, she will be hungry for the rest of her life. Let her drink of my tear, and she will be well."

The dragon lowered his head and tasted the air over the Queen's Guard and spoke as if to himself. "So weak and powerless. It is a wonder you have survived this long in Evendaar, little humans, with no magic of your own."

The Queen's Guard crowded around Adele, still held in Ohrig's arms. Lucky poured a mouthful of the tear between Adele's lips. The moment it hit her throat, her eyes opened, and she smiled to see the six men all huddled over her, their expressions changing from anxiety to relief in a heartbeat.

"You done lying down, Your Majesty?" asked Bear. "Because this dragon wants an honor guard to the surface."

Rainere's heart sank as they descended another stone staircase and he realized where they were being taken—the ingenious Marchant-designed prison hole called Hell.

Lord Orgustus stood in front of the great stone door to the prison and waved the large iron key, trying to find the keyhole on the ancient door.

"It's there, to the left," said the high magistrar as he pointed to the camouflaged entry. "Don't worry about the blue charms, my lord; they won't hurt you if you don't touch them."

Lord Orgustus instinctively pulled back from the door, but the glowing blue inscriptions were almost invisible to his eye. Rainere, however, could read them as clear as day.

"Those imprisoned behind this door and within these walls shall have their magic stripped and stolen, absorbed by the spirits who watch over this chamber of Hell—" he began, but was interrupted by the lord standing at his shoulder.

"Welcome to your new home, Your Highness," said Orgustus, enjoying his moment. "Your evil Marchant magic will be nullified down here, and you will be helpless as any commoner."

Orgustus opened the door, and as soon as Rainere crossed the threshold, he felt his magic recede, frozen and heavy as a rock underneath his heart. For the first time since his arrest, he felt a twinge of real fear. He knew from his studies of the Golden Palace that there was no escape from Hell.

The door opened onto a wide corridor lit by green-flamed wall sconces, the floor laid with flat paving stones. The right side of the corridor was lined with five cells divided by metal bars into separate cages. On the left side of the corridor was a stone wall with five doors. In the spaces between the doors were three hypnotized guards standing at attention.

"This sweet little chamber will be yours, Your Majesty," said Orgustus, pushing past the prince and opening a door on the left side of the hallway. There was only a tiny window cut into the top of the door, with a shutter to close it completely.

Charlie and Benjamin were shoved across the threshold behind Rainere, knocking into him.

"And how long are we to be locked down here, my lord?" Rainere asked. "Because when the queen returns—"

"That's a wonderful idea, Your Highness!" said Orgustus, gloating. "You will be locked in here until the queen returns, if she ever does, and then I will lock her down here with you too."

"You'll pay for this, Lord Orgustus!" shouted Charlie. "Queen Adelena is the rightful queen of Unisia, and the goddess Serena herself will see you burn for what you are doing to us and her."

Lord Orgustus narrowed his eyes at Charlie. "The goddess would never bother herself with scum like you," he sneered. "Now get in your cells."

"Prince Rainere, we can't let them hide us down here!" protested Charlie, aghast as he was shoved into a cage and the door was slammed shut. "Do something!"

"Seven days, Charlie," replied Rainere.

"But tell them they can't—"

"Enough, Charlie!" snapped Rainere. He turned his forest-green gaze on the young teenager and reached through the bars to clasp his hand. "We are Marchant men, Charlie, and a Marchant man will endure when he must endure and will fight when it is time to fight. In this moment, Charlie, we *must* endure, do you understand me?"

Charlie nodded, and Rainere could see in the boy's eyes a fear that mirrored his own. He decided in a moment that, though he had promised not to be violent with the St. Lucidis cretins, he had never promised not to be rash.

"Poor Lord Orgustus, he cannot know what he does, putting us down here, out of sight and sound of magic, Charlie," said Rainere, taking a step toward the lord. "It was not only the queen's children we rescued from the Boss's establishment last night. In fact, we took their whole stable of victims for the mines of Mount Ecrusius—fifteen children in all."

"Then where are these other children who could corroborate this story for you?" asked Orgustus.

Rainere raised a shoulder and dropped it slowly, noting how much his shrug infuriated the young lord. "What's important is that the Marchant Eldars will not get their victims in the mines," he said. "And that means that they will try to come here to find more."

Lord Orgustus blanched. "The Marchant Eldars are just a myth," he almost whispered. "They don't exist anymore."

Rainere stretched his lips into a thin smile. "Oh yes, they do," he corrected the lord. "And your high magistrar knows all about them. He's been servicing their needs with gifts of Marchant children for as long as I've been alive. Why don't you ask him about it?"

"Do you think I'm stupid enough to believe such horror stories?" spluttered Lord Orgustus, but his eyes flickered from Rainere to Charlie to Benjamin and back again. "There is no such thing as the Marchant Eldars," he repeated.

Rainere only looked at the ceiling of the prison, as if listening for something. "They'll come at night, you know," he said. "From the skies, and they won't stop coming until they have what they want."

"Get in your cell!" shouted Lord Orgustus, clearly furious not to have cowed his Marchant prisoners. "All of you will rot down here, and your green blood won't do you any good. Marchant Eldars, indeed!"

"Well, my lord, don't say I didn't warn you," said Rainere, stepping into his cell. "Be sure to come and get me if you see any monsters flying above Concordis." He even managed a dry chuckle just as Orgustus slammed the door in his face.

*　　*　　*

Lying on his back on the narrow cot, Rainere watched the shadows of the green-flame lamp dance on his walls, as he had done for hours. He had no hope of sleeping in the cold and dank atmosphere of the cell and instead was praying harder than he had ever prayed in his long life.

There was only enough space on the cot to tuck one hand behind his head, so Rainere rested the other on his stomach, tracing the muscles of his abdomen. His arm with the gunshot wound throbbed horribly now that the high wizard's opiate had worn off. Depression beckoned, but Rainere held it at bay, dreaming of Adelena and praying that his beloved was still alive and had managed to speak with a dragon tonight.

"Dearest goddess, Serena, you saved my life when I was lost among the stars, but in return I have failed to keep Adelena safe as you asked me to. Yet still I beg you, do not let Adelena die in this world," Rainere whispered to the dark. Adelena's face appeared in his mind, and the Mark on his side pulled, twisting his skin. "Adelena has done nothing wrong, yet the world of Evendaar has been so cruel to her. She only seeks to repair what was done to her child. Mother Goddess, please protect your daughter Adelena. Save her, please."

The magic came without warning, ripping Rainere's mind apart and filling every cell in his body with light.

"The last Marchant prince, I have heard your prayer."

The voice of the goddess paralyzed Rainere with its beauty. Though his body radiated the light of her magic, his vision was dark, and he couldn't make out her form, only hear her voice ringing urgently in his ears.

"My sweet prince, your love speaks so loudly, yet Adelena cannot hear it. My little angel is in terrible danger, and you must protect her. She has fallen under the gaze of my brother Dahk'hani, and he would have her raise him from beneath the earth. When Adelena comes back to you, do not let her have his child. Do not let her birth the abomination that will scour my beautiful Evendaar with its fire and piety."

"My goddess Serena," gasped Rainere. "Your will..." but he couldn't continue as the bliss swamped his senses, he spun back to his own reality.

Rainere sat up on his narrow prison cot, and for a long moment, it was the dank stone walls and flickering lamp that were the dream and not the vision that had shaken his very soul.

"I will," Rainere promised the cold emptiness in the cell, knowing his goddess could hear him. "I will protect Adelena, and she will never have another child again."

Promise made, he fainted dead away.

Chapter Fifty-Five
"The Path of the Goddess"

The journey back up the tunnel felt much faster with magical super strength powering her limbs and the glow of an enormous dragon clinging to her heels. When they came to the frozen entrance of the tunnel, Adele breathed in the thin air as if she were taking her very first breath.

Night had fallen while they were below the ground, and a carpet of stars lit the night sky. A sickle moon glowed lavender, reflecting the light of the heavy clouds of magic that made up the Path of the Goddess.

Behind her the dragon Sighmere stood in the entrance of his tunnel. His gaze was fixed on the heavens as his feet took their first tentative steps to freedom. "It is beautiful," he said. "I can hear the song of Serena calling to me."

The Chime Voices in Adele's mind sang the chorus of the song of the stars. She could hear it so much more clearly now that she had the magic of Sighmere screaming through her veins. Her heart filled with joy. Though she had come to the dragon, begging his favor, she had been able to fulfill his greatest wish and make his dream come true.

"Go to her," said Adele. "Your goddess has been waiting for you to join her ever since she left."

Jordansson and his brothers had stood frozen when Adele and her men came out with the dragon following behind, but now Jordansson walked to Adele's side, looking up at Sighmere, amazed to see a dragon before his very own eyes.

"Dahk'hani's people welcome the dragon Sighmere," said Jordansson, opening his arms as if to hug the dragon. "My people have watched over you faithfully for many thousands of years, as was the will of Dahk'hani."

"My little Dragon Hunters," sang Sighmere, casting his eye away from Jordansson to Tempestborn and Stormchaser. "Thank you for your service. I will grant you gifts before I leave this world of Evendaar."

Sighmere dragged a sharp claw across his chest. Black blood spilled out of the cut, and several scales clattered to the ice. "Paint your bodies with my blood for strength and hold my scale as your shield from danger." Sighmere looked down at Adele's Queen's Guard. "You too, little humans. Without magic you are like moths before the flame of power—one touch and you will be ash."

Each man stepped forward and picked up a scale of the dragon. Up close they were transparent, with an iridescent shine that dully reflected the glow of the dragon's light. Owens had the idea to empty his canteen of water, and he caught the blood of the dragon as it dripped slowly down the creature's chest. The rest of the Queen's Guard followed suit.

When the humans had finished collecting their gifts and offered their thanks, Sighmere raised his giant head to the sky and called out a long, chiming note to the roiling clouds of the Path of the Goddess. The heaving mass of clouds released shards of lightning into the sky, as if scenting the air, looking for the source of the music. The clouds sped across the tops of the mountains, and the temperature fluctuated wildly. Hot and cold winds blew hard on the humans standing on the top of a mountain of ice.

Looking up, Adele could see the electric streaks of portal doorways opening and closing within the clouds. A large portal opened directly above them, and through it, Adele could see the manicured gardens of the Golden Palace. "Look, that's our way home!" she shouted.

"Get on my back, and I will take you up to it," said Sighmere, and despite his gentle tone, it was an order, not a suggestion.

Adele gathered her men, and they studied the dragon, looking for the easiest way to climb onto his back.

"Queen Adelena!" Jordansson grabbed Adele's arm and turned her to look at him. "Keep your promise, please. I want to go with you."

Adele shook her head. "No, Jordansson," she said. "I'm sorry, but your god wants me to have your child, and I will not risk his interfering in my life again."

Jordansson was stricken. "But you promised!" he pleaded. "I showed you the way across the mountains, and you promised to take me back to Unisia with you."

"Take the boy, ugly angel," commanded Sighmere. "A daughter of Serena never breaks an oath, and his love for you is real."

Adele swallowed down her next protest that it wasn't Jordansson's love for her that she doubted, but his motives in general. Jordansson whooped with joy and leaped onto the leg of the dragon, clambering onto his back and clinging on for dear life. Adele followed him, sitting on the shoulder joint between the leg and the dragon's ribcage.

Sighmere didn't have wings but rose from the ground by levitating on air. He surrounded himself with a cloud of gold magic that protected his passengers from the buffeting winds and floated over to the portal that Adele had spotted from the ground.

"Here is your home, little humans," said Sighmere. "I will send you through and then find my own path to the Realm of the Gods. You have my gifts, and you have my thanks."

Adele felt her stomach drop away when she saw how high in the sky they were. For one terrifying moment, she tried to work out how she was supposed to leap into the portal, and then she felt herself lifted up by magic and pushed through, surrounded by her men and Jordansson. The magic of the portal burned with a savage heat, and Adele flailed wildly, trying to grab onto any of the Queen's Guard flying through the air around her. Then they were falling fast, out of the clear blue sky and toward the green space behind the Golden Palace.

Reaching within for her magic, Adele felt the gold power burst from her hands, capturing every man in a net of gold rope. A new strength joined the gold magic, and it was the white-hot power of the dragon's tear. Fighting gravity, Adele managed to push herself up, back into the sky, slowing the speed of their fall. The ground rushed toward them, but Adele fought her instinctive panic and continued to slow their fall. Concentrating with all her might, she felt the seams of her magic strain, and at the very last moment, the net broke, and everyone fell the last few yards to the ground, crashing onto soft, green Unisian grass.

Adele lay on her back, gasping air back into her lungs. She gazed up at the sky and watched the green slash of the portal shrink and disappear, taking the land of the ice mountains and the dragon Sighmere with it. She heard the sounds of someone laughing and someone else throwing up. She raised her head off the ground.

"I think I pissed my pants," chuckled Jordansson and slapped a heaving QG Bear on his back. "Don't worry, Bear. Strong men need to vomit all the time."

Adele cast a critical eye over her party. Everyone was sweat-stained and windblown. Their baggy clothes of fur and leather hung off them, and their cheeks were burned red from the strong mountain sun. They all looked terrible.

The relief was heady, and Adele actually giggled. "I vote we sneak in the back way so no one sees us," she said. "I just need to hug my children before I do anything else."

"Agreed," said Captain Lucky, who was the first on his feet. Adele took his hand gladly but was pleased to find that her legs didn't shake as much as she had feared they would.

"Just leave me here," moaned QG Bear, still lying on his back. "Go on without me, and don't look back. I can't move another step."

"C'mon, Bear, you great princess." Owens kicked his friend affectionately in the ribs. "The palace is only a hundred yards away."

"And it looks like we got some attention, anyway," said Ohrig, squinting at the group of purple-and-gold figures pouring out the main doors onto the terrace and running down the stairs toward them. "Get ready for your official welcome, Your Majesty."

"Just as long as there aren't any trumpets," groaned Adele. "I can't stand the trumpets."

"Can I ask why it's daytime now?" asked Pepper. "It was midnight on the mountain."

"It took time to get through the portal, even though we were moving so fast," said Adele, knowing she was right though she'd barely reflected on it. "The dragon's magic made it feel easy, but we have traveled an incredible distance to be home."

"Home," said QG Leith, sighing with relief. "Permission to take a day off today, Your Majesty? I want to go and find my mum and ask for an apology. She thought she was keeping me out of trouble getting me into the Queen's Guard, but I want to tell her that for once, she was dead wrong." He chuckled when Ohrig cuffed him on the back of his head.

"Oh, crap, that looks like Lord Orgustus at the front of the guards," said Adele. "And I think he's got Tilburn with him."

Adele and the QGs watched as the party came closer. Lord Orgustus led the charge, and Adele thought he looked angrier than usual as he streaked toward them, his capelet flying out behind him.

"Stand right where you are!" shouted Lord Orgustus as he closed the distance and pulled to a stop in front of Adele.

She looked behind the lord to the Household Guard, all holding manacles in their hands.

"In the name of the Crown of St. Lucidis, Queen Adelena St. Lucidis, you are being arrested on charges of despotism and using dark magic in the Golden Palace!" Lord Orgustus raised his chin and pointed a righteous finger in Adele's face. "You, my false queen, are about to answer for all your crimes."

Tilburn wrung his hands as he watched the handcuffs tighten on Adele's wrists. "Your Majesty, I am so sorry for this terrible welcome back to the Golden Palace," said her majordomo. "I personally am ashamed to call myself a servant of the new Lord Regent of the Court of the Golden Palace." He jerked his head in Lord Orgustus's direction, his lip curling in distaste.

"It's all right, Tilburn, I'm sure we can sort this mess out soon," said Adele evenly. She gave him a long look but could easily tell from his expression that he was still loyal to her. "Where are my children?"

"The children are safe with Mrs. Ollenby, Your Majesty," answered Tilburn. He hurried to walk by her side as the party started hustling back to the palace. "She has taken them somewhere secure and I will help her watch over them until this matter is dealt with."

"Please tell me that this isn't just a desperate grab for power by a former regent," said Adele, loud enough for Lord Orgustus marching ahead of her to hear. "I would love to know the real reason that I'm being arrested with my Queen's Guard."

"She was read the charges," Lord Orgustus shouted back over his shoulder. "Do not say another word to her without risking your own legal consequences, majordomo."

Tilburn buttoned his lips, and his eyes flashed with anger. "This is a travesty, Your Majesty, but two young squires were found dead at the stables two days ago," he whispered to Adele. "Prince Rainere is being accused of the crime, as there is proof they were killed by dark magic and he was seen at the site of the crime. Then he was seen leaving with Charlie and Benjamin from Belvoir in tow."

"Shut it, Tilburn!" Lord Orgustus stopped suddenly and grabbed the petite man by his collar. "I will throw you in prison with her if you say another word."

"It's all right, Tilburn," said Adele as they entered the palace. "Stay quiet, and come and see me after."

Despite the early hour, the foyer was teeming with courtiers and servants come to watch the incarceration of their newly returned queen. There was no way that Adele could believe they hadn't been called to witness her humiliation.

"Your Majesty," said Ohrig quietly. "What do you want to do here?"

Adele looked around at the crowd of whispering and jeering courtiers and tried to imprint all their faces on her memory. "They have my children, Ohrig," replied Adele. "Until I can get them out of the Golden Palace, this is the only place I need to be. Even if it is in prison."

Ohrig communicated Adele's wishes to the rest of the QGs as they were paraded down the corridor and a wide staircase to a narrow hallway, still followed by the crowd. Jordansson was getting his own fair share of stares and whispers, standing head and shoulders above everyone else like he did. Adele felt sorry that he had begged so hard to come to Unisia, only to be arrested in the first ten minutes.

She didn't recognize this part of the Golden Palace on the journey to the prison. They were taken through one hallway after another and down half a dozen sets of stone steps. In the bowels of the Golden Palace, the temperature dropped, and Adele felt her magics shrink into their places, under her heart and behind her neck. Only the dragon's magic still traced its white-hot lines through her veins.

Their party was finally pulled to a stop in front of a great stone door lined with blue magic runes, which glowed balefully at their approach. Lord Orgustus held a giant metal key, and when he turned it in the lock, the runes sparked, and the door opened wide enough for Adele to see through.

The prison corridor was lined with wooden doors on one side, each with a guard standing outside, and open cells with metal bars on the other side. "You will find your magic won't work in here, Your Majesty," said Lord Orgustus with a malicious smile as he stepped aside to allow Adele to enter the prison.

Adele rose to the bait. "And why is that, Lord Regent?"

"Because this room has been blessed by an ancient saint, and no magic—no matter how powerful—can be used within its sacred confines." He pushed past Adele to lead her down the corridor. "I thought you would be comfortable here, in this lovely cell." He opened the bars of the last open cell in the block. "No privacy, of course, but at least you can talk to the other prisoners."

"Your Majesty!"

Adele turned in surprise to see Charlie standing at the door of the cell next to hers. She walked into her cage, and Lord Orgustus clanged the door shut behind her.

"Comfortable, Your Majesty?" Lord Orgustus couldn't keep the gloat from his voice.

"Perfectly fine, thank you, Lord Regent." Adele forced herself to smile. "In fact, this is much nicer than where I've been sleeping lately."

"Yes, at least we are out of the wind and weather," remarked General Ohrig, standing with his feet planted and his arms crossed in the middle of his own cell. "Hot food on the way I hope, Lord Regent?"

Lord Orgustus snarled in disbelief at them all. "You will be called to account when the court is in session later tonight, Your Majesty. Until then, you may only receive visits from your lawyers. The high wizard has nominated himself for your counsel. Though if you don't mind me saying, it doesn't bode well to have the high wizard going up against his brother, the high magistrar in court. One could almost think he wanted you put away as much as the high magistrar does."

"Orestes is my judge?" Adele felt her insides freeze but struggled not to show any emotion. "Good to know, thank you, Lord Regent. I will be sure to remember those who stood against me at this time."

Lord Orgustus spun on his heel, his capelet twirling behind him as he stalked out of the room. A key turning in the lock sounded, and everyone began shouting at once.

"Charlie, it's good to see you." Adele raised a hand to silence the boy as he threw himself at the bars between their cells and tried to tell her everything that had happened since she had left. "But where is Rainere?"

Charlie pointed to the cell door across the corridor. "He's in there, Your Majesty. Don't worry about the guards; they're hypnotized and don't say anything. They've been instructed not to let anyone leave, but that's all. I was throwing my dinner rolls at them last night, and they didn't do a thing."

"Your dinner rolls, I see." Adele didn't understand anything, but she held her chin as if she was thinking very hard. She stared at Rainere's door. "And we cannot use any magic in here, yet we have hypnotized guards. Interesting."

Charlie blinked. "Your Majesty, the children are with Mrs. Ollenby, and we still think the high wizard is on our side.

Despite what Lord Orgustus said, Ohren isn't the Boss of the Underworld, but we think Orestes the high magistrar might be."

Adele didn't respond to Charlie's odd little collection of facts, only looked up to see the hulking figure of Jordansson standing outside her cell door. "My magic works," he said, as a tiny blue flash lit his fingertip and her door unlocked. "Should I open all the doors?"

Adele waved a hand as if it were just a pleasant suggestion. "Please do."

Charlie squinted at the giant tribesman as his cell door swung wide, and the stranger stepped into his cell holding out his hand. "My name is Jordan Jordansson of the tribe of the Valley of the Three Sisters. I greet you in your custom." He held out his hand for a reluctant Charlie to shake. "And now in mine."

Charlie yelped as Jordansson enclosed him in a giant bear hug. "All right, mate," he squeaked as the air rushed out of his lungs. "Nice to meet you. I'm Charlie, member of the Queen's Guard."

"Hey there, Charlie," QG Owens came out of his cell and into Charlie's to give him a slap on the back in greeting. "But tell him you're just a scamp, not a QG."

"Nope, General Beefy said if I got back alive from my job in the Gray Palace, then he would make me a proper Queen's Guard, didn't you, General?" Charlie's grin looked a little ghoulish under his wide eyes.

The old general raised a brow. "General *Beefy*?" He flexed his shoulders slightly as he thought about the name. "I've been called worse," he decided.

Adele smiled at her men, so brave with their false cheer. "Now, Charlie, can you tell me what really happened here?"

"Adelena."

Adele looked across the prison corridor, but his voice had already sent a crack right through her self-control. She drank in the sight of him.

Rainere's eyes raked her face, and hot pink dots bloomed on his angular cheeks. He had undone the buttons of his vest, and his shirt had been slashed on his right arm, where Adele could see stained bandages through the shreds of fabric. Rainere held on to both sides of the door frame of the cell, as if holding himself back from her.

Adele crossed the floor and stopped just in front of him. "You're hurt," she rasped and almost touched the bandage on his arm.

Rainere leaned into the space between them, and his dark green eyes studied hers. "As are you." His voice was a familiar rasp that sent chills over her skin. "*Cara mia*, I'm so very sorry…"

"Greetings, Prince Rainere!" Jordan Jordansson stuck his hand between Adele and Rainere. "My name is Jordan Jordansson of the tribe of the Valley of the Three Sisters, and I greet you in the way of your custom."

Rainere looked down at Jordan's proffered hand and then up into the face of the handsome tribesman. He looked back at Adele. "Did you bring back a souvenir?"

Behind Adele the men had fallen silent to watch the reaction of the prince to Jordansson, so they heard the insult. Charlie barked a laugh. "Now greet him in the way of your people, Jordansson."

Adele put her hand on Jordansson's arm, well aware of how Rainere would react if Jordansson tried to hug him. "Prince Rainere, this is Jordan Jordansson, a great hunter of the ice tribes. He helped us find the dragon's home. He has been a good friend to us on our journey, and I've only managed to repay his help so far by getting him arrested."

Rainere glanced at Adele's hand on Jordansson's arm. She saw the flash of jealousy and took her hand off immediately. "Prince Rainere, tell me what happened after I left for the tundra."

"Your Majesty, you're here!" Benjamin poked his head out of the cell door next to Rainere's and rushed to Adele, only pulling up short when the giant tribesman offered him his greetings.

Once Benjamin was back on his feet, he bowed before Adele. "We were so worried that you wouldn't make it back in time," said the handsome groom. His expression tightened. "They've accused us of treason and murder, Your Majesty. Please, you've got to get us out of here."

"They've arrested the queen too, Benjamin," said Charlie, annoyed at having to explain the obvious. "That's why she's down here with the door locked. It's a massive conspiracy against the Marchants, if you ask me."

Benjamin furrowed his brow, confused. "But the queen isn't Marchant; she's a pure-blood St. Lucidis royal," he said. "Why would they put her down here with us?"

The gravity of the situation suddenly hit Adele like a ton of bricks, and she returned to her cell, sitting down on the narrow bunk before she fell down. Rainere followed her in and sat next to her on the thin mattress. It took all of Adele's strength not to lean against his shoulder and cry her eyes out. Instead, she allowed herself to brush the side of his hand where it rested on the mattress and enjoy the pulse of electricity that leaped through her, heading straight for her core and heating her through. Rainere threw Adele a glance, and the corner of his mouth quirked up in the way that always made him so irresistible and utterly kissable.

The lock in the prison door grated, and slowly the door was pushed open.

"Who goes there?" shouted Captain Lucky as he and the QGs formed a barrier across the corridor.

"For goddess's sake, it's me! I'm here to see the queen," said High Wizard Ohren. He shut the door quickly behind himself. "Why are you all out of your cells? And who the hell is this?" He pointed at Jordansson, and his eyes traveled up and down the length of the tribesman for a moment before he made his way down the corridor to find Adele in her cell.

"Excuse me, Your Majesty, you have a visitor," announced Captain Lucky formally, making Ohren wait in the doorway of Adele's cell. "Would you have time to take an appointment with High Wizard Ohren?"

Adele appreciated Lucky's attempt to protect her dignity even though they were all sitting in a dank prison. She thought it showed the strength of his character and sense of humor, that he would still hold to protocol, even though Ohren was shifting impatiently and rolling his eyes at his behavior.

Adele waved her hand. "Thank you, Captain, you may let the high wizard in."

"Your Majesty, thank the goddess you are back so soon," Ohren clasped his hands and tried to hide the fact that his rings were sparking and glittering with green lights. "I have to ask—" But the image of Ohren had begun to flutter and blink.

"Ohren, what is this?" shouted Adele. She was on her feet in an instant, Rainere her shadow.

"The high wizard's disguise doesn't work in here, Your Majesty," said Rainere. He frowned at Ohren. "Why don't you just take it off, wizard? You are making Her Majesty uncomfortable."

Reluctantly, Ohren pulled off his rings one by one, and the awful flickering stopped. In his place stood a tall, lanky young man with electric-blue eyes and an ashamed expression. His blond hair flopped into his eyes, and he rubbed his bare chin. Nothing about him was familiar to Adele, except those eyes—they were Ohren's eyes.

"It's nice to lose the beard," said Ohren, chewing his pink bottom lip. "But I am sorry I have to shock you like this after you've had so many surprises today, Your Majesty."

"Yes, so very many *surprises* today," said Adele, her tone heavy with sarcasm. She narrowed her eyes at the high wizard. "I should kill you where you stand, you lying sack of—"

"Ah, we're all here, then!" Ripenzo Shale pushed his way into the prison, surprising everyone again. He paused at their shock. "The door was unlocked." He pointed behind him. "Hope you don't mind if I join this little party?"

"Excuse me, Your Majesty, but you have a visitor," called Lucky, glaring hard and stopping Ripenzo Shale with a hand on his chest. "It's the horse thief and thoroughly suspect character Ripenzo Shale who requests an appointment."

Adele waved Ripenzo in. "It's getting crowded in here," she remarked. "Please excuse the mess, Ripenzo, but I wasn't expecting to entertain in prison today."

Ripenzo nodded and looked around at their group. "You guys smell terrible, and you look worse," he remarked. "Hello, and who's this big fella?"

"My name is Jordan Jordansson," said Jordansson. He squeezed his way into Adele's cell and continued his greeting, making Ripenzo laugh—"Now, that's a hug!"—before introducing himself to Ohren in the same way. Adele only raised an eyebrow when she saw Ohren flush bright red and hide a smile at the ebullient greeting.

"And you finally decided to lose the disguise," said Ripenzo to Ohren. "You *are* a good-looking kid. What were you, twenty, twenty-one, when you were cursed?"

"This is irrelevant," Ohren snapped at Rip's teasing tone. He turned back to Adele, piercing her with his sharp blue gaze. "Did you get the dragon tear, Your Majesty?"

"Of course I got the tear, and a lot more besides," answered Adele. She took her seat on the narrow prison bunk with all the dignity she could muster. "I always keep *my* promises. How about you, High Wizard? Did you manage to keep any of yours?"

But it was Rainere who went down on his knees in front of Adele, claiming her attention. "Your Majesty, I will tell you everything that has happened from the moment you left."

Adele sat back on her bunk and braced herself. "This better be good, Your Highness."

Chapter Fifty-Six
"Old Enemies Revealed"

Hours later, Adele stood at the bars of her cell and held them so tightly her knuckles were white.

"So, to be clear, you were forced to rescue my children from the Boss and Pere Raven because they were going to be sent to the mines to feed the Marchant Eldars or worked to death making this Gift of Life." Adele sucked in a harsh breath. "Charlie knows this is true because Pere Raven kidnapped him from the Gray Palace and took him to the mines, where he met Ripenzo. Ripenzo came back to the Golden Palace after I met him in the Black Mountains because he thought I was an idiot to leave my children with Prince Rainere.

"Poor High Wizard Ohren knows nothing about anything because, despite running the Golden Palace and being an immortal wizard, it's his own brother who you think is the Boss of the Underworld and the man who tried to have me killed. Lord Orgustus is furious with me for bringing all these Marchants into the Golden Palace, so he has launched a coup to have me ousted, and Ohren has to be seen publicly to support both his twin and the lord regent, or he loses his golden popularity."

Adele looked at the men surrounding her. Charlie was pale from having to recount the horror of the mines, the tears still drying on his cheeks. Rainere, crushed by guilt, was on his knees, his shoulders hunched as if braced for her to do him violence. Ohren had crossed his arms across his chest and was leaning back against the bars of the cage, humiliation and defensiveness making an ugly expression on his young face. Benjamin just looked miserable, his eyes on his shoes, though he had done nothing wrong. Only Ripenzo gave Adele a jaunty grin.

"Well, when you use that tone," he said, "anything is going to sound stupid."

Adele didn't smile. "Now the man who has been trying to have me killed will sit in judgment on me for my crimes against the crown, giving him the perfect excuse to have me legally murdered." Her voice faltered. "And after he imprisons and kills all my allies along with me, my children will be friendless, and no one will stop them being sent to the mines. But not Stella, because she doesn't have any magic, so they'll just let her die."

Adele felt herself crushed against Jordansson's chest, his arms tight around her. "Yes, this is bad, Queen," said Jordansson as he rubbed her back. "But you are the friend of the dragon Sighmere and twice blessed by the great god Dahk'hani. No one will let you die here in a cell or let the leaders of the tiny people kill you."

Rainere climbed to his feet. "You are a friend of the dragon?" His dark gaze took in Adele's comfort in Jordansson's arms. "And you were blessed by a god?"

Adele nodded. "Twice." She pulled away from the tribesman to escape Rainere's accusing stare and started pacing the corridor. "If we can all agree that this will be a kangaroo court upstairs, then we shouldn't be wasting any more time in this prison now."

"Your Majesty, this is a Marchant-designed prison. There are no secret exits, and no magic can be used in here," said Rainere, clearly reluctant to give her any more bad news. "I have studied it before. The saint who cursed this place didn't use any known magic."

"Please accept that a forced escape is simply not an option, Your Majesty," protested High Wizard Ohren. "The proof against you is mostly circumstantial, and I'm sure I can drag this out for days, or weeks, if I have to, giving us more time to smuggle the children out of the Golden Palace to safety. Then you can take all the time you need to find the evidence against the Boss and bring him to justice, even if he does turn out to be my brother."

Adele felt a flash of fury at Ohren's stubborn desire to follow all the rules of the system that had failed her so completely. Both her magics spiked through her blood, mixing with the dragon's magic and igniting a white-hot rage that filled her vision and exploded out of her hands into a nearby door. The heavy metal door flew off its hinges and banged back against a wall.

"There's your fucking 'no magic' rule blown to bits," she snarled back at Rainere. "And in case you hadn't noticed, Jordansson was able to unlock all the cell doors, and we can use him to—"

A movement out of the corner of her eye made Adele shift her gaze back into the dark cell. She froze as something crawled toward her on its hands and knees. Adele gasped when glowing green eyes blinked at her in the gloom. "Abomination!" it hissed.

Adele swore and leaped back as if she'd been bitten. "Grottonski!"

Rainere flashed to Adele's side, and everyone stared as Grottonski, the prince's malicious manservant, crawled out of the cell and pulled himself up on the wall, only to fall on his knees again. "Master, you have forgiven me! Please, tell me you have forgiven me."

Grotto wept into his hands, the tears trickling between his knuckles as he covered his face. His greasy scalp gleamed in the light of the torches, and his old black suit hung in rags on his undernourished frame. "Please," he begged a horrified Rainere, clutching at his master's boots. "Please, Grotto has always loved you, his dear boy and only charge—Rainere, the very last Marchant prince of Unisia."

"Oh, shit," Ohren swore under his breath. "I forgot about Grotto."

"You knew Grottonski was *here*? I asked you a dozen times, and you said you didn't know where he was," said Adele as she turned to face the high wizard, raising her hands above her head to direct the fury that was burning through her veins and the magic that filled the atmosphere around her. "Give me just one goddamn reason why I shouldn't kill you right now before you can tell any more lies." Ohren gaped, but no sound came out, as what he saw in his queen held him frozen with fear.

Ripenzo Shale stepped into Adele's line of vision. "Easy, tiger," he said calmly, holding his hands up in a gesture of peace. "It looks like you've learned some fancy new magic, and I'm proud of you, darlin', I really am." Ripenzo smiled and let the deep gold band that had been obscured by indigo irises spin around his pupils. In that moment Adele remembered how vast and magnificent Ripenzo's magic actually was. Her own gold magic responded by flooding her mind, bringing calm where anger had been.

"Don't kill the golden boy, Adelena," said Rip. "You know it'll just set this snake pit hissing, and he's the only one who can help clear your name. You want to stay here, don't you? It's nice being queen of your little realm, isn't it? This is your destiny, Adelena, but you have to trust it. You don't need a prophecy to know what's right and wrong in this situation because you have your heart to tell you."

Ripenzo reached up to take hold of Adele's shaking hands. He winced as the magic sparked at him but covered her hands with his warm, callused fingers.

"Your human heart is your greatest gift, darlin', not all this magic," he said. "That is what Serena wanted you to have. It's why you had to leave Evendaar and grow up on Earth, so that when you came back, you would see through all the catshit of these wizards. You must defend the throne from them, her Favored, and protect those thousands of people who have no magic anymore. If you don't, then all those lovely commoners will be wiped out by the wicked few in power, and no one will be strong enough to stop them."

Adele shook her head to try to dislodge all Rip's words, which were now spinning around her mind like so many butterflies. "This is too much," she whispered. "Ripenzo, I'm not strong enough for this!"

"Yes, you are, *cara mia*," said Rainere. "With me behind you."

"With *us* behind you, Queen Adelena," corrected Ripenzo. He stretched his lips into a shaky smile. "Now think, darlin'. What should we do first?"

Adele took a deep breath and felt the magics twine in her blood, still raging, so she looked to her heart for a path. The faces of her three children were front and center. "I will give a dose of the dragon tear to Ohren so he can go heal Stella and get her out of her coma," Adele said, pulling her hands free of Ripenzo's. She pushed her shoulders back. "That will remove the issue of dark magic surrounding her. Then I will have Mrs. Ollenby take the children to the Belvoir Estate to keep them safe from magic, and Ohren, you will put out a warrant for the arrest of Pere Raven and the man they call the Boss, whoever that may be."

High Wizard Ohren swallowed hard and nodded. "Yes, Your Majesty, at once."

Adele turned to Rainere. "Prince Rainere, we might not be able to escape our prison, but I imagine we can escape whatever courtroom we are taken to in the Golden Palace. You will draw us a map of any possible routes we can take through the walls of the palace to get away if this legal battle gets violent."

Grottonski started cackling, the madness clear in his glowing eyes. "A pretty plan, but the Eldars are coming for my prince," he said. "With no Grotto to watch over him, they will come to take him home." Grotto pointed at an amulet around his neck. "Grotto's dead, and now you all are too."

Adele resisted the urge to kick Grottonski in the face where he kneeled at her feet. "Is what he says true, Rainere?" she asked.

Rainere bent down and took the amulet gently from Grotto's neck, ignoring the manservant's grateful blubbering, and examined it.

"I'm almost certain that this crystal is charmed to hide a person from the eyes of magic, any sort of magic." He dangled the amulet by its string. "It's not like a shield, but actually renders the wearer invisible to magic. Grotto would never voluntarily have put this on. If he is invisible to magic then the Eldars would believe my elf guardian to be dead, and then they would come for me as the last remaining Marchant prince, and I would be taken to the Eeyrie. You and I both know that's not what Grotto wants for me."

Charlie slipped next to Rainere. "You mind if I have a look at it, Your Highness?" he asked. "I had one of these before, but it was stolen." He almost smiled when Rainere handed it to him and quickly placed it around his neck, hiding it under his shirt.

"Who did this to you, Grottonski?" asked Adele, staring down her nose at the servant groveling at Rainere's feet.

Grotto pointed at High Wizard Ohren, which Adele had expected. "And that filthy traitor, Prince Gorrik."

"Gorrik? The old history teacher?" She turned to Ohren and saw his apologetic shrug. "And you lied about him being a history teacher too, I suppose, High Wizard?" Adele clasped her hands in front of her chest to stop them filling with magic.

"Night falls," sniffed Grotto. "The goddess Lune is rising now."

"You worship the goddess Lune?" asked Jordansson. He crouched down next to Grottonski on the floor, his expression soft with pity. "You are one of the tribes that the dragon made, aren't you? It will comfort you to know your creator lives and has returned to the goddess, elf."

Grotto recoiled from Jordansson's proffered hand to help him up. "Get off me, you stinking great peasant," he snapped. "Do not seek to pity me, when I am your better." The hurt in Jordansson's eyes made Adele want to kick Grotto in the face again.

"Your Majesty, I think what Grotto meant was that Lord Orgustus will be coming for you," interrupted General Ohrig. "Night has fallen, and the court will convene soon. We need to work out what you're going to say and do."

The words had just left his lips when there was a loud clanging at the prison door, and the sound of shouting could be heard. The door opened, and Tilburn almost fell forward, just ahead of Lord Orgustus and a handful of Household Guards. Lady Olivia pushed her way through the crowd of men, her arms full of silk and lace, carrying a makeup box in her hand.

"What are you all doing out of your cells?" shouted Lord Orgustus, but his cheeks were as white as his lips, and the lord looked terrified.

"Your Majesty, welcome," said Lady Olivia. She dove in front of Adele. "Please, we haven't much time."

"Your Majesty, you must come now!" shouted Tilburn, holding his side as if it ached and yanking down his disheveled waistcoat. "Something terrible has happened, and only you can fix it."

Adele felt fear clutch her heart. "The children?" she whispered.

Lord Orgustus stood before Adele and looked down at her. She saw the pride war with his terror as the gold band spun around his pupils, and she actually felt her gold magic reach out to his in sympathy.

"Your Majesty, Marchant Eldars have been sighted in the sky above Concordis. No reports of any deaths yet, but we cannot wait." Lord Orgustus's gaze flickered to Prince Rainere. "Your Majesty, you must make the Marchant prince help us. I know he is your lover, and I know he will listen to you!"

Lord Orgustus looked back to Adele, and his face crumpled. "I have always understood politics. Do you know, I can feed the entire population on a budget that doesn't even cover the cost of your shoe collection? Every day, I keep the factions within the court on even terms so the population of Unisia gets to live without the threat of civil war. And all my life, I have worked to keep the wizards and their meddling out of education and public government, but Marchants..." He drifted off, despair catching his last words.

Adele raised her chin and looked hard at the man who up until now had been trying to steal her crown. She understood that Lord Orgustus was a ruler who desperately loved Unisia and would do whatever it took to protect it, even beg the help of the woman he hated.

"If I do as you ask and help you to contain the Eldar threat," said Adele, "do you agree to stay out of my way and let me heal my daughter Stella first?"

Lord Orgustus's mouth twisted as though he tasted something sour, but he saw immediately that arguing would be useless. "Yes, anything! I can take you to the child," he said. "She is in my quarters."

Adele raised her eyebrow, and Lord Orgustus actually flinched from her expression. "I had to move her," he said. "But the child is still stable in her highly illegal dark magic coma. No harm has come to her by my hand, I promise you."

The matter decided, Lord Orgustus impatiently gestured to the open door to indicate that they should hurry, and Adele was only too happy to follow him out of the prison.

She felt her mental strength returning as High Wizard Ohren and her Queen's Guard gathered around her. Rainere marched by her side, and Charlie, Jordansson, Benjamin, Lady Olivia, and Tilburn brought up the rear.

When they reached the first populated floor of the palace, Adele was appalled to see the chaos in the hallways. Everywhere people were banded together in large groups, following the shouting Household Guard or running around, their arms filled with belongings.

"Where are the people all going, Lord Orgustus?" asked Adele, narrowly avoiding a troop of Household Guard rushing past her.

"To the lower levels," replied Orgustus. "It is known that the Marchant Eldars don't like to go underground, so they think they will be safe there."

"And where are Natalie and Aaron right now?" asked Adele, but it was Tilburn who rushed to answer.

"The prince and princess are with Mrs. Ollenby, Your Majesty," said the majordomo. "We honestly feared for the children's lives, and Mrs. Ollenby said that she would take them to a location where they would be safe. Though she wouldn't tell me where that was, she also told me that General Ohrig would know the place."

"Mrs. Ollenby will keep them safe," said Rainere, and Adele felt better that the prince trusted the lady too.

It took time to get through the press of people, but eventually their party reached the upper levels of the royal suites, and Lord Orgustus flung open the door to his apartment.

"The child is through there," he said, pointing to an inner chamber door.

Adele wasted no more time and raced to the side of the bed. Stella was lying peacefully on top of the covers. Her white nightdress was arranged to cover her feet, but her little toes still poked out.

Adele scanned her baby, drinking in the sight of her after such a long absence. The virus had bleached Stella's hair from blond to white, and her soft pink skin had a sheen on it, like she was made of china. Clear as day, Adele could see the net of green magic that surrounded Stella, protecting her from harm and keeping her life locked in—like a held breath.

Adele sat next to Stella, careful not to touch the spell matrix. She heard High Wizard Ohren organizing the room behind her. He cleared out everyone except Jordansson and Prince Rainere and retrieved the dragon artifacts that Lord Orgustus had stored in a messy pile in the corner of his office.

"Your Majesty, I have to warn you," said Ohren as he gently touched Adele on her shoulder, making her turn to him. "I have never seen this type of magic before." He had decanted some of the dragon tear into a clear glass bottle, and the liquid sloshed in a viscous mass. "I have no idea how to activate the tear once we have given it to Stella. Did the dragon give you any information on how to use it?"

"When the dragon read my memories, it was so violent that it almost destroyed me," said Adele. "Then Sighmere advised Ohrig to let me drink his tear. I didn't hear any chanting or a spell, but maybe there was something he did. I don't know, it was all so rushed and confusing." She frowned, anxious that now they were so close to healing Stella, they might need another key to unlock the cure that she'd found.

"I will help, Queen Adelena," said Jordansson, seating himself on the other side of the bed. "The dragon's magic is already inside me, and you know I can hear the magic sing, just like you can."

Adele was surprised at Jordansson's words. Yet when she took a moment to concentrate on pushing back her fear, there it was under the confusion in her mind—the quiet song of the dragon tear in the bottle as it called to its magic already in her blood.

"Yes, I hear it," she said, nodding at the high wizard. "Ohren, Jordansson and I will direct the magic when you give the tear to Stella."

"Well, if you think you know what you're doing, Your Majesty," said Ohren, giving her a doubtful look, "we'd better get started."

Adele leaned over Stella and the green spell matrix lit up at her presence.

"Administer the kiss, Your Majesty," said Ohren quietly.

"Mummy's here, baby," whispered Adele as she closed her eyes and pressed her lips to Stella's tiny rosebud mouth. She felt the fizz of the magic burning her for a moment before Rainere's stasis spell cracked and fell to pieces. Stella suddenly took in a deep, chest-rattling breath.

"Now I will administer the dragon tear," said Ohren. He leaned over Stella to carefully pour the liquid into her mouth. "Your turn again, Your Majesty."

Adele reached out for Jordansson's hand and clasped it over Stella's chest. Together they closed their eyes. Adele felt the song of the dragon's magic vibrating through her and the Chime Voices singing in time with it. Her green and gold magics remained curled out of the way as the dragon magic raced through her blood. Adele could see her daughter in her mind's eye. Stella was glowing as the dragon's magic spread over her skin.

Make her stronger, chanted the Chime Voices. *Give the baby to the dragon's magic. Nothing will be able to ever hurt her again. Make her strong, make her whole.*

Adele reached out for Jordansson and saw him behind the black lines of his dragon blood protections. Then she heard his words and saw the protections move aside for her. Invading Rainere or even Ohren had always felt like standing on the shore of an ocean of power, but inside of Jordansson, Adele saw an ice cave. Jordansson's natural magic was frozen and cold to her psychic touch. Yet she could see the pearlescent veins of the dragon's magic running through the frozen walls. *But how can I get at it?*

In the real world, Adele heard Jordansson intone a chant intense with words of power telling Adele how to take his power for her own. Delighted, the Chime Voices repeated the instructions, and Adele wrapped Jordansson up in her power, using his strength like a tool to push the magic through the pores of Stella's skin and down into her body, saturating every cell with the powerful, healing magic of the dragon's tear.

Only when Adele was certain that the dragon's magic inside Stella was stable did she release Jordansson from her grasp and withdraw from his body. Back in the world again, Adele took a deep breath, calming the chanting Chime Voices and the racing white magic in her own blood.

"Mummy?"

With a gasp Adele opened her eyes and looked into Stella's bright blue gaze. A pearlescent circle of power ringed the baby's pupils, slowly spinning as the magic claimed its place in her tiny body.

"Stella!" Adele cried. "Sweet Christ, finally you're all right, my darling Stella."

Stella reached out to her mother, and Adele gathered her baby to her chest, hugging her tightly. "My Stella Bella! My baby girl, you're well again!" Adele pulled back to stroke Stella's head and chest, checking for any trace of the damage that had given her so much pain before.

Adele looked up and locked eyes with Rainere. A radiant smile spilled across his face and chased away his shock. In a few steps, he was by Adele's side, holding her and the baby in his arms.

"Rainere, we did it!" said Adele. She leaned into his embrace, and all at once, she felt like she was home again. "We finally saved Stella."

"No, you did it, *cara mia,*" corrected Rainere. He brushed the hair out of Adele's eyes, stroking her cheek. "You did the impossible, finding this dragon and taking his tear. As always, you are infinitely incredible, Adelena."

Adele smiled into Rainere's loving gaze. "If you hadn't helped me keep Stella safe, I would never have been able to search for the cure," she said. "And for that, I thank you, Rainere, from the bottom of my heart."

"Your heart…" Rainere leaned a little closer, tilting his head to the side, his lips only a fraction from Adele's. "Adelena, your heart is everything to me."

"Your Majesty!" A shout from the doorway made Adele start away from Rainere. Lord Orgustus stomped into the room.

"Your Majesty, how does the princess fare?" asked the lord as he paced to the window, looking out at the night.

"She is healed, Lord Orgustus," said Adele, shifting her body so he could see a happy Stella smiling in her mother's embrace. "The magic worked, and Stella is perfectly healthy again."

"Brilliant! May the goddess Serena bless you both," said Orgustus quickly, but his face was pinched with worry as he stared into the night sky. "If all is well with your daughter, perhaps you can now deal with the matter of the Marchant Eldars flying over Concordis?"

Adele exchanged a single heavy glance with Rainere and climbed to her feet, shifting Stella to her hip. "Then let's go." She walked out to where her Queen's Guard, Charlie, Benjamin, and Tilburn were seated in Lord Orgustus's combined office and sitting room. The terrace doors had been opened to let in the fresh evening air, and Adele could smell rain on the breeze.

"Your Majesty!" Ohrig shot to his feet and clapped his hands to see Stella sitting up in her mother's arms, smiling around at all her favorite men. "By the grace of the goddess, you did it!"

"Yes, Stella is well again!" Adele thought she would never get sick of repeating it as she let the cheers wash over her and delighted in Stella's happy giggles.

Carrying her baby to the open doors, Adele joined Rainere, Ripenzo, Lord Orgustus, and Ohren where they gathered on the narrow terrace. With a flick of her head, Adele signaled to General Ohrig to accompany her too. From the balcony she could see the thousands of twinkling lights of Concordis and the great blazing bonfires dotted in every square. The largest fires were in the Lower Districts. Though the sky above them was littered with stars, they shed little light, and the moon was covered with dark clouds.

"What are the fires for?" asked Adele.

"To keep the dark away," answered Lord Orgustus. "The Eldars cannot stand the light."

Ripenzo snorted, as if he might know better, and Adele turned to him, curious, just as she felt heavy drops of rain fall on her head and automatically shielded Stella against her chest. A peal of thunder rumbled across the sky, and a flash of green lightning ripped the darkness where there were no clouds.

"You see, Rip, this is another one of those storms I was telling you about." Adele prodded Ripenzo's arm. "Do you have any advice for me this time?"

Rip looked back over his shoulder at Adele and gave her a lopsided smile, but his eyes were tight. "Run," he suggested. "Far away."

"No, you see, I just can't do that." Adele stared out over the capital city. "A queen doesn't run from her troubles, plus there's this stupid prophecy about the end of the world that I'm still trying to solve."

"But your stupid prophecy has nothing to do with the Marchant Eldars," said Ripenzo, though he didn't sound happy about it. "It is impossible to know how—"

"But, Rip, impossible is what I do," Adele said confidently. "Come along, gentlemen, we'll dodge this storm yet."

Then Adele turned on her heel and took her baby back inside, out of the rain.

TO BE CONTINUED...

Acknowledgements

This book was created with the support of my dearest Reader. Thank you for all your words of encouragement and enthusiasm for this our world of Evendaar.

Thank you as always to the wonderful Monica Hall, under whose all-seeing eye this story was crafted into a book.

Thank you to the team at The Artful Editor for their hard work and incredible attention to detail, which helped make this book a much better book.

And a thank you to S. Critchley for giving me a devilish little bit of inspiration. You were an excellent beta reader!

Thanks to my wonderful family and dear friends who supported all the wailing, gnashing of teeth, and endless times of quiet that all come with trying to be around an author who is trying to write a book.

To find out more about the author A.R. Winterstaar or the World of Evendaar please visit:

www.evendaar.com

A. R. Winterstaar on Facebook